DOPE

DOPE

Thierry Sagnier

Fourth Lloyd Productions, LLC
Burgess, VA 22432

Book and cover design by Richard Stodart

Fourth Lloyd Productions, LLC
512 Old Glebe Point Rd.
Burgess, VA 22432
www.fourthlloydproductions.com
4thLloyd@gmail.com
Phone: (804) 450-4595

Printed in the United States of America.

ISBN: 978-0-9889391-8-9
Library of Congress Control Number: 2019955341

Acknowledgments

Writing a sequel is odd. The main characters already exist with set personalities and quirks. I was allowed to invent new bad guys and new situations, and wander around new neighborhoods. I also had the privilege of creating a few new good guys, including an outspoken 13-year-old who nearly causes the downfall of my heroes. That was fun.

As always, I've discussed ideas and chapters with other writers and at one point had a roomful of them telling me—with charts, no less—how I should end my book.

I'm a strong believer in writers' groups where works are critiqued and often improved. As such, virtually all of *Dope* was dissected and scrutinized by other eager writers. They contributed greatly to what I think is a pretty good plot and were instrumental in making my characters and situations believable. I'm grateful to the Arlington Writers Group, the Mosaic Writers, and the Chain Bridge Writers for taking the time to read my work with critical eyes. I am especially grateful to Melanie Dixon and Patricia Buckley, both editors *extraordinaires* who pored over *Dope* and found its shortcomings. My many thanks to Nancy Stodart for showing great patience during multiple revisions and to all the friends who listened to my lectures on drugs and addiction. And, of course, I am grateful to an untold number of 12-step program people who will remain anonymous but have, over the years, imparted amazing knowledge.

It's often said that writing is a lonely business, but in reality it isn't. My many thanks to all who tolerated, assisted and supported me as I tried to put words on pages. I couldn't have done it without you.

Thierry Sagnier,
Vienna, VA,
September 2019

Fairfax Sees Six Deaths by Overdose in a Week

FAIRFAX. Police said Friday that six people had died of drug overdoses in Fairfax County in the past week and that five of the deaths may be related to batches of heroin laced with lethal opioids.

The victims were between 22 and 34 years old, Fairfax County police said in a statement.

The first of the string of opioid-related deaths occurred last Friday in Alexandria; the second Sunday in Fairfax Station; the third and fourth deaths, Wednesday in McLean and Clifton; and the fifth death, Thursday in the Fairfax City area.

The deaths may be related to batches laced with fentanyl and carfentanyl, synthetic opioids that can be lethal in small doses.

"In my 20 years in Narcotics, I have never seen anything like this," said Second Lieutenant James Carlson of the Organized Crime and Narcotics Division.

There have been 402 overdose fatalities in Fairfax County in 2017, police said, up from 212 in 2016. According to state medical examiners, overdoses claimed the lives of over 1,200 Virginia residents last year.

Prologue

LeBron Johnson was a happy dealer of illegal drugs. The night before, he had scored a thousand bucks' worth of top-notch heroin from his source, a mean-looking Salvadoran with an acre of prison tats on his hands, arms, and neck.

The man, short, swarthy, aggressively unsmiling, had sat behind a scarred Salvation Army desk in an otherwise empty studio apartment on the wrong side of the Potomac and counted the ten one-hundred-dollar bills three times with effort, moving his lips as he went. Then, he'd folded the thin wad of money and stuffed it into his shirt pocket.

LeBron was deathly afraid of the Salvadoran, who was said to have beaten a brother to death with an empty Yoo-hoo bottle. LeBron, in fact, was discreetly seeking another source of drugs, one who might be less threatening and handier with numbers. The operative word was 'discreetly.' It was not a good idea to switch services with a lot of fanfare. Suppliers—Salvadoran or others from four-syllable Central American nations—were jealous, very possessive of their clientele, and unbelievably violent.

After cutting and redistribution, LeBron figured his $1,000 would fetch close to $4,000, which was not a bad return on the investment. Subtract one grand for his own dealers, and there'd still be $3,000 for LeBron, or a clear, untaxed profit of $2,000. All in three or four hours, with luck. Turn that over, and in a week LeBron stood to make about twenty grand, which would lead to a much bigger buy and commensurate profits if everything went well, and why shouldn't it?

LeBron had taken a few business admin courses at Northern Virginia Community College and gotten all As. He'd thought of becoming an entrepreneur before realizing he already was one. The world of money held no mysteries for him. You got money, you made money, and when you got even more money, you reinvested carefully. When the payoff came, you diversified or maybe left town. That was the plan.

He wasn't too worried about getting caught. He was a vet; he had served his nation in the Middle East—well, actually he'd dispensed uniforms at Fort Huachuca in Arizona, but no one ever asked—and if he were busted and got even slightly lucky, he'd most likely get off with a minimal sentence. After all, he had served his country, gotten a good conduct medal, and been discharged honorably. There were no meaningful priors except for a disorderly conduct. He was golden.

It amazed him how easy this was. A little stake, a little street smarts, and there he stood, well on the way to his first hundred grand. The sky was the limit, as long as he treated his clients with respect, gave them good value for their money, and stood by the quality of his product. This, he had learned, was what entrepreneurs did.

In order to ensure the quality, LeBron always cooked up a tiny amount of whatever new stock he had on hand and tested it on himself. He skin-popped, injecting a minute amount just beneath the skin of his right arm, and he could tell instantly how much the stuff could stand to be cut with baby laxative or whatever was on special that day at CVS. Occasionally he used confectioner's sugar, and once he'd mixed some Mexican brown with espresso coffee ground to a fine dust. One white girl from McLean swore she could taste Starbucks cappuccino after using. For a moment, LeBron thought of adding a couple of Splendas to the mix but then discarded the idea.

LeBron had shot up twice in his life and both times gotten sick to his stomach and thrown up in an alley. This was a blessing, he knew. It meant the god of the African Methodist Episcopal Church he'd grown up in on New York Avenue was looking after him, telling him in a no-nonsense way that intravenous use was a no-no. Needles were bad and, LeBron thought, completely ghetto.

LeBron glanced at his knock-off Rolex. Damn. Running late, as always. No time to cook the stuff.

He took a pinch of the latest product purchased from the frightening Salvadoran, held it to his nose and inhaled hard. The rush was like a giant white light, like being inside 4th of July fireworks on the Mall. Somewhere deep inside, LeBron went, "Ooooooh," like a kid at the grand finale.

Then he dropped dead.

1 "So what happened," said the scruffy man leading the AA meeting, "is that my wife took the kids and moved back to Minnesota. She left the dog, though."

Colin Marsh had stopped listening. He knew the man, and he knew the man's story. He knew the stories of every single person at the meeting, all twenty-three of them, because the stories never changed. People drank. One day they started drinking too much, and the day after or the day after that, they realized they *needed* to drink. Some started in the morning. They all kept it secret. They hid bottles in the basement, in the back of the closet, or under the kitchen sink. One day someone said something about the drinking: a boyfriend complained, a boss threatened, a wife got angry. The anger was met with righteous outrage, and the drink fueled the drinker's blamelessness because wouldn't you drink if you had a shitty job and a nagging partner and a seven-year-old Toyota with a bad water pump? Wouldn't you want a little bit of relief at the end—or even at the beginning—of the day, to escape the bills and asshole bosses and overdue insurance premiums? Of course you would.

Colin yawned. The leader was winding down.

"So anyway," the man said, "I'm glad I'm here."

"Thanks for sharing!" A dozen voices. Colin closed his eyes and sighed. Catherine, seated next to him, hissed, "Colin!"

"I'm not sleeping," he whispered. "Really."

Colin Marsh was in the basement of the Arlington Church of the Redeemer, in the back row on a folding chair, sipping a tepid cup of 7-Eleven coffee. The chair, he liked to say, had cost him a few hundred thousand dollars in wasted opportunities. It was his; he'd bought and paid dearly for it.

He had two years and seven months of sobriety now. One night's uncontrolled drinking had wiped almost fifteen years of clean time. He also had a cold.

In the past, a cold was a welcome opportunity to mix over-the-counter decongestants with shots of vodka and earn a pleasantly bleary buzz that could be justified and might last a few twenty-four hours, bolstered by cups of Ramen soup and Sara Lee frozen brownies.

Not any longer. Now he avoided cough syrups, cold pills, and anything that might trigger a need. He still liked Sarah Lee cakes and sometimes Ramen.

After the meeting, they went food shopping, and Catherine asked, "So I'm going with you to the funeral, right? I hate driving in Maryland. I always get lost."

They were pushing a cart at Safeway. He was loading it with green and red vegetables; Catherine had given him a juicer some weeks earlier. He had yet to see the machine's benefits, and she insisted he use it twice a day for a full three months.

They would be going to the funeral of Antwone, a youth their friend Mamadou Dioh had taken in.

"It's so sad. First Mamadou loses a sister, and now the boy. I can't imagine going through that." She looked down at her shoes. "I was going crazy when Josie was gone."

Two years earlier, Colin and Mamadou Dioh, a former policeman from Senegal, had saved Catherine's daughter, Josie, from a murderous drug dealer. Rescuing the girl did not go well. A policeman friend was shot and mortally wounded; the girl had been near death when they'd found her. In time, things had quieted down and Mamadou had more or less adopted Antwone, a troubled black youth in whom he'd glimpsed promise.

Three days ago, following an anonymous phone call made to the local precinct, the police found Antwone dead under a park bench in Northeast Washington.

"I know," Colin said. "That sort of thing makes you stop believing in God. I don't know how much more Mamadou can take. When I saw him yesterday, he looked a hundred years old."

"He's thinking of selling the limo business."

"And moving back to Senegal. Yeah, he told me."

They fell silent. Colin paid for his veggies at the automated checkout under the watchful eye of a sari-wearing employee. Catherine said, "I promise the juicing will start working within another week."

"You said that last week."

"I lied."

Mr. Snow waited on a side street near Columbia Pike in the Virginia suburbs, some eight miles from Washington, D.C. He was parked in an inexpensive rental car among other inexpensive cars, some dented, others polished to a high gleam, and many wearing cheap bolt-on chrome accessories from AutoZone and Pep Boys. The street on both sides was lined with two-story red brick apartment buildings that looked like former army barracks. In every other window, an air-conditioning unit hummed and wept. He was listening to an NPR program on dying oceans and wondering who really gave a shit if sea bass and barracudas vanished, because he certainly didn't. He'd never cared for fresh- or salt-water seafood, sushi, scuttling crustaceans, tanning lotion, or sand anywhere on his person. He reddened when subjected to sunlight and, when sunburned, itched and flaked and peeled in the most disgusting way, shedding strips of skin from his face and shoulders.

He was hoping, but only somewhat confident, that Lobo would not hang him by his *cojones* from a low branch. This was something Lobo had apparently suggested, hopefully as a joke, ha ha. It was hot.

Seatbelt removed, Mr. Snow ate from a bag of cold popcorn. He wished he were at the air-conditioned shooting range in Rockville squeezing off shots at a paper target.

The wait might last hours. He played a couple of CDs, classical and Beatles, and resisted the urge to exit the car and stretch. He found an AM station with a right-wing commentator—the Voice of Reason, the man called himself—railing against Obamacare. Jesus, thought Mr. Snow, where do people like that come from? He personally liked Obamacare and considered himself somewhat of a liberal even though, he knew, most people in his line of work were arch-conservatives who'd vote for Agent Orange.

After a while he turned the radio off and leafed through an old issue of *Wired* he'd taken from his dentist's office. He understood less than half of what was written and became annoyed by the magazine's confusing layout.

The world was moving too fast; he couldn't keep up with the technology. It was disconcerting, all these new sciences and inventions and discoveries fighting for space. He liked to think of himself as a man on top of things but the gadgets and equipment that blinked, buzzed, and talked back were simply too much. He scanned the magazine with diminishing interest.

Shortly after dusk, a teen-aged boy in overlarge black baggy pants and a hooded sweatshirt knocked on the car's passenger window. Mr. Snow rolled it down a few inches, and the boy asked, "You lookin' for somebody?"

Mr. Snow handed the youth a twenty and said, "Lobo. I want to see Lobo."

The boy was squatting next to the car. He took the bill and said, "Lo who?"

"Lobo," Mr. Snow repeated.

"Ain't no Lo nothing around here, man. Watcha want?"

Mr. Snow handed the boy another bill. "I'd like to see Lobo."

The boy pulled a large caliber pistol out of his pants, aimed it casually at Mr. Snow's head. "Ain't no Lobo or Bobo or Hoho or nothin' here for you, man. Really. Take my word for it. You makin' people here concerned, sittin' in your crappy car and eatin' popcorn, and these are nice people that don't need to be concerned 'bout nothing. You what, 'migration?"

The boy was probably at the bottom of the hierarchy, a sentry, not yet even a foot soldier in the system.

Mr. Snow tried a shallow smile. "Lobo lives around here, I know he does. I'd very much like to meet him and no, I'm not from immigration."

The boy shook his head, shoved the gun back into his pants. "You crazy. You stay here, some sort of white street zombie concernin' people with your popcorn, something bad for sure gonna happen." He stood, adjusted his pants, walked off and vanished in the shadows between two buildings.

Mr. Snow rolled up the car window and waited. He fiddled with the radio and found an AM station playing Big Band music. He had allotted six hours and $800 to this mission.

After another forty-five minutes, the boy came back accompanied by a very short man who could have passed for a child. The adolescent look was marred by a scar that traveled from the man's receding hairline, crossed his nose, ran haphazardly down his cheek and neck and vanished into a white T-shirt. His arms were sinewy and veined, covered with amateur tattoos.

Mr. Snow lowered the car window again. The short man said, "So wazis?"

Mr. Snow held a hundred-dollar bill out. "I need to see Lobo. It's important. My name is Mr. Snow. We're old friends."

"Snow?"

"Yes, Snow. Like rain, except it's Snow."

The man didn't touch the bill. "Don't know no Lobo, and if I did, he wouldn't have no friends like you."

Mr. Snow peeled off another hundred.

The man shook his head. "Why you offering me money? You think that's gonna help you?" Then he nodded at the kid who snatched the bills from Mr. Snow's hand.

Mr. Snow was unfazed. "Lobo's name is Geovany Sandino, or maybe Yann Sandrin. Or something that starts with a Y and an S. He's 41. He claims to be an Aztec. He has a wife, Carmen, but she's in Managua. He did four years for beating up a snitch. He got out in March. He lives in this neighborhood."

"Roll down the window some more."

Mr. Snow did and the little man stuck his head inside the car, looked around. "You got this from what, Rent-a-Piece–of-Shit-dot-com?" He withdrew his head then put out his hand. Mr. Snow handed over a hundred dollars.

"Tell you what, Mr. Popcorn. You come back in three days, same time, except you leave your car in the Rexall parking lot up at the intersection," he pointed up the street, "and you walk here, and you wait. And you wear shorts with no pockets, and a T-shirt, and shoes and no socks, and if there is a Mr. Lobo, which there ain't, and if he wants to see you, which he probably won't, and he don't hang you from a tree by your *cojones*, which I would enjoy seein', and which is possible, maybe something'll happen. Or maybe not. I wouldn't get my hopes up. That'll be another two hundred, Mr. Popcorn."

Mr. Snow handed him the money. The man and boy walked a short distance and turned into an alley. Mr. Snow nodded to himself. It had taken three hours and he was still under budget. Plus, his *cojones* were intact.

2 MAMADOU DIOH WAS IN THE DARKENED GARAGE where he kept AfriCars' four limos. The aging S-Class Mercedes he owned for personal use was parked outside. His Washington, D.C. neighborhood was quiet as if respecting the demise of one of its own. Someone was tapping on the door, but he didn't move.

After a short while, the tapping stopped and a square of paper appeared under the door. Mamadou lit a Gauloise with his silver Dupont lighter and poured an inch of brandy into a stained coffee cup. He sipped, inhaled, sipped again, then dropped the cigarette and ground it into the concrete flooring.

Eventually, he removed his blazer, found a rag and started polishing the chrome hubcaps of AfriCars One. He finished that and moved to AfriCars Two, which bore stubborn tar stains on its rocker panels. He used solvent on the rag to clean the tar off.

This had been Antwone's job, which the boy had done meticulously. Antwone had kept the cars spotless, vacuuming their interiors every morning before school and slipping little Christmas tree deodorizers beneath the front seats.

Antwone had pleaded to drive the cars, but Mamadou had said he was too young, maybe in a few months.

Antwone had then produced an OpenOffice spreadsheet showing how Mamadou's profits would increase if he, Antwone, were allowed to do small chauffeuring jobs. This would save Mamadou the expense of hiring a temp driver for half a day when the man only worked an hour or so. Plus, Antwone said, he had ascertained *conclusively* (Antwone's own words) that the occasional drivers were cheating Mamadou when they gassed up the limos. The receipts were inflated and, he told Mamadou, "the numbers simply don't match up. I can prove it."

"I'm sure you can, Ant. But the answer is still no, you can't drive until you have your license."

Antwone had wanted to argue. Mamadou threw him a warning look and the boy shrugged. "It's your money, *Monsoor*. You want to waste it, that's your business." He pulled a folded sheet of paper from a pocket and waved it in Mamadou's direction. "According to my calculations, we could be saving $8,241.76 annually if you just listened to me. But no, *Monsoor Le Grand Policeman du Sénégal* isn't going to take advice from some poor nigrah child that *Monsoor* rescued from the evils of the street." Then the boy had dropped to a crouch and polished the chrome headlight rims of AfriCars One.

Antwone had been a delight. That he died of an overdose was unthinkable.

Mamadou drained the cognac, poured a second, and looked into the cup. His eye teared and he hurled the cup away. It shattered against a wall and sprayed AfriCars Three with brandy. *"Crétin! Tu es un crétin! Tu veux devenir un soulard comme Colin? Espèce de con! Pauvre connard!"*

A quiet, elderly voice said, "You'd better wipe that car off quick. That rotgut you've been drinking is going to eat the gloss coat right off."

Mamadou didn't turn. "Hello, George." He sighed, found a clean rag and sponged off the car.

"I never learned French," George said. "Can you translate?"

Mamadou blotted up the last trace of brandy from the hood. "I was calling myself an idiot and a cretin. Also, asking myself—rhetorically— if I wanted to become a drunk like my friend Colin."

George was quiet for a space, then said, "That was a good thing, what you and him did."

"Saved one life, lost another."

"The policeman."

"Joe. Yes." Mamadou nodded, dropped the rag into a laundry hamper. "It's good to see you, George."

George was immaculately dressed in a suit from the 1940s. He was ageless, small-boned and chestnut-colored with slicked-down white hair and false teeth a bit too large for his mouth.

"I can't tell you how sorry Mim and I are. I just can't."

George sat down slowly on a folding chair, careful to preserve the crease of his trousers. "We're both sick at heart. Mim just loved that boy. Loved him like a grandson. She'd even opened a savings account for his college."

Mamadou looked up. "Did she?" He shook his head. "She never told me."

"Mim was pretty sure he'd get a scholarship. It was just so he'd have rent and food money, maybe get a used car."

"That was kind of her."

"He was a smart boy, Antwone."

Mamadou turned away and wiped water from his eyes.

"Mim can't go to the funeral, of course, but she'd like you to come by one day soon. Will you do that?"

Years ago, Aunt Mim had taken to her bed and never gotten up. Mamadou nodded.

"Good."

George got to his feet, came to Mamadou, and hugged him awkwardly, his arms barely encompassing the bigger man's chest.

"You're going to be all right? Anything at all you need?"

"I'll be fine."

George stooped, picked up the square of paper he'd slid under the garage door and folded it carefully.

"You come and see Mim, all right? She'll be expecting you, and you don't want to disappoint her. She's hard to live with when she's disappointed." He nodded once, adjusted his tie, smiled sadly, and walked away.

After George left, Mamadou took the bottle of brandy and emptied it into the bathroom sink.

The last death in his family had been Amélie, his youngest sister. She'd died at the hand of a drug-dealing youth who'd addicted and abandoned her. That had led to a necessary vengeance. Aunt Mim had told him how to find his sister's murderer.

And then things had taken a strange turn. Now, not that long after Amélie's passing, Mamadou gladly took the money of bad people to drive them around. He chauffeured men he knew were drug dealers, thieves, smugglers, and extortionists—there had to be a murderer or two in the lot. He made conversation with them, had been obsequious at times, and never once refused a large tip or an invitation to serve them again.

The hypocrisy wore at him. What to do? And, more important, would he allow Antwone's death to go unpunished?

No.

That would be wrong.

What worked well for Mamadou was revenge. He didn't exult in it, but it was obligatory.

On the 5th floor of the courthouse building in Fairfax, Virginia, Gloria Rose Nachtalyan sat in her office and sipped Caffeine Free Diet Coke. It was eleven in the morning, and she was already on the third can. A case was in the closet next to her umbrella, snow boots, and a purple rolled-up yoga mat. Only six Cokes were left. She'd have to replenish the supply during her lunch hour, which meant missing her noon yoga class, which she had already missed four times in a row. This, she knew, was how bad habits were formed.

There was a machine in the cafeteria that dispensed Caffeine Free Diet Coke, but at a buck twenty-five a pop, it offended her fiscal sensitivities. At Costco, a case of two dozen Cokes was $3.75 on sale, so where did the vendors get off charging county workers so much money?

This was one of the small indignities fate rained down daily upon Gloria Rose Nachtalyan. Others included the newly relined employee parking lot with the narrower spaces designed for tiny un-American foreign cars. Now it was hard to exit her 1993 Lincoln Continental without banging the driver's side door into the car next to hers. A third was the homeless man who leered at her when she came to work and made disgusting slurping sounds as she passed by. A fourth was, how in the world had her numbskull, maybe gay, boss risen so high? The man was a consummate bean-counter whose existence was justified by his unending battle to save the county pennies. He deserved a name tag: Ralph Charrette—Loser.

There were other, smaller humiliations. The empty toilet paper dispenser in the women's room stalls; Pete, the legume-spewing lacto-vegetarian who too often insisted on sharing her table at lunch; the *Washington Post* which no longer ran either *Broom-Hilda* or *The Far Side* in the comic pages but still had Mark Trail. *Mark Trail!* Who reads *Mark Trail?* Nobody, is who.

Despite grievances, Gloria Rose was not one to disregard her blessings. The Lincoln she had inherited from her stepfather ran like a top. She loved her cats, Sarah and Courtney, and liked her apartment, though she wished the trash chute weren't directly across the hall from her front door. For a woman with only an Associates Degree in Office Management, she was doing well. She missed having sex, but that was manageable. Sometimes at night she wished her ex, Clarence, was still there to hold her, but she'd bought a full-size body pillow on Amazon and a Rabbit vibrator and that helped.

The problem was, things got more expensive daily, and county salaries were frozen three years in a row before being raised a measly two percent across the board. There had been staff cutbacks at the Department of Management and Budget where she worked, so this was not the time to ask for a raise.

Thank Heavens for Mr. Snow and his $2000 a month.

Gloria Rose was reasonably certain she didn't have the full story on Mr. Snow. He had appeared a half-year ago claiming to be a consultant in a firm hired by a large pharmaceutical company. The company sought information about state and county funds spent to combat drug addiction. Mr. Snow needed numbers: How many addicts? How much drugs? Policing efforts, rehabs, interdiction programs, needle exchanges, ambulance services, and detoxes in local hospitals. And what about social services, child protection, job training for former addicts? How much did all this cost the community? The pharmaceutical company was spending a fortune on opiate replacement research, and the bean-counters needed dollar figures to justify costs to the shareholders.

He'd bought her coffee twice, then taken her to lunch at Ruth's Chris Steak House. While she was cutting the Porterhouse with her fork, he'd told her there was a choice. "I can spend a lot of money wining and dining your boss Ralph, or I can give you the money and get the same information. You already know what they know. So what do you think?"

She didn't need a lot of time to think. Her useless boss was making $115K annually, and she did most of his work. Mr. Snow would be paying her $100 a day for basic info on county expenditures. He asked only that she send him an email once a week outlining what she'd heard or seen. He'd even bought her an iPad and watched as she set up a Gmail account for herself under a fictitious name.

So she fed Mr. Snow snippets of information strewn alongside bits of material that might discredit her boss—long lunch hours, golf weekends with potential county suppliers, unreported vacation leave, wasteful use of office supplies—all of this despite his obsession with cost-cutting.

Mr. Snow bought her dinner once at Charlie Chiang's, and over cocktail and a bottle of excellent Cabernet, they both had admitted to very limited experiments with illegal substances in their youths, which was many years ago. Mr. Snow had tried cocaine, once, and sort of liked it. Amazingly, so had Gloria, once. Well, maybe twice. And occasionally now and again, if her now-former boyfriend happened to have some on hand which, she hastened to add, was very rarely.

By the time the after-dinner drinks came—brandy for him, Benedictine for her—they were old friends. Gloria admitted that she *really* liked cocaine. Mr. Snow said he wasn't even sure cocaine should be illegal. Gloria agreed; they were of one mind.

At work, she culled information for him. Most of it was available on the web. A hundred bucks a day just to surf the Net—not too shabby. It kept her in QVC money. And coke money. Not Caffeine Free Diet Coke money; the *other* coke money.

About three months earlier, or maybe a little longer than that, Gloria Rose realized she'd gone from recreational cocaine use to just maybe, possibly, a little bit dependent. One night after going through the last of her stash, she watched three episodes of *The Blacklist;* she adored James Spader ever since *Boston Legal.* If anything—or anyone—could soothe her wants, it was Spader. Binge watching him had gotten her through the breakup with Clarence, the man who'd introduced her to cocaine and provided excellent sex. As the evening wore on, she tried to deny the craving and found Spader powerless.

Halfway through the fourth *Blacklist,* Gloria Rose's heart was beating too quickly, and both legs were jumping up and down in time with the program's theme music.

She drank a can of Caffeine Free Diet Coke in two swallows. When she closed her eyes two white lines stretched like highway markers into infinity.

She got dressed and drove to the convenience store where Bong Bong, the small Filipino supplier—he wasn't a *dealer;* she didn't have a *dealer*—normally reigned behind the counter. Bong Bong was not there. It cost her $50 to get his telephone number from the other Filipino who worked nights and whose name she didn't know (Bing Bing?).

When she rang the number, it went unanswered for a long time. Bong Bong finally picked up, sounding both sleepy and irritated. He kept saying, "Who dis? Who dis," as Gloria Rose tried to identify herself and why she was calling. She was no dummy, she used the code word 'merchandise' in case someone was listening.

Bong Bong said, "You crazy lady? You calling me at home, wake up my wife and baby!"

She apologized, and he said, "This is gonna cost you. You got money? Cause you know, your lack of planning is not my emergency."

She said she did. He asked how much. She said $200. He told her to go to an ATM and get another $400 and he'd meet her in twenty minutes behind the Shop N Go on Lexington. She did as he said. It seemed like a lot, but then again she was saving a lot by buying her Caffeine Free Diet Coke by the case at Costco.

Bong Bong ran late and by the time he arrived she was desperately eager to give him the $600. She felt an overwhelming sense of gratitude; when she tried to hug him, he recoiled and said, "You go home now," and made shooing motions with his hands. He drove away in a 1996 Camaro.

In her 1993 Lincoln, she opened the little clear plastic bag. Not much to show for $600, but certainly enough to get her through a night or two.

She almost dipped a finger into the powder to rub it into her gums but resisted the urge. She'd wait until she got home to Spader. She drove slowly; the Lincoln was the sort of car cops stopped now and then just to talk, and she wasn't taking chances.

When she was back in her apartment, she used a Ginsu knife to make two fat lines of coke, then four.

Then she made two more, and then another two.

In the morning, she was surprised how little was left in the bottom of the baggie and when she blew her nose there was a little blood in the Kleenex. Her head hurt and her eyes felt gritty. That had been a strange night. Now, though, she felt she had things under control.

It was a question of willpower, no matter what anyone said.

She'd spent a few evenings researching cocaine on the Internet. She learned about half-life, the amount of time it took for half of the drug to be eliminated from her system. Cocaine's half-life was short; in under an hour, half the cocaine she used would be assimilated, which explained why she'd want more. That little piece of knowledge was strangely comforting. It wasn't that she was abnormal; it was that the drug itself didn't last long, like cotton candy at the circus.

She found out other things too. Some scientists believed cocaine dependence was not an addiction. That was good to know and bolstered her confidence. A few authorities thought its use should be legalized. She wasn't sure about that; not everyone had her degree of self-discipline; not everyone could handle cocaine, just like not everyone could handle booze. Her stepfather, God rest his soul, had been one of those quiet drunks who passed out every night while watching The Late Show. He'd died there, right in front of the flickering TV with a half-empty fifth of Old Crow nestled between his feet, a perfect example of the powerless drunk. Not her; she'd always handled booze well, and knew exactly when to stop.

Now she used coke only on Mondays, Wednesdays, and Fridays, and sometimes Saturdays if she felt the urge, which she did, more and more.

She'd have to ask Mr. Snow for a raise; hundred bucks a day simply wasn't enough. And she needed another supplier, preferably without a double name, who was more amenable to doing commerce at night.

Not 72 hours after his encounter with Lobo's people, Mr. Snow was thinking a hundred bucks wasn't what it used to be. He had several hundred dollar bills in his pocket, but nowadays, this was chump change.

He was standing in the street near Lobo's apartment wearing a T-shirt, moccasins without socks, and running shorts that didn't have pockets. His keys dangled from his left hand. He felt vulnerable. His forty-year-old legs were naked and fish-belly white; he tried to remember the last time they'd seen the sun but couldn't. He was less worried about his *cojones* than he'd been three days earlier and confident he would come out of the meeting unmaimed.

He'd been waiting twenty minutes. He knew a dozen or more sets of eyes were looking at him, and a score of phone calls probably had already been made by the ever-watchful community. There wasn't a soul on the street; occasionally a curtain moved. The neighborhood knew something was going on and was holding its breath.

A Fairfax County police cruiser crept past him, stopped, rolled back. The passenger window slid down and a black cop waved at him to come closer.

"Waiting for someone?"

Mr. Snow nodded. He looked at his wrist and realized he wasn't wearing a watch. "My girlfriend. She's late."

"Your girlfriend?" The cop's eyes opened wide in disbelief.

"Yessir. Fiancée actually."

"Fiancée? Imagine that!" The cop turned to his partner behind the steering wheel. "Man's waiting for his feeyonsay…"

The other cop laughed, said something Mr. Snow couldn't hear entirely but it sounded like 'Beyoncé.'

The first cop said, "Well now, you might want to go to one of those tanning salon places and get a little color on you. Fit better in the neighborhood, if you know what I mean."

Mr. Snow nodded. "Yessir. Plan on going to Acapulco for our honeymoon."

The cop had lost interest. He rolled up his window and the car drifted away.

Mr. Snow looked around. Still nobody. He wished the shorts had pockets. He detested wearing shoes without socks and wondered if his rental car would be safe in the Rexall parking lot. He admired Lobo's way of doing things, though; very professional. Make the other guy uncomfortable; take away any semblance of security and maximize unease. Get the upper hand by humbling him. Mr. Snow couldn't have done it better himself.

The police car returned. The passenger cop opened the back door on the street side and said, "Get in."

Mr. Snow said, "My fiancée…"

The cop said, "Your fiancée is probably giving blowjobs in an alley even as we speak. Get in."

Mr. Snow got in. There was a grill between the front and rear compartments of the car, and no door latches or window opening switches. The back seat was heavy vinyl and smelled faintly of urine;

the floor was lined with some sort of thick and tough sound-deadening material; a large metal o-ring was bolted in the middle of the floor pan.

Mr. Snow thought even more highly of Lobo; that was pretty slick, having the two cops working for him. He wondered how much that cost and decided a lot more than a hundred a day.

They drove a block to a red brick apartment house that looked exactly like all the others nearby. The car stopped and Passenger Cop pushed a button. The rear door popped open and he said, "Okay, get out. Stand on the sidewalk and don't move." Mr. Snow did as he was told. The cop car sped away. Soon the man from three days earlier with the facial scars and tattoos came out of a doorway.

"Mr. Popcorn! You're back! Follow me."

The man led him past a row of garbage cans to a door set deep within the red brick wall. Mr. Snow spotted several expensive surveillance cameras and nodded in approval. Nothing Kmart about those babies— top of the line Lorex night-vision units. He counted eight in all before the tattooed man said, "Ain't got all day, ya know."

He walked through the door… and was astonished.

He was in a large, airy room with walls painted a light grey. Mahogany wainscoting extended from hip height down to the baseboards. A twenty-foot ceiling was broken by skylights that let in the warm summer sunshine. Eight large fans hung down and spun slowly. Highly polished oaken slats lined the floor, and a row of Louis Poulsen lamps shone dimly. In the middle of the floor, if as an afterthought, lay an antique Persian Tabriz Sickle Leaf rug. Mr. Snow knew his Orientals. Eighteen to twenty grand, minimum.

To his right was a small drawing he recognized as a Diego Rivera. Next to it, a slightly larger Botero.

The tattooed man prodded him forward. "Yeah, they're the real thing, okay? You got no manners? Your momma never told you not to stare? It's not polite."

At the far end of the room, a thin man in a cream-colored suit sat at an ornate desk, flanked by two muscular bodyguards. The tattooed man held Mr. Snow's arm in a painful grip and said, "Wait until he tells you to come closer."

Eventually, the man behind the desk looked up and smiled; fifty-thousand dollars' worth of perfectly white teeth gleamed.

"Charlie Snow! Welcome! Welcome!" He motioned with his right hand, and the tattooed man stepped back. Mr. Snow approached. The bodyguards stepped closer, but the man waved his hand again and they retreated. "Charlie Snow," he repeated. "You're not going to try to hurt me, are you?"

Mr. Snow shook his head. "No, Lobo, of course not."

The man's smile grew. "Well then, come closer! I won't have to hang you by your *cojones*! Have a seat!"

One of the bodyguards brought a chair, placed it ten feet from the desk—smart, Mr. Snow thought—and motioned to it.

Mr. Snow sat, and sweat from his armpits dribbled down the sides of his chest. His *cojones* felt very vulnerable.

The man behind the desk grinned again and said, "You know, I don't think anyone has called me Lobo to my face in a couple of years. That brings back so many memories. Like the time you tried to kill me. Remember?"

Mr. Snow nodded. "An unfortunate event."

Lobo's smile didn't waver. "That took *cojones*," he said.

It was a bright blue day. The church was almost empty. Antwone had had no family save Mamadou, and Mamadou had few friends. His brothers and sisters had come in from five states across the nation but only one, Moustapha, had actually known Antwone well.

Colin noticed George dressed nattily in yet another suit from the 1940s; Aunt Mim, George's partner for more than half a century, had sent a monstrously large bouquet whose aroma overwhelmed the church. The regular AfriCars limo drivers were there, as were Catherine and her daughter, Josie, who stood close to her mother.

Colin had become uneasy when with both women. Catherine may have forgiven him the one night with her daughter, and Josie was not even aware that early in her sobriety, she'd spent the briefest of time in bed with the man who would become her mother's lover. Still, when he and the two women were together, Colin felt as if he were teetering on a mountain of shifting glass.

Mamadou was burying Antwone in the Cedar Hill Cemetery across the Potomac in Maryland. Earlier that day, he'd told Colin, "We never discussed death. Who discusses such a thing with a 15-year-old?" He'd wiped his eyes with a white handkerchief. "I'd like him to be someplace I can visit. And he always liked going fishing on the Maryland side of the river."

Colin nodded. "Does that mean you're going to stay?"

Mamadou shrugged.

Colin said, "I'm really happy to hear that. Catherine will be, too."

Mamadou stuffed his hands into his pockets. "I always thought I'd return one day, but there isn't a lot to go back to, Colin; some distant cousins in Dakar, but my parents are gone, and the rest of us are here in this country. Who was it who said, 'You can never go home again'? One of your writers."

"Thomas Wolfe," said Colin.

"It's probably true," Mamadou said, and then fell silent.

The service was brief. Mamadou, Colin remembered, was not a believer in any deity, Muslim, Christian, or otherwise. A young girl sang a song neither Catherine nor Colin recognized. The coffin was carried into the hearse by Mamadou's people, with George, slighter than the other men by half, pretending to hold up one corner.

Catherine and Colin followed the hearse across the river to Suitland. Colin's Porsche was third in the cortege.

"The last time Mamadou went through something like this," Colin told Catherine, "he just about wiped out a gang single-handedly."

"He has always scared me a little," Catherine said. "He tries to hide his anger but it's right there, just below the surface. I remember that from when I met him the very first time. I wouldn't want to stand in his way."

Josie spoke for the first time in minutes. "He saved my life." She was squeezed in the car's cramped back seat.

Catherine nodded. "I know."

Colin said, "He's fair, but he's a hard man. Some of the stories he told me about being a cop in Senegal..." He let the words trail off.

"Does anyone know what happened? With Antwone, I mean?" Josie had met Antwone a few times, had thought him cute and smart.

Colin shrugged. "He overdosed on heroin. That's the official cause of death."

Josie frowned. "That's hard to believe, you know. I've been in enough rehabs to know about heroin addicts, and I never met one like Antwone. He really hated drugs. He told me that once; we were talking about how his mom and dad were both crack addicts. They'd leave him alone for days with a jar of peanut butter and a box of crackers. He was maybe seven, eight years old."

"Mamadou thinks he was smoking it," Colin said. "When he went to identify the body at the morgue, he looked for tracks on Antwone's arms and legs. There weren't any."

Catherine shuddered. "God. I can't imagine having to do something like that."

Josie shivered and made a face.

Colin parked the car and they joined the small gathering. They stood near the grave with a dozen or so onlookers and listened to the preacher say the necessary words and intone a prayer. The coffin was lowered into the ground. Mamadou threw in a handful of dirt, as did his brothers and sisters. George followed, and then Colin, Catherine, and Josie.

The sky turned overcast and, in the far distance, a shudder of thunder rolled.

Colin noticed a tall, thin woman standing at the edge of the sparse crowd. Three exactly identical small boys encircled her, dressed in their Sunday best. Dark blue suits, white shirts and red ties, shiny black patent leather shoes. Each had a handkerchief folded carefully in the breast pocket of his jacket.

As people were returning to their cars, the woman and the boys approached. Mamadou was talking to George. The old man smiled at them, and the woman and her boys came forward.

The one in the center said, "We wanted to say we're really sorry about Antwone."

The other two blinked in agreement. The woman nudged the boy on the right. "He helped us with our homework."

The boy on the left said, "Especially with numbers. We're not good at numbers."

Mamadou nodded. "Yes. Antwone told me about you." He turned to the woman. She thrust out her hand. "I'm DiAngela Jones, Mr. Dioh." She pointed to the three in turn. "This is Dionne; this is Dewan; this is Darnell. We can't tell you how bad we feel about Antwone. He was a wonderful, beautiful boy. But you know that." She smiled sadly. "I still can't believe it. I keep thinking it must be some mistake."

"I know. I feel the same way, Miss Jones."

"*Mrs.* Jones."

"I'm sorry, *Mrs.* Jones."

She smiled at him. "Actually, I don't know why I insist on that. *Mr.* Jones hasn't been seen since these three were born…"

"Ah," said Mamadou, "I'm sorry."

DiAngela Jones smiled again, "I'm not. Worst thing that ever happened to me was him. Best thing that ever happened to me was them," she nodded towards the triplets.

"They're handsome boys." He bent down, put out his right hand. Each boy shook it formally.

"Antwone helped them a lot, and not just with homework. He taught them politeness and manners, and I'll tell you what, Mr. Dioh, I don't know how he did it. But the first time one of them opened a door for me, that was a surprise! Now they fight to do that. They say please and thank you and…" Tears welled in her eyes.

Mamadou placed a gentle hand on her shoulder. She gathered her boys and stepped back. "Antwone was a blessing, Mr. Dioh. A God-sent blessing."

She rummaged in her purse and found a card. "I know you're going to be busy, and you need your time to mourn. But if there's anything I can do," she handed him the card. "Anything at all. Antwone told us about your cars. The boys are good at cleaning and polishing, though you'd have to supervise them." She smiled again.

"Thank you." Mamadou put the card in his pocket. He looked around, said, "Excuse me. I have to talk to some of the other people before they leave. But thank you for coming. Thank you for telling me about Antwone and your boys. That was kind of you."

She nodded to one of the triplets, Dewan.

"We's real sorry, Mr. Dioh."

"*We're* real sorry," Darnell corrected his brother.

Dewan ignored him. "Well, we really is."

Dionne added, "Antwone be a real good teacher, Mr. Dioh."

Darnell opened his mouth to say something then just rolled his eyes.

As they were walking away, Dewan turned and ran back to Mamadou.

"Antwone said we was to keep away from Ru So. He said Ru So was a bad man and we should run if we ever seen him."

"Ru So?" Mamadou didn't know the name.

"Ru So," the boy said again. "We was to run."

Now DiAngela Jones and the other two triplets stopped and retraced their steps.

"We *were* to run," Dionne corrected his brother, "and it's *see* him, not *seen*."

"Were. See." Dewan repeated.

DiAngela Jones grabbed Dewan by the arm and pulled him away. "Don't you bother the man, you. He's got things to do!"

Mamadou looked at the woman. "Who is Ru So?"

She shrugged. "I don't know. But Antwone told the boys that, the last time they were together, about a week or ten days ago. And that's what they keep repeating now, 'Run if you see Ru So.' I'm not sure what it means."

DiAngela Jones looked at Mamadou sadly, shrugged once, turned and walked away, the three boys trailing after her like ducklings.

Colin and Catherine were talking with George. Josie was steps away smoking a cigarette and looking over the expanse of gravestones.

Mamadou said, "George, could you ask Aunt Mim something when you see her? If she's ever heard of someone called Ru So?"

"Ru So," George repeated. "Like the French philosopher?"

Mamadou looked blank.

George smiled tightly. "Jean Jacques Rousseau. Born 1712, died 1778. *The Social Contract. Discourse on Inequality. Confessions.*"

"Oh," said Mamadou. "Of course. *That* Rousseau," and smiled for the only time that day, then added, "No, it's probably not that Rousseau."

3 COLIN'S RELATIONSHIP WITH CATHERINE had barely survived his relapse. That one night when he had decided sobriety was not paying off, when he went to a bar and drank himself insensate, and when his wheelchair-bound sponsor, Orin, found him and brought him home; that night had been wounding.

The evening's intake—sixteen shots, according to the bartender—had stripped Colin's sobriety bare.

Catherine had been shocked. He had so many more clean years than she did, how could he throw it all away without a second thought?

He'd tried to explain things to her, how some alcoholics and addicts felt deep within that they hadn't been given the handbook of basic rules; they had to make it up as they went along. Invariably, they made it up wrong and suffered the consequences.

It wasn't marching to the beat of a different drum, he told her, but stumbling in the dark to constant cacophony. Time after time the same concept was brought up, discussed, and illustrated with drunkalogs. Both Colin and Catherine knew it was as if the non-drinkers, those clear-eyed and healthy earth people, had a set of rules known from earliest childhood, rules that made sense, that allowed travel from point A to point B without being manhandled or molested and left wounded by the roadside. The longer an individual didn't understand the rules or, worse, had no rule book at all, the harder it got.

Family and friends and lovers raced by with a set destination in mind, a well-delineated future with razor sharp horizons. The drunks, meanwhile, the shooters, the huffers and skin-poppers and inhalers of noxious fumes, those of inexplicable behavior, they had no idea. They witnessed the world as a place where velocity mattered, a place where others got a running start while they stood still and watched, bottle or pipe or pills in hand, barely capable of staying upright.

Their world was not a horizontal place; it was a landscape of massive ups and downs distressed by mudslides and tremors, a geography of peaks and abysses without a middle ground. There was elation and there was depression and there was nothing in between. So, of course, they drank or smoked or ate or gambled or drugged! And, if one or two among them were very, very fortunate, if at three in the morning in the darkness of winter they had an epiphany, a whole-body realization that there *had to be* another way, then and only then, might they end up in a church basement on a Friday night with a dozen or so sufferers of shared proclivities, others who understood their dim situations and suggested there might be an answer. Not an *easy* one, mind you, because the easy answers got you into the bottle in the first place—but a hard-earned solution leading to a modicum of peace.

Catherine's trek to AA had taken a different route than Colin's; no two drunks' roads were really alike, though the end destination was often the same.

She now had more uninterrupted and sober 24-hours than he had. She was good about it and never brought it up, except for the one time she said, "It's not like all those years are gone forever, you know. You still have them. You just took a little break."

Or, as his sponsor Orin said, he'd gone out and done more research. He'd backslid. He'd picked up. He'd slipped. He'd fallen off the wagon. He'd fucked up. Recovering drunks had more words for *relapse* than Inuits have words for *snow.*

For Colin, that one night at the bar had changed a lot of things, important and not so important.

He no longer exercised compulsively. He'd sold his weights and the leg-press machine on Craigslist and used the small sum gained to buy his car a new muffler. He ran once or twice a week. He went to more meetings and attended Al Anon on Saturday mornings. Sometimes, if they'd spent Friday night together, Catherine accompanied him. He still did writers' research for a living and had increased his prices without seeing a loss of demand for his services. "You're getting a reputation. People keep mentioning you in the forewords of their books. Other writers notice."

"Seems sort of silly now. You can find everything on the Net."

"Not everything," Catherine argued. "That's why they need you."

The relationship wasn't quite the same either. It had become more precarious, warier.

"That relapse scared me," Catherine told him. "It scared Josie, too. We both thought you were fireproof, you know? That you'd be the last person on Earth to go out and get drunk."

That annoyed him at first, and Catherine saw it.

"That's a compliment, you know."

"No," Colin said, "not really. It's an expectation. I don't want to be Mr. AA. It surprised the hell out of me too, but it was a lesson. I was starting to believe I'm above all this program crap, and I'm not."

Catherine didn't speak of it again, but Josie did.

After the funeral, Colin dropped them off at Catherine's house. Josie stayed in the car and said, "I'll be in soon, Mom." To Colin, she said, "Are you in a hurry?"

He shook his head.

"Good." She climbed from the rear of the aging Porsche into its passenger seat. "You got to get a better car, Colin. This thing is really *déclassé*." She pronounced it 'dayclassaye' on purpose. "Let's go to Greenberry's."

The roads were miraculously clear, with 66 West wide open. Colin floored the accelerator. The car hesitated, backfired, and slowly picked up speed.

Josie looked at him. "This is a Porsche?"

He nodded.

"Aren't they supposed to, like, go fast?"

"Not this one. Small engine, many miles, and in need of a complete rebuild."

Josie looked out the passenger window. "That Toyota station wagon is passing us. The people in it are laughing. I'm pretty sure it's at us."

Colin smiled. "I'm driving with skill, not speed."

"Yeah," she said, unconvinced.

She let a few beats pass, then asked, "So you and mom, you're still sleeping together." A declaration, not a question.

Colin made a face but before he could speak, she said, "Jesus, what's embarrassing about that? You think I'm what, twelve years old?"

"That's an… indelicate question."

She laughed. "My experience is that sex is generally indelicate. And when you start talking about parental sex, you cross the line into the weird."

He nodded. "So let's not."

She grinned, "You mean not talk about you fucking my mom?"

He looked up, eyes angry. "Enough!"

She was unimpressed. "For God's sake, Colin, don't be such a prude. *Fuck* is a perfectly acceptable word. And gender-free, too."

He veered into the Tyson's exit ramp, drove two blocks, then turned right and parked the car in front of a Petco store.

"Josie, listen to me; I don't want to have this discussion with you more than once. How you talk to your friends is your concern. And I don't care how you and your mother talk to each other. But when you talk to me, if you want a response, you'll have to watch your mouth. Are we on the same page here?"

Josie stared at him hard, her lips a tight line. After a second, he reached across her and opened the car door.

"All right, out you go. It's only a couple of miles to your house. You can walk."

She didn't move. He shoved her.

"Hey!"

He pushed her again, "What, you're deaf? Get out of the car! I don't like kids with potty mouths."

She stared at him. "Did you just say, *potty mouth?*"

He didn't answer.

Her laugh started as a giggle, then erupted. "*Potty mouth?* Oh my God!"

In spite of himself, Colin smiled. "A perfectly valid expression…"

"If you were born in 1890! Even nuns don't say *potty mouth!*"

She stifled her laugh, wiped at her eyes. "Thank you, Colin. That was great! All right, I apologize; I won't use the f-word in your presence anymore, okay? Promise." She closed the car door. "By the way, you should know, I sorta prefer girls."

"Girls?"

"Yeah, like to be with? Like, for sex? Guys, I don't know. You people are just so… messy."

"Messy?"

"Jesus, Colin, are you gonna just repeat everything I say? Yeah! Messy! You slobber, you ejaculate, it's sort of disgusting and messy. Maybe it's because your junk is just hanging out there. Our stuff is neatly packed inside us, so we're a lot…" She paused, searched for the perfect word. "A lot tidier, you know?"

She looked at him and smiled. "Now can we get some effing coffee?"

The autopsy of LeBron Johnson was cursory. Young black males found dead in the Nation's Capital are assumed to have been victim of physical violence—shootings and stabbings, for the most part—or of drug overdoses. Since a bag of what was obviously heroin was found on his person, the cause of death was a foregone conclusion.

His discovery by neighbors coincided with a multi-alarm fire that killed a family of four and its eight dogs in a Michigan Avenue row house.

LeBron's body ended up at the morgue on E Street, Southwest.

It was placed in a cooler. The paperwork filled out by the Washington, D.C. Medical Examiner's office was electronically misfiled with that of the deaths by asphyxiation of the house-fire fatalities.

No one came to claim LeBron. After 30 days, his body was handed over to W.H. Bacon Funeral Home, where it was cremated. His ashes went to the Blue Plains Potters Fields, also known as the Smallpox Grounds Cemetery. And that was it for LeBron.

The heroin was placed in the D.C. Police evidence warehouse. Like much of the drugs in police custody anywhere, it vanished, replaced by a baggie that looked almost exactly like it and wore an identification tag bearing a date, case number, logging officer, weight, and content. Since there would be no police inquiry into Lebron's death, that small bag of white powder was incinerated along with a drug seizure from the Washington Marina of what might or might not have been eight ounces of cocaine.

"So here's the deal, Colin," Josie said, stirring a fourth Splenda into her coffee. "I know."

"Know what?" Something dreaded stirred in Colin's gut.

She leaned closer to him. "I *know*..."

And he knew she did.

He'd been fearing this moment for two-and-a-half years.

"I suppose that's why I think it's funny that you're such a prude. That the word *fuck* offends you. Cause, you know, we did, you and me."

He blinked.

"Mom doesn't know I know. And that's fine. Let sleeping dogs lie, and all that. I don't see any reason to tell her."

He nodded.

"And I didn't bring it up to embarrass you. It happened, it really wasn't that important an event, you know? No offense or anything. We had sex, once, and it took me a really long time to sort through the memories. You didn't do anything wrong. I was really frightened when that asshole attacked me, and you got rid of him. I was shaky. I wanted to feel safe, and you made me feel safe for the time that I needed. That's all." She paused. "Are you going to say something?"

"I'm honestly not sure what to say."

"Okay. I understand. But now it's out in the open. So you don't have to put on an act every time you see me. It happened. It won't happen again, are you good with that?"

He nodded. She smiled, wiped her lips with a paper napkin. "Good. Hey! I'm hungry. Can I have three bucks for a cinnamon scone?"

Later that evening in his apartment, Colin tried the juicer once more; he held his breath and drank down the foul greenish liquid.

He felt a vast sense of relief, tempered by guilt. What had happened with Josie in the dark had taken on the brushstrokes of an illusion. He could not remember the feel of her; he hadn't even seen her body. She'd been a wraith, there and gone in minutes. He wondered how much she recalled. Something, obviously; his face or smell or touch, or perhaps simply the violence before he stepped in, wrestled the drunk off her, and took her to his apartment.

He considered calling his sponsor but knew exactly how the conversation with that dislikable man would go.

Orin: "It happened, Colin. You made your amends to the girl?"

"Yes, and to the mother, a while back..."

Orin: "Fuck the mother, Colin. Oh. Wait. You already did, didn't you?" Followed by Orin's lewd guffaws, and finally, "Let it go, Colin."

He needed a new sponsor.

He cleaned the juicer, scraping out the pulped green stuff that smelled vaguely of rotting vegetation. Catherine had warned him. "You're going to be, well, gassy, for a while."

"Wonderful."

"But not very long, Colin. Promise."

"Great."

"Maybe two or three weeks. Until your body adjusts."

"It's sounding better and better."

"After that, you'll feel like a new man!"

He needed a new sponsor and he needed to get rid of the juicer.

"So," Lobo asked Mr. Snow, "how much were you paid to kill me?"

Mr. Snow allowed the slightest smile to show. "Well, let's be exact. *I* didn't try to kill you. Someone I hired did."

Lobo nodded, put his hands out in a *yes, of course,* gesture.

"I think it was $150,000 plus expenses," Mr. Snow said.

Lobo nodded again. "That's a lot of money."

Mr. Snow thought, *Not to you, it isn't,* but said, "It is, yes. But you're an important person. And everyone knows it's not easy to kill an Aztec."

Lobo bobbed his head again. The Aztec reference pleased him; he did have Aztec blood. He was an important person, but not a half-a-million-dollar-to-kill important person, and Mr. Snow was not an important half-a-million-dollar-person killer. That irked Lobo slightly.

"And how much did they pay when your man did not manage to kill me?" Details like that were important in establishing one's worth.

"Not a cent," said Mr. Snow shaking his head.

"And did they repay your expenses?"

"They did not."

Now Lobo's smile was all large white teeth. "So, all in all, how much did it cost you not to be able to kill me?"

"Right around fifty big." Now Mr. Snow smiled openly too. He knew Lobo's ego.

"See," said Lobo, "now that amuses me!" He turned to the bodyguards on his left.

"And, of course, you dealt with your killer *manqué* yourself. I heard about it. That was a very fine piece of work."

"Thank you," Mr. Snow answered. He made a mental note to see what *mankay* meant. "It's always better not to have any loose cannons rolling around." It had been a bit messy but without consequences.

"Cannon? Ah! Yes! Very funny!"

Mr. Snow bowed his head slightly in acquiescence.

Lobo snapped his fingers. "*Café, para mí y mi amigo!*"

"*Con leche, por favor,*" added Mr. Snow.

"So we are not enemies anymore?"

"We are not, and we never were. This was business, nothing more." said Mr. Snow. "In fact, I am now hoping we can become great friends."

"Wonderful," said Lobo, accepting a cup of coffee from the bodyguard, who placed the second cup, *con leche,* on the desk as well.

"So, Charlie Snow, I wonder... Oh, can you stand up for a second?"

Mr. Snow did. The bodyguard on Lobo's right approached him with a smile and launched a left hook that smashed into his jaw and lifted him off his feet. Mr. Snow crumpled and was propelled backwards, sliding on the polished floor. The bodyguard approached him again, looked at Lobo who frowned and nodded. The bodyguard aimed and launched a kick that caught Mr. Snow squarely in the kidneys.

Lobo said, "*Basta.*"

The bodyguard helped Mr. Snow up and gently deposited him back in his chair.

Mr. Snow was bleeding from the mouth. Three teeth were loose; he could feel them wiggle when he prodded them with his tongue. He'd probably be pissing blood for a day or two, but nothing was shattered. That was important.

Lobo said, "That was necessary. I'm sure you understand."

Mr. Snow nodded. He did understand.

"As you said, business."

"Bishnesh," Mr. Snow agreed.

"If you need dental work, send me the bill and I'll take care of it."

Mr. Snow said, "Shank you."

"So," Lobo stood, "get some rest, take aspirin, and use ice on your jaw. Come back in a day or two after you feel better, and we'll talk."

Mr. Snow said, "Shank you," again.

He'd been hit harder and kicked harder before. In fact, he thought the bodyguard was not particularly skilled at inflicting bodily harm. Lobo was slipping; a good thing to know. Snow was sore in a dozen places but broken in none.

Everything was going according to plan and he was still under budget.

4 IT WASN'T MUCH PAST SIX IN THE MORNING when the phone rang. Colin knew before opening his eyes it was Orin. No one but his sponsor ever called so early. He really did need a new sponsor.

"So two more croaked last night," Orin said. "They're fucking dropping like flies. That means two more funerals, and you're coming with me."

"It's sort of early for this kind of news, Orin."

He heard the fat man snort. "Never too early for death. Never too late, either. Anyway, Rambler Ernie, heart attack, apparently. Jeez. Only sixty-seven." Orin had just turned sixty-five. "Sixty-seven. That's not old!"

Still holding the phone, Colin went to the bathroom, ran some cold water, washed his face and peered at himself in the mirror. Then he asked, "What happened?"

With thirty-four years in the program, Rambler Ernie didn't ramble much. His wife Norma might be constantly traveling—cruises to the Holy Land and Egypt and the Caspian Sea—but Ernie had never been farther from his Arlington, Virginia, home than Ocean City, Maryland, for the Sessions by the Sea AA convention in 1988. If asked, Ernie would tell you he couldn't find a single reason to go more than five miles in any direction from the chair he occupied daily in the AA meeting room. Everything he'd ever wanted was here.

Ernie owned a pristine mustard-colored 1951 Nash Rambler Country Club two-door hardtop automobile—hence his nickname—he drove daily to the Liberty Club noon meeting on Davis Avenue. On the day he won the Virginia Get Lucky lottery with a ticket bought at his neighborhood 7-Eleven, he had planned to have his usual lunch at Joe's Pizza & Pasta with a couple of the guys, talk briefly with his sponsor and maybe roll a game or two in the afternoon if he could find someone to go to Bowl America with him. Instead, the Get Lucky Lottery gave Ernie such a massive coronary, the doctor who signed the death certificate would later write about Ernie's destroyed heart in a medical journal. Rambler Ernie was stone dead before his knees hit the floor of his home, the phone still clutched in his hand.

Half a world away aboard the cruise ship Centurion, his wife Norma was shouting, "Hello! Hello!" into her cell phone. She thought the call might have been an accident, "butt dials," people said, and she was slightly annoyed since it had interrupted a winning hand of canasta. She turned her phone off for the rest of the evening.

Albert F. found Ernie. Albert had a key to Ernie's house, and when Ernie didn't make the noon meeting the next day, Albert walked the three blocks from the Liberty Club to check on his friend, and there was Ernie, eyes wide open, a grimace on his face and the winning Lottery ticket on the coffee table.

The ambulance came and took Ernie away; Albert made a phone call to Ernie's sister. She in turn notified Norma, who would book the first plane from Istanbul to Dublin and then to Washington, D.C. Then Albert noticed Ernie had opened the *Washington Post* to page B2 where the winning lottery numbers were listed. No surprise there, Ernie had bought a six-dollar lottery ticket every week for ten years and never won anything more than twenty bucks, but this time Albert saw that Ernie had copied the winning numbers onto a piece of scrap paper, and that the numbers corresponded exactly with those on Ernie's ticket. Ernie had won $84.1 million dollars.

To Albert's credit, there was not a thought given to stealing the ticket. Instead, he drove to the Union Trust bank and put the ticket in his rented safety deposit box. He told no one about Ernie's winnings; he would save the news for when Norma got back. He planned to pick her up at Dulles International Airport, and he hoped her sudden wealth would somehow offset the tragedy of Ernie's death, which, it turned out, it did.

"Who else died, Orin?"

Colin, phone cradled on his shoulder, had made coffee and poured cereal and milk in a bowl. Ernie's death was unfortunate, but he was leaving a happy widow.

"That old black man, the one who played guitar in front of the Metro station."

Colin put his cup down. "Willie?"

"Yeah. Him. OD'd."

"Willie OD'd? No. That can't be right."

"That's what I heard. You were sort of friends with him, weren't you?"

Colin sat down hard on the sofa. This was not the kind of news he wanted to hear from Orin. "I've got to go, Orin. I'll call you back."

He clicked off the phone, walked twice around his living room, then twice more. Too many deaths, he thought. Why do they always come in threes?

Actually, not three. Five. There had been two funerals a month ago for AA friends. One man had skidded and wrapped his car around a tree; the other had developed pancreatic cancer and was gone within a month. And now Antwone, Willie, and Ernie.

The last conversation he'd had with Willie was, what, a month earlier? Ah, Jesus, it had been coming back from the cancer funeral. He'd given Willie a ride, and the old black man had slid a CD of his own songs into the car's player.

Willie played mostly slide on his ancient Gibson acoustic. He had a rusty voice that lacked the depth of a Lead Belly or Howlin' Wolf, but the message got across; stories of pain and poverty and drugs and drunkenness told in simple words and chords. Willie had once played at the Kennedy Center with a host of other, old black men gathered before a largely white crowd. He'd recorded the CD locally at Cue Studios, hustled it after meetings in the club parking lot, and probably given more copies to women than he'd ever sold. He called the CD his "afrodisiac," stressing the *afro* part and cackling. He'd once said to Colin, "You a good man, but that sponsor of yours, Orin? He's sheer downright nastiness. Maybe you'll do him some good."

They'd both laughed. Willie had added, "Man always says the wrong thing to the wrong person at the wrong time." Willie knew Colin was Orin's last sponsee; Orin had fired or been fired by all the others and didn't care. To Orin, everyone was an asshole until proven otherwise.

Colin found Willie's CD in the Porsche's center console. The songs sounded better at home than in the car. Willie's voice scraped out of the stereo speakers, something about his days and nights with the White Lady heron, and how he could never go back to the greatest love he'd ever known; how the Lady had broken his heart, ruined his life and left him lying on a sidewalk, eyes shut and mouth wide open to the rain. There was a long, raspy slide solo that ended in a dangling minor chord and Willie moaned, "No, no, no, no." Colin hit the replay button.

Ernie and Willie B's funerals were on the same day, Ernie's in the morning, Willie's in the afternoon. Colin drove Orin's van with the handicapped tags and listened to his sponsor complain about the traffic. This was one of Orin's favorite grievances, how Northern Virginia had become a center for idiots who didn't know how to drive and shouldn't have licenses in the first place. Every three minutes, Orin pointed out one of the idiots, and once he flashed a middle finger at an SUV that passed them on the right. "Driving while Asian! Jesus, we beat 'em in Japan and in Korea and in fuckin' Vietnam and now they're here!"

Colin didn't correct the historical inaccuracies; Orin was a vet who remembered things differently than most people.

Ernie's service was a quick Lutheran thing followed by a reception at his home. Ernie's wife, Norma, had already told everyone she would be moving to Florida as soon as the estate was settled. Colin and

Orin paid their respects; Orin steamed through a dozen hors d'oeuvres and five deviled eggs and then said, "Take me home, Colin. I'm done mourning for the day. You can go to the other service by yourself. I didn't hardly know the man."

Colin drove the van back, parked it in Orin's garage, and took the Porsche to the Shiloh Baptist Church in Washington. That morning, the *Washington Post* had carried a death notice for William Herbert Booker paid for by Willie B's family, with the picture of him from the CD cover. No age or cause of death mentioned, but a long list of survivors, children and grandchildren, some eighteen in all when Colin counted. Willie would be buried in the family plot adjoining the church; contributions to be made to the Afro-American Blues Musicians Fund that Willie had helped create in 1981.

When Colin got to the church, he noticed a group of white men standing across the street. He recognized some of them from the Liberty Club. One approached him. "Hey, Colin! Man, it's all black folks in there. I'm not sure we're going to be welcome."

Colin looked at the church's entrance. "I'm sure we will." He crossed the street; the other men followed.

The crowd was entirely black, entirely well-dressed, the men in well-tailored grey, navy blue, or black suits, starched white shirts and muted ties, shoes buffed to a high shine. The women all wore hats and skirts mostly below the knees. When Colin and his group were spotted, a young man detached himself from the crowd and led them to three empty pews. They filed in, sat quietly, looked about.

It was a century-old church that smelled of God, wax, and incense, with exquisite stained glass and burnished woodwork. Willie B's coffin was oak and brass, and just to the left of it were two seated guitarists and an upright bass. Colin could just make out the strains of *Yellow Morning*, one of Willie's songs.

Soon the church filled and quieted, the rustle of skirts and the creak of wood under weight subsiding. A tall and thin minister walked to the dais, faced the congregation, cleared his throat and began to speak with a decidedly Southern accent. His address was brief and followed by a poem read by an elderly woman wearing a plumed hat and white gloves. Colin thought it might be something by James Emanuel, whom he'd interviewed years ago. Several more speakers addressed the crowd, none for more than four minutes. There was an invocation, a prayer, and then six large men rose from one of the front pews, shouldered the casket down the center aisle of the church, down the steps and to the adjoining cemetery.

The grave had already been dug, a blue plastic tarpaulin covering the red clay dirt. The congregation followed silently, heels tapping and scraping on the marble floor.

Colin felt a hand on his arm. "Mr. Marsh?"

Her name was Emily Jameson Martin, and she was Willie's granddaughter. Her skin was the exact color of cane sugar, her hair hung loosely to her shoulders and she was just short of five feet eight in medium heels. She wore a simple and loose black sheath dress and a small pillbox hat with a veil.

Colin would later learn she was one of the seven girls and eight boys Willie's own six children had sired. Her mother was white from a large German-Pennsylvanian mining town; her father was Willie's middle son, a good man killed in a traffic accident two decades earlier, and the inspiration for one of Willie's best songs, *Fine Boy Down*.

She said, "You *are* Mr. Marsh, aren't you? My grandfather spoke of you many times." She smiled, shook his hand, turned and vanished into the crowd leaving a trace of perfume, a scent both woodsy and feminine he wasn't familiar with.

The interment went quickly; the casket was lowered into the grave, and each member of Willie's large family threw a clump of soil into the hole. Colin watched as Emily bowed her head, saw her lips move in a silent prayer. There were tears in her eyes as she dropped her handful of dirt, nodded one last time, and stepped away.

She approached him as he was walking to the parking lot with the group of men from the Liberty Club. Her eyes were dry now, her composure serious. She handed him a card, a thick rectangle of paper that bore her name, a single telephone number, and the words *Data Mining/Information Technology.*

"Mr. Marsh?" Again, her hand touched his arm. "I have to go to the reception, but would you call me later this evening? I'd very much like to talk with you." Then she turned and walked away. One of the men with Colin's group hissed a long whistle under his breath. Colin glared at him.

He dialed her number around seven p.m., left a message, and then rang again an hour and a half later. She called him back at 10 as he was doing push-ups in his living room. He was breathing hard when he picked up the phone.

"Goodness," he heard her say, "Have I called at a bad time?"

Colin felt a bead of sweat roll into his left eye. "I was doing push-ups." That sounded moronic, so he added, "You know, exercising."

She said, "Ah," and paused.

Colin found a once-white towel and wiped his face.

"Do you always exercise at night?" He could sense she was smiling.

"Generally, yes. It's quiet then and I can concentrate."

"So you're sort of a night owl."

"I suppose. Nights are generally more interesting than days."

"Excellent," she said. "I've just looked up your address." She asked for his apartment number, added "I can be there in twenty minutes."

That caught him by surprise and she hung up before he could respond.

He dashed in and out of the shower, straightened the cushions on the couch, hid the laundry basket in the bedroom closet, rinsed the coffee cups left in the sink, and then she was at his door.

"I hope it's not too late to come calling," she said. "The gathering of the tribe lasted much longer than I anticipated; it's still going on, I think. Lots of drinking by this time, Grandfather would not have approved." She paused again, "He was a popular man."

Colin ushered her in to the apartment, glancing around to make sure all things needing to be removed had been. "He'll be missed. Everyone liked him," he said. "He was a good man with a lot of wisdom."

"And a lot of time in your AA program as well," Emily Jameson Martin said. "Although he struggled. Did he speak with you about that, Mr. Marsh? How hard it was for him?"

Colin shook his head. "I didn't know him that well, just gave him rides to meetings occasionally. And I liked his music a lot. I was listening to it just yesterday. To be honest, I'm surprised he mentioned me at all."

She took in the apartment with a noncommittal look. Colin noticed, shrugged. "I was never much into decorating. I thought I'd be here a short time and never got around to it."

"And how long have you lived here?"

"Twelve years."

That made her smile. "Not long at all." She sat on the sofa, crossed her legs, rummaged in her purse for a bottle of water. She'd changed from the dress she wore at the funeral to a pair of well-tailored tan slacks, a green silk blouse, and white leather sandals. Colin thought her sheer presence made his apartment cheerier but didn't say so. He went to the kitchen and returned with a glass of iced tea.

"Grandfather turned eighty-nine three weeks ago. There was a small celebration—he wanted the big one to be when he turned 90, so there weren't that many people there. Still, we had a fine old time. Six of the grandkids who play instruments came, but he looked tired, worn out. Usually when he sang or played with the family, well, he lived for that, for passing the music on. This time, I had the feeling there was something wrong, and, it turned out, there was."

She unscrewed the top from the bottle of water, took a long drink, placed the bottle between her thighs. "My grandfather was in AA for close to forty years, but he never really managed to become what you call an old-timer. He never once picked up an anniversary chip. You know why?"

Colin shook his head no.

"Because he thought it was plain silly to give a man a medal for *not* being a screw up. It didn't make sense to him. He came from a generation that took on responsibilities and did what they had to do, so the concept of being rewarded for doing what you're *supposed* to do in the first place, that struck him as ridiculous."

She took another sip. "Every six or seven years, he'd have a slip. The relapses never lasted more than 48 hours, and he never, ever, spent money that his family needed. Every penny he earned, whether from music or digging ditches—he did both—went to his family. He put his children through college, and later on he helped his grandkids, like me. He gave me enough money for all my college books, for five years. But then something would happen, and he'd buy some heroin and we wouldn't see or hear from him for a day or two. He'd hole up in a motel, do the drugs and play his guitar. Then he'd come home and he'd be shaky for a while. Once he signed himself into a hospital to get detoxed but he never had insurance, and when he found out how much it would cost, thousands of dollars for an overnight stay, he just went home and did it cold turkey.

"Have you ever relapsed, Mr. Marsh?"

He refilled his iced tea and told her he had, the before and after of it, and she nodded her head. "My oldest brother, Jared, he's been in and out of rehabs and detoxes for years. Alcohol ruined his life. His wife left and took their two kids, and I can't say I blame her. Jared is a big guy and he got violent a couple of times; he was jailed twice, then he lost his job. We don't know where he is right now. Half the family wants to help him, half says to let him be until he straightens out. What do you think we should do, Colin?"

They talked, meandering from subject to subject. Around midnight he said he was hungry and fixed an egg-white omelet with feta cheese and tomatoes, and they ate at his kitchen table. She left shortly after one-thirty; he insisted on walking her to her car, a late model no-nonsense Audi. She pecked his cheek with her lips and extracted a promise that he would call in the next few days. He returned to his apartment thinking, *there are no coincidences*, and afraid to consider anything past that.

5 IN THE MORNING COLIN ATE AN ORANGE, choked down two tablespoons of apple cider, drank a cup of coffee, stretched, and leafed through the newspaper without interest. He paid his bills—rent, health insurance, cable, and Visa—and remembered an earlier time when he hid the incoming statements from the woman he was once married to. The bills back then were huge, mostly from bars, liquor stores, and restaurants, and he could barely afford to pay for the cheap wine with bad lunches and the endless shots of Jack during and after work.

He'd often cover the Visa bill with his Mastercard, then both with the Amex, deferring the inevitable and skimping on other payments. One month the trash people stopped emptying the bins left on the sidewalk; a few weeks later the house phone was turned off. He invented excuses, made good on the debts, saw services restored. His account with a major department store was closed for non-payment, to the shame of his then-wife whose credit card was seized and cut into pieces by one of the store's cashiers. Letters from creditors crowded his mailbox; he threw them away unopened. He padded his expenses, small as they were, invented fares for cabs never taken and charged the newspaper where he worked for meals never eaten.

His major worry, on an hourly basis, was being discovered for the cheat he was. It corroded him and occasioned panic attacks, soured his stomach, made dealing with those around him—family, friends, colleagues at work—an immensely painful necessity that left him exhausted and in need of a drink. Life was a raw cycle as hard and as set as the rhythm of the planets, an existence without fulfillment save for the small yet crucial moment when, arriving home, he would reach into the freezer, pull out a bottle of vodka and drink deeply, hungrily, feeling the alcohol burn his throat, detonate in his gut, and bring peace, quiet, and serenity for all too short a time.

When he got sober, family finances were one of the first things he attended to. He called the people to whom he owed money and arranged payment plans. He went to the bars and settled tabs, closed store accounts, rid himself of his ATM card, obtained a new Visa with a $1,000 limit. It took longer than he had hoped, but he finally got squared away, and when he did, his spouse left him, saying that, all in all, it had been easier to live with him as a drunk than as a sober man obsessed with righting his life. He hadn't seen or heard from her in ages; she'd moved to a vowel-full Midwest state and, he was told by a mutual friend who called once a year, she had remarried well, an architect or maybe an accountant, the friend couldn't remember.

Colin hadn't remarried. He had found the involvements that strayed outside the 12-step world were dangerous, while those staying within it were sadly predictable.

He arrived late to the noon meeting, took a chair in the back, half-listened to a woman whose name he'd forgotten share about the difficulties encountered in sobriety. She had less than a year in the program, spoke rarely, but when she did it was about family, a husband who still kept a bottle of Gilbey's gin in the fridge, and a teenage daughter who'd twice been caught smoking marijuana at school. He remembered in his first few months sharing the same story with small variations about his wife, and how she'd figured out how to make life work in spite of his addiction and couldn't quite fathom existence without it.

He put a dollar in the basket when it came around, spoke with a few men after the meeting ended. One, a lawyer who worked for the county, asked, "Is it true Willie B OD'd? I wanted to go to the service but I was stuck at work…"

Colin ignored the question. It was unlikely the attorney would have found his way to the downtown Baptist church under any circumstance. "It was a nice ceremony. Willie had a lot of friends."

He spoke briefly with a sponsee and agreed to meet for coffee at five that evening, shook hands with a couple of old-timers, and ate a quick lunch by himself at Jason's Deli.

More and more, he was discovering, he liked an emptiness about him. His sponsor would call it isolating, a cardinal sin within any 12-step group, but Colin thought of it more as a declaration of independence, an acceptance that his own company was often more worthwhile than that of others. One could enjoy the freedom of solitude without incurring too deep a loneliness.

In the past few months he'd fallen into a routine that could justify his seclusion. This time, he walked home taking the long way through Cherry Hill Park, down the W&OD trail that had once been the raised bed of a railroad track, and along Lee Highway, stopping for a quick coffee and a handful of roasted cashews at a Starbucks. He jogged twice around the block, felt his legs loosen, rejoined the trail, and did a couple of wind sprints that left him breathing hard. Then he cut through the baseball diamond adjacent to the local high school and found the county playground that seldom saw children. He did an alternating series of push-ups and pull-ups on the jungle bars, fifty in all, until his arms burned. He drank from the fountain, wished he had a cigarette, settled for a red Lifesaver, and did another set.

He thought about Catherine. He enjoyed her company but sensed a growing lack of passion on both sides. Despite his promise to Josie, he doubted things would last. Catherine was enjoying her single life, her sobriety, and the attention paid her by men other than him.

When he got home there were two voicemail messages—one from

his sponsee who had forgotten a prior commitment and wouldn't be available tonight, the other from Emily Jameson Martin who asked if he might be free around seven.

The gods were smiling.

She arrived carrying an expensive attaché case made of scaly lizard skin, and when she saw Colin look at it oddly, she said, "African crocodile. Probably saved some hapless native bathing in Lake Tanganyika from being eaten alive. Not endangered." She put the case down on the dining room table, snapped it open. "Also, considering the price I paid for it, I probably fed an entire village for a month. I do not feel guilty. At all."

Colin nodded, smiled. "Never did like crocodiles. All those teeth…"

She took out a handful of manila folders, each bearing a name, arranged them alphabetically on the table. Colin picked one up—Andrue Winston—and opened it, saw a police report, a mug shot, and some hand-written notes. The next one, LaRoche Washington, had a shot of a young, smiling black woman holding a baby. No police report, but a Commonwealth of Virginia death certificate. Ali Stuckey wore a baseball cap sideways and sat on an inner-city stoop. Derrick Swann looked stern and potentially dangerous. Tureena Johnson's eyes were unfocused, her lips were bruised, and her hair was a mess. There was one white man, Richard Baron, and one white woman, Susan Compton. They were a couple but each had a folder. Their photos had them in jeans and T-shirts from a U2 concert. Baron, grinning and showing not enough teeth, held a 16-ounce can of Coors Light aloft. Compton looked both bored and annoyed. There were other names: Tamarius Wright, Quashawn Graham, Frank, La'Tasha, Toreena, Amir, Jahmeen…

Colin put the folders back on the table, looked at Emily Jameson Martin, said, "Dopers."

She nodded. "Dead addicts. All within the last couple of months. All heroin overdoses, according to the coroner's reports." She took a long look at the folders, squared them. "But you know what? My grandfather, he said most of those people didn't overdose. He said they were murdered."

She picked up one folder, handed Colin the photo within. "This one, Portia Cox, I knew her a little bit. God. We used to make fun of her name in school. Her mother lived down the street and went to church every Saturday night and Sunday morning and afternoon. Her mom and my grandfather were friends." She smiled, shrugged, "Maybe a little more than friends. Anyway, I wasn't allowed to hang out with Portia; she was 'the wrong type of nigrah' is what my father called her. But her mother told my grandfather that Portia never used heroin. That girl was into everything else under the sun, but never heroin, never anything with needles. There was an open casket ceremony, and her arms were bare. No tracks…" She looked up, made a gesture with a hand. "I know what you're going to say, Colin, she could've been smoking it, or shooting up between her toes, or whatever, but she wasn't. She wasn't." She paused, nodded, "Someone killed that girl."

They ate diner in a Thai restaurant that smelled of peanuts and curry. She had glass of cabernet and ordered it without asking if it was okay to drink with him there, which he appreciated. That was one of the things about eating a meal with normal people, this belief that a nearby glass of wine might offend or set him off, that he might leap on top of the table like a crazed rhesus monkey, snatch the drink, and run. He had a Diet Coke with a slice of lime. The waiter brought their drinks and automatically placed the cabernet in front him. Colin slid the glass across the table and retrieved his Coke.

"Why would anyone want to murder a bunch of addicts?"

She speared a morsel of chicken out of her bowl of soup, brought it to her mouth, and took a swallow of wine.

"I don't know. I'm pretty sure it's not a new dealer trying to establish himself. I read about that in the papers, how that happens sometimes."

Colin knew. It was more common some years earlier when the

heroin market wasn't as strictly controlled by the Asians, the Mexicans, and the gangs from Central America. A new dealer wanting to establish a quick reputation would sell a few batches at a loss, keeping the product so pure it would kill a junkie or two. Word would spread on the street that the new stuff was so good it was lethal. Sales would spike. When a clientele was well established, the dealer would go back to cutting his product. If sales lagged, the death of a few more junkies was sure to produce renewed interest among the users. And sometimes, there were accidents.

In 2010, when Colin was researching a book on the Russian mafia for a client, there'd been such a spate of deaths, eighteen within a week, spread across Montgomery and Prince George's counties in Maryland. The newspapers had barely noticed, and only the local Fox affiliate had run a brief piece noting the deaths and quoting a member of the PG County Narcotic Enforcement Division who said, with a shrug, "These things happen."

Curious to see if the murders might be linked to the Russians efforts to take over the East Coast trade, Colin had looked up a Montgomery County cop he'd befriended at an AA meeting in Bethesda and, in time, had received detailed information on the investigation.

The case involved not Russians but Chechens living in Bladensburg, a bedroom community adjacent to the nation's capital.

According to police files and public records, on April 12, 2010, a number of Chechen youths led by twin brothers Buvaizar and Alhazur Udugov raided the storefront clubhouse of a dozen Salvadorans loosely affiliated with the MS-13 gang. The incursion occurred because one of the Latino boys, earlier that day, had bumped against a Chechen girl at the Food Lion, pressed one hand against a breast and a second against her blue-jeaned crotch, squeezed and muttered "Puta!" The girl's cousin knew what the word meant and shoved the boy through a six-foot tall Chicken of the Sea Tuna display. A melee ensued. Security guards stopped the disturbance from spreading, but the Chechens sought revenge later that night.

Shots were fired at the clubhouse, but no one was seriously injured, and the Chechens withdrew after pummeling the Salvadorans with aluminum baseball bats stolen from the local high school. The loot they took from the raid included three loaded revolvers—worthless Saturday night specials—and, unknowingly, a Nike athletic bag containing two pounds of Mexican heroin the Central Americans were holding for a middle-level dealer.

The Chechen boy who seized the bag had seen one just like it at the local Foot Locker store but could neither steal nor afford it.

The same boy traded the bag, contents unseen, for one of the pistols. The bag's new owner was somewhat older than his cohorts and immediately realized what he'd just acquired could spell either moderate wealth or great troubles. He sold it to a Chechen grownup for $1,000, and the man turned it around for $5,000 in less than an hour. By the next morning, the two pounds of Mexican heroin had changed hands five times and were worth $20,000.

The penultimate buyer, an Azerbaijani immigrant, knew exactly what he'd lucked into but had no distribution network, so he sold the heroin in four separate packets of eight ounces to a Russian who paid $40,000 for the lot. The Russian, his girlfriend, her two brothers, and an unrelated woman spent the night repackaging the drug, and by morning 220 small bags of pure heroin were on the street. Most were bought by seasoned addicts who immediately spotted the drug's purity and quickly tripled the weight by cutting it with baby formula. Twelve unfortunates cooked and shot the drug in its pure form, and seven of these died within minutes, succumbing to the slowing of already damaged hearts and, shortly thereafter, asphyxiation.

The Prince George's police paid only scant attention. They interviewed known junkies and learned the heroin had appeared without warning, sold at a more than fair price by a small army of nickel-and-dime dealers.

One of the deceased users was the 19-year-old nephew of a black county detective with two decades on the force. The nephew had been in trouble with the law since he was a kid, but still, he was family, and it appeared he was getting his life together. The young man's death infuriated the detective. He took it upon himself to find the drug's source and in a very short time discovered who had sold his nephew the killer dose.

The trail quickly led back to the Chechens and Salvadorans.

The Chechens lacked subtlety. They operated as they had in their home country with undiminished violence, and in the States they had discovered the aluminum baseball bats, which they used with joyful abandon. For all the talk of silence and pride and family ties, when told they were facing quick deportation, the Chechens rolled over on their brothers and cousins with startling speed.

The Salvadorans, far better versed in the nuances of American law, were tougher to crack, until the county detective came up with a brilliant and devious ploy.

The youngest of the Salvadorans, a not very smart boy barely eighteen and with minimal English, was sequestered without food, water, or legal representation for eight hours. Then two plainclothes cops informed him he was to be deported within hours, but not to his native country. No; he would be sent to Chechnya and left there. It was winter in Chechnya, he was told, and the followers of Islam had little love for Christian drug dealers. The boy had no idea where Chechnya was, but he had watched ISIS beheading hostages on YouTube with unhealthy fascination.

Within an hour he had delivered names, addresses, and telephone numbers. The Prince George's County police swooped down on the apartment complex where most of the Salvadorans lived. They arrested seventeen men and women and recovered three pounds of cocaine, one and a half pounds of heroin, and 5,000 hits of crystal meth dyed blue to look like Breaking Bad drugs.

The Prince George police gave the black detective a raise and took most of the credit for the bust and seizures; the county police chief mentioned in post-bust interviews that he was considering running for State Senate.

He did, and lost.

The next few days Colin spent at the library using one of the county six-year-old computers, a machine that far outstripped in speed and dexterity the Windows 7 PC he owned.

He began by looking for drug-related deaths in the past twelve months in Fairfax City, Vienna, Arlington, Alexandria, Falls Church, and other northern Virginia cities within 15 miles of Washington, D.C. The search yielded an amazing number of names, more than 250 in all. Colin stuck a thumb drive into the computer's USB port and created several file folders into which he downloaded relevant information. He found that fully half the deaths were more violence-related than drug-induced, so he created sub-folders. He listed the names and some accompanying information, then looked for mention of particular drugs—heroin, cocaine, methamphetamine, marijuana, crack, and miscellaneous but deadly concoctions like Spice. Three meth deaths had occurred when a basement drug lab outside of Manassas exploded, killing two of the chemists instantly and leaving the third in a coma. Days later, a follow-up paragraph in the *Washington Times* noted that the surviving culprit had suffered third degree burns over seventy-five percent of his body and died of cardiac arrest in the hospital.

There were several shootings, some fatal, others not, and one stabbing death occasioned by a dispute between two addicts over the last speck of crack in their possession.

He widened the search and entered "death heroin coroner Northern Virginia" in Google and Bing, then in a couple of private search engines for which he paid a small membership fee. He worked with several variations that included arrests, trials and convictions, police and lab reports. He read court documents, then spent the better part of an afternoon gathering information on local gangs, the most prominent of which was MS-13. He learned that the gangs were not as large as most people thought and that their reputations far outstripped their numbers. Members were savagely dedicated and wantonly violent. They employed guns and machetes, with the latter a popular way of inflicting punishment. They were not above raping and murdering pregnant women or teenagers, and their main income came from drug trafficking, underage prostitution, and extortion.

Colin traced the gang's activities from Los Angeles to El Salvador and back to Virginia. This in turn led to a mention of a Nicaraguan offshoot calling itself Mara21. Mara21 was reputed to control thirty percent of the heroin trade in Northern Virginia and was involved in constant skirmishes with the Vietnamese White Dragons gang, which imported large quantities of opium products from Asia.

Variations of a first and last name appeared in four stories. Geovany Sandino was quoted as a knowledgeable source on Central American gangs. So were Yann Sandrin, Johannes Sanders, João Sandano, and Ian Shaunder.

Three years earlier, Colin read, Ricardo Delgado, Steyr Tactical Machine Pistol in hand, had pumped thirty rounds in Geovany Sandino's SUV as Mr. Sandino waited in a Sonic parking lot for his chauffeur/bodyguard to get a SuperSONIC Bacon Double Cheeseburger combo. The armored SUV survived the onslaught, as did Geovany Sandino. The alert chauffeur/bodyguard dropped his meal, lunged into the SUV and drove off at top speed.

A nearby cop car saw the SUV flash by, pursued it, lost it, found it again, and stopped it. There were bullet holes in the vehicle's flank.

Confusion ensued. Mr. Sandino maintained that the entire incident was a sad mistake, most certainly a case of mistaken identity. He was alive, unarmed, quite healthy, and uninterested in pursuing the culprit, if culprit there was. His driver was charged with speeding but maintained he was unaware that a police car was giving chase.

The case had garnered very minor notoriety since the apparent target of the assassination refused to cooperate with the authorities. The latter had noted an odd fact: Mr. Sandino's SUV was armor-plated, an unusual option for a vehicle owned by a coffee importer.

The perpetrator, Ricardo Delgado, was simply unlucky. He chose a stolen Toyota Camry for his escape on the assumption that, among a million other Camrys, his would be invisible. This particular Toyota had been recalled, but its parsimonious owner, fearful of hidden Japanese charges, had never taken it to the dealership. As Mr. Delgado was speeding from the scene of the failed assassination, the object of the recall, a faulty and loose ball joint, separated from the rest of the steering assembly.

Delgado lost control of the vehicle. It careened into a Starbucks, shattering the storefront and showering the baristas with boiling soy milk. Delgado banged his head painfully and suffered a minor concussion and three broken ribs.

He freed himself from the car's safety belt, staggered out of the Camry, and was limping away when a police car finally arrived with wailing sirens and a screech of tires.

Delgado turned to face the cops and dropped the Steyr, but not before one of the two responding officers drew his service revolver and shot him four times in the chest. The autopsy would show that two bullets had lodged in Delgado's heart and two more in his lungs.

The obligatory inquiry following a police shooting exonerated the responding cop. Officer Charles Snow had responded appropriately given the situation. He was put on leave with pay for three weeks and underwent mandatory psychiatric counseling. Eight months later, Officer Snow scored in the top percentage of applicants and was promoted to sergeant. His test results demonstrated a strong general aptitude and knowledge of police procedures, as well as above-average decision-making, managerial, and supervisory skills. His courage under fire was also mentioned.

6 It had taken Birch Carroll several years to enjoy being disliked. Now a bunch of liberal people really hated him, and it made life worth living.

"Mike from Manassas! You're on the air and I'm listening. You're talking to the Voice of Reason!"

Carroll's radio show was broadcast on twenty-two stations in Virginia, Maryland, and Delaware, where the listenership was growing by small increments. In Washington, D.C., what Carroll liked to call Sodom on the Potomac, his numbers were distressingly low.

His name had once been Mark Carroll but Birch had a good tone to it on the radio, and it reminded listeners of the John Birch Society, or so he hoped. Actually, he suspected this generation of conservative listeners had probably never heard of the JBS. They weren't the sharpest tools in the shed.

"Mike, I'm glad you called! I love Manassas, and I can't help but be horrified to learn that your lovely, lovely town has been invaded by do-nothing Mexican dope users and welfare cheats who expect you to take care of them!"

Do-nothing dope users were among Carroll's favorite targets. Welfare cheats—which was pretty much anyone on welfare—ran a close second.

"It's a crime, Mike! An absolute crime! I don't understand why your elected officials don't do something about it! They're Republicans!

They're elected! They're officials! Welfare mothers and terrorist dope-smokers sitting on their front stoops waiting for the checks to come in! How did this happen? How did the good people of Manassas *allow* this to happen? If you ask me, we don't need a wall on the border. We need a wall around Manassas! How did this invasion happen?"

Carroll knew exactly how such things happened. He was relatively well versed in the societal and financial causes of events, but he rarely referred to them. The blame for the sad state of the nation lay squarely on the sloping shoulders of left-wing liberals, college professors, gays and lesbians, the past President and the one before the one before that, legal and illegal immigrants from countries with tropical weather, Social Security, Obamacare, Medicare and Medicaid, public housing, and all the crime-allowing climate-warming Democrat yahoos who had originally come up with the Miranda Rights and sought to weaken police authority.

"Mike, I bet you've worked hard most of your life. Of course, you have! It's law-abiding folks like you who call in, not deadbeats! And I can tell by your voice that you're nearing retirement age, aren't you? Now, here's what I want to know: What are you going to do when the government steals your savings and starts taxing your IRA? What're you gonna do when the dope-smokers and transsexuals and pansexuals and cross-dressing Haitians move into your neighborhood? Because they're coming, George! They're coming! They're loading up their U-Haul trailers and hippy vans even as we speak! What're you gonna do when your little grandchildren can't play in your own front yard?"

Carroll took a quick breath, swift enough that Mike from Manassas didn't have a chance to comment. He had developed a breathless, machine-gun style of delivery that implied imminent disaster. The Mexicans and Haitians were coming to your neighborhood *now.*

"You know, Mike, a couple of days ago I was talking to my good buddies Bill and Rush, and they told me they were shocked at what was happening in this area. Shocked!"

Carroll had never in his life spoken to either Bill O'Reilly or Rush Limbaugh, though he had once run into Don Imus in the men's room of the Dulles Expo Center during a gun show. It didn't matter. He knew what Bill and Rush and Don and Mike thought. They were all on the same wavelength. This great country was being stripped of its entrepreneurial soul. As he liked to remind listeners at least once a week, "Folks, that feeling of impending doom that you're feeling is impending doom!"

He took a breath. "So you agree with me, don't you, Mike? Good. I knew you would! Thanks for calling and God bless!"

It was tiring sometimes. There were an awful lot of people out there who simply had not a clue. Not that they were stupid, they weren't, not really, though Carroll secretly doubted any two listeners' cumulative IQs reached three figures. No, not stupid though sometimes a little dense, a little slow on the uptake. What it was, was they'd been co-opted. Get them laid once a week; give them a big screen TV, Netflix, a tray of nachos, and a six-pack of Miller Lite, and they'd be perfectly happy to let it all go to hell while watching *America's Got Talent.*

"You're on the air, Molly. I'm listening. This is Birch Carroll, your Voice of Reason, always on your side!"

Molly was having problems with her Social Security check and suspected her Asian mailman of stealing it. Carroll sighed. This was not the sort of person he wanted to talk to on the show, and the assistant who vetted the calls shouldn't have let her through.

"Well, Molly, that's one of the issues, isn't it? Our government giving away American jobs to foreigners. I'll tell you what, Molly, stay on the line, give us your address. I'll send you a copy of my book, *America! Live it or Leave it*!" Carroll pushed a button, cutting off Molly's, "Thank you, but—"

"Hello, you're on the air, this is the Voice of Reason! Telling it to you like it is, when it is!"

Carroll's back was beginning to hurt. Two hours a day, six days a week, plus a pre-recorded Sunday show; it didn't matter how comfortable the chair was or how many times he got up to stretch during the commercial breaks. He could feel the muscles start to tighten. The pain was worsening daily. Vicodin time.

"Talk to me, Sam from Richmond! How's the weather down there? What can I help you with? This is Birch Carroll, the Voice of Reason."

His back was really beginning to throb. Carroll told people it was an Armed Services injury, but in fact he'd hurt himself a decade earlier falling off a ladder while cleaning the gutters of his two-story townhouse. The fall and the injury had been followed by a deep sense of depression, which he was still medicating.

He half-listened to Sam's complaint that the cops weren't doing enough in the neighborhood; there'd been a mugging two days ago and a drug bust four houses down a day before that. Plus, Sam's streets were always littered with empty beer cans and Taco Bell wrappers.

Carroll found the small pill box in his shirt pocket, shook out a five milligram Vicodin. Into the microphone, he said, "Keep talking, Sam, I'm listening."

He swallowed the pill, chased it down with a mouthful of club soda. Carbonated water seemed to make the meds work faster.

Another man was talking about the police.

"What can I tell you? This is happening all over the country, nice neighborhoods being taken over by druggies and criminals, and the policemen's hands are tied! They can't act, they can barely make arrests anymore because the ACLU..."

The pain was beginning to dull. Carroll was tempted to take a second pill but resisted. He could feel the slight drying of the mouth that told him the drugs were starting to work. That weird feeling of being separated from himself would kick in any second. He looked at the studio clock. Jesus. Another forty-five minutes. He took another gulp of club soda.

"Lenny! How are you?"

"Lieutenant Leonard Baskey! Northeastern Defense Militia! How are you, sir?"

Lenny Baskey was one of Carroll's favorite listeners. He was an ardent patriot and pharmacist at a nearby Wanker's Drug Store, which regularly advertised on the radio station. Baskey called once a week—the assistant was instructed to let him through—and was surprisingly well-informed for a white supremacist.

"What's new in the militia world, Lenny?"

Both Carroll and Baskey knew well enough to limit their on-air conversations to acceptable topics. No overt racism, talk of violence, or overthrowing anything or anyone.

Baskey had a head for statistics. "Sir, did you know there are almost five million emergency room visits every year by drug addicts?"

"And alcoholics," added Carroll. "Don't forget the alcoholics."

"Yes, sir. Alcoholics, too…"

"I read that, Lenny. And it costs millions."

Lenny loved statistics and always had a bunch of them on hand. "No sir. Not millions. Billions. Illegal drugs are $181 billion. Alcohol is $224 billion."

"And that comes out of our pockets, doesn't it, Lenny. Yours and mine and the pockets of all those good folks who work for a living and pay our taxes. Makes you wonder, doesn't it?"

"Yes sir. Billions and billions of dollars."

Carroll, too, loved numbers like that, staggeringly unimaginable figures, and he liked to make it easy for the little man listening to his broadcasts to understand. In a voice full of wonder, he said, "A sum like that would allow us to fund more than 900,000 police officers. We could make our streets safe, and deport all those illegal wetbacks! Whoops! I'm not supposed to say that! That's not politically correct. My bad! Billions, right Lenny!"

"Yes sir, that's correct."

"But we know the police would have their hands tied when it comes to arresting criminals…"

"Yes sir. That's why we need militias."

"Well, Lenny, you know I can't speak to that, though the constitution does."

"Yes sir. 'A well-regulated militia, being necessary to the security of a free state, the right of the people to keep and bear arms, shall not be infringed.'"

"Our Second Amendment!"

"Yes, sir."

"Thanks for calling! It's always good talking to you, Lenny!"

"You're a great American, Mr. Carroll!"

Damn. The pain was growing again. Carroll had been told by four different doctors that a back operation might be the best option, but all the surgeons available through his HMO were foreigners, mostly Asians with name like Nguyen, Kim, and Singh. He swallowed a second Vicodin.

"Jimmy from Rehoboth, you're on the air! Jimmy, I was in Rehoboth not long ago and you could hardly be on the boardwalk because of all the gays and lesbians and transvestite sickos! It was disgusting!"

Jimmy from Rehoboth chortled. "Only in the summer, Mark, when me and the wife go away. We rent our house out and go to Minnesota."

"You rent your house? Please don't tell me you rent your house to those people?"

"Well, yes we do, Mark. And I'll tell you, I wish you wouldn't be so hard on the gay people. They're not bad and—?"

"And they sleep in your bed? The gays? *In your bed? And they use your bathroom?*"

"Well—"

"Let me get this straight. You're not a homosexual, are you, Jimmy?"

"No, no! I'm married, I have three kids, I—"

"And your wife's not some sort of confused lesbian lady?"

"Jenny? No, course not! We've been married fif—"

"Well then, let me ask you this, Jimmy-who-rents-his-house-to-homosexuals, who wears the pants in your family?"

"What? What-"

"What are you, Jimmy, some sort of debauched pervert? My God! I feel dirty just talking with you!"

Once a week, Carroll picked a caller to flay on air. It enlivened the conversation and kept his right-wing bona fides healthy. People like Jimmy-who-rents-to-gays were a gift. Birch allowed his voice to rise, the outrage unfeigned, his Midwest accent taking on an edge of disbelief.

"And you have three children? *Three* children? What're you thinking, Jimmy? I mean, letting a bunch of pederasts sleep in *your* bed in *your* house with children around... And use your bathroom? Has the concept of diseases ever crossed your mind? AIDS? HIV? Zika? Where do you think you are, Jimmy, in France? What's *wrong* with you? What's wrong with your wife? Your neighbors should call the police on you! Not that the police could do anything... You know what? I'm ending this conversation. I'm feeling sick to my stomach." He pushed a key on the keyboard in front of him; there was the sound of an old-fashioned phone handset being slammed back into its cradle.

A bolt of agony shot through his spine. Jesus! What the hell was going on! Spasms of pain racked his lower back and shook his shoulders; it brought tears to his eyes. He signaled the engineer to cut to an ad. He rushed to the bathroom ready to throw up and didn't through sheer will; vomiting would vacate the Vicodin. He swallowed hard, splashed water on his face, stood straight, and stretched. The pain eased slightly. He took a Vicodin, returned to the booth and slipped on the earphones. The engineer had cued an ad for *America, Live It or Leave It*. Birch Carroll took a deep breath through his nose, nodded to her, and exhaled through his mouth.

"Dan, you're on the air. This is Birch Carroll, the Voice of Reason! Do you believe that guy who just called? Jeez! What kind of country is this becoming?"

Gloria Rose Nachtalyan had spent a terrible and sleepless night. In the morning, a migraine headache plagued her; the faintest light hurt her eyes and her temples were soft with pain. It was only around eleven that she began feeling normal again.

She seldom had migraines and wondered if the onslaught had been due to too much cocaine, or not enough cocaine, the night before. The latter possibility concerned her slightly.

She'd called in late, which she rarely did, and planned to make it to the office after lunch.

Now it was close to noon and she was waiting for Bong Bong next to the convenience store Dumpster. It crossed her mind that this was not what a woman of good social standing should be doing, but it was only a fleeting thought. She waited.

Bong Bong came out, hands in pocket and apprehensive. He said, "Come behind store."

She followed him. It smelled of rotting fruit and wet cardboard. There were wooden pallets stacked alongside a wall, and she thought she saw a rat.

Bong Bong handed her a small plastic baggie. He whispered, "Three hundred!"

That was a hundred more than the norm. Gloria shook her head. "That's a lot!"

"New stuff. Super good! Need only half to do twice as much!" Bong Bong had his hand out.

"Why is it brown?"

"Not brown," he said. "*Gold*. From very special gold coca plants. Hurry now!"

She fished out the emergency $100 kept in the secret compartment of her purse and added it to the other bills. Bong Bong snatched the money and buried it in his pocket. "You go now. Go! Go!"

She went.

It felt good having the coke. Lately, when she was close to running out, she'd become anxious, and one time she hyperventilated so seriously she had to lie on the floor of the apartment until her heartbeat subsided. With the small baggie nestled beneath the front seat of the Lincoln, though, she felt herself relax, allowed her shoulders to slump and took a deep breath. It was a gorgeous day; the sky was postcard blue with cottony clouds, the traffic moved along at a steady pace, and she caught most of the green lights. She didn't even mind going almost all the way to the top tier of the parking garage to find a space.

She locked the car, walked to the elevator, paused and turned back. What if one of the parking lot attendants jimmied the lock to the Lincoln and found the cocaine? What if the Lincoln was towed, or, worse, stolen? She retrieved the baggie and slid it into the now empty secret hundred-dollar-bill compartment.

In her office, the gold coke sang to her and she hummed along. *"Every little thing, gonna be alright!"* Who was it who sang that? Jimmy Buffett? No, one of those Rastafarian guys from Jamaica, the one with dreadlocks. *Don't you worry, about a thing.*

Gloria was not worrying; she was planning her evening with James Spader, Miss Tan Cocaine, a bottle of Chablis, and a foot-long cold-cut sandwich from the Italian Store. She decided that on her way home she'd buy two of those expensive little tins of cat food for Sarah and Courtney. The three of them would celebrate the evening in style.

The day took forever. The little baggie occasionally changed tunes, once segueing into *Yes, We Have No Bananas*, which made her giggle. Her boss was his usual asshole self, commenting on her cheerfulness. "My! Someone must have had a good time last night!" Moron. She wondered if that was enough of a statement to pursue a sexual harassment case. That would fix his ass.

Actually, every little thing was probably gonna be all right except for sex, which she missed. Crap. She didn't like thinking about sex during working hours, because Clarence, the ex, worked less than a mile away and that had been his one redeeming quality—he was good in bed. Which was odd because he didn't look it; nobody seeing him in the street would say, "See that man? He's probably great in the sack!" But he was, especially for a thin, little, light-skinned black guy who probably didn't weigh 140 pounds. Gloria smiled. He really was *good!* And he truly appreciated women! The smile faded to a frown. He was so good, in fact, and so appreciated white women that he couldn't keep his dick in his pants and had to share his goodness, notably with JoAnn Sabatini who was so white she was almost see-through. Sex, she thought. Rhymes with ex. She sighed.

She found a couple of items that might interest Mr. Snow and copied them into a folder she'd forward to him later. She answered a few phone calls, mostly redirecting the callers to other numbers and offices. She monitored her department's email but found nothing of interest or urgency. When her boss popped his head into her cubicle to say he was leaving for the day, she smiled, wished him well, and left the building ten minutes after he did, navigating the big Lincoln down the parking garage's ramps and curves and humming to herself.

Once home, she stripped and showered, applied cream to needy spaces on her body, then stood naked in front of the closet mirror. Not bad. She could stand to lose a few pounds but no one was going to toss her out of bed for eating Saltines.

She slipped into a loose sundress, brushed her hair, and pumiced her heels. She thought maybe it was time to make an appointment to get waxed, but why? It hurt like hell, left her red and tender, and anyway, it wasn't like there was anyone to appreciate it. She spent a few minutes trimming her pubic hair with a pair of cuticle scissors because, who knew? She might meet a guy in the laundry room. You had to be prepared. The pre-cocaine anticipation was building nicely.

She let it build, fed the cats their special meal, slowly sipped her wine, and nibbled on the sandwich. *Don't you worry, about a thing.* Her willingness to wait, to delay gratification, proved she wasn't one of those dope addicts who couldn't help themselves.

She was making thin, gold lines of cocaine on a cake dish that had belonged to her mom when the phone rang. She recognized the number immediately and knew she shouldn't answer but did anyway.

Clarence. The man was like a bad penny. Ever since their breakup eight months ago, he'd called her every three or four weeks. So far, she'd resisted his plea that they get together; coffee, maybe dinner, just to catch up. She shouldn't have answered the phone.

"Hey Gloria! How are you, beautiful?"

"I'm fine, Clarence. What do you want? I was just leaving."

"I was walking by. I saw the Lincoln parked. I've been thinking of you. A lot."

Ah God, that voice. She should hang up right now.

"Do you think I could come up for a minute or two?"

"No!" It came out a yelp. She took a deep breath and closed her eyes. Mistake. The image of Clarence on top of her, the *smell* of him; how it felt when he was inside her.

"Just for a minute, Glo, really, I just want to see your face."

She took another breath. "That's not a good idea, Clarence. Plus, I'm going out."

What the man could do with his hands, with his mouth!

"I've really missed you!"

"Go away, Clarence. I don't want to see you."

But she did.

"Let me just come to the door, okay. Just to say hello, that's all. I really need to talk with you. About stuff that happened. And then I'll leave."

"Nothing to talk about, Clarence. You fucked JoAnn Sabatini when I was out of town. You lied about it. We talked it to death. End of story."

There was silence on the other end, then, "Please, Glo. Just for a minute or two."

Gloria sighed. She and Clarence had really been good at sex. Sex and coke. Actually, coke, then sex. She'd never done coke until he'd come along, and it was so much *fun!* And it would have kept being fun, too, if Clarence hadn't been such a duplicitous horndog. She'd really cared for him, loved him, maybe, though neither had ever used the word.

"Glo, are you there?"

She let the silence between them ring.

"I'm so sorry," he said. "I didn't even like JoAnn. I just wanted to get even with her husband."

"Which makes you an even bigger prick."

She heard him sigh. "I know. I know."

She was going to hang up, but instead she said, "Call back in a half-hour, Clarence. I'll think about it."

"Half an hour."

"Yes."

He hung up.

This was a mistake.

She swept the gold cocaine back into the baggie and dropped it into the pocket of her sundress.

Seeing Clarence would serve no purpose whatsoever other than make her feel bad afterwards.

She applied a trace of lipstick and a hint of eyeshadow.

Neither of her cats even *liked* Clarence. *She* didn't like Clarence, at least, not anymore. And JoAnn Sabatini? The woman had a mustache, for God's sake. How insulting was that, your prick of a boyfriend fucking a circus freak-show woman? Somebody pretty, you could sort of understand. But JoAnn? Okay, she had huge tits and wore T-shirts two sizes too small. But the mouth on that bitch! What did that say about Clarence? What did that say about Gloria herself, for being with Clarence?

Maybe she should put on something else. She wasn't wearing a bra or panties under the sundress and Clarence would notice. He would grin at her with *that* smile. Probably the same smile he'd used on JoAnn.

Screw him. That would serve him right. He could look all he wanted. She'd give him an eyeful and then throw his sorry, pale black ass out.

She sprayed a touch of Victoria's Secret Very Sexy Fragrant Mist between her breasts, and squirted a bit more down there. She finished her glass of wine and poured another. She wrapped the sandwich and put it in the fridge, then emptied some M&Ms into a bowl.

For sure he wasn't going to get any of her coke. Although, in retrospect, that was one of the nice things about Clarence, he never took more than his share. She'd do four lines to his two, and he never complained, even when it was his dope.

Jesus. Was that all she could say about him? He was great in bed and he didn't hog the drugs?

She let him into the apartment twenty minutes later. He had brought a cheap bouquet of flowers from Trader Joe's. She could see the price tag, $5.99.

He said, "My God, you're gorgeous," and hugged her. In four minutes they were in the bedroom. He lifted the sundress off her and the little baggie fell from its pocket to the floor.

"Hello, what's this?"

She grabbed it. "None of your business!" She stood, naked, and wondered, where do you stash coke when you're not wearing anything? Damn! She knew this would be a bad idea!

"I'm clean, Glo. If that's what I think it is, I wouldn't want it even if you offered me some."

Her laugh came out nasty. "You're clean? Gimme a break…" She slid the baggie into her panties drawer.

"Two months last week," he said. "No coke; no dope; I even stopped smoking. And I'm going to the gym. I've changed, Glo."

"I don't believe it."

"True fact." He slipped his Polo shirt off but kept his jeans on. "God, you're beautiful. I'd almost forgotten. Come to bed."

It was just as she remembered except better. He even did the thing with his tongue and his thumbs.

With a little coke, it would be *incredible*.

She came hard a couple of times, and then once again, and when he was through too, she pulled the coverlet over herself and asked, "So why did you quit?"

He was silent, then said, "Well, I haven't really quit, like, totally. It's not like I'm an addict or anything. I've just cut way back. And I did stop smoking."

They got up and shared the sandwich from the Italian Store, and finished the bottle of wine.

"Where are the cats?"

She shrugged. "Hiding, I guess."

"They never liked me. I still can't figure out why."

"They don't like liars."

He looked hurt. "C'mon, Glo. Let it go. It didn't mean anything. You were always the one."

She had put the sundress back on and was feeling good. Her parts still tingled. She wondered if maybe there was something still there to be had with Clarence. Maybe he really *had* changed.

She asked, "You want to try a little of this stuff?"

He shook his head. "Nah. I really shouldn't. You know what they say, it's the first drink that gets you drunk."

"No, it isn't. It's the fifth or sixth."

"That's what they say in AA. That it's the first."

"You've been going to AA?" She hadn't expected that.

He looked a little embarrassed. "Just a couple of times. It's not like I'm an addict. I can take it or leave it."

"Still," she allowed. "I'm impressed."

"I even got a sponsor," Clarence added, a little self-conscious.

"Wow," said Gloria, not quite sure what a sponsor was but not wanting to appear dumb, either. "A sponsor. Wow."

He changed subjects. "What is that stuff, anyway?"

"Bong Bong said it was gold coke."

He laughed. "You're still buying from Bong Bong?" Clarence had introduced her to the Filipino.

She nodded, opened a second bottle of wine and poured. "It was expensive." She took a healthy slug. "It's supposed to be really good."

She retrieved the baggie and handed it to him.

"Gold coke, huh?" He paused, peered at the bag closely as if trying to detect its secret.

"Imagine that! Good old Bong Bong." He held the baggie up to the light. "It really is a sort of interesting color. I wonder what they did that made it that way."

"Bong Bong said it's a golden plant."

"Hmmm. I think I've heard about that, but I've never seen it." He kneaded the baggie between index and forefinger. "I wonder what it's like?"

Gloria sat down next to him, her leg pressing against his. "Amazing, is what Bong Bong said."

He looked at her, smiled and shrugged. "What the hell. Yeah. Let's do some! I've been good for weeks…"

Gloria always thought watching Clarence cut cocaine was like witnessing the creation of great artwork. The lines he fashioned were perfect, uniformly spaced and containing an exact amount of drugs, to within a microgram, she was sure. He was methodical and didn't waste a single movement and when he was done he sat back and inspected his work, then nodded.

"Beautiful," Gloria breathed.

Clarence rolled up a twenty dollar bill and offered it to her; she was still feeling good and tingly and generous. "You first."

He bent over the table, snorted one line, then two. His eyes bugged out. He said, "Oh my God, Bong Bong wasn't kidding! This is amazing sh—"

He dropped to the floor in a disjointed heap.

Gloria laughed, said, "Asshole!" but fondly this time. Clarence could be such a joker!

He didn't move.

"Get up, Clarence! C'mon!" Then she added, "I have to pee. Be right back."

She went into the bathroom, peed and flushed, and looked at herself in the mirror. That idiot, Clarence, always had to be the center of attention. She smiled. Her parts still felt happy and good.

One of the cats, Courtney, had snuck in and approached Clarence's head. Clarence didn't move. The cat sniffed at his hair, his mouth, his ear. It looked up at Gloria as if questioning the large hunk of meat on the floor.

Gloria whispered, "Clarence?" Then, a little louder, "Clarence? What're you doing, Clarence?"

The cat returned to the bedroom, its tail an exclamation point.

Gloria nudged Clarence's side with a bare foot.

She hesitated, then dropped to her knees.

Clarence was definitely not breathing.

She gently placed the index and middle finger of her right hand where the big artery in Clarence's neck should have been pulsing.

Nothing. She pressed her fingers harder into his flesh. Not a quiver. "Ohmygodfuckme!"

She laid him on his back and applied pressure to his chest as she'd been taught to do in CPR class to the tune of *Stayin' Alive*. *Ah* **press!** a*h* **press!** *ah* **press!** *ah* **press!** *staying alive* **press!** *staying alive* **press.** *Well, you can* **press!** *by the way I use my* **press!** *I'm a woman's* **press!** *no time to* **press!** *Music loud and women* **press!** *I've been kicked a* **press!** *since I was* **press!**

She did that for three minutes, getting tired and panicky. Courtney the cat emerged once again from the bedroom, sat on its haunches, and watched with feline indifference.

She stood. Clarence had dropped the twenty dollar bill and she picked it up, bent over the two leftover lines of coke and reared back just in time. Did Clarence have a heart attack or had Bong Bong's coke done that to Clarence?

She stared at the lines of brown powder.

"Shitshitshitshitballsackfuckfuckfuck!"

Instinct took over. She went to the kitchen and retrieved the yellow Kitchen Maid rubber gloves she used to clean out the cat box. She moistened a dishrag and swept up the coke, wiping in a circular motion until it was all gone. Then she applied Windex to the coffee table and cleaned that too, just in case. She rinsed the cloth in the sink and washed her gloved hands using dish soap and very hot water.

She looked at Clarence. Had he moved? No. No, he had not moved. Clarence, she knew with utter finality, would never move again of his own volition.

He had pissed his pants. Gloria crinkled her nose. Disgusting, and so typical of a man to make a mess before leaving!

She got a thick beach towel from the linen closet, knelt next to Clarence's inert form, and pushed and lifted until he was on his right side. She slipped the towel beneath him as far as it could go and repeated the process on the other side. She loosened his belt and tucked the towel in.

Gloria felt as if she had to pull air into her lungs. She drained her wine glass. She found her cell phone and hit 9-1-. And stopped.

The ambulance people would come, and then the police, and they would determine the cause of death, and Gloria would have to explain why Clarence was in her apartment with a noseful of something that had killed him. They'd find evidence of sex, drug possession and use, and undoubtedly they'd search her office, too, and her computer, and they'd bring up the Mr. Snow folder. And that would be that. Fired, no retirement, no health insurance, maybe even implicated in Clarence's death.

She took three deep breaths and suddenly felt extraordinarily calm. Her forehead creased in concentration.

She grabbed Clarence by the ankles and pulled him toward her hallway door. It was surprisingly easy. She propped him in a sitting position against the living room wall, then thought better of it. He would stiffen up, left like that. So she took his ankles again and pulled until he was on his back on the floor. His head made a bonky sound when it hit the rug. He farted, a long, sad, bleating sound, and she made a face. Fucking Clarence! Just like him, put her in an impossible situation like this! And fart, the pig.

She returned to the kitchen, poured the rest of the bottle into her glass, and ate a handful of M&Ms. She turned Netflix on and watched James Spader outfox the government agents and occasionally flash his strange, feral grin. She set her clock for two a.m., went to bed and stared at the ceiling. She dozed off feeling her heart pound in her chest and woke up from a dreamless sleep ten minutes before the alarm went off.

Clarence hadn't moved. His skin was sort of gray now, and his lips had turned pale, like someone had drained the blood from them. She took his wallet and his cell phone and emptied all his pockets. His fly was undone; she zipped him up.

She sized up his narrow shoulders, which were slightly wider than his hips. Yes. Clarence would fit.

She laced her hands behind his head and lifted. Clarence wasn't quite as stiff as she expected. His neck bent. It appeared, though, that his legs were locked at the knees. She lifted, struggled, shifted her weight, then his, and got him to a standing position leaning against the wall. Good.

The trash chute serving her wing of the building was across the hall behind a door marked *Trash Recycle*. She wedged it open by jamming Clarence's wallet under the door's bottom edge.

She grabbed him in a bear hug across the waist and waddled them both to the chute room. She propped him up again. His head bobbed and a long thread of saliva hung from the corner of his mouth like a thin icicle. She pulled open the chute door. A little lever allowed it to stay open so tenants could dispose of several bags of trash. She wrapped her arms just below Clarence's butt and lifted. Clarence wanted to tip forward. She set him back on his feet and thought about it for a moment. Head first, maybe? That would be more... streamlined.

She lifted Clarence from the knees and allowed his head to fall forward into the chute door. There was room to spare on either side. She slowly lowered him, and when his waist was in the chute, she let him go. Clarence vanished almost without a sound. She thought she heard his head bang a couple of times against the chute's metal lining, but that was faraway and muffled.

Back in the apartment, Gloria started shaking from head to toe. Her teeth chattered as if she were standing outside naked in a blizzard.

There was an unopened bottle of scotch whiskey in the hall closet. She'd won it in an interdepartmental charity raffle and never opened it. Now she did, and took a long pull that burned all the way down to the bottom of her stomach.

"Jesus Fucking Christ in a tow truck." She said it aloud. Where the expression came from, she had no clue.

The trembling turned into giggles and then into laughter. Then it turned into sobs.

7   MAN'S BODY FOUND
WEDGED IN TRASH CHUTE

THE STORY APPEARED ON PAGE FIVE, BOTTOM LEFT, of *The Washington Times* two days after the event. The *Post* had a much smaller article buried below the fold on the third page of the Metro section.

There wasn't much to report. A woman on the fifth floor of a building in Fairfax, Virginia, noticed that the trash chute had backed up, something not unusual and which she privately ascribed to the number of immigrants living in the building. She called the super. The super determined the blockage was between the second and third floors. Shining a powerful flashlight in the chute and peering up, he saw what looked like a fuzzy brown bowling ball. The super cursed in Albanian, his native tongue, because people should know better than to throw things like bowling balls into the chute. Americans were so wasteful! If he could dislodge the ball, he'd give it to his teen-age son who almost lived at Bowl America.

From the floor above, looking down into the chute, the super could see the soles of a pair of running shoes apparently suspended in midair. When he used a broomstick to try to dislodge the shoes, he realized they were attached to something, possibly feet, though he sincerely hoped that wasn't the case. Fairfax volunteer firemen proved it was.

Gloria read the story and shuddered. In the forty-eight hours following Clarence's untimely death and disposal, she had tried hard to persuade herself it had been an act of God, and that she had been involved only in the details. Quite obviously, Clarence was meant to die and she, a modern Charon, merely eased his way across the rivers Styx and Acheron, or, in her case, the apartment hallway. But she stopped short of being convinced, and the ensuing two nights had been nightmarish. She was terrified of going to Bong Bong; God only knew what the Filipino savage might have in store for her. Out of cocaine with no replenishment in sight, she drank herself insensate and woke up a dozen times gasping, panicked, the bedsheets soaked from terror sweat.

No one else much noticed the death. Colin saw it reported in the online version of the *Washington Post*. A follow-up filler appeared three days later; **Body Found in Trash Chute Investigated.** A three-inch story said the Fairfax police thought foul play might be involved. Colin called Michael Wilkie at the *Post*'s Metro desk.

Wilkie was a legend for having survived three newsroom reorganizations by keeping a subterranean profile. Having been in the newsroom close to twenty-five non-threatening years, he earned a six-figure salary with innocuous reports on the weather's highs and lows, animal-related events focusing mostly on rabid raccoons and unusual pets, centenary birthdays, spelling bees, Potomac River drownings during spring thaws, shootings and stabbings in the far suburbs, and the occasional two-paragraphs death no one cared enough to explain. He was a compendium of information, and like many recovering alcoholics, had dabbled with drugs decades earlier.

In an otherwise open newsroom without walls, the better to foster communications, Wilkie had somehow gotten a windowless and broom-closet-size office of which he was inordinately proud. Colin saw him at AA meetings two or three times a year.

"Colin! How are you? Still straight? How much time, now?"

"That's why you're such an exemplary reporter, Michael. You always ask the right questions."

"So how long?"

"A little more than two and a half years."

"Excellent," said Wilkie.

"Day at a time. Listen, the guy in the trash chute—"

"Isn't that great? The police suspect foul play!" Wilkie laughed and coughed. Colin could hear him catch his breath.

"Still a pack a day?"

"Half. I've cut down."

"And you have how much time?"

"Thirty-two years!"

"Oxygen tank yet?"

"Stop being a pain in the ass, Colin. I opened the window, okay? Anyway, what do you want to know?"

"Were there drugs involved?"

Wilkie laughed again. "Colin, a young black man ends up in a trash chute. That would be a really original way to commit suicide, wouldn't you say? Of course, there were drugs involved! Lethal stuff, too, according to the coroner. Coke and heroin, your standard speedball, with a little added zip."

"What?"

"Don't know. Something nasty. Rat poison was popular in the past, but you really have to be one mean son of a bitch to do that. Fertilizer. Cyanide. Cement, even. Sometimes a powdered version of that crap you spray on your tomatoes to get rid of aphids. A lot of Fentanyl, too. The stuff's about fifteen times more potent than heroin and looks just like it so when people use, their lights go out."

"No tests?"

Wilkie sighed. "Running tests to figure what's been cut with what costs a lot of money, and so does the equipment. Depending on how thorough you want to be, there're instruments like spectroscopes and such. But for something like the guy in the trash chute? I'm not sure anyone's really interested. He's still a John Doe. No ID and apparently no record, so no prints either."

"So what do you think the cops are going to do?"

"Do?" Colin heard the scorn in the reporter's voice. "You read the paper, Colin? Have you kept up with what's happening out there in happy drug land? Heroin deaths have quadrupled in the past decade. There was an FDA report that came out a few months ago that no one paid attention to, and the bottom line is, you've got an epidemic going on here, people dying left and right from overdoses. Heroin and prescription opioids alone were good for 25,000 deaths, and probably double that many, realistically, since a lot of deaths are written off as accidental. Grandpa didn't *mean* to take all pills; his bunions were killing him. So to answer your original question, what are cops going to do? Nothing. *Nada.* Zilch."

Colin thought about that for a second, and then asked, "Could the MS-13 gangs have been involved?"

"Hang on."

Colin knew Wilkie was lighting a forbidden cigarette for a quick puff. He heard the rasp of the lighter, the inhale and exhale.

"Better?"

"Much," Wilkie answered. "I truly hate all that new corporate health crap. I actually got a memo from personnel saying I should exercise." He puffed again. "So MS-13? No. Very unlikely. Those gang guys are mutants, you know? They like machetes and hammers and stuff that cause blood to splatter. So the trash chute, that's not their style. You want my humble opinion?"

"Absolutely."

"Guy died while visiting one of the tenants in the building. They were hootin' and tootin' and got their hands on some nasty composite drug, maybe some new designer pharmaceutical that a genius in a trailer park didn't quite get right before he put it out on the street. The guy dropped dead, and whoever he was doing this stuff with disposed of him in the chute. A sad but unoriginal tale of the new suburbs. But that's only my opinion."

Wilkie paused, took another secretive puff. "But you know who might be able to get some better info? That Latino lawyer, been in the room for years and years, whatsisname, Eduardo? Ricardo?"

"Angelo?"

"That's him! Angelo from Guatemala, right? He lawyered a bunch of would-be gangbangers about six months ago. They weren't MS-13, because those people have loads of money and they can afford the best, and Angelo is not exactly an attorney *extraordinaire*, but he's pretty good. I think those boys got their money's worth. You got his number?"

Colin did. He thanked Wilkie, promised a future lunch, his treat, and hung up.

It took eight calls to reach Angelo Vasquez, Attorney at Law. The eighth time, Colin left a message that said, "It's Colin. I'm a friend of Bill's. I need to talk to you." This, he knew, was cheating. A "friend of Bill" was code for a friend of Bill Wilson, the late cofounder of AA, and therefore a member of the fellowship, possibly in need of fast assistance. Angelo believed it was the duty of a recovering alcoholic to help another recovering alcoholic anytime, anywhere. He called Colin within an hour and was irritated.

"You mean, you're okay? You're not going to drink or something?"

Colin admitted to the subterfuge. The lawyer sounded maybe a little disappointed.

"So why'd you call? You need a lawyer?"

"No, Angelo, but I'd be grateful if I could just ask you a question or two."

"Hey," Vasquez said with hope in his voice, "I heard you went out?"

"More than two years ago. I'm all right now."

"Hmm," said Vasquez, his voice heavy with doubt.

Colin asked about the MS-13 gangbangers Angelo had recently defended.

"Those boys? Listen, I can't talk about the details, confidentiality and all that, but those kids were never MS-13. What they did, they got MS tattoos, which was a very bad idea since the real MS frown on that. And then they held up an Einstein Bagel store using cap guns. They didn't even make it out the door. There was an off-duty cop there and he nabbed all three of them."

"Did they do drugs?"

Vasquez's laugh was a bark. "Of course, they did drugs! You know any kid who's not smoking a little something now and then? They all do. But serious stuff? No. Listen, Colin, one of them was nineteen with the IQ of a gerbil. The two others could barely speak English. Believe me, they weren't MS-13 material."

Colin was about to end the call when Vasquez asked, "Why are you interested in these kids?"

Colin told him about the body in the trash chute.

"Oh yeah, I read about that," Vasquez laughed without humor. "No, none of the people I know would do that sort of stuff. And my guys, they're in one of those progressive camps for juveniles, serving out their sentences. They're making flower boxes and macramé oven mitts. They wouldn't have the imagination to stuff someone in a trash chute."

Just before hanging up, Vasquez asked again, "So Colin, you sure you're okay?"

"I'm fine, Angelo. And I have a sponsor, thanks."

"Oh yes, that's right. You've still got that madman, Orin? Him now, wheelchair or not, I could see him stuffing someone in a trash chute."

8 THE LITTLE MAN IN THE BACK SEAT of Mamadou's limo seemed lost in the expanse of leather, glass, and vinyl. It was his first time in America; he'd arrived the day before from Mombasa via Dublin, and Mamadou had picked him up at Dulles airport. The little man wore an ill-fitting suit of too-shiny material, inexpensive shoes, and a red tie with a large mustard stain on it. He gazed out the window with unabashed curiosity.

"I never thought America would be so green. It reminds me a little bit of home." If he hoped to raise a question from the limo driver, he was disappointed. "Of course, in Kenya, it's the rainy season, so everything is soaked. But in my real home, in Conakry, we don't get that much rain."

That got the driver's attention. "Conakry?"

"Yes. Guinea. Actually, just outside of Conakry. A village, three hundred people, last time I was there. It's not there anymore. And I know what you're thinking. Ebola. Don't worry. I have been tested and tested again, five, six times. The last time at the airport in Dublin, and then again, here. I don't have it."

"I wasn't thinking that," Mamadou lied.

The little man laughed. "Of course, you were! It is all right; now, you say Guinea or Sierra Leone or Liberia, people think, *Ebola!*"

He turned serious. "It's under control now, according to the UN, but if it's under control, why are there people still dying, you might ask?"

Mamadou didn't ask, concentrated instead on negotiating a turn and was stopped dead by a double-parked truck.

"Now *that's* Africa," the little man laughed. "Trucks stop in the middle of the street. The driver breaks for lunch and just abandons his vehicle."

Mamadou steered the limo around the obstacle to a chorus of horns. It was just past noon, and he'd driven the little man to various Washington, D.C., tourist spots.

"You're West African too, aren't you? Ivorian?"

"Senegalese."

"You're fortunate. No Ebola there. Or here, now that I think of it."

Mamadou nodded. "No. Here the killer is drugs."

"Twenty-five people in my parents' village died," the little man said. "They all went into one grave, and then the government came and burned the village down. They used flame throwers."

Mamadou muttered something. The little man said, "Excuse me?"

Traffic stopped again. Mamadou said, "They should use flame throwers here."

The little man leaned forward. "Here? Why?"

"Because," Mamadou hit his horn again to no avail, "Because here, drugs are our Ebola."

They drove in silence towards the Kenyan Embassy until the little man asked, "Have you lost someone to drugs?" He was sitting back now, once again looking very small in the back of the car.

"My..." Mamadou hesitated. Antwone had been, what? A protégé? A ward? No. A future. Antwone had been *the* future. "A very close family member, almost a son."

"I am so sorry," the little man said. "I shall put you, and him, in my prayers. What was his name, if I may ask?"

"Antwone."

"Antoine? A very French name!"

Mamadou didn't correct him.

They reached the embassy on R Street. Mamadou opened the rear passenger door and the little man got out. "Well," he said, "that exhausts my discretionary transportation funds and my leisure time in Washington. I always wanted to ride in a limousine, like the Mercedes *wallahs* in Nairobi, and now I have. Thank you, Mr. Dioh. I shall pray for you and your Antwone. *Inna lillahi wa Inna Ilaihi Raji'un.*"

Mamadou nodded and translated the Muslim expression of condolences. "Surely we belong to Allah and to Him shall we return. Thank you."

They shook hands. Mamadou refused a twenty-dollar tip and drove back to the AfriCars garage.

He was about to park the limo when his cell phone rang. It was George. "Do you have a minute to come and see us today? Mim may have some information."

Aunt Mim's house in Northeast Washington was impeccably well kept. Mamadou knew the neighborhood took care of its most notable person, and so the yard was mowed in the summer, raked in the fall, and fertilized in the spring. At the first sign of a winter snowstorm, a horde of small boys appeared with shovels; the man who lived two houses down drove a city snowplow, and so Aunt Mim's street was ice-free even before Embassy Row was.

Mamadou parked the Mercedes in front of the house in the space he knew would be there, since he was expected. A lanky teen with dreadlocks appeared and said, "I'll watch your car, sir." Mamadou gave him the car keys without the slightest hesitation. The boy asked, "You want me to wash it?" Mamadou gave him a ten-dollar bill. "No. Just make sure no one drives off with it."

The boy pocketed the bill and smiled, showing widely gapped teeth. "No sir. That just ain't gonna happen."

George met Mamadou at the door and ushered him in. Aunt Mim's house smelled of Johnson's Lemon Pledge Wax, cigarettes—Mim smoked Tareytons, Mamadou knew—and Gallo Hearty Burgundy wine.

George scowled. "She's still smoking, and she's still drinking. Doesn't seem to matter what I say!"

Mamadou followed George up the stairs. The Tareyton smell grew stronger. Mamadou entered Aunt Mim's room.

She sat up in the large bed, opened her arms wide. Mamadou gave in to her hug. Aunt Mim said, "I am so sorry about Antwone, Mamadou, I just don't have the words…" She wiped at her eyes with a lace handkerchief, and Mamadou knew the tears were real. She released him, and he sat on the edge of the bed. George took his appointed seat by the window and picked up a thick book. Aunt Mim pointed her chin at the man she'd been with more than fifty years.

"Fool's reading a medical encyclopedia now. Imagine that. Crazy old man."

George looked up, adjusted his glasses. "Wasn't all that crazy when you had the gas, and I knew what to do, was I?"

Aunt Mim dismissed him. "Oh hush up, George. Don't you talk about a lady havin' gas. That's rude!"

George returned to his tome.

Aunt Mim took Mamadou's right hand in both of hers. "How you doing, Mamadou? You healing? Have you prayed?" She sniffed and didn't wait for an answer. "Course you haven't. That's okay. I prayed enough for both of us."

Mamadou poured her some wine from the jug by the bed.

She took a sip. "I don't know what's happenin' anymore. Young folks like Antwone; he was such a wonderful boy. A little rough when you took him in, but so smart, wasn't he George? Wasn't Antwone smart as a whip?"

George looked up, nodded.

"He was a good boy, but them drugs," Aunt Mim said, "they're just getting worse and worse every year. We losing a entire generation. Even right here, on *my* street, some dealer started hangin' around the corner. We chased him off, but then some others came, and we called the police, and they run those nasty men off too, but they were back the next day. Had to put a curse on them, and I *never* like doin' that."

Mamadou looked quizzical.

Aunt Mim raised her eyebrows and her forehead crinkled, deep and shallow lines etched across the brown skin. "You see any drug dealers on the corner when you drove by? You didn't, did you?"

George said, "Mamadou's an educated man, Mim. He doesn't believe in curses."

Mamadou, who did believe in curses, kept silent.

"He was a good boy, Antwone," she said again, this time more softly. "I had hopes for him."

"Antwone wasn't using, Aunt Mim. There weren't any marks on him. Not one. I checked."

"Hmm." Aunt Mim drank deeply from her glass; Mamadou refilled it.

"He *wasn't.*" Mamadou was insistent.

"Don't matter much at this point, does it? 'nother good boy gone." She put the glass down on the night table. "There's sadness. All the time there's sadness. Just seems that's all there is, nowadays." She lit a Tareyton. "So you wanted to find out 'bout someone called Russo?"

George had been right, the man's name was Rousseau, just like the French philosopher, but there all similarities ended.

Théophile Bienaimé Rousseau was a 32-year-old Haitian from Croix-des-Bouquets, a suburb of Port-Au-Prince. He liked to say that the rapper Wyclef Jean was a cousin but this was a lie. Théophile was the son of a small-time gangster who himself was the son of a *Tonton Macoute,* the feared private police force employed by both the dictator Jean-Claude Duvalier and later his son, Baby Doc Duvalier, when he came to power.

Théophile had begun dealing drugs when he was seven years old. A charming boy with a toothy smile, he sold single joints to tourists and used the profits to build a solid, small business employing other kids. By the time he was twelve, he regularly bribed the police and was moving pounds of product weekly.

He'd fled Haiti when he was nineteen following the ill-planned murder of a competing dealer, and arrived in Miami with $5,000 and the phone number of a Cuban heroin importer who'd been impressed with the young man's work ethics.

The importer put Théophile to work after procuring him a French passport that claimed Théophile lived in a suburb of Paris and worked as an interpreter. He kept his name.

Théophile engineered drug deals with Russians, Canadians, Marseillais members of the Union Corse, Tunisians and Algerians, Vietnamese and Laotians. He was responsible for two showy and unsolved assassinations done artfully with very sharp knives. He was smooth, persuasive, trustworthy, and urbane. He did very well. In fact, he did too well. In the third year of Théophile's service, a coup led by one of his employer's bodyguards overthrew the Cuban, whose headless and handless body was found in the Dumpster of a Seminole casino on the Tamiami Trail.

Théophile thought it wise to leave. He paid the former bodyguard $200,000 for the right to do so and not be hunted down. That left him $50,000, a large suitcase of summer clothes, and a 2012 BMW 435i. There were no hard feelings; business was business, and in fact he had every intention of relying on the new Cuban network for product. He went to Washington, D.C.

"Jesus CHRIST!" said the advance guy. He was thirty-two, and four years earlier he'd finally gotten a job in politics like he'd always wanted. It had been fun. Now this.

"Jesus, Jack. You *asshole!* What've you done now?"

The candidate was forty-seven. He was white, pudgy, balding, and his boxer shorts were around his ankles. He was slumped on the floor of a W Hotel Marvelous Suite, two grades below the eighth-floor Extreme WOW Suite, whose cost he had not been able to justify in spite of a little family money of his own. There was a syringe sticking out of his left arm, which was turning blue. A length of surgical tubing was tied tight just above the syringe.

Huddled in the corner of the room, a bare-legged girl in an open kimono that revealed young breasts was holding her head in her hands and crying softly. The advance man wondered how long she'd been there.

"I didn't do anything. I told him I don't do drugs. I didn't want any. He said to wait. I went into the bathroom." Her voice trailed off.

"Ah shit," said the advance man. He looked around the room. The bed was disheveled. There was a half-empty bottle of Jack Daniels on the nightstand next to an open 10-pack of Trojan Studded Bareskin condoms. The candidate's shirt, suit, tie, and well-shined shoes were carefully laid out on an adjoining sofa.

The advance guy knelt beside the girl. Her nose was running and the make-up around her eyes was ruined.

"C'mon, honey, stand up. You gotta get dressed and get out of here…"

How old was she? Sixteen? She had the soft round features of an Iowa farmer's daughter. Her skin was pale with a bridge of freckles spanning her nose. She had on bright red five-inch stiletto heels.

"C'mon, honey! You don't want to be involved with this. Get dressed. You have to go *now*."

The girl looked at the candidate. "Is he—"

Fourteen or fifteen, the advance guy thought, judging by her voice. He took her right hand and pulled her to her feet. She tottered and the kimono slipped off. Oh jeez. She was perfect, absolutely flawless. He tried hard not to stare and failed. Her breasts were tipped with cartoon-pink nipples. Even her navel was impeccably round and perky in the center of a child's belly. She was shaved smooth, the slit of her sex a sealed vertical line.

Jesus… How much had she cost? A couple of thousand? No, more. This was Washington, D.C., and the kind of carnal pleasures the farmer's daughter could provide didn't come anywhere near that cheap. The suite was just above a grand a night, the girl, probably three, maybe even four.

"What's your name, sweetie?"

She sniffled. "Candy." Then she wiped her eyes on the hem of the kimono and said, "No. My name's Mary Anne. Mary Anne Sweeney." She blew her nose into a tissue. "I want to go home." She started sobbing like a kid and he held her. When he felt himself growing hard, he pulled back.

He helped gather her clothes, handed them to her and watched as she stepped into thong panties and a very brief skirt.

"Where's home?"

She settled her breasts into her bra. "Watertown, Ohio."

"Go wash your face."

"I have to pee."

"Do that too, but hurry."

Shit, shit, shit, shit, shit. The advance guy knew the candidate was dead. He'd done two tours as a medic in Afghanistan and knew exactly what the bodies of overdose victims looked like.

He pulled the syringe out of the candidate's arm, untied the rubber tube. The skin beneath it was red, the flesh indented.

He wrestled the candidate into the bed, arranged the sheets and covers. He took the bottle of Jack Daniels and walked into the bathroom. The girl was sitting on the toilet rubbing her eyes. He ignored her and dumped the rest of the alcohol into the sink, then ran cold water.

The girl wiped herself and flushed. She went to the sink, threw water on her face, and examined it in the backlit mirror.

Back in the bedroom, the advance guy found the candidate's briefcase. He took a folder from a side pocket—the speech the candidate would now never give—and arranged it on the writing desk. Then he dumped the bottle, the box of condoms, the syringe and rubber tube into the briefcase.

The girl was now fully dressed and standing uncertainly near the door. She has holding a bright green knapsack with *Disney World* embroidered on the flap over a smiling Mickey Mouse. God. Could she be *younger* than fifteen?

He asked, "You have money?"

The girl shook her head, *no*. The advance guy peeled ten hundred-dollar bills from a wad of cash, than added a fifty. He handed it to her and put his hands on her shoulders. She was still shaking slightly. Her cornflower eyes were focused on the floor.

He said, "Look at me."

She did, trying to get her bearings.

"Okay. Don't ask questions, just do what I say. Walk out of the hotel. Don't talk to anyone. There are cabs out front. Get in one and go to Reagan National."

He squeezed her shoulders lightly. "You following me?"

"Walk out of the hotel. Don't talk. Take a cab to Reagan National. Yeah."

"Go to the United Airlines counter and buy a one-way ticket to Chicago. When you're there, go to Midwest Air and find out the best way to fly to Watertown. Is there an airport there?"

She nodded.

"Okay. You got all that?"

She nodded again.

"Okay. Go. Don't ever come back here, all right? Go back to high school or whatever, but never come back to D.C., and never, ever, talk to anyone about this. Promise."

The girl nodded. She was back in control. "Okay. Yeah. I promise."

She took a deep breath and squared her shoulders. Her breasts pushed hard against the fabric of her blouse. The advance guy thought, *perfect,* again, and sighed. She looked at the money in her hand. "Can I have a couple hundred more? You know, if I have to stay in a hotel or something in Chicago."

He peeled off three more bills. She took them, smiled, pecked him on the cheek, and left.

He did, too, minutes later, knowing he had contributed to at least a half-dozen crimes. He left the Do-Not-Disturb sign where it was on the room's doorknob. He took the candidate's briefcase, which he would later toss into a construction site Dumpster. He went home to his month-by-month rental apartment, an Adams-Morgan walk-up about half the size of the W Hotel suite. He took off his suit and hung it in the bedroom closet, then wadded up socks, underwear, and shirt into a ball that he threw into the laundry hamper.

He took a long shower and washed his hair twice. He heard the phone ring three separate times. They'd be looking for the candidate by now and he was the first person they'd reach out to. It would probably take a day or two for the hotel to check on its guest, and there would be a minor scandal, the sort of thing that got on the front page for a few days and ended up in the Metro section. The candidate wasn't well known, and the office he'd been running for was of little importance in the Washington greater-scheme-of-things.

The police would talk with him. He'd profess minimal knowledge; he was just an advance guy for a third-tier politician. It was only a job, he had no idea what the man was doing in a W Hotel suite. Drugs? Ridiculous!

The candidate had been divorced a decade earlier, thank God, so there would be no furious grieving widow giving tearful interviews to the *Fox News at 5* people on the evils of the Nation's Capital.

He thought about the one political truth he'd taken to heart during his brief career, an axiom he'd read in a biography of Richard Nixon: Never be associated with a loser. And was there anything that shouted *loser* more loudly than overdosing in a hotel room with a whore?

Mind you, he thought, *there are worse ways of dying.*

"Did you read the story? About that politician in the suite downtown?"

Colin nodded. It was a minor piece, a page three below-the-fold item, about the same degree of unimportance as the guy in the trash chute.

Today Emily Martin was in jeans and a loose T-shirt that read, "Elect an Inept Woman to National Office! (Then We'll Really Be Equal)". Colin had read it, smiled, and struggled and failed to keep his eyes from Emily's chest. They wandered there anyway and if she noticed, she didn't mention it.

"That's another unusual death," she bit into a blueberry scone, and crumbs stuck to her lips. "A white guy running for county commissioner, Charles County or Welford, but it's still weird. His handler said he never knew the guy had a problem."

Colin shrugged. "He could hardly say anything else, could he?"

Martin swallowed, took another small bite. "On Fox News, they said the police thought there might have been someone else in the room. And he definitely had some fresh needle marks on his arm."

"Maybe he was diabetic, had to use insulin or something. Plus, the guy was sort of liberal. Not the kind of politician Fox would endorse."

"Still," Martin said.

"If he was a liberal, and an addict, Fox will have a field day."

They had agreed to meet at a coffee shop near Dupont Circle. It had taken Colin twenty minutes to find a parking space, and the aged Porsche's temperature gauge had hovered over the red.

"I'd really like to find out more about this," she said. "It's an epidemic. Even the papers talk about it, and there are full-page ads from the big drug makers saying it's not their fault. But I still think of my grandfather dying like he did. And then those other people; your friend's ward?"

"Antwone. For Mamadou, he was almost like a son."

"You don't believe the boy was an addict."

Colin smiled sourly. "I don't know what to believe. I didn't know him well, but I know Mamadou, and if Antwone had been using drugs, Mamadou would have known and have done something about it."

"So," Aunt Mim said, taking a sip of wine and tapping her Tareyton into an ashtray, "That's what we found out about Mr. Rousseau. I don't know if that helps you or not."

Mamadou thought it might.

"The man is sort of a fool," George said, looking up from his medical encyclopedia. "Comes into town and he's dressed like a French pimp—"

"George!" Aunt Mim objected to strong language of the mildest sort.

"Well it's true. And talking with an accent like Maurice Chevalier—"

"Who?"

George frowned. "An old French singer, Mim. He was in *Gigi*."

"Well, why di'n't you just say that?"

"I did, Mim. That's exactly what I said."

"No you di'n't, George! You said *pimp*."

"Well he did look like—oh never mind." Now he addressed Mamadou. "So this is what people have been saying. This Rousseau cut quite a figure in the neighborhood. And then he got a bunch of bad boys, gathered 'em like apples. Boys who had all done things and gotten caught and been sent away, and he organized them, thieves and muggers and minor dealers and men with domestic abuse issues. There was a rumor that Rousseau killed a couple of these men, just to make an example for the others, but there never was proof, so maybe it was just hearsay."

"Hmph," said Aunt Mim. "Where there's hearsay, there's always a grain of truth."

Mamadou wasn't so sure. On the streets, he knew, stories were like weeds in sidewalk cracks. Addicts would chase down new products on the vaguest of tales that somewhere in Prince George or Calvert or Susquehanna County, a dealer was selling high-quality goods just in from New York, or Boston, or Tallahassee.

Addicts were strange people, Mamadou thought. They killed themselves slowly and were eager to do it faster.

He left George and Mim and heard George say, "Pimp is not a bad word, Mim. It's a perfectly acceptable term…"

He drove back to his garage and found an unknown 10-year-old SUV parked in the driveway. Standing and leaning against a fender, DiAngela Jones and her triplets watched him open the garage door with a remote and drive the car in.

"You live in an interesting neighborhood, Mr. Dioh."

Mamadou could remember the names of two of the tree boys, Dionne and Dewan, but not of the third.

"Well," said Mamadou.

The woman pointed to her sons. "Antwone told them all about your cars, Mr. Dioh, and this morning Dewan got it into his head that he wanted 'to pay his 'spects' to Antwone. Dewan and Darnell thought it was a great idea, so here we are. I hope we're not disturbing you."

One of the boys stepped forward. Darnell? "I told him it wasn't 'spects. I told him it was *respects* but he never listens to anything I say."

"We can wash the cars," the second small boy stepped forward.

"And dry and polish them, too," added Darnell.

"We's really good at that," said Dewan.

"We *are* really good," said Darnell. Then repeated with even more emphasis, "*Are*, not is."

DiAngela Jones laughed. Mamadou thought it was a light, happy sound. She had on jeans and a loose blouse. The boys wore identical blue shorts and white tee-shirts. "I put up with this 24 hours a day," she said. "Darnell corrects them, and they ignore him."

"A perfect relationship," Mamadou said. "Who's the oldest?"

"Darnell," she nodded her head towards the boy. "By three minutes. Then Dionne then Dewan."

Mamadou addressed the boys. "Are you ready to do some work? I'll pay you each five dollars for each car. There are three cars. How much does that make for each of you?"

"Seven," said Dewan tentatively.

"Twelve!" Dionne was more certain.

"Fifteen," Darnell sighed dramatically. "It's fifteen." Then to Mamadou, "I'm sorry Mr. Dioh. Antwone did teach us math. But they," he nodded in his brothers' direction, "they don't ever pay attention."

"Do, too!!" Dewan and Dionne said in unison.

Mamadou showed them where to turn on the water hose and found three buckets and rags. He poured a little Turtle Wax Car Wash liquid in each. The boys filled the buckets and got to work.

He and DiAngela Jones sat in the dingy office.

"How are you feeling? I hope showing up unannounced wasn't too brash on my part."

Mamadou fixed coffee in the stained pot. "No. I'm glad you're here." They talked about the weather, about his business, about hers— she was a legal secretary for a major downtown firm and was studying to become a paralegal—about the weather again. Then Mamadou said, "I found out a little about who the boys were talking about, Ru So."

He'd spoken for less than a minute when Jones opened her mouth, then shut it, then opened it again. "Oh my god," she said. "I know exactly who that is, now that you describe him. I just never knew his name. There are lots of flashy young men with money, or at least who pretend to have money. I'm almost certain I know who you're talking about."

She paused, closed her eyes and rubbed her forehead. "I went out with him. Once. For coffee." She rummaged through her purse. "He gave me his card, but I'm not sure I kept it." She found a small leather case and emptied it, then rifled through its contents. "Ah! Here it is." She handed it to Mamadou. There was a name, an email address and a single phone number in heavy script on a thick and creamy rectangle of paper.

Mamadou blinked.

The man she thought was probably Rousseau had identified himself as Nicholas Boissy, a Haitian from a good family, churchgoing, land-owning and friends of the Port-au-Prince ruling class. "I met him at a church social." She smiled, embarrassed. "There aren't a lot of places I can go with those three. They can get rambunctious."

The three in question were splashing soapy water mostly on each other but also on one of the limo's sides. "The church offers childcare for a few hours while single parents meet. He was very polite. We started talking. He told me he had a son in Miami. Then he said he was a cousin of Wyclef Jean, you know? Hip hop?"

Mamadou knew the name, but no more.

Jones continued. "I thought that was sort of interesting, though I'm not into rap, personally. Anyway, he seemed nice, until he started asking a lot of really personal questions, and I looked at him and knew he wasn't what or who he said he was. I mean," she held her hands palm up, "I'm sure he was Haitian, I've met a few and I recognized the accent, but I'm almost certain the rest of everything he said was nonsense." She frowned. "Why are you looking at me like that?"

Mamadou looked up, snatched back to the present. "I'm so sorry! I was thinking of what I'd been told about him by a friend. I think you did well to get away; if it really was Rousseau, he's not someone you want to be around, or," he looked towards the triplets, "your boys. He's a bad man."

And he told her about Aunt Mim.

Later, she asked, "Do you really think he had something to do with Antwone's death?"

Mamadou was handing each of the boys the money they'd earned. He looked up. "I don't know. But I have every intention of finding out."

9 On Monday in the early morning, Birch Carroll sent an email to the radio station calling in sick. He'd woken up at two a.m. with agonizing cramps in his lower back, managed to down three Vicodin dry, and then fallen back into a fitful sleep that left him exhausted.

The Voice of Reason had several hours of pre-recorded programming that could be aired at any time. That was the great thing about ultra-conservative radio: There was never a lack of subject matter, and whatever was broadcast didn't need to be news. Any number of tried and true issues could find a receptive audience. Carroll's personal favorite was the international Muslim conspiracy, which involved several well-known American personalities, starting with Barack Obama and including, but not limited to, the Kardashians, Ralph Nader, various Senators with foreign-sounding names, Mexicans who might actually be Arabs, Turks, French, and Armenians, the Greek Orthodox Church, and OPEC as a whole.

This morning, conspiracies were far from his mind. He'd awoken for the second time that morning in a sweat, the bedsheets tangled around his legs and a bitter taste in the back of his mouth. His back was a field of pain.

He got to his feet painfully, did an unenthusiastic set of morning stretches designed to loosen the cramped muscles linked to his spine, and limped to the kitchen.

He shook two more Vicodin tablets from the plastic vial and swallowed them with a mouthful of Mountain Dew.

There were only four pills left. The refill date on the prescription's label was two weeks hence. That surprised him. Had he really taken that many?

He had. The past few days had been hell. No doubt, his back was getting worse, but the notion of surgery terrified him, and surgery performed by a minority physician was even more petrifying a thought.

He made toast, microwaved yesterday's coffee and eased himself down into a chair. He sat at the kitchen counter and practiced slow and even breathing.

In the past two years, he had sought help from a dozen sources. Chiropractic adjustments provided temporary relief. Yoga did the same, but he seldom went. Being in a room with so many women made him self-conscious. Once, while doing a downward dog, an escaping and silent blast of intestinal gas had made the ladies on either side wrinkle their noses. He'd never returned to that studio, even though he'd paid for a six-month membership. Plus, deep down he suspected yoga was sort of foreign and maybe even gay.

He had tried massage of every kind including deep tissue, hot stone, *effleurage, petrissage, tapotement,* Swedish, Norwegian, Thai, Shiatsu and, shamefully and only once, Korean with a Happy Ending. Nothing worked for longer than an hour or two. Except for Vicodin, and even the hydrocodone's benefits seemed to be diminishing.

Carroll got Leonard Baskey's number from the radio station by saying he was thinking of putting together a roundtable of the best telephone callers. Leonard Baskey, officer with the Northeastern Defense Militia, super patriot and, by the way, pharmacist, was the best.

Nor, when reached, was he hard to persuade. Birch Carroll was Baskey's hero and after Carroll explained exactly the nature of his emergency, the pharmacist swung into action. Probably, he explained, Carroll was simply becoming resistant to the drug's benefits. This commonly happened among chronic pain sufferers. He recommended an opiate rather than hydrocodone, as opiates' pain-killing virtues were less likely to decline in the long term. Did Mr. Carroll have asthma, or any other breathing difficulties? No? Wonderful.

Leonard Baskey even delivered. "I'll be there in forty-five minutes," Baskey said.

That sounded great to Carroll. "Let me give you the address."

"I already have it sir. I took the liberty of looking you up before I called your program the first time."

Now *that* sounded a little creepy, Carroll thought.

Carroll, on crutches for good effect, met Baskey at the door but did not invite him in. He tried to give the pharmacist militiaman money but Baskey refused. "It's an honor to come to your assistance, Mr. Carroll. And if you ever need anything but can't reach me, you can call this gentleman." He handed Carroll a card with the name Dr. Mario on it and a phone number. Then he left.

Carroll hefted the small white paper bag Baskey had given him. He opened it and found a medium-size bottle of Advil and his heart sank. *Advil? What the fuck?*

He uncapped the bottle and tipped it over on the kitchen counter. *Holy Shit!* He tried to count the pills. More than forty. He noticed for the first time that the Advil bottle bore a small sticker, *OxyContin 80mg.*

Oh my, thought Birch Carroll. *Oh my, my.*

He inspected the tablet. Wasn't eighty milligrams a lot?

His back was *really* hurting.

If eighty milligrams was a dangerous dosage, no doubt the pharmaceutical companies would not manufacture such pills. And certainly, Baskey was a responsible professional, a man employed by a reputable company that advertised on Carroll's station. Birch Carroll swallowed a pill with a gulp of water.

Within minutes, he felt the pain in his back ebb away like a gentle tide. An hour later, Carroll decided he was well enough to be The Voice of Reason. He called the station to say he would be in to work.

He spent the rest of the day in a state of pain-free joy. Why had no one told him about eighty milligram Oxycontin?

He took a second pill at six p.m. and a third at eleven. He slept. He dreamed of sex with a long-ago girlfriend. He woke at five in the morning and felt a slight twinge. Another capsule took care of it. Four doses in less than a full day? Was that too much?

"So you got me thinking, Colin," said Michael Wilkie, the *Post* reporter, "about the guy someone stuffed in the trash chute, and some other strange stuff that's happened in the last few months, you know, not just in D.C. but in Virginia and Maryland, too. And I asked a couple of the boys and girls who work the regional desks if they'd heard anything. Hang on."

Colin heard the snick of a lighter and an inhale. Wilkie came back on the line. "Sorry. Anyway, it turns out they've sort of been talking among themselves, but nobody really wants to go to the trouble of writing a story about it, the deaths, that is. There's a whole bunch of them, but it's a real pain in the ass research nobody wants to do anymore for something that'll wind up on B5, you know?"

Colin knew. Journalism had changed drastically since his days in a newsroom. Most young reporters wanted the sort of story that exploded across the Internet and was picked up by the *Huffington Post, Google News,* or *World News.* The death of a bunch of junkies in the Washington area wouldn't ring many bells.

"So some of these young hotshots are comparing notes," Wilkie inhaled again.

Colin interrupted. "They tell you all this stuff?"

Wilkie laughed. "I'm a legend, Colin. They love getting close to me! They think I can tell them how to survive in a rat's nest like *The Post.* Did I tell you I know this girl on the Style desk, she's twenty-six and when we f—"

Colin cut in. "Spare me the details, Michael."

Wilkie sighed. "I was going to say that when we *find* time to have lunch, all she can talk about is the old days. Hell, she wasn't even born then, but she wants to talk about the Berlin Wall and the Rodney King verdict, and I'm just about the last person in the newsroom who remembers all that stuff. I'm a hero here! I make 140 grand a year to write about planes that *don't* crash and people who live to be a hundred. So yeah, they talk to me all the time. Can I continue now?"

Colin nodded into the phone. "Sorry I interrupted. I thought you were going to say—

"That I'd fucked her. You have a filthy mind, Colin. So back to the dead druggies." Colin heard Wilkie light another cigarette.

"I started calling people in the program, people who go to the meetings I used to go to years ago when I was a lot more active and traveled around. Like to Winchester and New Market and Sunrise and Poolesville. Some of the real old timers remember me; I call them a couple of times a year. So I ask them, any new young people going to meetings and they start talking about how it sure seems like a lot of addicts in their small towns are getting really sick or dying. Eight in Rockville, six in Germantown, five in St. Michaels. I started writing it down. Hang on."

Colin could hear Wilkie shuffling papers. "Yeah. So four in Hagerstown, six in Leesburg, seven in Ellicott City, twelve, *twelve!* in Lynchburg. Now I'm beginning to think this is really scary."

"And the police aren't doing anything?"

"Small town police, they've got a bunch of other things to do. And these are junkies, remember? Who gives a shit about a few junkies? Now get this, in Riversboro, they get eleven dead in four months. Riversboro has like 100 residents. Only two of those who died are locals, a boy and a girl, both sixteen. The rest appear to have been passing through and whatever happened to them happened there."

"I researched something about that town a few years ago," Colin said.

Wilkie shuffled more paper. "Every house is old, like, a hundred, two hundred years. People there are real proud of that. And almost all the houses are made of stone. There's a famous old school there."

"And a farm that's been in the same family since 1735. I remember now." Colin had researched the town for *Smithsonian Magazine.*

"That's the place," Wilkie said. "Not all of them croaked within the town limits. There are woods nearby and two died in some sort of makeshift camp. Three were in a car accident. Driver apparently passed out and there were passengers, and they were killed too. All the bodies tested positive for drugs, according to the coroner. Two drowned; one was a gun accident, some kid was playing cowboys and Indians and shot his buddy in the head. Then he apparently decided he should get more fucked up to get over the trauma of having killed his friend, and he overdosed."

Colin asked, "So are you going to write this up?"

Wilkie laughed. "Me? Oh, hell no! My longevity here comes from *not* writing stuff. Nope, nothing from me. I was just curious, after your call and all."

"So maybe somebody on the local desk will do it."

Wilkie grunted. "Hunh. Doubt it. That's the sort of piece that's got no traction at all. You spend a ton of time and end up on the back of the Metro page."

"Times have changed." Colin recalled much lesser stories that had elicited much greater interest.

"That they have. Part of the problem is the cops, too. A story like this, nowadays they won't even talk off the record. Used to be, they'd give you some stuff without attribution, you know, the old wink-wink nod-nod. Now with lawsuits and procedural boards and everybody hating cops for weekly shootings of some poor unarmed black guy, they just clam up. But then again, none of these kids even bother developing sources any more. When I was doing the cops, I'd hang out at the police station and the bars they went to and just talked to guys, have coffee with them, and they got to know me, and if something happened, I knew who to call. They don't do it that way anymore."

They spoke for a few more minutes, getting back in touch with the good old days which both knew had never been as good as they remembered. Colin hung up, copied the notes he'd taken as Wilkie talked, and made the scribbles legible.

Later that day Catherine called him and came over. She went straight to the kitchen, fixed tea and, when she sat down, said, "Josie told me she told you." She paused and sipped. "I'm not sure how I feel about it, but I think with everything out in the open, maybe now's the time to all go our own way…"

She wasn't looking at him; her glance went somewhere over his right shoulder.

He sat next to her. "This is sort of sudden, isn't it?"

Now she looked at him. "No. Not really. We haven't been close since your relapse, and that's quite a while ago. I think we stayed together because we both felt guilty about Josie. And grateful, too, at least, I was, I still am, you know that."

She rummaged in her purse and found a tissue. "Crap. I really didn't want to start crying." But she did, and when she was gone eight minutes later, leaving the apartment key he'd given her, Colin sat down heavily on the worn sofa and tried to figure out if he was sad or relieved. He decided he was both, with the emphasis on the latter, and guilty, too.

He looked around the apartment and remembered when Catherine had come by unannounced and rearranged the furniture. The place had looked better, no doubt about that, but he had enough manly pride to shove the furniture back where it had been. A month later, good sense overcame stubbornness and he'd moved the furniture again, exactly as Catherine had placed it.

He wondered if she'd met someone else, decided that was a distinct possibility. Catherine was smart and had a sense of humor that had often caught him off guard. She was attractive and, when Josie had vanished, proved herself capable of not falling apart in the darkest times. Plus, and there Colin smiled wryly, her divorce had left her well off. Actually, exceedingly well off. Josie's father had hidden assets which Catherine's very good lawyer discovered. The divorce settlement had been in the high nine figures.

He went to the chest of drawers where she kept a change of clothes. Empty. When did that happen? She had a key to the place; had she come by when he wasn't there? They'd last spent the night together two weeks ago. In the morning he'd gone for a run and found her gone when he returned, which was the norm. She'd probably taken her clothes then.

He wondered if Josie knew, and decided the girl probably did. Since the kidnapping, Josie and her mother had grown much closer and there were few secrets between them.

He thought about Emily Jameson Martin and immediately felt awkward, so he tried focusing on Willie B, but that didn't work. It seemed wrong to be thinking about the late Willie B's grand-daughter when the scent of Catherine still lingered in the room, but he did it anyway.

A basic truth Charlie Snow had discovered—albeit too late, he would tell anyone listening—was that he did not need to concern himself with things he did not understand, or that had little relation to his actual well being.

When, two years earlier, he had been hired by one of Lobo's competitors to *terminate* Lobo, he had given only five seconds' thoughts to why the man hiring him had used the word 'terminate.' To Snow, this sounded like a term someone in a bad novel would use. It was silly and screamed of government jargon or of cheaply produced spy movies where in the end the agent got the girl who was really a Russian mole. Snow didn't bother pursuing the matter much past those first thoughts. You want someone *terminated?* Snow would *terminate*, or at least try to.

The operation had been a fiasco, and he had been forced to step in, firing his service revolver four times and executing the man he had hired to kill Lobo. Charlie Snow had not gotten paid for services not rendered. Instead, he suspected his name had been put on some secret file identifying fuck-ups who couldn't get the job done, and he'd never again been contacted to *terminate* anyone.

He assumed the recent beating Lobo had instigated settled things between them. As he'd told Lobo when they met and prior to getting manhandled by the bodyguard, it had been business, nothing more, and there was no call for ill feelings so long after the fact. Charlie Snow needed Lobo. He hoped bygones could be bygones.

Meanwhile, he waited in Lobo's dentist's badly decorated anteroom. The walls and carpet were mustard-colored. The newest magazine was a coverless seven-months-old issue of *Dental Health,* and the receptionist—also mustard clad—hummed to herself loudly and popped gum. Charlie Snow no longer thought of Lobo as a class act.

"I don't think it's just the synthetics," Emily Martin told Colin later that day. "I've read up on those, and I know there've been some deaths, but those were kids, Colin." She looked abashed. "Oh God, that sounds terrible. That's not what I meant to say."

She was lying down with her head on the arm of the couch. He was sitting on the floor.

"I've read about JWH, John—"

"John W. Huffman," Colin said.

"Yes, him, and how he synthesized drugs, and it got away from him."

"Cannabinoids."

"Stop interrupting, please." She said it with a smile. Colin kept silent.

"And I know there were something like a hundred deaths. Spice, that's what the synthetics were called. I know the statistics, too, how overdoses went from less than fifty to more than 400 in a couple of months. But still, I *know* that's not what caused my grandfather's death. He wouldn't have fooled around with that stuff, believe me."

She sat up, swung her feet to the floor. "But then again, maybe I'm being unrealistic. Maybe my grandpa was just an old junkie. Old junkies die just like he did." She sighed and shrugged her shoulders. "Jeez. I am just full of wisdom and cheer today."

Colin stood. It seemed natural to reach for her. She folded into his arms; he could feel her warmth against him.

"This is probably not a good idea." She stepped back, put some distance between them. "You're with that woman, right? The one whose daughter you rescued?"

He shook his head. "Catherine. No. Not anymore."

"Oh."

"We… ended it a couple of days ago."

"Oh again."

They stood facing each other for an uncertain moment, and then she moved away. "Then you need a little time, I'd say." She kissed him on the cheek and went into the kitchen. He heard the refrigerator door open and close, and she returned with a glass of ice water.

"So what do you think it is?"

"The deaths?" Colin went to his desk and shuffled through some papers. "I think a lot of it is fentanyl. I downloaded this last night." He handed her several sheets of printout.

The top one read:

TWO THOUSAND VIALS OF FENTANYL STOLEN, REPLACED WITH TAP WATER

VICTORIA, Australia—Victorian police are investigating the disappearance of large amounts of a powerful, highly addictive painkiller from the state's ambulance service.

An internal investigation found that more than two thousand vials of the drug Fentanyl, which is up to 100 times more powerful than morphine, had been stolen and replaced with tap water.

Fentanyl is a potent narcotic and commonly administered by syringe to give patients pain relief.

A paramedic has been stood down.

The Ambulance Employees Association says the union is helping the paramedic.

"It's a tragedy on so many fronts," said a spokesman.

"I guess there are people who are susceptible to these sorts of drugs and I guess the opportunity arose, and so, unfortunately, he may have an addiction."

The union has criticized the ambulance service for letting the theft go unnoticed for some time.

"But that's Australia," Emily Martin said.

"That theft, yes. Read the other stories."

She leafed through the papers. All were reports of fentanyl thefts from hospitals, pharmacies, veterinarians, nursing homes, and doctors' offices. There were dozens of reported instances.

"Look at the last one."

"The *Baltimore Sun?*"

"Yes."

She read, Truck Carrying Drugs Hijacked

"When did this happen?"

"Three months ago," Colin said. "Right in our back yard."

She moved her lips as she read. "Good God! Twenty-five *thousand* doses? How come we haven't heard about this?"

"It's not really that important, I guess. Twenty-five thousand doses will fit into three medium-sized suitcases."

"It says here the driver of the truck was a suspect."

"Yeah," Colin nodded. "But in a later piece, the paper reported there was no evidence, so he wasn't charged. And anyway, that wasn't the first or last time that happened. I found six other reports, all the same."

"All fentanyl?"

"Yes. Best bang for the bucks. I'd bet at least three of those hijacks were by the same people. The stuff is transported like tomatoes or hamburger meat, no security at all. The thieves waited until the driver made the pickup from the distributor, followed the truck in two cars, and forced it to stop. They wore masks and took the drugs at gunpoint. The driver wasn't about to resist. No fuss, no muss. Each time, there was a surge of deaths within a week of the thefts."

"And the police?" Martin was still staring at the papers.

"Not much they can do. There are truck hijackings every day. I looked it up because it seems to be pretty much unreported, as a crime. Everything gets stolen. Cars, electronics, furniture, lumber, automobile parts, school supplies. There was one a month ago that got three tons of beef, and another where they took 1,000 live Maine lobsters. And four hundred pounds of frozen shrimp. The best was 8,000 bags of processed cow manure headed for a Home Depot warehouse."

That made her laugh. "What, they unloaded all those bags?"

"No," Colin laughed, too. "That one, they took the truck, too. Someone phoned in an anonymous tip, and the semi was found abandoned and empty the next day on a side road. The driver was tied up in the back, and the thieves left a note on the windshield. It read, *No More Bullshit.*"

"Bet that didn't make the paper."

"No," Colin said, "but it made Fox News."

They talked and went out for dinner at a local spaghetti place. Emily had a vodka martini full of green olives and two glasses of wine. They talked about relationships, about her broken engagement a year before, about Colin and Catherine.

When they got back to his apartment, she said, "Okay, I think you've had enough time." She took his hand and led him into the bedroom.

10 THE LIMOS ALL BORE TRACES OF SMALL HANDPRINTS and unwiped wax. AfriCars Three had suffered the most at the ministrations of the triplets. There were water marks on the hood and windshield and the limo's rear hubcaps hadn't been washed. By the time they'd finished tending to the first two cars, the boys had lost interest in the job.

A mound of damp rags towered between two of the cars. One of the boys had spilled—what? Leather reconditioner? —on the garage floor. The water hose lay uncoiled. The boys had used it to good effect soaking each other from head to toe.

Mamadou and DiAngela Jones had watched the triplets' antics with amusement. They spoke of earlier years, Mamadou as a policeman in Dakar, Jones as a theatre major at DePaul University. "Do you know where that is?"

"No."

"Chicago. Have you been there?"

He hadn't. "I haven't traveled much. No time so far, but I'd like to."

Twice, Mamadou had stepped in and aimed the hose at the triplets, and once he showered their mother, to the boys' delight. "Much better than Kings Dominion," DiAngela Jones had noted, "and a whole lot cheaper."

Later that same day, he'd taken them all to the National Zoo in one of the limos. The boys had been impressed to the point of silence. He'd fed them hot dogs, hamburgers, French fries, and milkshakes, and Dionne had gotten sick behind a bush, to the vast amusement of Dewan and Darnell.

"I'm so sorry," Jones had said. "I should have told you Dionne's got sort of a weak stomach. Between the food and the excitement, getting sick was unavoidable."

So Mamadou carried Dionne past the lion's compound and the green space housing the giraffes and elephants. The boy sipped a Coke to settle his stomach, and after a while began to squirm so Mamadou put him down.

"You're going to have to carry the other two now," she told him. "That's how it is with triplets. No favoritism."

So he did that, too, and by the time they were driving back to the garage, Mamadou realized that only once had the despair and sadness of loss swept over him; that was when they stood before the cassowary's cage. The bird had been Antwone's favorite. The triplets had cowered behind their mother when the prehistoric avian with its monstrous claws approached the retaining fence.

"Jeezuzcrist," Darnell had muttered, looking at the bird's talons. That earned him a light swat across the back of the head. "Hush up! Taking the Lord's name in vain!" Dionne and Dewan had snickered. Their mother's glare silenced them.

On the way back to the garage, the boys fell asleep in the back of the limo.

Mamadou and Jones were quiet until the car got on Rock Creek Parkway and she said, "You're a good man, Mr. Dioh."

He'd demurred. "I'm not sure you'd say that if you knew what I was thinking."

Her smile turned mischievous. "Well now, let me guess. If you're thinking about me, I can guess your thoughts and agree with them. But nothing will happen for a little while. I hope that's all right with you."

He'd nodded, taken by surprise.

"I know. That's very forward of me. I'm not sure if that's a shortcoming or an asset." She tilted her head and continued, "If you're considering doing something," she looked at him intensely, "against whoever hurt your boy, please know that I'll help any way I can."

They pulled into the AfriCars garage. It smelled of oil and gas and leather cleaner. Mamadou and DiAngela remained in the front seat of the car, a good two feet separating them. In the back, the triplets seemed to breathe in unison. Dewan was sucking his thumb and Dionne had thrown a small protective arm around Darnell.

"They're going to be talking about this for months, you know. The animals, the cars, the food. That was a lot for one day." She reached and took Mamadou's right hand into both of her own.

Birch Carrol used up his entire supply of painkillers in less than a week, but it was a terrific week. His shows were livelier than ever; one in particular triggered a flurry of Twitter comments that made their way to Bill O'Reilly, who called live on-air to say the Voice of Reason was the sort of show everyone ought to listen to. He called Birch 'my man.' Not bad.

Being free of pain gave Carroll wings. Even his engineer, a generally lackadaisical and apolitical millennial, noted the increased audience participation. She gave Carroll a bright smile and a high five at the end of a show and said, "Phones were off the hook, man. That was cool. Too cool." The compliment pleased Carroll immensely. She was cute in a chubby way, and he'd lusted for her a little, but when he'd made his interest known, she'd turned him down. Maybe give it another try?

The drugs were running out faster than he could account for; one day there were forty tablets, and the next he was down to twelve, then six. Now he had four. But being pain free was such a miraculous relief! He'd heard the expression 'feel like a new man' and had always thought of it as, well, an expression. But that was exactly what he felt like— new, stronger, smarter, and wittier. And perhaps even taller, he wasn't sure. It certainly appeared as if everything he looked at seemed as if at a greater distance. He had an *overview,* is what it was. Things were clearer; ideas were more sharply defined and easier to understand.

It amazed him that a simple pill, a simple *few* pills, could have such an effect.

He had the number Leonard Baskey had given him. He found the slip of paper. Mario. Would it be better to call Mario or Baskey?

But Mario, that was Latino. Mexican maybe, though Carroll supposed it might conceivably be Italian, which was somewhat better.

He dialed Baskey's number and hung up before the voice mail came on. He dialed Mario's number and was pleasantly surprised when a decidedly Anglo woman's voice answered. "Doctor Morales' office. May I help you?"

"Would that be Doctor *Mario* Morales?"

"Yes sir. May I help you?"

"Ah. I'd like to speak with him. Leonard Baskey suggested I call."

The woman's voice became uncertain. "I see. Can you hold on?" She clicked off before Carroll could answer and returned a minute later. "Can Doctor Morales call you back? He's with a patient right now."

So Doctor Morales was a real doctor, not a doctor of history or English literature. That was good. Carroll told the woman his name was John Smith and he gave her both his home and cell number. Then he broke one of the remaining Oxycontin pills in half and swallowed it dry. As soon as the half-pill went down, it struck him that he wasn't in pain and in fact hadn't been for a while, actually. He congratulated himself for practicing preventative medicine.

When Dr. Morales called back, Carroll picked up the phone on the first ring. Dr. Morales said, "Tell me you are in unbearable pain."

"Yes," said Carroll, "I am."

"So please tell me you are in pain, Mister, Smith, is it?"

"That's correct," said Carroll.

"Ah," said Dr. Morales with a hint of impatience and an accent decidedly not from south of the border. "We are not understanding each other, Mr. Smith. In order for me to help you, you must tell me you are in terrible pain."

"But I—oh," said Carroll, finally understanding. "I am in excruciating pain!"

"How unfortunate," said Dr. Morales. "Perhaps I can be of assistance. Is it your back, you neck, or your appendages?"

"My back, doctor. My back. Terrible, terrible pain," said Carroll, getting into the spirit of things.

"I see. Well, I suggest an office visit, and then we can discuss possible courses of actions."

Carroll had not thought a visit would be necessary. As if reading his mind, Dr. Morales said, "A very brief visit. I must see a patient before I can prescribe a solution. Can you be here within an hour?"

He could and was. Carroll pulled into the parking lot of the Buena Vista Medical Center forty-five minutes later. Dr. Morales's office was on the third floor. He signed in and took a seat.

Dr. Morales was unquestionably not Latino. Carroll stared; the doctor smiled. "Ah, I see your questioning look. I get it from patients who come here for the first time. I am from Israel, but Arab. When I obtained American citizenship, I decided Mario Morales was a better option than Ma'ruf Marzuki. I certainly could not pass for a John Smith, now could I?" He winked, unexpectedly.

"Now. Your back; am I correct?"

"Terrible pain," said Carroll. "Unbearable."

"So you said. Stand up."Carroll did.

"Balance on your left foot."

Carroll did that too. He was about to switch to his right foot when the doctor said, "That won't be necessary." He scribbled on a prescription tablet and handed it to Carroll. "There you are. This should alleviate your discomfort." He stuck out his hand. Carroll shook it. It was dry, strong, and smooth. "Come back in two weeks. You can make an appointment with my receptionist." He turned and walked away.

The four-minute visit cost $375. Dr. Morales did not take insurance, though his receptionist gladly accepted Carroll's MasterCard.

"We'll see you in two weeks?" She was a strong-looking woman with a fixed, pearly smile and perfect blond hair that looked only slightly artificial.

"I can't just phone in to get the prescription refilled?"

The woman smiled icily and shook her head. "I'm afraid not. Dr. Morales likes to monitor his patients closely." She looked down at her appointment book, traced the dates and times with a finger.

"Will the seventh at 10 a.m. do?"

Carroll nodded.

There was a pharmacy on the building's first floor. An Asian man in a white coat asked, "Generic do?"

Carroll wasn't sure. "Is there a difference?"

The man said, "About a hundred dollars."

"Generic is fine."

The morning had cost Birch Carroll close to $500, but he was set for at least a couple of pain-free weeks, and in his mind, this was all that mattered.

11 Danee James Watson was a good kid in a neighborhood where it was hard to be a good kid. Most of the other 13-year-olds on his street had already spent time at the Juvenile Detention Center on Mt. Olivet Street. He hadn't, which made him a pussy. His survival depended on a quick wit, a willingness to defend himself when absolutely necessary, and an instinctive knowledge of when to back down, such as the time a 12-year-old wannabe gangster threatened him with an unreasonably large gun.

Danee was painfully aware of his surroundings, his background, and his tenuous prospects. His mother was a heroin addict and an only partially successful whore, who often said she'd be much richer if she didn't give it away every other night. His father was in prison for robbery, aggravated assault, and general stupidity; the fifth conviction, so he'd be there a good, long while. There were few friends; the only one who'd mattered, Antwone, had been found dead. OD'd. Which was strange because, while alive, Antwone had been adamant about not using drugs.

He'd also promised Danee a future, "I'll hook you up with my friend. His name is Mamadou. He's African. He'll help you." They talked about it over two weeks and Danee got excited. The African ran a limo service, and Danee loved everything with a motor and wheels. He routinely made a few dollars washing and waxing cars. He could help maintain the limos, he knew how to check the oil and tire pressure. He and Antwone would work together, which sounded almost too good to be true. The African could be a godsend.

"But I'll tell you what," Antwone had told him, "don't you never lie to that man. He's got some Africa juju thing. He can tell when you're lying."

When Antwone saw doubt on Danee's face, he'd added. "This one time? He was out working, and I knew he'd be gone all day? So I took one of the cars out. Just drove it around the block once is all, ain't nobody seen me, and then I cleaned it super good." Antwone took a deep breath. "Well the next day, he come up and he says, 'Antwone, what'd you do yesterday?' And he looked at me and he *knew!* It was that Africa juju thing; he looked me straight in the eyes and he *knew.*"

"So you told him?" Danee was fascinated. This was one powerful man.

"Course I told him! I ain't no fool!"

"Did he hit you or something?"

Antwone shook his head. "Naw. He don't do that. He never touched me. Not once. Tell you what, he don't have to! Man looks at you with that juju look, and it make you shake all over."

Antwone also told Danee of another man, Ru So, for whom he ran errands once in a while. He'd pointed to his brand new Air Jordans. "Man pays well, but I tell you, he scare me. It's a different scare from the African. A scarier scare. Like he wouldn't hit me, but he could kill me."

Antwone paused, sighed, and shrugged. He went to a library shelf, pulled down a book.

They spent a half hour looking at pictures of the most expensive automobiles in the world, then Antwone said, "The African, he has *three* limos *and* a Mercedes."

Danee had really wanted to meet the African, but it never happened; he was disappointed. Another unfulfilled promise.

Danee read a lot; he was a gangly boy with glasses that gave him a prematurely intellectual look, and huge hands and feet. He spent at least ten hours a week at the poorly served William O. Lockridge Library. Danee had read everything there about being a lawyer, a doctor, a car mechanic, a cop, a paramedic, a counselor, a tree surgeon, a large animal veterinarian, and a drug dealer.

There wasn't much information about the last, mostly articles in magazines often defaced by youths with little to do but make life more difficult for people. That was okay; Danee had no intentions of becoming a drug dealer. There were a dozen or so in his neighborhood alone, and not one seemed to have two dimes to rub together. Mostly, they struggled like everyone.

Danee kept a small spiral notebook in his back pocket where he recorded the events of the day and, on the back pages, the deaths of people he knew. Lately, a lot of young men and boys had died. Counting Antwone, twenty-two, in a three-month period. Seventeen directly drug related, three by gunshot, one by stabbing, and one by television.

A teen-aged boy had dropped an ancient Panasonic from the third-floor balcony of his apartment building onto the head of another teen, a rival for the affections of a 15-year-old girl named LaTrina who everybody knew would fuck for a bag of Doritos.

The murder had been messy. The victim's head looked like a leftover pizza, and it took the ambulance more than an hour to get there. The hospital wouldn't send medics to the neighborhood without a police escort, and the cops weren't that eager to enter the courtyard where the boy lay, oozing blood and smelling bad, with a sixty pound television where his head used to be.

Danee was right there, not twenty feet away when the television hit. It made a sound like a watermelon falling off a truck, and the boy didn't even have time to howl. Danee heard a voice above him yell, "Take that, motherfucker," and another voice went, "Whoa!" and within less than a minute there were fifty people in the courtyard, all staying a careful ten feet from the corpse. Some took photos and videos with their phones, uploading them to Instagram, and one man kept shouting, "WorldStar! WorldStar!" Someone said, "Man, that was a *old* teevee!"

Danee knew the dead boy slightly. His nickname was French Fry because that's what he ate most of the time, and he'd never amounted to much; mostly he wandered the neighborhood park and threw stones at birds and squirrels. He was an amateur arsonist and inept shoplifter who'd been caught a dozen times but rarely prosecuted because of his age and the insignificance of his thefts. He lived with his great-aunt and two cousins in a street level two-bedroom apartment and hung around bigger boys when they'd let him. Danee was sure French Fry's demise wasn't important enough to warrant vengeance of any kind. And getting killed over a girl like LaTrina was plain stupid.

When the ambulance got there, they didn't even try to see if French Fry was alive. The EMT people just slid him into a body bag, lifted the gurney into the back of the ambulance, and left without turning on the sirens or lights. The cops stayed a while longer, and a plainclothes detective talked to a few people but no one had seen a thing. That old Panasonic had just dropped out of the sky. Danee left before The Man could question him.

Danee missed Antwone, who was smart and wanted out of the neighborhood too. Danee wished Antwone had stuck around long enough to introduce him to that African. He also wished Antwone had never mentioned the other man, Ru So. Just the day before one of the courtyard boys had found him, "Yo, D! Man been lookin' for you," and handed Danee a slip of paper with a phone number. "Man say you gotta call him. His name Lu So, or Mo Fo, or So So. Dress real good, but got a weird accent." That, thought Danee, couldn't be good.

Danee knew who Antwone's African benefactor was. He'd once followed Antwone to the AfriCars garage, seen the limos and their owner, a tall, very black man who wore his chauffeur's uniform with authority. Danee had almost stepped forward but the man was so imposing, it was almost like he was white, and Danee did not approach white people.

That night in the apartment, Danee listened to his mother and one of her 'friends,' a stooped, round-bellied man who came by once or twice a month. They were talking and laughing in the master bedroom, with long pauses between conversations.

Danee had no problems with this friend who did not get drunk or threaten violence or bring heroin. This friend usually arrived with food from Popeye's, enough for the three of them, and a twelve-pack of Miller Lite. He asked Danee questions and seemed interested in his answers. He complimented the boy on spending time in the library, and talked about sports and cars until Danee's Mamma suggested it was time for Danee to go to his own room and watch television.

Danee knew his mom would do a little heroin while the man drank a beer or two. They'd have not-very-energetic sex and eventually his mom would do more heroin and nod off. The man would get dressed, gather what was left of the twelve-pack, and leave.

After the man was gone, Danee checked on his mother. Everybody knew heroin people shouldn't lie on their backs after shooting up; they might choke on vomit or on their own tongues, so Danee made sure his mom was lying on her side and breathing evenly. He placed pillows on the front and back of her so she wouldn't roll over and suffocate. When she was safely swaddled and propped, he went to the kitchen to see what was left of the Popeye meal. There weren't any wings, so he made do with watery coleslaw and a couple of hushpuppies.

He took the note with the phone number out of his back pocket. There wasn't a single good thing that could come from calling Ru So. Danee knew this as a fact and basic truth. Not a single good thing. He took the slip of paper, wadded it up and dropped it into the kitchen sink. He used the spray attachment to chase it into the drain and turned on the garbage disposal.

The next day, some three weeks after Antwone's death, Danee James Watson put on his good jeans, a clean T-shirt, and his church shoes. The sky was the color of dead fish, and he rode his bicycle the three miles to the AfriCars garage. He circled the garage slowly twice and, when he was satisfied no one was there, he hid his bike behind some bushes, stacked a couple of empty wooden boxes under one of the windows, climbed up and looked in.

There wasn't much to see—two large shiny cars took up space, as did shelves of cleaning liquids and spare parts. There was a stack of seven wheels, and another stack of a half-dozen tires. He was on tip-toes trying to see more when he felt something very small and solid prodding his back.

"You move, you're dead." The voice was elegant, deep, and very foreign and frightening. Danee didn't move for what seemed a long time, and then said, "I wasn't going to steal nothing. I just wanted to see."

The pressure on his back didn't let up. "Is that your bicycle in the bushes?"

Danee nodded. "Yessir. I'm a friend of Antwone's." He caught himself. "Was. Was a friend."

The pressure twitched and Danee held his breath. Then the voice said, "You knew him?"

Danee answered, "Yessir. I'd see him at the library. We'd talk."

There was a pause. The pressure on his back lessened.

"You're Danee?"

"Yessir."

"You didn't come to the funeral."

"Nosir. I didn't have no way of getting to Suitland. I don't even know where that is."

"It's in Maryland."

"Yessir."

"Come down from there."

It hadn't been a gun after all. It was a tire iron. The African man held it loosely in his right hand. He stared at the boy.

"How do I know you are who you say you are?"

Danee fumbled for his wallet, a worn leather thing he'd stolen a year before from a Target store. He took out his library card and handed it to the African, who scrutinized it.

"Why are you wearing your Sunday shoes?" The African pointed at Danee's feet with the tire iron.

The boy shrugged. "Antwone told me that if I ever met you, I had to make a good impression."

The African smiled for the first time, but it was a very thin smile.

"Have you ever been arrested?"

Danee was sitting in the garage, sipping a strawberry soda. "Naw, I..." And then he remembered Antwone's admonition. *Don't you ever lie to that man! He got that Africa juju thing! He can tell when you're lying.*

He caught himself. "Yessir, once."

"What did you do?"

Danee tried looking everywhere but at the man's face.

"I took some dog poop, and I put it in a paper bag, and I put the bag on Missus Bella's doormat, and I lit it on fire, and then I rang the doorbell and ran away." Danee was staring at his church shoes.

The African leaned closer. "You did what?"

Danee repeated the details of his crime, adding, "That Missus Bella, she's a mean old woman! She's always spying on everybody! She called the cops, and she knew it was me that done it, and when the police came to take me away, she was laughin' and cacklin' like some old witch."

The African got up and said, "Excuse me for a minute."

Mamadou went into the bathroom, closed the door, turned the tap in the sink on full and flushed the toilet. Then he started laughing, and when he started he couldn't stop and the tears ran down his face and soaked the collar of his white dress shirt. He remembered doing exactly the same thing when he was twelve in Senegal, except it was cow dung, and he'd gotten caught and his mother had thrashed him with a handful of river nettles. It had hurt, but he had no regrets. The flaming cow dung story had people laughing for weeks.

He washed his face, wiped it dry, and put on a stern expression.

12   The police spoke to everybody on the second and third floor of Gloria Nachtalyan's apartment building. She'd not done any drugs for three days but had finished the bottle of scotch and a plastic half-gallon of Popov vodka bought at an ABC store the day After Clarence. That's how she thought of everything now, always in light of Before or After Clarence.

She was a little bit drunk when the detective came, which worked to her advantage. She could sense he wasn't really that interested in finding out what had happened. She caught him staring at her breasts.

He asked, did she know what had happened? She did, sort of. She'd come home from work and there were a lot of people in the parking lot, and a tenant said someone had been found in the trash chute. The super was there and told her it wasn't anybody who lived in the building, thank heavens.

Had she heard anything? No, she hadn't; she generally turned in early after watching Netflix for a little while, adding that she took melatonin to sleep through the night.

Had anyone come to see her that night? No. She'd eaten a sandwich, had a glass of wine, maybe two—she smiled at the detective; yes, she was naughty, she drank two glasses—and retired. She was planning to get up early next morning and go to yoga class.

Had she? Gone to the yoga class? No. She smiled sheepishly. No, she hadn't. The detective had glanced at her breasts again and handed her his card, saying, call if you think of anything else.

She smiled at him one last time; he was a good-looking man in a sort of stocky cop way, though she could have advised him on his choice of suits. He wasn't wearing a wedding ring.

Inside, she'd been dying of fear and curiosity. She wanted to ask the detective if the dead man had been identified, and if anyone was a suspect. She wanted to suggest he question the really fat and unfriendly woman three doors down who never said hello, even when they were picking up mail in the lobby at the same time. She wanted to ask maybe they could meet for a drink one day? The last thought took her aback. Even in the light fog of alcohol, she knew this was delusional. What am I, nuts?

The evening with Clarence had taken on an aura of unreality. It now felt like the out-of-body experiences some people claimed to have, where they floated over events and watched themselves perform acts as if on a stage below.

Had she really done that? Really? Stuffed a grown man into a trash chute? And not any grown man! A man she'd had sex with just hours before!

The day before the policeman, she'd looked through Clarence's cell phone address book—the fool's password was 1 2 3 4—and found JoAnn Sabatini's number. He'd called the bitch twice the same day he'd come over. That made Gloria's breath catch in her throat. That cocksucker! It had also put her mind, if not at ease, at least at a modicum of rest. The pig had deserved to die, and she'd had nothing to do with his death, only his... disposal.

In the days that followed, Gloria felt as if a door had been slammed on the entire situation. Clarence was gone. Good fucking riddance. And she would never do cocaine again, and that was good riddance too. Only two questions still smoldered in her mind: Did Bong Bong know? And, more important, had Clarence fucked JoAnn Sabatini before coming over that night?

"Don't look at me like that, Colin. That boy is *not* a replacement for Antwone." Mamadou frowned at Colin, was about to say something else but didn't.

"I never thought that, Mamadou. It didn't cross my mind." But it had and both knew it.

Danee had gone to the men's room, clearly uncomfortable in such surroundings. Mamadou said, "Aside from fast food places, I'm sure he has never set foot in a restaurant, much less one where a white person will wait on him." He sipped at his water.

"Where's Catherine? I thought she'd come?"

Colin was evasive. "Ah. Well, we're not really together anymore."

Mamadou bowed his head briefly but didn't comment.

Danee returned, wiping the palms of his hands on his trousers. He sat, looked uncertainly about.

Mamadou regarded him with mock sternness. "Relax, boy! Here," he pushed a glass of Pepsi toward him. "Drink this, then tell Mr. Marsh what you told me."

"Colin," said Colin.

Mamadou acquiesced. "Colin, then. And take your time, don't skip anything."

Danee emptied his glass in one long pull. Mamadou motioned to the waiter for a refill. When it arrived, Danee said, "Where you want me to start?"

"Tell us when you met Antwone."

Danee thought for ten seconds. "We both liked the library. I go there two or three times a week. It's quiet. I read magazines. I had *Upscale* and—"

Mamadou interrupted, "A magazine for rich black people."

Danee looked from one man to the other, unsure if he should continue.

Mamadou said, "Go ahead."

"*Upscale,* and Antwone come to my table and says, 'I was going to read that,' and I say, 'I'll be done with it in a sec,' and I thought if that boy was gonna cause trouble, I could probably handle him, but he sat down and said for me to take my time and we started talking. And that's how we met, about six months ago."

Their food came. Danee had ordered a monstrous cheeseburger. He picked it up to take a bite when Mamadou said, "Knife and fork, please."

Danee picked up the implements reluctantly.

"So we got to be friends."

He cut a large chunk of the sandwich and stuffed it into his mouth. Colin picked at a salad; Mamadou had ordered a bowl of half-vanilla, half-chocolate ice cream. "Tell him about Rousseau."

Danee chewed, swallowed, and sipped his Pepsi. "So one day Antwone wearing some Air Jordan 11 Retros and—"

Mamadou explained for Colin's benefit, "Foolishly expensive athletic shoes."

"Yeah," said Danee. "Where I live, people get beat up serious for shoes like that. Anyway, so I ask him where he got those and he tells me he's working with this man, Ru So, helping him out, you know? Running errands and like that."

"I didn't know any of this," Mamadou said. "Antwone never wore shoes like that around me. He knew I'd ask questions."

"So I didn't mention it again 'cause I didn't want him to think I was envious of his Airs or nothin'." He speared some French fries and bathed them in ketchup.

"And then one day, about a month ago, we're in the library and he says he's gonna go away for a while, and I ask him why and he gets real quiet and he says, 'Ru So after my ass.'" Danee looked at both men, shrugged, "Those were his words, true fact."

He cut another bite of the burger. "And then he was dead."

Mamadou flinched. Danee noticed and muttered, "I'm sorry."

"That's it?" Colin asked. "Nothing more?"

"Well," Danee looked at Mamadou, who nodded.

"Go on."

Danee put his knife and fork down. "A couple of days ago, a boy told me there was a man looking for me. He said he had a accent. It's Ru So, I'm sure. So I decided maybe it's time to see Mr. Dioh."

Colin leaned across the table. "You think this Ru So person had something to do with Antwone's death?"

Danee chewed slowly. Around a mouthful of cheeseburger and fries, he said, "Big time! Fuck yeah!"

Then he caught himself. "Sorry. I meant, yessir. And now he want me too. Sir."

Danee's shoulders were hunched as if expecting a blow. His eyes were scanning the room for a way out.

Mamadou placed a large hand over the boy's smaller one. "Sit up, Danee. It's all right. You haven't done anything wrong. Finish your food. Mr. Marsh and I have to talk for a few minutes. We'll be right over there," he pointed to the bar ten feet away.

Danee stopped chewing, his eyes wide. "You leavin' me here?"

Mamadou rose to his feet. "We'll be there, Danee," he pointed again. "Anyone asks anything, you tell them to talk to me."

Danee's eyes followed the two adults to the bar.

They took adjacent stools; Colin asked for ginger ale. Mamadou sipped from a glass of Chablis and recounted his meeting with Aunt Mim and George. After he'd answered Colin's questions, he asked, "Can you take Danee in, Colin? Just for a few days. This Rousseau character, he scares me. Anyone willing to kill a child…" He looked back at the boy who had picked up the cheeseburger with both hands and buried his mouth in it. The boy looked up and grinned, a mustache of mayo and mustard framing his mouth.

"He's a good kid, Colin. He's smart, and he's responsible. And it'll only be for a few days." Mamadou stood. "I know it's a lot to ask, but after Antwone, if anything happened to this boy…"

Colin nodded. "Yes, of course, as long as you want."

They finished their meals. Mamadou drove off in his Mercedes, and Danee looked doubtfully at Colin's car.

"This a Porsche?"

Colin nodded. "A 924. You know cars, right?"

Danee nodded. "This one of them cheapo Porsches. Got like a tractor engine in it, right?"

When they got to Colin's apartment, Danee called his mother. The boy didn't say much. When he got off the phone, Colin asked, "Is she okay with things?"

Danee shrugged. "She with somebody. I'm pretty sure she been using. She probably won't remember I called. I'll try again in the morning."

"So. So far it looks like the experiment has worked," Charlie Snow said to Lobo, "and now we need to know if you're on board to take this even further."

Charlie Snow was vaguely angry. He did not like being summoned, and he resented Lobo's toothy smile. His own teeth still did not feel entirely right. When he prodded the back molars on the left side of his mouth, he could detect what he was sure was a tiny crack in the enamel. His mouth still glowed with a dull grey pain from the blow by Lobo's bodyguard. He wanted to cup his cheek with a protective palm but that would show weakness. He felt cheated; a deal was a deal, and Lobo should have done better than the dentist with halitosis and a mustard-colored waiting room. When all this was done, Lobo decided, he would avenge his own teeth, rearrange Lobo's if he had the opportunity, which he knew he wouldn't. Lobo would soon be history, and Charlie Snow had plans to spring for an entire mouthful of pearly caps for himself.

"How many dead," asked Lobo.

"Ah. Well. That depends…"

"No, it does not," Lobo smiled without pleasure. "People are either alive, or they are dead. There is no 'depends.'" He smiled again, bright white teeth positively glowing. "You liked my dentist? He fixed you up properly?"

"Magnificently," said Charlie Snow, showing teeth of his own and lying through them.

"Dead. Or not dead," Lobo repeated.

"Well then, about 300 dead."

"Three-hundred drug users?"

"Possibly a few gunshot victims as well, but mostly drug users and maybe a dealer or three."

"I read something about a politician?" Lobo kept up with the news.

"Yes. I did as well."

"Not an important man, though."

"A very minor cog," Charlie Snow agreed, and let a silence stretch between them.

In time, Lobo said, "There was a man in a trash chute."

"Ah," Charlie Snow said, "I'm not sure I know about that one. Was it recently?"

Lobo pretended to smile. "Probably of no significance." He took a small sheet of paper and a very expensive gold fountain pen from the drawer of his desk. "So how many people are we talking about?"

"Between two and 3,000."

"That is a lot of people."

"Yes," Charlie Snow said, "but you have to look at the larger numbers."

Lobo arched an eyebrow.

"Six million dollars. Maybe a tad more."

"What is *a tad*?"

Snow explained.

Lobo's eyes widened imperceptibly and Charlie Snow thought, *Gotcha, you tooth-loosening greedy Aztec motherfuckin' greaser son-of-a-bitch.*

"You got any chocolate milk, or soda, or deli stuff?" Danee stood in front of the open refrigerator, inspecting the contents. He frowned and gave Colin a sidelong glance. "Is this what you call white people food?" He picked up a plastic bag of greying leafy matter. "Ew! What this?"

"Kale." Colin took the bag dropped it in the trash. It had been more than two weeks since he'd juiced anything and now the tomatoes, peppers, and avocados were misshapen and rotting. Only the carrots and celery perhaps remained edible. "You can't be hungry! You just ate."

Danee frowned briefly. "That was hours ago. You got cookies? Milk maybe? A candy bar? I like Kit Kats."

Colin had nothing. "We'll get something to eat in a little while. I'm expecting a lady friend, and she'll come with us."

"Your girlfriend?"

"No."

"Can I watch TV?"

"Sure. The remote's on the sofa."

"You get SHOWTIME?"

"No. Just basic cable."

Danee turned the set on. "BET?"

"What?"

"BET. Black Entertainment Network. You ain't heard of BET? Everybody know BET."

"Not me."

"Jeez," said Danee. "You poor? You can't afford the good channels?"

"No. I just don't watch TV a lot."

"How come your TV so old?"

"It's not."

"Older'n me."

The kid had been talking non-stop and had questions and comments about everything.

"That's a old computer, too."

"Not really."

"Yes, really. What, it like Windows Zero?"

"Windows 7."

"At this library in Virginia, I heard they got Windows 10, with touchscreen. How come everything in your apartment is old?"

"Not everything."

"Yeah, it is," Danee pointed to the sofa, "that's old, and the chair, and the TV, and everything in the kitchen. Even the food is old!" He said that with a note of wonder, then added, "And some of it smells funny.

"You got comic books?"

Colin didn't.

"Graphic novels?" None of those either. The kid sat down, dejected.

When Emily Martin arrived, Danee stood up and asked, "You his girlfriend? He says you ain't."

She glanced at Colin, arched an eyebrow, looked back down at the boy. "Really? He said that?" She wore a vulpine smile. "Maybe he just doesn't know it yet."

Danee said, "You're black."

She nodded. "So?"

"He ain't."

"And?"

"And nothin'." Danee saw the two adults were staring at him and fell silent.

Emily said, "Does he always talk this much?"

"I have no idea," Colin said. "We really just met."

"I may ask you an enormous favor," Mamadou said to DiAngela Jones. The triplets were asleep in a heap on the floor of Mamadou's apartment.

She nodded once.

"I might need your help to lure this Rousseau person somewhere so I can… talk with him."

DiAngela was unfazed. "I can do that."

Mamadou looked at the three boys. She said, "That's how they sleep. I've given up putting them in separate beds; they always end up in one heap. Darnell's the oldest, so he's on top to protect the other two. Dionne's in the middle and Dewan's on the bottom. How he manages to breathe is beyond me."

"They're beautiful."

"Yes, they are. They're amazing." She drew closer to him and took his hand.

The two-week prescription, rationed carefully, lasted six days. Birch Carroll hadn't really bothered to keep count of the pills he was taking. He felt great, rejuvenated, smarter if occasionally sleepy, and funnier even, cracking jokes on the air that had the station manager raising her eyebrows but not complaining. The listeners loved him. O'Reilly phoned again and called him, "My man, The Voice." He'd even gotten laid! A woman who saw him in the Safeway parking lot recognized his face from a photo on RightWingNews.com, took him home, fed him, and screwed his brains out! Could life get better?

And so it was with a troubled mind that when he went to shake two of the OxyContin out of the little plastic bottle, he only found one. That made no sense.

He searched his pockets, looked in his desk drawer, and decided he must have left the pills at home, except that he knew he hadn't.

This was not good.

He called Dr. Mario and made an appointment for later that afternoon. When he got there, the receptionist told him Dr. Mario had an emergency but had left a prescription for him. Carroll looked at it. The script was for twenty pills.

"There must be some mistake," he told the receptionist.

She shrugged. "I don't think so, sir."

"But it's not enough. I'm sure the doctor knows this. Can we call him, straighten this out?"

"I'm afraid not, sir. The doctor can't be disturbed."

Carroll felt nausea and panic stir his stomach. He thought he might throw up, swallowed hard and managed a sickly smile.

"All right. When can I see Dr. Mario again?"

"In two weeks, sir. Shall I make an appointment?"

"Next week would be better. Early next week."

The receptionist shook her head. "I'm sorry, Mr. Smith, is it?

I really am. But those are the doctor's instructions. Twenty pills, two weeks."

Birch Carroll thought he might start crying. "Please…" He withdrew a hundred dollar bill and dropped it on the receptionist's desk.

The woman made it disappear, glanced around, and when she knew no one was looking, scribbled something on a slip of paper. "I really shouldn't be doing this." She handed it to Carroll. "If you're really in a bind, you can try calling this number."

Carroll looked down, saw a 703 number and the words Bong Bong.

Bong Bong?

What the fuck is Bong Bong?

For Mamadou, the night was one of quiet wonder.

His last encounter, almost a year earlier, had been a hurried coupling with a grateful call girl in the rear seat of AfriCars One. Earlier that night, he'd ejected the drunk client he was chauffeuring from the back of the limo; the man had tried a bit too assertively to familiarize himself with the breasts and ass of the working girl he'd hired. Newly arrived from a recently renamed nation, the drunk, a minor diplomat, had cursed in a tribal language Mamadou vaguely recognized as Kpelle; Mamadou, in turn, had emptied the man's wallet and given its contents to the girl. He'd then dropped the diplomat off at the intersection of Wisconsin and Massachusetts Avenues in the northwest section of Washington, D.C., a mile from Embassy Row. The man could hail a taxi from there. The girl had been appreciative.

With DiAngela Jones, things had progressed with exquisite languor. He worried the boys might wake up but she reassured him, "When they're down, they're down. You won't hear a peep from them until the morning."

And so he and Ms. Jones made love three times over the course of the night. It was effortless, punctuated by her assertion that really, the boys would *not* wake up. He thought they would and tried to stay quiet, though at one point he was sure his gasping must have echoed through the apartment. He had forgotten the feel and softness of a woman's body beneath his hands, and he might have been overly careful not to press too hard or lunge too deeply. She murmured in his ear, little sounds of pleasure with here and there a squeak that made him laugh.

At four in the morning they showered, toweled each other dry, returned to bed and fell asleep quickly. He awoke to find her head on his shoulder; she was breathing so lightly he thought there must be another word for it.

He tried to extricate himself but she murmured, "You're not going anywhere. Do you have the makings for breakfast?" He nodded. She got up shortly after that, put on his worn bathrobe, and disappeared into the kitchen.

He was shirtless and pulling on his pants when Darnell opened the bedroom door, stuck his small head in and announced, "Momma says breakfast is ready and please don't eat all the bacon or pancakes 'cause there aren't that many and we're all hungry. And also, Dionne and Dewan, they want to know if we're going back to the zoo today." He crinkled his forehead, "Dionne said he wouldn't get sick again, but I know him and he might."

When they'd finished eating and the boys were cleaning up, DiAngela Jones pulled him aside and said, "I don't want you to think I behave like this casually. I don't." She looked hard into his eyes. "That doesn't mean I'm asking anything from you, like to commit or whatever, because I'm not. But," she draped her arms around his neck, "if you'd like us to visit again soon, I'm sure the boys would love it." She kissed him lightly. "The mother would, too."

On his way to the garage, Mamadou thought how fortuitous it was that Danee had sought him out, that one triplet, Dewan?, had remembered Rousseau, that DiAngela Jones seemed to be interested in him, and wasn't it strange? He finds her, and Colin loses Catherine. And, the thought made him grin, his friend acquires, even for a day or three, a small talkative houseguest.

Mamadou Dioh felt almost guiltily happy. He was still in mourning, yet the grey film coloring his life for the past month was fading.

She was, he thought, a magnificent woman.

Mamadou's familiarity with sex was limited. In the suburbs of Dakar, Senegal, where he'd grown up, educated middle-class families were terrified of AIDS. Though his West African country had not been as victimized as other nations on the continent—more than three million afflicted in Nigeria; one-and-a-half million in Tanzania; a million in Zambia—still, fears ran high. Senegal had kept the illness at bay through massive education and awareness programs that stressed the use of condoms and monitoring the nation's legal sex workers. Religious authorities openly preached sexual responsibility and marital fidelity in a polygamous society. Premarital sex, in his social circles, was deemed unseemly. As a policeman, opportunity had been rife, but a combination of fear, mores, and familial pressure had kept him celibate.

When Mamadou left his country of birth, it was to a chorus of warnings from aunts, cousins, and neighbors on the dangers of promiscuous American women, white or black; all, it was said, were tainted by the disease and eager to engage with African males, particularly such sturdy specimen as Mamadou Dioh, the feared Dakar lawman. Such were the beliefs in Senegal.

Mamadou arrived in the U.S. a virgin and remained so for a year after settling in Washington. Finding work, taking care of the brothers and sisters who also came to America, buying his first used limo and setting up AfriCars, all had taken time and energy.

The two or three fleeting encounters with women had been satisfactory but little more. And now, DiAngela Jones.

It would be easy, he thought, to lose himself in the newness of this woman, this instant clan of mother and children eager to enfold him. He could do as his friend Colin always recommended—Let Go and Let God. But then, he'd often found his friend's AA sayings a little simplistic, even infantile. The maxim might be easier to apply had he actually believed in a deity, which he generally did not. No decent god, he had figured out as a boy, would allow the suffering that blanketed the world.

In his own life, another admonition—one learned at the family table—reigned: Vengeance is a meal best served cold. A good saying he'd first heard voiced in French.

It had been almost a month since Antwone's murder, and it was time for retribution.

Théophile Bienaimé Rousseau was also thinking of retribution, but of a lesser kind.

Someone had been asking about him, an old black man named George. Questions were rarely a good thing and needed, as he liked to say, to be nipped in the butt.

George wasn't hard to find. He made a daily trip to his neighborhood convenience store where he bought a pack of Tareytons and two bottles of Gallo burgundy for Mim, as well as a Babe Ruth candy bar for himself. Rousseau followed George and when they reached an alley, he walked quickly, caught up with the older man and said, "George?"

George turned around, so Rousseau knew he had the right old guy.

He pushed George into the alley and slapped him hard once. George's glasses flew off his nose and he dropped the paper bag with the wine and cigarettes. One of the bottles broke, and red ran on the alley's cobblestone.

Rousseau grabbed George by the shirtfront and lifted him up. George stood on the tip toes of his shiny brown wingtips, his eyes unfocused. Rousseau said, "What do you want to know about me, old man? I'll be happy to tell you…" He hit George in the face again. "My name is Théophile Bienaimé Rousseau. In my country I would bury you alive and destroy your soul." He hit him a third time, more lightly. "I am a very dangerous man, George, and you should pray that we never meet again."

He let George go. George crumpled to the ground like an empty burlap sack and Rousseau kicked him the ribs twice for good measure. It felt like kicking a bundle of dry sticks.

The owner of the convenience store was putting out the trash when he found George, still face down on the ground. He phoned for an ambulance, closed his store, and accompanied George to the hospital. He called Aunt Mim from there. Within half an hour the hospital waiting room was full. Among the crush of individuals awaiting news on George's status were two doctors, one an orthopedic surgeon, the other an osteopath; their medical school studies had been partially underwritten years earlier by Aunt Mim.   There were also three registered nurses, two cops including a detective, three churchmen, and a bevy of large church ladies.

George was fortunate. Two cracked ribs would pain him for a couple of months but there was no internal bleeding. He had a black eye, and a cut on his forehead required four stitches. When he spoke to Aunt Mim on the phone, he still wasn't sure of what had happened but he did remember Rousseau's name.

Mamadou arrived at the hospital in the late afternoon. By then, most of the crowd had left. George was sedated and asleep. He looked very small in the bed and the tubes running from suspended IV bottles to his arms and from a catheter into a green plastic jug made him appear even frailer. A nurse noticed Mamadou's worried look and said, "You're one of Aunt Mim's people? Don't worry, he's a tough old bird and he's gonna be fine though he'll be sore for a while. Those are just to keep him hydrated and peeing. I'll tell you what, I haven't seen so many people show up here so quick since, well, ever…" She adjusted George's pillows and added. "Is it true some drug dealer did that?"

Mamadou nodded. "Yes. That's what I heard."

The nurse's eyes flickered. "Well I do hope someone cleans that man's clock real good. *Real* good."

Théophile Bienaimé Rousseau's two serious mistakes were, one, not killing George outright; and two, not taking Aunt Mim into consideration. When some of his friends found out what he'd done, they suggested his ill-advised actions were certain to bring heat, and added that it might be a good time to lay low. Rousseau was told that George and Mim, his consort, were not people one could attack or injure with impunity. There would be repercussions.

Théophile Bienaimé Rousseau said he was no pussy and not about to hide from the wrath of two old people, but his protestations lacked conviction. George, he was told, had once killed a man with a pen knife, and Aunt Mim, back when she was plain Mim, carried a straight razor in her purse and was known for her deft use of hatpins. Rousseau decided it might be wise to get off the streets and spend some time at a cousin's empty rental apartment in Anacostia.

Mamadou found Aunt Mim's room strangely empty without George in it. A large black middle-aged woman was occupying George's chair, and two others flanked Aunt Mim's bed. It was the day after the assault, and Mim looked as if she hadn't slept well. The wine glass on her nighttable was empty and the ashtray was gone; Mamadou thought this might be in deference to the three women, serious Baptists even Aunt Mim wouldn't dare defy.

One of them moved away from the bed and Aunt Mim said, "Come here, Mamadou. We got to talk." She nodded to the women, "If y'all don't mind?" They left but Mamadou knew they wouldn't go farther than the other side of the door.

"So, George, he's gonna be okay. I talked to the doctors this morning. They're moving him to a private room, and there's gonna be an off-duty policeman right outside his door all the time, in case that bad boy decides to come back, which I don't think he will but you never know." She sat up a little, lowered her voice. "Pour me a little wine, Mamadou. The bottle's over there in the closet." He did. She swallowed deeply, handed him the glass to refill. "Those three out there, I've known 'em all fifty, sixty years, and if they see me with a little glass of somethin', I'll never hear the end of it!" She drained the glass, replaced it on the nighttable. "Gimme that roll of breath mints."

Aunt Mim wrestled two Clorets out of their wrapper and popped them into her mouth. "What do you think we should do, Mamadou? You can't let things like that just happen."

"I'll take care of it, Aunt Mim."

"And I don't need to know no details…" She dropped another Clorets into her mouth and chewed vigorously.

"You do not."

"All right. You're a good boy, Mamadou."

"It was my fault, Aunt Mim. If I hadn't asked George to get information, none of this would've happened."

Aunt Mim shrugged, slipped deeper under the bedcovers. "Life happens. Nobody gonna hold nothing against you, 'specially not George, and 'specially if you do what needs to be done."

She reached under the bedclothes, pulled out her pack of Tareytons and a Bic lighter. "I can't smoke in my own house. What kinda wrong is that…"

She lit up, inhaled deeply. "George would find that really funny." Her eyes misted over and she whispered, "Silly man. Silly old George… Hiding them Baby Ruth candy bars, thinkin' I don't know." Her voice trailed off and her expression hardened. "You're gonna take care of that devil, hurting an old man that way!"

"I will. You have my word."

"Well, good." They were both silent. She took two more puffs, stubbed the cigarette out in the ashtray. She handed it to Mamadou who emptied it in a waste basket and shuffled some papers to hide the butt. She smiled for the first time.

He was on his feet and leaving when she added, "By the way, I heard you were keeping company with a fine woman; DiAngela Jones? She got those three little boys? That right?"

"I might be."

"Well good. You know, I think she's the cousin of Arthur Cooke, who was my brother-in-law's grand-nephew. She a *good* woman. Ain't that amazin'? How small the world is?"

Mamadou drove back to the AfriCars garage suffused with a strange, violent joy. Danee may have been mistaken in his identification of Rousseau as Antwone's murderer, but there was no doubt that the dealer had attacked George, and that was reason enough to act.

After parking the car, Mamadou shifted a large Craftsman rolling toolbox away from the rear wall of his garage. Behind the toolbox was a small shelf, and on the shelf was a case of Quaker 10W-30 motor oil. He opened the case and pulled out his FN Five-seveN semiautomatic pistol. It was wrapped in a terrycloth towel, a slight sheen of oil still glowing on its barrel. He'd purchased it a year earlier at a Virginia gun show where it had not been necessary to furnish identification other than a driver's license. He'd also bought several boxes of ammunition and three twenty-round magazines. He'd paid cash and possibly too much, almost $1,900 for the weapon, ammo and a cleaning kit, which the gun-seller said was a bargain.

"You gonna need any accessories with that?" The seller was large, bearded, and wore a friendly smile.

"Accessories?"

"Holster? Trigger guard? Suppressor?"

"Suppressor?"

"A silencer," the large man said with a genial smile. "A lot of people don't like to make noise when they shoot. You know, like, they don't want to disturb the neighbors. It wouldn't be, like, polite!"

The suppressor had cost $600 and was delivered by UPS a week later. It was an ugly black tube precisely machined to fit the barrel of the FN.

Days later he'd checked the firearm registration process in the District of Columbia and found it byzantine. Forms and more forms, certificate for this and lease for that, rental agreement for his apartment, test procedures, fingerprinting, driver's license, and background check. He never got around to registering the weapon, but he did take it to Blue Ridge Arsenal in Chantilly, Virginia, thereby violating laws prohibiting the transport of an unregistered firearm across state lines. Mamadou, now a criminal, fired the pistol sixty times. The last fifteen shots almost found the center of the paper target at fifteen feet. That was good enough.

A week after that, he chose an overcast morning to take the gun, suppressor and some ammo to a forest near Occoquan. It was a bad day for hiking, for birding, or for nature walks. The weather was unfriendly and soon turned to rain with a cold wet wind blowing off the Potomac. He walked through woods for ten minutes until the only sound was of water hitting leaves. He found a small hollow in the forest, unpacked the gun, fit the silencer to the barrel and taped a paper target to a tree trunk. He fired off a box of ammo. The gun made a short, dry coughing sound whenever he pulled the trigger. There was almost no kick to it and the silencer didn't appear to affect the aim.

13 GEORGE WAS TOLD ON THE PHONE BY HIS DOCTOr that he'd need a cane for a while, but the way the doctor spoke, Aunt Mim, listening in, knew it would be a *long* while, maybe forever.

George had heard this twice before, once in person from the same doctor, and once from a nurse who specialized in geriatric care. He hadn't told Mim who, when she heard, was adamant he get one that very day. He placated her and using an ancient IBM laptop computer, ordered a Super Strong Mahogany Derby Walking Cane from FashionableCanes.com. When it arrived, the thing was not quite to his liking, and so he had an acquaintance with a basement woodshop modify it. It came back a thing of beauty with a brass collar and a pointy gold metal tip. George walked around the block, feeling quite pleased and dapper. Even Mim said the cane fit him. "You look like one of them Harlem gentleman from the thirties," she said, which pleased him hugely.

Anacostia was… nice, in a preppy sort of way. Théophile Bienaimé Rousseau was in a small furnished one-bedroom on Martin Luther King, Jr. Avenue.

This was vaguely amusing since he'd lived in an apartment on Martin Luther King Boulevard while in Miami. Out of sheer nothing-happenningness, he Googled streets named after the famous civil rights leader. There were more than a hundred spread across the fifty states. Rousseau had a vague notion of who Martin Luther King was and little interest in learning more. He was impressed, though, by the man's popularity. Otherwise, he was bored.

Within walking distance were a deli, a grocery store, a CVS, and a couple of restaurants. He'd gone into the Players Lounge for a late night meal and been deafened by the noise and disappointed by the food. No one looked at him, though he was well groomed and stylishly dressed. That was unusual.

Twice a day he received phone calls from his people, and the news was always the same. The old man he'd beaten up had been released from the hospital and was walking with difficulty. A nurse was with him at all times. The man's wife, or friend, or companion, had mobilized more than a dozen people and posted a substantial reward for information leading to Rousseau's whereabouts. Now *that* was interesting.

He obtained her phone number and was tempted to call, maybe find out why the old man was worth such efforts, but reconsidered. And so he remained bored, which is why when DiAngela Jones called him, he answered.

They had a nice conversation. Of course he remembered the church social! He liked her voice; it was soft and without the overly round accent of so many local black women. He agreed they should get together the following day. Coffee, maybe lunch. He never questioned her motives; he was a handsome man whom women liked and he did not ask himself why DiAngela Jones should call after more than a month's silence. Women were like that, quirky, prey to mysterious emotions and, he assumed, the phases of the moon.

Still, he hadn't stayed alive this long without taking precautions. He told her to come alone by Metro, use the Green Line. They would meet at the MLK Café. He might be a few minutes late, there were calls to be made to the West Coast and the time difference always caused delays. She said she'd wait, she had all afternoon, the kids were with their grandparents; she was looking forward to seeing him. He could have sworn she purred.

She put the phone down. "How'd I do?" They were sitting in folding chairs in the garage office.

"Well. Very well." Mamadou was taken aback. DiAngela Jones was entirely *too* convincing. Could she indeed be looking forward to seeing Rousseau?

She enjoyed his discomfiture. "You seem a little concerned, Mr. Dioh. Is something the matter?"

It took him a second to respond. "No. You were… very good."

"Theatre training. I was Ruth in *A Raisin in the Sun*. When I was in school."

"I'm sorry. I haven't heard of it. It's a play?"

She nodded. "Yeah. You'd like it. There's a limo driver in it."

"Really? A play about a limo driver?" That amazed him. Who would want to write a play about a chauffeur? "Was he a good man? In the play?"

DiAngela Jones thought about it. "Sort of. He's ambitious. But he gets duped."

"Duped?"

"Taken in. Someone steals his money."

"There are fools everywhere." He rose from his chair, straightened the crease in his trousers. "But not me. I am *not* a fool."

Jones stood too. "No. You're not."

Rousseau planned for the meeting.

He bought a pack of good ribbed condoms, some wine and two stemmed glasses, a bag of sea-salt-and-vinegar chips, a scented candle and a bouquet of flowers. He cleaned the apartment as best he could and, having forgotten air freshener, went to CVS a second time for a spray bottle of Febreze and, on impulse, a box of Whitman chocolates.

Colin and Emily took Danee to dinner at Joe's Place Pizza and Pasta on Lee Highway in Arlington. The boy returned to the buffet four times and ate an entire medium pie, a dozen meatballs, and a plate of rigatoni. Then he had some of Emily's eggplant parmigiana, followed by a piece of apple pie à-la-mode. He drank four large diet Pepsis and talked without pause.

"That was really good. When we have pizza with my mom, it always from some carry-out place and it cold by the time we get it cause ain't no store gonna deliver where I live, that's for sure! And why're you goin' out with a white man? I seen black men with white women, and pretty often they're really fat, you know, the women, but you ain't fat. Can I have some of that bread? Thank you."

And, "Hit him right on top of the head with a big ole teevee, dropped it from the balcony of the third floor, and I heard later that those two boys waited three days for it to be just right, for French Fry to be—"

"Who?" Emily and Colin asked at the same time.

"French Fry, the boy that got hit by the teevee. Cause he always smell like McDonalds, you know? An' I was sayin', those two who dropped it on his head, they waited three days for French Fry to be standin' exactly where he was, and when he got hit, oh man it made a mess, I was right there, not five feet away and—"

"Someone dropped a television set on somebody's head?"

Danee put down his fork with aggravated patience. "What I been tellin' you? Yeah, of course, right on his dumb old head!"

"Was the boy all right?"

"All right?" Danee looked at Emily as if she was slow. "Course he wasn't all right! Someone drop a teevee on your head, you think you gonna be all right?"

And, "Somethin' I forgot to tell you that Antwone told me about that man, Ru So, is, he always carry a gun. Always. And he got a knife, too. Got some sort of knife holder in his back pocket, so's he can whip it out real fast."

Danee made a 'real fast' move with his hands. And finally, "You and Mister Africa gonna do something about that man, right? Cause I know he the one that hurt Antwone. And I don't want him hurtin' me, too."

Colin had an inflatable mattress he'd bought at K-Mart, and he and

Emily put the boy to bed in a corner of the living room. Danee wanted to stay up but was asleep within minutes.

"When was the last time you had a 13-year-old sleepover?"

"That would be never," Colin said. "Thanks so much for being here. I think I'd have sealed his mouth with duct tape. I've never heard anybody talk so much."

She nodded and smiled. "I don't think he has an audience very often."

The phone rang and Colin picked it up. The conversation was muted. Emily went to the window, looked outside at the streetlights and the sparse traffic. In the distance an ambulance wailed; closer, a motorcycle whined, changed gears, and whined again. A minute later, Colin hung up. He turned to her and said, "That was Mamadou."

"Danee's…?"

"Yes."

She was silent and then asked, "Do I need the details?"

He sat. "He wants my help. He's setting a trap for that Rousseau character."

She canted her head. "Isn't that dangerous?"

"No," Colin lied. "I'm sure it won't be."

Bong Bong, Gloria was told, no longer worked at the convenience store. "He quit. Three days ago. He says he found a better job." The other Filipino, Bing Bing?, was mopping a spot where someone had spilled coffee. "No warning, just said he was leaving."

"He didn't say where?"

"No. Just left."

"I tried to call him. The phone just rings and rings. No voicemail, even."

The Filipino stared at her. "Why'd you want to talk with him?" He looked up, stopped swishing the mop and spreading the coffee, then bobbed his head. "Ah. Never mind." He dropped his voice to a whisper. "No more drugs here. You understand? No more!" He turned his back on Gloria and walked away. She saw him open a closet door and lean the mop against the wall. "No more drugs," he mouthed, then turned away again. *Jeez*, thought Gloria Rose Nachtalyan, *does everybody know?*

But Gloria was almost relieved. Part of her thought the poisoned dope was meant for her, though that made no sense at all, but then neither did Clarence keeling over. The part of her not relieved was the part that desperately wanted some cocaine. Or something.

The first few days After Clarence had been fine, relatively speaking. The interview with the detective had gone well. There'd been no changes at work; her asshole bean-counting boss Ralph was still an asshole. The cats were healthy. She'd been drinking too much, but couldn't be faulted for that, considering what she'd gone through.

Now there was a little gnawing inside, a little *need*. At first, it was difficult to identify where the distress was coming from; she really had thought she was through with cocaine, with drugs, with powders of any type and any color. But then it became more obvious that what was missing was that little jolt she so looked forward to, that mixed feeling of wisdom and hyper-awareness that came from two or four lines.

Watching a rerun of *The Blacklist,* she found herself angered by James Spader's unvarying expression of vague superiority. She got mad at the cats for no reason other than their unemptied litter box. Alcohol dulled her; what she wanted was vibrancy, sharpness, *life*. Which is what had brought her back to Bong Bong, who didn't answer his phone and was no longer where he should have been. Gloria Rose had no coke, no contacts, and a bad case of the nerves.

The next mid-morning, after Emily went to work, Mamadou picked up Colin and Danee, DiAngela Jones, and her children in the Mercedes. They dropped the triplets and the boy at Aunt Mim's where a trio of church ladies would tend to them, and then drove across the river to Anacostia. Mamadou let Jones out at the Anacostia Metro station on Howard Road. She'd take a cab to the café.

He parked beneath a giant elm, on a side street of renovated townhouses with kids' toys in the napkin-sized front yards. He and Colin walked to the MLK Café, ordered a coffee, iced tea and two scones, and when they were served took a small table near the door.

"You know," Mamadou said, "I've been living here many years now, and I still don't understand drugs." He sipped his coffee and his gaze traveled the restaurant, the street, the half-dozen customers sitting at outdoor tables. Colin sucked at his iced tea through a straw.

"In Senegal, they have khat. Actually, in most of Africa they have it. People chew it; it keeps them alert. I tried it a time or two, but," he shrugged eloquently, "I didn't see the appeal."

Colin put his drink down. "Back when I was using, there were drugs I tried but didn't like. Pills, for example. I *never* liked pills."

"Hmph," said Mamadou. He made a face. "Pills."

Colin looked away. It was impossible to explain addiction to someone who'd never been addicted, so he no longer tried.

"In Africa, people don't kill for that. It's just a part of life."

"Well…" Colin said.

"Here, they kill. People pull out guns and shoot each other over ten dollars' worth of drugs. Children have guns! How did this happen?"

Explaining gun ownership was as useless as explaining drug addiction. Colin said, "Well," again and stirred the ice in his drink.

"Children with guns, crazy people with guns, criminals and drug dealers with guns—"

"Large West African men with guns," Colin said and looked away.

That made Mamadou pause but not for long. He smiled. "Sane, adult, responsible West African men. Former policemen West African men who have had training with firearms."

"And are vengeful. Let's not forget vengeful."

"That, too," Mamadou agreed.

"There she is."

DiAngela Jones walked in, swept past without looking at them, and sat at a table in the back.

"Beautiful woman."

"Yes," Mamadou stirred his coffee.

DiAngela Jones was tapping a message on her iPhone. Seconds later, Mamadou's phone pinged. He read the message and grinned.

Colin's eyebrows rose quizzically.

"She says hello."

"That's all? Just hello?"

"The rest is private."

"Ah." Colin slurped his drink and rattled the ice with the straw. He broke a small piece of scone and ate it.

An elegant black man soon joined her. She rose; he kissed her on the cheek.

Colin watched Mamadou's reaction. The African remained almost motionless, but his hands tightened on the table's edge.

Now DiAngela Jones was leaning forward. The man they assumed was Rousseau was grinning; he reached a hand out and touched Jones on the shoulder.

Mamadou was glaring in their direction. Colin swept the African's car keys off the table and whispered, "Pick up the keys and stop staring!"

Mamadou did.

Colin said, "Now look outside."

Mamadou did that too, but with difficulty. When he brought his gaze back into the room, his eyes were flat and his lips pressed together tightly.

"Jesus, Mamadou! Relax!"

Mamadou hissed, "That man radiates evil. I can feel it from here."

"Just eat your pastry. You look like you're ready to kill someone!"

Mamadou made a show of laboriously cutting his scone with a fork. "It's not very good."

Colin agreed, "It tastes like sawdust. This place won't get a good Yelp review."

"What?"

"Keep chewing."

Rousseau and Jones pushed back their chairs and stood. She

gathered her purse. They walked past, Rousseau with a hand lightly on Jones's elbow as if guiding a blind person. Mamadou chewed with profound concentration; Colin smiled at Jones who looked through him.

Mamadou swallowed and grimaced.

DiAngela Jones was frightened. The fear curdled in her belly and worked at her knees. She fixed a pleasant expression on her face and walked toward the door.

She ignored Colin's smile. Mamadou's gaze was fixed on the intersection of a wall and ceiling, and he was chewing and frowning as if trying to defeat a piece of gristle. She allowed herself to be led by the elbow until she and Rousseau were outside, then she stepped lightly away from his touch.

"I do hope you live around here?"

"Just down the block." He was trying to be charming but he still scared her. Only the presence of Mamadou a few yards away allowed her to keep walking.

"Good. I couldn't walk a long distance in these shoes."

"Very elegant," Rousseau said. His stare evaluated her calves and thighs. He was glad he'd bought the condoms, already picturing himself on top of her between her spread legs. He would be gentle at first and maybe a little rough just before coming. The thought made his penis twinge.

Mamadou pushed the half-eaten scone away. He put his cell phone on the table. "If we don't hear from her in ten minutes, we go and find her."

"Do you know his address?"

"No."

"That might complicate things."

"No matter." Mamadou's face wore a hard cast Colin remembered the time when they'd waited in a car for something to happen and almost everything had gone wrong.

She walked up the stairs ahead of him and knew he was staring at her ass. She tried to keep her hips from moving as she took each step; she could almost visualize the images in his head, and she shuddered ever so slightly.

He said, "Second door to the right, 33B." He pulled out a key and turned the latch. "Not very chic, I'm afraid. But it is only temporary."

As soon as she entered the apartment, she asked where the bathroom was and locked herself in. She took out her phone, scrolled to Mamadou's number and texted, *5482 MLK dr 33B*. She waited, flushed the toilet once and then a second time. In seconds she got a response, *on our way*.

It was a shabby little place, she thought, poorly furnished and smelling of Febreze air freshener. There was a worn leather sofa, stained wall-to-wall carpeting, a framed poster of Tupac Shakur with his signature bandana wound around his head and knotted in the front. It reminded her of photos she'd seen of old black cleaning ladies in the South. Tupac looked very stoned.

Rousseau was looking at her looking at Tupac. "Wine?"

She nodded and sat on the sofa. He went into the small kitchen; she heard a cork pop. He returned with two good half-filled wine glasses and placed one in front of her on a scarred wood coffee table. "There's chocolates, too." He pointed to the unopened box of Whitman's. She smiled without commitment.

He raised his glass. "*A ta santé,*" he said. "That means, to your health."

She took a sip. "I know. I took French in high school and college."

That pleased him.

He sat next to her, draped an arm over her shoulders and leaned over to nuzzle her neck. She moved away with a forced laugh. "Give a girl a little time…"

The hand on her shoulder tightened its grip. His other hand went for a breast. She pushed it away. He turned, half rose to his feet and slapped her once hard.

The blow was completely unexpected. Her head whipped back and bounced against the back of the couch; her mouth was a round, disbelieving O.

His arm was raised to hit her again when there was a knock on the door.

He hissed at her, "Stay exactly where you are," turned and shouted, "What?"

"FedEx delivery." A white voice.

"Leave it by the door!"

"I can't. I need a signature."

"Come back later!"

"It says 'perishables' on the package." The voice was whining.

"I just need a signature. It won't take a second."

Rousseau said, "*Putain!*" He glared at Jones. "Don't move!"

He unlatched the door and had it ajar when it exploded open, knocking him back. A large black man stood in the entryway, pointing a gun.

The man glanced at Jones, said, "Get out."

Jones, cheek still stinging from Rousseau's blow, found her feet and grabbed her purse.

Rousseau shouted, "Sit down, cunt!!"

She froze, looked from one man to the other. Mamadou nodded slightly. "Go. Now." Then she was at the door, glaring back at Rousseau. "You didn't have to hit me, you bastard!" She slammed it shut as she ran out.

Colin was a short distance down the hallway. He motioned to her and whispered, "Mamadou said we should go to his car. Come on."

In Rousseau's apartment, neither man moved. Rousseau let his shoulders sag. "I don't know what you want but you just ruined a perfectly good afternoon fuck."

Mamadou waved his gun in the direction of a chair. "Sit." Rousseau did, asked, "What is it you're looking for? There's no money here. Nothing worth stealing."

Mamadou stared hard at Rousseau. "Why did you hit the lady?"

"The lady?"

"The woman who just left. She said you hit her."

"Lying bitch," Rousseau said. "I didn't touch her."

Mamadou sighed, "You're lying." He levelled the gun. "And you killed my boy."

"What? What boy?"

"Antwone."

"Who?" He looked at Mamadou shrewdly. "Where you from? Not here. I can tell. Africa? Côte d'Ivoire? Mali?" And then, *"Tu parles français?"*

"No."

"Yes, you do. *J'en suis sûr.*" He threw some familiarity in his voice.

Mamadou stepped back to lengthen the distance between them, reached into his pocket, withdrew the silencer, and deftly attached it to the gun.

"You're going to kill me?" Rousseau was amused.

"Why did you hurt my boy?"

"I don't know what you're talking about, *nègre.*"

"And George. Why did you hurt George?"

"That old man? Is that what this is about? He's alive, isn't he?"

"Antwone isn't."

"I don't know—"

"You have three seconds. *Tu comprends? Trois secondes.*"

Now Rousseau smiled. "I knew you spoke French!"

"Un."

"You're not going to—"

"Deux."

Rousseau's eyes narrowed. He could see Mamadou's finger tighten on the trigger.

"Trois."

"WAIT!"

Mamadou shot him once in the left thigh. The gun made a sound like an old man coughing. Rousseau grunted, fell back in the sofa and slid to the ground. There were tears in his eyes.

"*Salaud!*"

He rolled onto his side and clutched his leg.

"You have five seconds."

Rousseau said, "I'm bleeding."

"Three seconds."

Rousseau swallowed.

"One."

Rousseau closed his eyes. "Antwone saw me cut the drugs."

"Cut?"

"Alter."

"Antwone saw you poison the drugs. And then you tried it on him."

Rousseau nodded once. "He wasn't meant to—"

"Why?"

Rousseau was trying to get to his feet. Mamadou said, "Stay."

"I'm bleeding bad!"

"No. You're not. Tell me why. Why poison the drugs?"

"Money." Rousseau squirmed, sat up, and reached behind his back as if to scratch an itch. Mamadou saw a flash of silver and twisted away, shot once. The gun coughed. Rousseau's body jerked as if kicked and Mamadou shot him a second time.

There was a searing pain in his right shoulder. Rousseau's scalpel-thin stiletto had pierced Mamadou's jacket and shirt and sunk an inch and a half into flesh. If he hadn't moved, the knife would have nicked his heart.

Rousseau's right eye was gone and a small black hole in his temple seeped a thin thread of blood.

Mamadou breathed, "Ah. Ah." He closed his eyes briefly, dropped to the couch, and shook his head. He unclipped the silencer from the gun's barrel and stood up. The gun went into his right pants pocket, the silencer in the left. Both were warm. He pulled the knife out, dropped it into a jacket pocket.

He tore a two-foot length of paper towels from a roll on the counter next to the sink, wadded it up and pressed it against the wound. There wasn't much blood there either. He wedged the compress beneath his shirt and against his skin.

He emptied the wine bottle and glasses into the sink, dumped them into a plastic grocery trash bag. He hadn't touched anything except the roll of paper towels and the doorknob so he wiped it clean with a paper towel and pocketed that too. He looked down at Rousseau's body and thought, *this will not be the end of it.*

Make it look like a robbery.

He tossed the couch cushions on the floor. A small bag of white powder slid out. He pocketed it. He tore off another length of paper towels and wrapped it around his left hand. In the bedroom, he opened the chest of drawers and dumped the sparse contents on the floor. He tore shirts and trousers off hangers in the closet, upended a shoe rack and wrestled the mattress off its box spring. He returned to the kitchen and emptied silverware drawers on the floor, then overturned the trash can. He looked around the disheveled apartment and felt, what, remorse? It went away quickly.

He went into the bathroom; that must have been where DiAngela had texted him. He wiped the toilet seat, the tank handle, the faucets and the sink, the door handles on both sides of the door. He flushed the paper towel. Then he stepped into the hallway, trash bag clutched in his right hand. He closed the door and paused. Marvin Gaye's *My Girl* was playing in one of the neighboring apartments. He walked down the stairs, exited the building, and looked both ways. Twenty yards off, a young woman was pushing a baby carriage. He walked past her and nodded, and she smiled back. His shoulder was numb. He reached inside his jacket and held the makeshift bandage in place. He dumped the garbage bag in a municipal trash can. Four minutes later, he reached the Mercedes.

"Can you drive, Colin?" Mamadou's face had turned ashen.

"My God!" DiAngela Jones eased him into the back seat of the car. "You're hurt! We have to get you to a hospital!"

"No!" Mamadou barked the word. "Get me to Aunt Mim's. There's a nurse there taking care of George. You can pick up the boys, and Colin will drive you home."

They crossed the Potomac on the 11ᵗʰ Street Bridge.

Colin asked, "What happened?"

Mamadou lied. "He stabbed me. I shot him in the leg."

DiAngela Jones looked at him oddly. "In the leg?"

"The first time."

The flat statement hung in the air. Finally, Jones asked, "And the second?"

Mamadou sighed, closed his eyes. "My shoulder really hurts."

14 GEORGE'S NURSE PATCHED MAMADOU UP. She was a slender dark woman who'd spent a decade in a downtown ER, so little surprised her. She cleaned the wound, dabbed antiseptic and put in twelve neat stitches, saying, "That was easy. Whadja do, get into a fight with a surgeon? So don't lift anything for a few days; try not to get the bandage wet. Come and see me in a week, and we'll take the stitches out."

Danee, protesting vociferously, was told to go play in the back yard.

When the nurse was done, George said, "I think one of Mim's nephews left some clothes here a while back. Let's see if there's something you can wear. That shirt of yours isn't gonna get clean; you can never get blood out of fabric, I've found. Might as well throw it away."

They found a short-sleeved Hawaiian shirt. Mamadou felt ridiculous. George nodded, said, "That'll do." Then added, "I'm going take a nap. My chest hurts every time I breathe. Makes me tired."

When George left the room, Aunt Mim asked, "You done what you had to?"

He bobbed his head.

"Get a couple of glasses and the bottle from the closet. We're gonna have a toast."

He did, poured more for her than for himself. She gulped, he sipped.

"It don't bother you much, does it?"

"Dealing with people like Rousseau? No. They're a cancer. They infect everything."

"You know, about 50 years ago, George had to take care of some business. There was this man who was hurting women, beating 'em up and putting 'em out on the street. Killed one, maybe even two. And George put a stop to it. Man was three times as big as poor old George and mean as custard. George still has nightmares sometimes."

Mamadou shook his head. "Not me. I didn't have any bad dreams that last time, with the daughter of Colin's friend. I'm not going to lose sleep now. I've known men like Rousseau all my life. They somehow always manage to slip away, and they return, and they're always worse when they come back. He's not going to come back, and that's good."

"Sort of like you did society a service?"

"Sort of like that, Aunt Mim. Yes."

He finished his glass and reached into his pocket, brought out the baggie of white powder from Rousseau's apartment. "I found this. I'm not sure what it is. It might just be drugs, but it might be something else, maybe poison. Maybe this is what killed Antwone."

She put out a hand. "Lemme see."

She opened the baggy, sniffed it. "Don't think it's drugs. Least, not heroin. And not cocaine, either."

She sealed the bag, opened a drawer in her nightstand and dropped it in. "Lemme see what I can find out. I got a boy works in a lab analyzin' people's water for drugs."

"You mean urine?"

"Yeah. That." She nodded, embarrassed. "I'll pass it on to him, ask his opinion."

Mamadou poured more wine for her and leaned down to kiss her on the cheek. "I have to go."

"Your white man friend got your car, right? Hang on. I'll find someone to drive you and the boy home."

Colin drove the Mercedes and took DiAngela Jones and her triplets home to a neat two-story townhouse in Bailey's Crossroads near NOVA Community College. There was a handkerchief front yard with a small patch of flowers and a coiled garden hose on the front stoop.

"Pull the car into the driveway. The neighbors will be impressed by the Mercedes, even if it's an old one."

The home's interior was sparse but tasteful. Colin noted framed prints of works by Palmer Hayden and Laura Wheeler Waring. He commented on them, and DiAngela Jones said, "You know them? That's sort of unusual."

"I once did research for a man writing a book on black painters."

She sent the triplets to their room and told them they could listen to the radio.

"The radio?" Colin was charmed.

"They're not allowed to watch television unless I'm there with them. And there's only three or four stations they can listen to."

"NPR?"

She smiled. "Of course. And Pacifica."

She busied herself making herbal tea, and when both were served, she said, "Tell me about your friend. I like him a lot. He likes me. He seems to like the children, too. But his intensity," she paused, frowned, "if that's the right word, it frightens me."

So Colin told her what he knew: Mamadou the Senegalese cop, the immigrant, the successful entrepreneur, the avenger. He told her about the night they'd rescued Catherine's daughter, Josie, and how Joe the Cop had been slain. He told her of Mamadou's sister who had been killed by drugs, and how Mamadou took revenge on the dealer who'd addicted her, how he'd been cleared of charges following the deaths of the dealer and his gang. Through it all DiAngela Jones stayed silent. Finally she said, "He's not a cold man."

Colin agreed. "He's not. But he doesn't have the reactions you or I might have to things. Some of us get anxious, we get scared, we panic. He gets calmer and more focused. He was devastated by his sister's death. He planned and exacted a terrible revenge. Antwone's death was shattering. He'll avenge it; that's what he does. He has no sense of remorse if he thinks he's acted," Colin paused, searched for the word, "justifiably. He's not religious, but he believes in the Old Testament. An eye for an eye."

"Do you really think he killed Rousseau?"

"I'm pretty sure, yeah." Colin looked at Jones with a humorless smile. "Old Testament again. And he's no dummy; he knew Rousseau would be armed. He went into that apartment knowing exactly what he had to do." Colin blew on his tea to cool it, then took a sip. "We'll read about it in tomorrow's paper. There'll be an item about a man found dead in an Anacostia apartment, and then a day or two after that, there may be a small item about how the man found dead was suspected of being involved in the drug trade. And the police will put it down to this endless war among D.C. dealers and gangs, and very stupid people with guns, and that'll be the end of that."

"That's what Mamadou is counting on, isn't it?"

"He's a planner," Colin replied.

DiAngela Jones gave that some thought. Colin saw her frown again.

"Don't get me wrong, I think Mamadou is a rare type of man who'd go to the ends of the Earth to do what he feels he's got to do. You really like him?"

She nodded.

"That's great. I don't think you could find a more honest person."

She nodded again. "He wouldn't hurt us…"

"No. He wouldn't. Never."

"But he's still frightening."

"He is."

"The boys are crazy about him. He's all they talk about."

"I think Mamadou genuinely loves children. He was born into a large family, and he's the most responsible person I know. You couldn't want a better man as a father to your kids."

"Probably a little too early to start thinking about that." She smiled, then laughed, "But I have anyway. I just wish he wasn't so… intense."

Colin agreed. "Tell you the truth," he said, "sometimes the man scares *me*."

She nodded. "He asked if I knew how to shoot. I said I did; I had a boyfriend who was a cop and he taught me. He gave me a gun, Mamadou did. He said he'd feel better if I had one." She opened her purse, brought out a small revolver. "It's a Smith & Wesson. He said it was a good gun for a woman."

Colin looked at the thing, shook his head. "Does it make you feel safer?"

She shrugged. "Three little ones here, I have to be even more careful. So no. Not really."

The next day Colin drove Danee back to the AfriCars garage. The boy had spent a restless night—"I ain't used to sleepin' on no flo', and I like to get somethin' to eat in the middle of the night, and you ain't got nothin' worth eating"—and talked a steady streak the entire way.

"So she *is* your girlfriend, Emily, that's a pretty name. I knew she was your girlfriend right from the start, an' she's nice, I like her. Though a white man and a black lady, that's sort of weird, you know? You gonna have kids with her you think? Maybe not, I guess you're too old for kids, and you ain't got nothin' in your fridge that a kid could want. Kid would be bored to death living at your house. And probably starve, too!

"This a *old* car! Man! I don't think I ever met anybody with so much old stuff. You got old furniture, and old TV, and old *food*... Even your clothin' is old! You ought to look at that magazine I told you about, *Upscale*. They got nice men's clothing there. You could get some, you know?

"It's a Porsche? How come it ain't fast? Porsches supposed to be fast! This slow as a slug and makes funny noises too.

"So you think it's gonna be all right with that Ru So man? He ain't gonna come after me?"

"He won't. You've got nothing to worry about."

"What'd y'all do, kill him?"

That was unexpected. Colin said, "Kill him? Jesus, Danee, of course not! What gave you that idea?"

Danee looked at him shrewdly. "Cause Mr. Dioh, he look like he could kill people. You, not so much, but him, yeah, for sure. He got that Africa *juju* killer look. Can we stop and get something to eat?"

They went to McDonald's. Danee had two fish sandwiches and large fries. Colin nursed a coffee.

"Plus," Danee continued between bites, "Mr. Dioh ain't the type to forgive things. And that Ru So man, he for sure killed Antwone, so if you're tellin' me I don't have nothin' to worry about, that mean Ru So is gone." He chewed, swallowed. "I mean, like *really* gone."

And then, "Don't you worry. I ain't gonna tell anyone."

Mamadou greeted them at the garage entrance. "Did he behave?"

Colin thought about it, glanced at Danee who wore a worried look. "Yes. He did. A very pleasant houseguest. Talks a lot, though. And has some strong opinions."

Danee shrugged, "No such thing. Just makin conversation." Then he looked from one man to the other. "So Mr. Marsh says y'all killed Ru So, huh?"

The killing was reported the next day in the *Post* as Colin had predicted.

Rousseau had apparently set up an evening date to follow his meeting with DiAngela Jones. The other woman showed up, knocked on the door and, when there was no answer, called Rousseau's phone. She could hear it ringing in the apartment until Rousseau's voice mail answered.

She called three more times with the same result, then went outside, flagged down a passing police car, and voiced her concerns. The cop, heading back to the precinct at the end of his shift, called in to dispatch for instructions. He was told to knock on Rousseau's door and announce himself as a law officer, which he did. Still nothing.

A Howard University medical student who lived in the apartment above Rousseau's told the woman and the policeman that there was an emergency number in case something went wrong in the building.

The policeman called the number and reached an unhappy older man who indeed had a passkey for the apartments. The older man did not want to be disturbed. He was watching WrestleMania and had a minor bet on the next fight. The policeman exerted the power of his position, and the older man arrived within minutes, opened the door and left without looking in. The policeman saw the corpse and cursed his own bad luck; the paperwork would take hours, and the pasta dinner his wife was preparing would be stone cold by then.

Rousseau's date saw Rousseau's lifeless body and screamed. She tried for a fast exit; this was not the sort of event she'd planned for the evening, but the policeman insisted she stay. After a while, she slumped against a wall. "Well, shit. Poor fuckin' Nicholas." To herself she added, "Now what am I gonna do for dinner?"

"That his name?" the cop asked.

"The name he gave me," the woman said.

She and the cop were standing by the open door. The cop nodded, "Did you know him well?"

The woman considered the question carefully. She was in her late-twenties, chocolate-colored, and heavy-assed.

"Wellll," she drew the word out. "I guess not, not really. We fucked a time or two. So no. Didn't know him well at all."

The cop looked to see if she was kidding. She wasn't.

"He wasn't from here," she added.

The cop said, "Do tell." He decided he didn't like the woman. He was used to strong language but even after years on the force, it shocked him a bit when it came from women. He thought her comment indelicate in the face of death.

"He was from Haiti." She pronounced it Hate-ee.

When the cop had nothing to add, she fished in her purse, found a cigarette and lit it.

In the end, they both missed their evening meals.

More cops came, as did an ambulance and the forensic folks who said this was a pretty simple deal. Rousseau was shot with a medium caliber gun, from three or four feet away, and death was instantaneous. One of the bullets was lodged in his skull; the other had gone right through, made a hole in the rug and then slid a foot or so, creating a shallow furrow in the cement floor. When the body was rolled over, it showed that Rousseau had a gunshot wound in his left thigh and an empty knife sheath looped in his belt at the small of his back.

The man himself was not robbed, which was odd. His wallet contained $342 and his phone was in his pocket. And though robbery seemed an obvious motive, the shooter hadn't been particularly thorough in his search of the apartment. One of the forensic guys found $4000 hidden in a plastic baggie in the toilet tank. This oversight by the shooter was unusual, and the detective assigned the case wondered if perhaps the robber had been in a hurry; either that or the disheveled state of the apartment was a scam and there was another motive for the shooting. Revenge, maybe. Or business.

It didn't really matter.

The detective had worked more than a hundred such killings, and knew that this one, like so many others, would never be solved. There were budgetary and manpower constraints, and despite the mayor's recent assertion at a press conference that all lives mattered, the reality was that some lives mattered less than others. Young black men got killed daily in Washington, D.C., a sad and unalterable fact in the Nation's Capital.

15 AT A QUARTER AFTER TEN, COLIN FINISHED A LAST SET of push-ups with the TV tuned to *America's Got Talent* and muted because he couldn't stand either Howie Mandel or Mel B. He didn't much like Heidi Klum either.

Shortly after his relapse, he'd given up the weights when his then-girlfriend had said he looked like a wedge of cheese on two toothpicks. Catherine hadn't meant anything by the statement, but it had stung. Now, instead of pushing barbells and dumbbells around, he stuck to a daily regimen of body weight exercises and three-mile walks. He was slowing down. It was noticeable when he climbed stairs in a hurry, when he went from a walk to a run to a sprint.

He was thinking about Emily Martin, wondering if the joy he felt when she was around would last and scared to consider the possibility that it might not. He really, *really*, liked her. There was a quality to the woman he hadn't encountered in years—a sort of spontaneity that most alcoholics, recovering or not, had suffered from sometimes in their lives and now avoided. She seemed to delight in his discomfiture; he liked that. He liked that she padded around naked in his apartment, asked embarrassing questions, and was disarmingly comfortable with who she was. She made him happy.

He was enjoying the reveries when the phone rang. He didn't recognize the number though the area code was local. When he picked it up, a voice with the slightest of accents said, "Mr. Marsh? You don't know me? I'm a friend of Clarence? The man you sponsor?"

"Clarence?"

"He said you were his sponsor?"

It took three seconds for him to remember who Clarence was, a tall, thin, light-skinned black man in his thirties who'd shown up for three meetings, asked that Colin sponsor him, and had neither been seen nor heard from again. Not unusual within the rooms, Colin knew. In his years in the program, he'd sponsored more than a dozen men who'd vanished.

"Clarence? Ah, yeah. Right. Clarence."

"My name is JoAnn Sabatini? I'm a friend of his?" The woman spoke in question marks.

"Yeah?"

"Well, he gave me your number? When he started going to meetings? He said I was to call you if I ever saw him using drugs or drinking?"

The question marks were getting annoying. Colin sat on his couch, wedged the phone between his head and his right shoulder.

"I have to tell you, I never heard from Clarence. He never called me."

"He didn't? He told me did?"

"I'm sorry. I'm sure he meant to. He just... didn't."

Colin could smell Emily's perfume from where she'd been sitting on the couch a day earlier. He tried to chase thoughts of her away and concentrate.

There was a snuffling sound, and Colin realized the woman on the other end of the line was crying.

"Well," she said. "The thing is, he's sort of disappeared?"

"I'm sorry to hear that, but—"

"So I thought I'd call you?"

Colin exhaled. "Have you tried the police?"

The woman hiccupped; her voice changed subtly. "I can't."

A declarative sentence with no question marks. Colin said, "I see," though he didn't.

"I think something bad happened to him?"

"Well." The question marks were back.

"I think this nasty woman hurt him? I'm sure of it?"

Emily's perfume was maddening. He'd call her as soon as the questioning woman hung up. Maybe they could have dinner.

"Well, can you take my number? Just in case?"

He found a pad of paper and a pen. "Sure."

"It's JoAnn. One word. Capital J, capital A." She dictated a number. "If you hear anything? Anything at all?"

Colin said, "I will?" God! It was catching—the question marks.

"I will," he repeated, flatly.

That night he took Emily to the Caribbean Grill on Lee Highway, and they both ate black bean soup and Cuban sandwiches. She had a 10 Saints beer; he had an expensive bottle of ginger ale that purported to be real and made by ginger ale artisans though it tasted a lot like Canada Dry.

She asked about Danee and his whereabouts.

He told her, "I have a feeling Mamadou is going to try to take him in. Plus, he's seeing DiAngela, and she has her triplets, so he'll be knee-deep in kids. He'll enjoy it."

They drove back to his place with the ancient Porsche's engine clattering like a coffee can full of steel bolts.

She asked, "Is it supposed to sound like that?"

"Yeah," said Colin, "It's a Porsche."

"Really?" She wasn't convinced. "It's a really old piece-of-shit Porsche," he admitted, "and most of them do sound sort of… iffy."

"Iffy?"

"Yeah." He floored the accelerator. The car considered it, then lumbered forward.

They were nuzzling on the couch when Wilkie called from *The Post*. Colin was set to ignore it but she said, "Go ahead. I need to use the bathroom."

He picked it up. "Hey, Colin, it's Michael Wilkie. Am I disturbing you?"

Colin looked up, saw Emily stark naked sidle into the bedroom.

"Ah, well, it's a little—"

"Won't take a minute. Just wanted to tell you that the guy in the trash chute? They identified him. I knew you were interested, and it's not gonna make the paper because there's been a rash of shootings in Oxon Hill, like six gangbangers who took over a Red Robin, can you believe that? And there's no space in the Metro section. Anyway, his name was Clarence Durocher. That's D U R O C H E R."

Colin said, "What? What?" Emily had kept the bedroom door open and was leaning forward, her perfect breasts not ten feet away.

"What?"

Wilkie said, "Are you okay? Colin? Ah shit, I interrupted something. I can tell. Man, I'm sorry. So listen, trash chute. Durocher. Clarence Durocher. Call me tomorrow if you'd like."

Colin said, "What?" again but Wilkie had hung up.

"What was that about?" Emily had slipped into one of Colin's T-shirt. It covered her to mid-thigh.

"A guy died. Turns out I knew him. That was Michael Wilkie, a friend from the *Post*."

"You were just standing there going, 'what?', 'what?'. It was sort of funny."

"It was hard to concentrate…"

"Drug death?"

"I don't know. I'll have to call Wilkie back."

"Do it now." She wasn't smiling anymore.

He went to her, lifted the T-shirt. "In a little while."

She hesitated, then smiled. "In a little while."

The spent an hour fooling around; they watched television and fooled around some more, and then they went to sleep.

He did call the next morning. Wilkie wasn't in the newsroom and he left a voicemail. He wondered if the Sabatini woman knew, if he should call her as well, and while he was debating his responsibility, she called him.

"He was killed," she said without preliminaries. "That bitch Gloria killed him! I know it! He went to see her and she killed him! With drugs!"

Emily came out of the bedroom wrapped in his old bathrobe, her hair wet from the shower. She raised her eyebrows questioningly; he shrugged.

Joan! Jeanne! What the hell was her name? "JoAnn, listen, start from the beginning, okay?"

The woman took a deep breath that hissed on the phone. "It was on Fairfaxunderground dot com? About Clarence being found in a trash chute? A friend called me, and I looked it up, and there it was." He heard her take another breath. Then, controlled, she added, "That bitch killed Clarence. Gloria Nachtalyan, is who."

"Gloria who?"

"Nachtalyan. I'll spell it out," and she did.

"You should go to the police. That's important information."

The woman laughed, a harsh sound. "I *can't* go to the police. Jesus, for a sponsor, you're not very smart. No wonder Clarence never called you."

"I don't under—"

"Oh for God's sake," JoAnn Sabatini whispered into the phone, "I'm married! Now do you get it?"

He didn't for a second, then did.

"Oh."

"Yeah, oh," Sabatini echoed dryly, "but *you* can go to the police. You were his *sponsor*. Tell them about Gloria, that bitch, tell them she killed him." And she hung up.

Emily was looking at him. "That was sort of a strange call."

He sat on the couch, looked at the piece of paper where he'd spelled out Gloria Nachtalyan's name. "It was. Yeah. It really was."

He went to his computer, entered Gloria's name in the Google search box and navigated to Whitepages.com. There were two: one in Long Beach, California, another in Fairfax. He copied the Fairfax address, then went to the *Washington Post* local page website and entered, *man's body in trash chute fairfax va.*

The article appeared in seconds.

He scanned it, looked at Emily and said, "Humph."

"Humph?"

"Look," he pointed first to the note, then to the screen. Clarence's trash-chuted body had been found in Gloria Nachtalyan's building. Imagine that.

Emily left later that morning with the promise that she'd be back that night. Colin went to a meeting.

He'd always preferred church basement meetings to the large AA clubs that had sprung up in the 1980s and '90s. The yellowed linoleum floor tiles, hissing coffee pots, the rickety folding chairs set up before each meeting, even the fluorescent lighting that gave all in the room a deathly pallor, these were the hallmarks of Alcoholics Anonymous.

Church basements had another advantage. Older churches were rarely handicap-accessible. Colin's sponsor, Orin, being wheelchair-bound, could not attend meetings there. Colin knew his gratitude for such a strange blessing was ill-founded, but was increasingly thankful for Orin's absence. The man's barely hidden racism, his chauvinism and sarcasm were becoming hard to stomach.

After the meeting, Colin spotted the custom-built van Orin hated straddling two parking spaces, and Orin himself squatting in his motorized chair, a frowning obese genie expelled from his bottle. He was smoking his pipe in front of the *No Smoking in the Parking Lot* sign and ignoring the annoyed looks of other drivers.

"Imagine running into you here, Colin!" Orin pushed out a foul cloud of blue Carter Hall Premium Virginia Tobacco smoke. "How come you always seem to go to meetings I can't get into? I'm starting to take it personal."

Colin offered Orin his best disingenuous smile.

"Any coffee left in there? Get me a cup? Cream, two sugars. And a stirrer."

Colin reentered the church and got to the coffee urn just as the coffee guy was pouring it out. He thrust a cup beneath the stream of jet black liquid, dropped two Splendas in and a dash of instant creamer and grabbed a little wooden stick stolen from Starbucks.

In the parking lot, Orin had secured his chair into the van's passenger seat. He motioned to Colin. "You drive. Let's go get some food."

They went through the drive-in lane at the Wendy's off West Street. Orin ordered two pulled pork sandwiches and large fries. Colin got the Mediterranean salad.

Orin didn't eat his food; he fought it. If they went to a spaghetti place, by the end of the meal, Orin's shirt would be a battlefield pockmarked with red stains. He was rude to wait staff and a poor tipper, regardless of the service quality; Colin was glad they were eating in the van.

Orin shoved a quarter of the pork sandwich in, chewed with his mouth open. Colin looked away. The sounds were almost as ghastly as the sight, but he couldn't close his ears.

"So you been very quiet, never a good sign. You haven't called me. What's going on?"

No sense lying to Orin. The man had an uncanny talent for spotting bullshit. Colin said, "I'm trying to find out what's going on with all these deaths. Dead dopers. My friend Willie. A bunch of other people; it doesn't make sense."

Orin swallowed, bit into the sandwich again, and dabbed at a dribble of pork juice from his chin. "Willie was just an old nig—" he caught himself, "An old black heroin user. People like that die every day."

"No. There were others. Remember my friend Mamadou? A boy he was taking care of died too. There's been dozens, and nobody's paying any attention."

"Jesus," Orin wiped his mouth, crumpled the napkin and dropped it into the take-out bag. "And you're gonna make it right? That it?"

"Well, no, but—"

Orin cut him off. "May I remind you the last time you and your African buddy decided to help others, a cop died, who was your friend. And your sponsee, I might add. And the only reason you're not doin' time, Colin, is because the people who know about it haven't talked. And," he found a last French fry and popped it into his mouth, "and you got drunk. I'm sure you remember that part. Or maybe you don't. I had to come and get you, pay your bar bill, and you puked in the van." He pointed to the van's floor. "You can still see the stain."

This wasn't technically accurate. Colin had paid several hundred dollars after the fact to make Orin's van spotless again. There was no puke stain, but this wasn't a good time to discuss it. It *was* true that he'd ended up in a dive, gotten drunk, and lost years of sobriety in one binge. It was also true that Orin had gone to the bar, paid the tab, seen to it that Colin was safely strapped in the passenger seat—where he'd puked—and taken Colin home to dry out for a few days. All that was accurate.

Orin said, "Rescuing people doesn't work real well for you, Colin."

He tossed the greasy take-out bag out the window.

Colin frowned. "Jesus, Orin."

"Biodegradable," Orin said.

"Not," Colin corrected.

"Then it fuckin' well should be," Orin held. And that was the end of that discussion.

Colin drove the van back to the church parking lot and helped Orin shift to the driver's seat. Orin said, "Thing that pisses me off, Colin, is that whatever I say don't matter, does it? You're going to do what the fuck you're gonna do and that's that." He shifted the van into drive. "Try not to get yourself killed. Or drunk. I won't be coming to save your sorry alcoholic ass a second time."

Some six hours later, Colin was at the locked door of Gloria Nachtalyan's apartment building.

He did the pizza delivery thing, punching intercom buttons on the call box until someone in the building buzzed the front door open. He found the mailboxes in the rear of the lobby. Nachtalyan was in 706.

He knocked on the door, waited, and knocked again. An irritated and slightly woozy woman's voice asked, "Who is it?"

He looked at his watch. Seven p.m. Did Gloria hit the bottle? He was familiar enough with drunken voices to recognize one.

"I'm a friend of Clarence."

Silence. Then, "Clarence didn't have friends. And anyway, I don't know any Clarence."

Nothing ventured, nothing gained. "JoAnn Sabatini said you do."

"WHAT?"

"She told me you and Clarence were an item."

"GO AWAY!!!"

"JoAnn Sabatini said you killed him."

The door flew open. A woman, Gloria, he assumed, blew a cloud of vodka vapors into his face. "JoAnn said WHAT??"

Colin took a step back. The woman's hands were balled into small fists ready to strike.

She leaned forward unsteadily. "Who the fuck are you?"

"I was Clarence's AA sponsor."

Gloria's fury evaporated. "Son of a bitch." She hiccupped, stepped away from the door. Colin entered, closed it behind him.

"Son of a bitch," Gloria said again.

She picked up a glass half-full of ice and clear liquid, drained it, stepped into the kitchen to refill it. She raised it in Colin's direction.

"Drink?"

"No thanks."

She gasped a laugh. "Well duh! Of course not!" She dropped to the couch. "Fuckin' Clarence." Then added, "Fuckin' JoAnn Sabatini." And finally, "Did she really say that, that bitch? That I killed him?"

Colin nodded, sat at the other end of the couch. "She did. Is that what happened?"

She looked at him shrewdly; her eyes slipped past his. "No. Nothing happened. What're you talking about?"

"So it's all a coincidence? That he was found in the trash chute of the building where you live?"

"Absolutely!" She hiccupped, laughed, sipped and said, "Fuckin' coincidence…"

"And that's what you told the police?"

"Police? What police?"

Colin took a stab in the dark. "The police that came to ask you if you'd seen him?"

She paused a long time, looked around the room. Her eyes teared. "Ah fuck."

"Look," Colin scooted closer to her. "I'm not with the police. I didn't know Clarence that well. He asked me to sponsor him, and I feel a certain… responsibility."

Gloria Rose looked at him oddly, her head tilted to the right.

"Why? Clarence was a fuck up. He really was, you know. A liar and a charmer and a fuck up." Then, almost to herself, "I can't believe that bitch said that!"

Colin let a moment pass. "So it's not true?"

Gloria drained her glass, looked into it and said, "I'm drinking waaaay too much.

"Course it's not true. I really liked Clarence. He was a fuck up but I really liked him." Two large tears rolled down her cheeks. "Jesus."

Colin let the silence build. Finally, Gloria said, "It's his entire fault." She sighed theatrically. "That stupid man. That stupid, stupid man…" She stood, teetered, sat back down. "Crap," she said, "I'm drunk." She peered at him, craning her neck. "You're sure you're not the police?"

He nodded once.

"Lemme see your badge!"

"I don't have one."

She sighed, deflated. "That was just a test. If you were a cop, you'd say, 'Here it is.'"

He waited. She sighed again.

"He came here. I didn't want to see him. Except I sort of did." She looked up, searched Colin's face for disapproval and found none. "He had some cocaine," she lied, "and when I reminded him that he was in AA, he said cocaine didn't count, only alcohol did. He asked if I wanted some. Of the cocaine. I said no."

Colin's face was blank.

"So I said no because I don't like drugs, and he took some himself, and then he dropped to the floor and I thought he was joking, 'cause he used to do that, joke around, I mean, except that he wasn't. He was on the floor and he wasn't breathing."

Gloria's words came out painfully. "So I tried CPR like I'd learned, but it didn't help. I did it for a long time like they tell you; you use *Stayin' Alive* and I did but nothing worked. He was very dead.

"So then I got really scared." She stopped talking, stared at the floor, stood, and paced.

"He brought the drugs?" Colin asked.

She hesitated; she was lying. "Yes, of course!"

Gloria went to the kitchen, dumped some ice in her glass and picked up the vodka bottle, then paused, shook her head and filled the glass with water from the sink.

"So then what happened?"

"Whaddya mean?"

"How did Clarence end up in the trash chute? It must have been hard to wrestle him in there."

Gloria face fell. "Poor, stupid Clarence.... You're gonna tell and I'm gonna get arrested."

"No, I'm not. I don't think you killed Clarence. I think some bad drugs did, and that's what I need to know. He's not the first to die, Gloria. And I don't care about the police. I want to find out who's killing people and why."

Very softly, Gloria said, "I need help."

"Tell me what happened..."

She said, "Fucking Bong Bong is what happened!"

He said, "Bong Bong?"

She nodded. "Bong Bong. That fuckin' little convenience store Asian, Bong Bong; that's who killed him."

So more of the story came out, an edited version, Colin knew. He asked, "So that was it?" and she looked mildly insulted. "I wouldn't lie to you! You're a *sponsor!*"

Just before leaving, he reassured her again that he wouldn't go to the police. "I don't think you committed a great crime, Gloria. You maybe disposed of a body in an... unusual manner, and you should have told the police the truth. But this is nothing you'd go to jail for."

At the door, he looked into her eyes. "Do you think you might have a problem?"

She nodded. "I'm pretty drunk." In a loud theatrical whisper, she added, "And I'm out of cocaine."

"Ah." He asked for a piece of paper and pen and wrote down an address. "Stop drinking, make some coffee, and when you're sobered up, go there. They'll help you."

As soon as he left, Gloria decided she couldn't wait; she hadn't had that much to drink. She Siri'd the address Colin had given her; it wasn't that far away and sort of near the Costco she liked. She splashed some water on her face, inspected her teeth, then got into the Lincoln and steered it to 66 West, off at the Fair Oaks exit and followed 50 to Chantilly. She thought it was really nice for poor old stupid Clarence's sponsor to help her out. Maybe when she was calmer in a day or two, she'd go to an AA meeting; there might be some nice men there.

She turned left on Walney, and parked the car in front of a long, low brick building with shaded windows. She rang the bell.

Soon a thin, tough-looking young woman appeared and cracked open the door. "Help you?"

Gloria whispered, "I was told to come here for cocaine."

The woman smiled and nodded, opened the door wide. "Sure thing. Come on in. Sit over there," she pointed to a wooden chair, "and I'll be right back."

Gloria sat and waited. Soon an older, black woman came. She said, "Cocaine?"

Gloria bobbed her head. The woman handed her a clipboard with a questionnaire. "Fill this out."

Gloria thought that was odd. "Why? I've never had to do that before."

The black woman was silent, stared hard at Gloria, and lowered herself into the adjoining chair. "Whaddya here for, honey?"

"Cocaine," Gloria repeated softly.

The woman paused. Then, "You mean, like to buy?"

Gloria nodded.

The black woman rubbed her eyes. "I think there's been some mistake, honey. This is A New Beginning. We're a county rehab."

Ralph Charrette estimated that in his twenty-two years with the county, he had saved his taxpayers $73,571,827, give or take a buck or two. He was proud of this and had a couple of plaques on his wall attesting to his skills. He'd been commended by the county commissioners with certificates that read:

WHEREAS: RALPH CHARRETTE has been a major contributor to the successful implementing of the County budget because of his integrity, winning personality, and hard work.

WHEREAS: RALPH CHARRETTE played a critical role in his department's success by conducting budget comparison research in the performance-based budgeting process and served as a pivotal part of the department's overall effort.

WHEREAS: RALPH CHARRETTE provided the leadership necessary in building support and enthusiasm for the budget.

WHEREAS: RALPH CHARRETTE exemplifies the County's Values to "Embody Honesty, Cooperation, Good Will, and Integrity in our Conduct" and "Show Excellence and Pride in our Work".

NOW, THEREFORE, WE, County Commissioners, do hereby recognize, give special tribute to, and commend most highly RALPH CHARRETTE for his outstanding contribution to the County and we congratulate him for being honored with the APRIL 2014 OUTSTANDING EMPLOYEE AWARD.

Ralph also had a commendation for July, 2011. Both were expensively framed in cherry wood and hung prominently in his office.

Others might call themselves innovators; Ralph was a "dennovator". He was a short man with the bitter mouth of a bureaucrat, and it was his job to spot waste, over-costs, spendthrift actions, and excess expenses, and to flag projects unworthy of county expenditure. He did this with a verve rarely seen among mid-level government employees. He was single, lived alone, and occasionally played karaoke clarinet in his living room. He owned a $2000 Hämmerli SP20 22 caliber target pistol which he was pretty good with, and a low-end Martin guitar bought on a whim and played only three times because it hurt his fingers. He loved his work.

In the past year, he had persuaded the County Commission to veto new mattresses for the county jail as well as additional towels and bedclothes for the inmates. He had overseen the purchase of 10,000 gallons of bile green paint for county buildings at a dime a gallon less than a more cheerful lemon yellow. He had originated the defunding of an art program for teens from low-income families and the closing of three sparsely attended swimming pools in Section-8 housing complexes. He had fought hard—and lost the battle—against body cameras for cops, and ached in his heart over a program that increased the basic cost of school lunches for the neediest by eight cents per serving.

He had a small staff of accountants and a tenured secretary he did not much like but could not get rid of. She didn't like him either, and he was reasonably sure she was a drinker and perhaps even a substance user; lately, she had come to work shaky and bleary-eyed with alcohol on her breath. He could not act upon his suspicions since the county did not have a drug-testing policy for secretarial staff. He was stuck with Gloria Rose Nachtalyan.

He was nearing mandatory retirement and putting together his masterpiece.

It was complex work that had begun with a consultants' study of health-related costs incurred by the county's addict population estimated over a six-month period. Ralph had been astounded by the figures, overwhelmed, even. A second study corroborated the findings of the first.

Ralph did numbers well. He tabulated costs suffered by the police, the sheriff, and the courts. He added those involving family, neighborhood, and community services, a staggering amount in and of itself. Then there were the ambulances, the emergency rooms and hospitalization detoxes and rehabs, job training and placement costs not paid for by community services or insurance. The list went on, more than a hundred-and-fifty entries in all. All told, addicts—their pursuit, arrests, trials, imprisonment, feeding, paperwork, health care, retraining, and other expenses that involved testing, interdiction, and education, the list seemed endless—cost the county $28,387,943 a year. Give or take a few bucks. And that, thought Ralph Charrette, in the face of massive budgetary shortfalls, was completely unacceptable. Intolerable, actually.

Aunt Mim told Mamadou that the white powder he'd found in Rousseau's apartment was a variation of scopolamine. "But not regular scopolamine, whatever that is. Here, talk to George, he'll explain."

George said, "It's normally used to treat Parkinson's disease, and sometimes nausea, but only in very small doses. Some people call it Devil's Breath, or burandanga, and there's all sort of legends about how toxic it is. But the sample you gave Mim was some sort of altered version. The boy at the lab said he'd never seen anything like it. He said it had to be manufactured privately, not by a company; it doesn't have any use commercially. It's really nasty stuff. It'll kill people in a heartbeat."

16 A month passed.

Colin told Emily he loved her, and she said she loved him too. They talked about the oddness of being a biracial couple; both thought even talking about it might not be politically correct, but they did so anyway. They started noticing the number of similar duos, Asians with whites, blacks with Asians, Indians from the subcontinent with blacks or whites, and permutations thereof. They broached the idea of maybe getting an apartment together and began looking at two-bedrooms in Arlington or Alexandria, just to see what was out there. The rental prices astounded them.

"We'd be better off buying," Emily said without realizing the implications. Colin agreed, and liked what purchasing together might suggest.

She needed to be near a Metro station; he didn't care. He wanted some green space not too far away and a trail where he could run.

Colin got a long-term contract to research a series of articles for *Wealth* magazine on rich people who lived in Virginia. There were thirty billionaires and more than 60,000 millionaires within state lines.

Emily was spending four nights out of seven at his apartment, and had taken over most of the bedroom closet by pushing the few items he had on hangers to one side.

Orin, when he heard about the living arrangement, maintained his peace. He congratulated Colin but privately let it be known that he wasn't sure a man and a woman of different colors should be sharing a home; it was against the laws of nature, he believed. Raised on a visceral fear of blacks, Orin warned Colin of black women's propensity for doing horrible things to their mates. "When their men are sleeping, mostly. I read about it, how some black woman in Richmond poured boiling oatmeal on her husband when he was taking a nap. Gave me nightmares for a week!"

Colin told him neither he nor Emily liked oatmeal.

Gloria Rose gave up drugs and alcohol. She signed up for an out-patient program and began attending AA meetings. There were some interesting men, but she was told it was thought unwise to begin a relationship in one's first year of sobriety. She made a few women friends and got a sponsor.

She slipped a few times. Her last episode was one rainy night when, depressed, sure she'd be forever single, and burned out on *The Black List* and James Spader, she drank an entire fifth of Grey Goose vodka and passed out with her chin resting on the toilet bowl. She never told her sponsor.

She kept feeding information to Mr. Snow and the checks appeared in her mailbox every Tuesday, but now she put the money into a special vacation account. She had heard good things about Belize from a woman in the program who said the young men there were gorgeous, safe, and cheap. Gloria would go there as soon as she'd accumulated $5,000 in play money. She was amazed by how much she saved giving up coke and booze.

George healed, though he walked with a limp and now used a cane. Aunt Mim tried to make him feel better by saying a cane looked elegant but he wasn't convinced. He finished reading the medical encyclopedia that had occupied him for months and started on Will and Ariel Durant's *Story of Civilization.* "Eleven volumes," he told Aunt Mim. "I'll be reading this when I die."

She shuddered and crossed herself. "Don't you say things like that, you silly old man!"

Mamadou took Danee in. Danee's mother was pleased; she knew neighborhoods like hers were murderous, regardless of a child's promise. Mamadou enrolled Danee in a Montessori school where he thrived and soon developed a tolerable private school accent. He was known to drop his g's when excited and experience a linguistic relapse if scared. DiAngela Jones' triplets idolized the young teen. Mamadou had never been happier.

He bought a fourth car, a 2007 Lincoln Town Car stretch limo with 70,000 miles and in excellent condition. He hired a full-time driver, a young Senegalese from Dakar whose family he knew from the old days.

The peace and quiet ended with a phone call from Danee's mother.

"There's some men came here last night looking for Danee," she said. "I was on… a date. So they asked the neighbors. They said they'd be back tonight. I don't know what to do."

Mamadou thought about it. "Give them my number. They want to talk to Danee, they talk to me first."

Then he called Colin. "My friend," he said. "I need your help again."

Colin said, "Uh oh."

Ralph Charrette had met Charlie Snow for the first time two years earlier at Gilbert's Indoor Shooting Range in Rockville, Maryland, an easy twenty-five-minute drive from Fairfax if you took the Beltway and the traffic was light. Snow was shooting a cheap Smith & Wesson 22S Sports Series with a 5.5-inch barrel. Compared to Charette's Hämmerli SP20, Snow's Smith & Wesson looked like a rock.

They'd gotten to talking, as gun owners do, and pretty soon they knew each other's names and marital status—both were single; Snow thought Charrette might be a little gay; Charrette worked for the county, Snow was a security consultant, and politics—both were Republicans of the non-coddling variety when it came to minorities, welfare, illegal immigrants, drug addicts, and Planned Parenthood. Both confessed that in spite of their political affiliations, they thought Trump was an asshole. "Maybe even crazy," said Snow, who had known many crazy people in his days as a cop.

They were friendly but nothing more. Snow's gaydar occasionally beeped; Charrette had a strange way of moving sometimes. There was a certain cant to his hips when he was shooting, and the tiny leaps when he got off a good series, all were, well, *suspect*.

Charrette, for his part, thought Snow might be a crook, but an interesting one. Both were more right than not about the other's tendencies.

After a particularly successful afternoon at the range, Charrette let Snow handle the Hämmerli, and Snow was impressed. Charrette fired Snow's S&W and was not, but he praised the weapon anyway because it wasn't politically correct to criticize another man's gun. They had beer and fries and bacon cheeseburgers at a local eatery, and the conversation got a little more personal. Charrette explained that saving the county money was both his job and his passion, and voiced frustrations regarding the stupendous waste of funds allocated to worthless people and projects. He told Snow about arts programs for brain-damaged youths. "Almost a half-million bucks a year for kids who drool. I stopped that one dead!"

Snow nodded. As a former police officer, he had seen breathtaking waste, particularly in the court system. He told Charrette, "We'd pick up a guy at noon for dealing. He'd spend an hour in a holding cell, go out on bail, and be back on the streets by four. There was this one guy, big dude, half Cherokee and half Jewish. Everybody called him Running Schwartz. I got him three times in two days. He wouldn't even bother changing corners! Judge thought it was funny, said to him, 'We have to stop meeting this way! People will talk!'"

"I've seen figures on recidivism," Charrette noted.

"Unreal," agreed Snow. "But you know what they used to say in Vietnam: 'Kill 'em all and let God sort 'em out.'"

Charrette snorted. "Humph. If only."

"That's what the Chinese did with the opium addicts." Snow had read a lot of history books. "Killed 'em all. Tell you what, though. That sure solved that problem."

Charrette looked up from his burger. "Save a hell of a lot of dollars…"

"Damned straight. And the Chinese had more addicts than we ever will. Millions and millions of the little yellow bastards nodding out. Chinese did the right thing!"

They finished their burgers, but the conversation continued on and off for the next few months. One would think of an important detail, a necessary action, and the other would offer solutions. They were smart men, one with street creds, the other with a deep knowledge of how town and county governments worked.

And then one day, damned if they didn't have just the beginning of a plan. Theoretically, of course.

The search for Bong Bong was not going well. The first time Birch Carroll called the number the nurse had given him, it rang and rang and then died. The second time it went straight to an incomprehensible voice mail greeting. When he tried to leave a message, the phone cut him off with a dial tone.

The third time a nasty little voice answered and said, "Whaddya want?"

Carroll, hesitantly, said, "Bong Bong?"

"Maybe." Definitely not the sort of happy voice one would expect from someone named Bong Bong.

"Ahhh. Doctor Morales' nurse said I should call you."

"Why?"

"Ahhh. She said you could help me?"

"Five hundred dollars," said Bong Bong.

That seemed like a lot.

"Going to hang up now. Good bye."

"No, no, no, no! Not hang up, not hang up!"

"Meet you, half hour, front of doctor's office. Five hundred dollars. Understand?"

"Yes. I'll…"

Bong Bong was gone.

Birch Carroll went to an ATM and withdrew $400. He'd haggle with Bong Bong. Asians liked that he'd been told. He thought about it for a second and withdrew another two hundred. He couldn't be certain Bong Bong was Asian, and making ethnic assumptions was dangerous.

Carroll had no idea what Bong Bong might look like, but there was only one impatient Asian in front of the doctor's office.

"Are you—?"

"Yeah. You got money?"

"Yes." Carroll fumbled in his pocket and brought out a sheaf of twenty dollar bills. Bong Bong took it, counted quickly and said, "Not $500 here. Only $400."

Carroll looked around and lowered his voice. "I thought maybe we could come to an arrangement."

Bong Bong let the money fall to the ground. "Fuck arrangement. Cheap asshole, waste my time. Dickhead." He turned and started walking away.

Carroll dropped to his knees and recovered the bills, saying, "No, no, no, no. I have five hundred! Five hundred, see?"

He fanned out the original amount and took another hundred out of a pants pocket.

Bong Bong said, "Asshole," again. He snatched the money and in one smooth movement dropped a small bag of white powder into Carroll's empty hand.

Carroll said, "This isn't OxyContin. I wanted—"

"This is better than OxyContin. Snort." Bong Bong made a snorting sound with his nose. "You understand?" He was twenty yards away and turning a corner before Carroll sought to respond.

"Snort? Whaddya mean, snort?"

But Bong Bong was gone and Birch was $500 poorer.

"Well, fuck me," said Birch Carroll. And then more softly, "Fucking little slanty-eyed, illegal, motherfucking, immigrant, dickhead." But holding the bag of powder, he said it without much conviction.

This was to be Bong Bong's last deal.

Bong Bong was a modest man with well-established likes and dislikes; he had never considered himself either an asset or a liability. He led a small life, was a good husband and an even better father, and he sent money home to his mother in Biñan in the Philippines.

He was one of many small-time dealers whose illegal activities did not come close to bringing wealth. Most of his drug profits went to prosaic ends—diapers for his twin daughters, new brake pads for the Camaro, a night out once a month with friends, and a mistress he shared with three other Filipino men. He neither liked nor made much use of her, but she was a distant cousin of his wife's, and he felt duty-bound to contribute to her well-being.

Bong Bong knew selling drugs was against the law but had never considered himself a criminal; he met a demand, and did so as efficiently as possible. His profit margin was small but adequate.

And he was cautious. If he thought a client might be unsafe, he ceased dealing with him or her, as he'd done with the crazy white woman who'd called him at home and insisted on meeting in the middle of the night. He'd dealt with her one last time, changed his place of employment and refused to answer her calls. He was proud to be a capitalist and an entrepreneur, an American, almost, but he was careful, too.

His downfall came when his supplier, a Haitian man named Rousseau, was murdered. Bong Bong had seldom exchanged more than a few words with the man, whose body was found in an Anacostia apartment. The slaying scared Bong Bong. He knew drugs and violent endings went hand in hand, but had hoped that by being remote from the mainstream of trade, he might avoid getting embroiled in its more vicious moments. It didn't work out that way.

It took a little time for Rousseau's people to regroup after his death. There was infighting, politics, two murders, and one victim-free drive-by. The group's new leader was a man named Meat, whose first official act was a call to avenge Rousseau's killing.

A Vietnamese gang with which Rousseau's people had tangled a time or two over turf rights was a natural target. Suspicions were aroused when one of the late Rousseau's employees sought out Bong Bong and learned the man had quit his job suddenly. Bong Bong was the only Asian dealer in Rousseau's network and that fact alone did not work in Bong Bong's favor. The fine distinction between Vietnamese and Filipino was overlooked. Asian was Asian.

Cue, a hot-headed young man with ambitions, a very junior member of the organization, found Bong Bong, followed him around for half a day, and saw him sell a bag of product to a white man in front of a medical building in Manassas. When Bong Bong walked away and turned a corner, the young man was there. He allowed Bong Bong a few dozen yards, then silently ran up behind him and fired two shots from a Ruger SR22 into the back of the Asian's head. It sounded like a small Japanese car backfiring. Bong Bong dropped without a sound in the empty parking space next to his Camaro. The young man took Bong Bong's phone; iPhones had high street value. He also took the money but left the wallet; it was important that the dead man be identified. Then he ran; he was fleet, having competed on his track team in junior high. He jumped into his own car, a stolen 2013 Honda Accord, and was back downtown within an hour. He would later boast that what his friends had called a "Smurf gun" had worked very well, thank you.

The medical building where Bong Bong's murder occurred had a security camera above its main entrance. When the police came, a replay of that morning's events showed a very-much-alive Bong Bong being handed money which he dropped to the ground. The camera caught a white male kneeling to gather the bills, and further discussion between the two men. Bong Bong handed the white male something that could not be identified but might have been drugs. Then he walked away. The other man hurried away as well and both were soon lost to the camera's range.

The killing was covered in the next day's news. If the murder of young black men was commonplace, that of Asians was not. Gloria Rose saw it on Channel Four's News-4-You and immediately knew it was Bong Bong. She was sick with fear and didn't go to work the next day. She called Colin to tell him that though she'd initially forgotten Clarence's dealer's name, she now remembered it. Yes, Bong Bong *was* an odd name, and even odder was that Bong Bong had been shot dead in a Manassas parking lot.

There was really no hard proof that Bong Bong was in any way responsible for Rousseau's death, but he was Asian, and therefore sneaky. For some of the gang, Asian meant Korean, and Korean meant the owners of neighborhood stores whose cash registers were behind metal grills. These unpopular Asians overcharged, refused to give credit, and spoke a language incomprehensible to anyone but themselves. A dead Asian, therefore, was not a great loss.

Meat, who had taken over Rousseau's organization, praised the young murderer for his motivation but demoted him to the rank of driver for acting without thinking things through. The man accepted his punishment knowing he'd impressed the people who needed to be impressed.

Birch Carroll never learned of Bong Bong's demise, nor did he know that detectives pored over the security camera images showing him as pale, faceless, and unidentifiable. Had the camera lens been clean, there might have been better resolution, but the maintenance man was afraid of electronics and heights, and avoided ladders whenever possible. Never once had he bothered to wipe the lens clear of grime and dust.

Carroll was wary of the drug he'd just bought and so in the privacy of his bathroom and feeling like a street junkie, he snorted only the tiniest amount. The stuff jolted him; it was powerful and did the job, but he got a nasty headache and stomach cramps. Obviously, he simply wasn't used to it. When he'd first started taking anti-depressants a few years earlier, the gearing up procedure had involved bouts of sleeplessness or drowsiness, anxiety, and lethargy. This was probably the same.

Mamadou spent the next few days at the garage tinkering with the cars and keeping an eye on the street. He was relatively sure that two vehicles had driven by the garage repeatedly, taking stock of the place and, indirectly, of him.

He'd dealt with gang members before. Years earlier, his apartment had been attacked by four men that included the Zulu, a powerful D.C. drug dealer. Things had not gone well for the men. The Zulu had escaped and resurfaced days later with evil intentions, and Mamadou had killed him in an epic battle still referred to with awe by cops and witnesses at Baltimore's Harbor. The policemen had walked away shaking their heads; Mamadou had never been charged though there had been intense questioning by a variety of authorities, ranging from an unhappy harbormaster to a Coast Guard Chief Petty Officer.

He still had the weaponry used to defend himself against the home invasion: two shotguns—a Remington 870 and a Mossberg 500—with seven-shot mag extensions for both, barrel shrouds, front and rear assault grips, and folding stocks. Five boxes of shells remained. Everything was stored in a locked metal chest kept in the back of the walk-in closet in his apartment. There was one gun, a Beretta 92 FS, that he kept in the garage should someone try to break in while he was there. That gun was in his desk, in a drawer with a false bottom he had built himself, along with a box of ammo.

He drove home from the garage, wrestled the chest from closet to car, drove back to the garage and moved the chest again. He closed the automatic doors and shaded the windows. Then he took apart the two shotguns and cleaned them carefully though they were already spotless. That done, he reassembled the weapons, wrapped them in old moving blankets, and slid them beneath AfriCars 1.

A man who identified himself as Meat called him in the evening as he was driving home.

It was a brief conversation. Meat said, "We need to see the boy. Just a few minutes. Need to talk to him, is all."

"Why?"

"Got a few questions."

"About what?"

The man on the other end remained calm. "Actually, ain't none of your business, motherfucker."

Mamadou parked the car, lit a Gauloise and asked, "Why are you calling me names?"

Meat ignored the question. "Where the boy at?"

Mamadou pressed the off button.

Meat called back within seconds. "You wastin' my time. We just got a couple of questions. Why you makin' this difficult?"

Mamadou said, "I'm quite sure the boy isn't interested in talking with you, Mr. Meat. As a matter of fact, he told me so. But you can talk to me anytime."

The man grunted, then laughed dryly. "I see you, nigger, it ain't gonna be to talk."

"That would be fine, too." Mamadou hung up again.

Ralph Charrette and Charlie Snow's plan developed at roughly the same pace as their relationship, which meant slowly and painstakingly. It wasn't a *real* plan, more like the strategy games that existed before everything went video. It was something fun to talk about; it gave them an excuse to get together.

Charlie Snow had always liked men. He hadn't spent much time thinking about it; it was simply a part of his make-up. He wasn't overtly gay, nor was he opportunistically sexual. He could take it or leave it and mostly did the latter. Sex did not much interest him, and when it did, it was always for a very short time.

Ralph Charrette had spent hundreds of hours and several thousand dollars trying to figure himself out. When it became apparent that his preferences focused on his own gender, he had gone through a long and tough period of solitary shame, and then signed up for intensive one-on-one and group therapy. There, he was told he was neither sinful nor depraved; that millions shared his penchants; that he was a young man who should enjoy life. He wasn't sure whether to be relieved or further aggrieved.

An older guy in his therapy group seduced him. There was a brief encounter which Ralph was far too nervous to enjoy; his few involvements over the years were no better.

With Charlie Snow, the emphasis wasn't on sex, it was on conversation, guns, and a strange sort of companionship that neither chose to question. *The Plan* was what they came to call their initiative, and it became for both a serious focus of attention long before either admitted it. It was Charlie Snow who, over bottles of craft beer at an Irish pub, looked deep into Ralph Charrette's eyes and said, "You know, this could work. We could get rid of all these useless fucks and nobody would know."

Ralph began taking a spiral notebook to their meetings. One night he suggested they involve Gloria. "But without her knowing," he said. "She's a wiz on the computer. She can run figures all day, tell you exactly what costs how much. But she doesn't like me. That's pretty obvious." And then, with a mean little smile that didn't reach his eyes, he added, "Plus, I think she might be an alky. Lots of times, she comes in the morning for work looking pretty worn out." *And*, he thought to himself, *it's always good to have someone between you and whatever is happening.*

Eventually Charlie Snow said, "I know a guy." And he did, a man known as Lobo who, a year earlier, Charlie had been tasked with assassinating by an up-and-coming competitor in the trade. The attempt had failed, and Charlie had lost a respectable amount of money.

Lobo was an importer of South and Central American hollow things—pottery, toys, fake artifacts, bricks, books, and cans of tuna and tomato soup and coffee, and other items that could—and often did—contain illicit substances. He, personally, never got close to the shipments. There were at least three cut-outs between him and the drugs; these people took the risks; they earned and deserved incomes that would make a pop singer blush. Lobo also made an extraordinary amount of money and lived a discreet life.

Charlie Snow put out the word that he'd like to see Lobo and tender his excuses for trying to have him killed. Lobo, he was sure, understood that business was business; there had been nothing personal in the failed murder attempt. And now Charlie had something to offer, a deal that would make Lobo smile, he was sure. Therefore he, Charlie Snow, hoped bygones could be bygones. There was money to be made.

A month later, Charlie heard that his proposal had been met with great glee by Lobo, and that it was the subject of conversation over several late night dinners. Not the meeting itself, but what should be done to Charlie when he was found. Lobo had proposed hanging Charlie by his testicles from a low tree branch but it was decided his testicles were probably too small, if he had any at all. Lobo ventured that Charlie's *cojones* were probably no larger than garbanzo beans.

But Lobo's men weren't after him, and Charlie's balls remained intact.

"I know a guy," Charlie told Ralph Charrette, "but it's going to cost a little money. We'll have to pay your secretary for whatever information she gets, and then if things work out, the guy will probably need a pretty good hit of cash."

Charrette thought about it and smiled. "There's some money available," he said. And they left it at that for the evening.

But they revisited *The Plan* almost every time they met. Fine points were honed even finer. Snow hired Gloria Rose who did come up with a lot of useful information about spending and the county budget. He knew dealers from his cop days and enlisted a few of them whom he supplied with less than perfect product. And it worked! In the middle of a heroin epidemic gripping the East Coast, a few extra deaths in one or two Virginia counties didn't make much of a stir. Snow had reasoned correctly that the police wouldn't pay much attention to a demise here and there. "They're already over-burdened. Thousands of new people moving into the suburbs and no budget for more cops. Hell, you know about that better than I do!"

This was true; Charrette had advised the county commissioners that hiring additional law enforcement officers was hardly necessary. It would cost millions when in fact the existing force was always willing to work extra hours. In the stupidly costly Virginia suburbs, most cops could hardly make the payments on their recreational Harleys or Ford Super Duty trucks. They worked second jobs providing security in malls or at EagleBank Arena and the Jiffy Lube Live concert grounds. Overtime was always welcome.

"So the police force is already stretched," Charlie Snow continued, "and not that interested in dead junkies, take my word for it." He shook his head in wonder. "You would not *believe* the paperwork involved! And on top of it all, the assholes always manage to die just before shift change…"

Shortly thereafter, Charrette and Snow mixed their first batch of drugs.

Charlie Snow knew a lot of people, many of them not reputable. His years as a cop had brought him into close proximity with second-story men, stick-up artists, swindlers, dealers and users, meth chemists, auto thieves and mechanics who could strip a car bare in two hours, cigarette smugglers, and a couple of moonshiners who made tolerable whiskeys and vodkas with stills hidden in national parks. He also knew poachers and truck hijackers, phony doctors, other bad cops, detectives and politicians on the take, pornographers, 12-year-old whores, and 13-year-old pimps, people who ran illegal restaurants and after-hour bars, disbarred attorneys, bogus real estate agents, and crooked accountants. He knew murderers and assassins, too, and a variety of strong-arm men gifted in the use of pliers and pipes.

Over the years he had developed a live-and-let-live attitude, realizing that being a policeman could be lucrative if one did things right. That meant arresting the right person, not the wrong influential one, or the one who had money. Or the one who could do something for you. Even such a simple thing as a traffic ticket, handled well, could be useful or remunerative.

He knew never to be impulsive, to think things out. That was the problem with the cops who wanted more out of life than a salary most people could barely live on. It wasn't smart to buy a pair of Yamaha Wave Runners for you and your girlfriend, or a cabin on Lake Anna, or take elk hunting trips to Colorado. He personally liked the story of the D.C. cop, who during a drug bust took personal custody of a briefcase full of hundred dollars bills. Nobody saw him; he stashed the briefcase in the closet of an adjacent empty apartment and retrieved it hours after the crime scene team had left. Then he spent a weekend in Las Vegas and returned with stories of a fabulous night at the tables. Problem was, poker playing cops knew him as a piss-poor gambler who routinely bet on bad hands and developed a tic in his left eye anytime he held two pairs or better. Busted.

So survival had everything to do with being cautious, and Charlie Snow thought of himself as a very cautious man.

The first batch of altered drugs was mixed in Charrette's two-bedroom apartment in Landmark.

Using Charrette's money, Snow had sought two acquaintances who supplied him with a quarter-pound of cocaine ($7,000), an eighth of a pound of B+ tar heroin ($9,000) and a quarter-pound of fentanyl ($3,200). He had Charrette purchase a quarter-pound of scopolamine analogue online from Alibaba.com for $2,800. This was called sharing the risk.

Both wore disposable latex gloves and surgical face masks with ear loops. They'd had a couple of drinks and the bottle of Scotch was on the kitchen counter.

The three powders were dumped in a sturdy shoebox that had once held Charrette's rarely used hiking boots. Snow mixed them together using a wooden spatula. He did this carefully for five minutes, and then handed the spatula to Charrette. "Softly and gently. This has to be exactly proportionate."

Snow watched Charrette mix. Charrette was holding his breath. All told, Snow thought, a lifelong bureaucrat mixing lethal doses of drugs with a wooden spatula in his own apartment showed more balls than Snow had earlier assumed the man had. They were committing a possession-with-intent-to-distribute felony that carried many, many years in prison.

"Gently," Snow repeated, "gently."

"Have you ever tried this stuff?" Charrette looked up, his hand soft on the spatula.

"A long, long time ago. Never liked it, though. Made me throw up."

"I haven't either. I just don't understand the attraction."

"I do." Snow moved away from the table, stripped off his mask and poured himself a liberal amount of alcohol. "There's a bunch of reasons," he said, "and I guess it depends on who you are." He sipped, pursed his lips.

"Most people are pretty stupid. Also, unhappy. Something that gives them pleasure, escape, that's always gonna be welcome. And nobody ever thinks they're gonna get addicted. They're too smart, or too strong, or too whatever, too different from everybody else. And then they *do* get addicted, and it's adios, baby." He thought for a moment, and then added, "Plus, there's all the people who were using painkillers, you know, like after getting a wisdom tooth out, or surgery. Back pain. Sciatica. They get way too much drugs from their doctors, it's ridiculous, really, and after a little while, when they're not hurting anymore and can't get the prescription refilled, they go from Vicodin or OxyContin to heroin. It's a really easy step."

He took a last swallow of the Scotch, replaced his mask. "All right then. I think we're just about ready."

He and Charrette used an electronic postal scale to weigh the drugs. They had almost nine-tenths of a pound. Snow asked, "You got flour?"

Charrette nodded and went to the kitchen. He returned with a five-pound bag of Gold Bond flour. "I like to bake sometimes." He said it almost apologetically.

Snow added flour to the mix until they had an exact nine-tenths of a pound.

"Okay. Let's measure out an ounce per baggy."

It took twenty minutes to fill fourteen baggies. Snow poured the leftover mix into a separate baggy and dropped it into his shirt pocket.

"Gotta call some people now," he said.

17 DANEE WENT TO COLIN'S APARTMENT AGAIN, complaining the entire time. "That man's got nothing to eat, nothing to watch, and makes me sleep on the floor. An' everything he has is *old*!"

"But you like Miss Emily, don't you?"

"She's okay."

"It's only for a couple of days," Mamadou said. "I want to make sure Rousseau's people leave you alone."

Danee squinted at him. "I thought you'd taken care of Rousseau?"

Mamadou stared straight ahead, guiding the Mercedes through traffic. "What do you mean?"

Danee made a gun out of his thumb and forefinger, pulled the trigger twice. "You know..."

"No. I don't." Mamadou frowned, added, "Don't go spreading stories like that, Danee. You'll get people in trouble."

Danni nodded. "Yeah. Right." He was silent for a minute or two. "I never did thank you for, you know, getting my a—, my butt out of a jam. And I guess I never did tell you how I miss Antwone, too." He wiped at his eyes. "He was really a good friend, you know? It was wrong, what happened to him."

Mamadou turned into the driveway fronting Colin's building. "I know, Danee." They sat in the Mercedes side by side, man and boy, and finally Mamadou said, "You behave yourself, all right? Don't go making fun of Colin. You be polite, do what he says."

Danee made a face. "Sure."

"I mean it!"

Danee opened the car door and stepped out, then stuck his head back in. "And you, you be careful, now. That's a mean bunch of people. I don't want to be losing another friend." He straightened up, and closed the car door. Mamadou, in spite of himself, couldn't help but watch Antwone walk away.

"So Mr. Dioh said I wasn't to sass you."

"That's good advice." Colin was stacking the breakfast dishes into the dishwasher.

"Miss Emily spent the night, huh?"

"She did."

"I could tell 'cause there's more than one person's dishes there."

"You're a smart kid."

"Yeah. I am."

The boy said it so seriously that Colin turned around. "Something the matter?"

Danee shrugged. "I'm sort of worried about everybody. Mr. Dioh. My mom. Those are bad people out there. Real bad. And they're not very smart, most of them, and they got guns, and not very smart people with guns is always gonna be trouble. I learned that a long time ago."

Colin wiped his hands on a dish towel. "You're really worried? About your mother, I mean?"

Danee shrugged, maybe embarrassed. "I guess so. Those people, if they can't find me, they might hurt my mom. I don't know."

"Is she at your apartment now, do you think?"

"Yeah. She don't wake up until ten or eleven, normally. Particularly if she been with somebody, last night."

Colin looked at Danee. The boy was trying to be manly.

"All right then" Colin grabbed his car keys, stuffed his wallet and phone into pockets. "Let's go get her."

In the Porsche, Danee said, "Man, we'd better hope those people don't come. I don't think this nasty car could help us 'scape."

"What was it Mr. Dioh said about sassing?"

"Oh. Yeah."

When they got to Danee's apartment building, he said, "This may take a few minutes. She's gonna have to get some clothes and stuff together." He squirted out of the car and scrambled up the stairs.

Mamadou had moved three limos out of the AfriCars garage and parked them in a nearby underground lot. He drove the fourth car, the Lincoln stretch, to a space he rented behind a neighboring townhouse, and walked back to the garage. He arranged two stacks of tires into a barricade, brought the weapons he'd cleaned and oiled, and placed them on a nearby workbench. He threw a blanket over them and stacked the ammo within easy reach.

Meat's people would come soon; there would be three or four of them, and they would think he was alone in the garage. Or perhaps they hoped to find Danee there.

He opened a bottle of Perrier water and lit a Gauloise with his gold Dupont. He waited.

Danee's Mamma was short, a shade past plump, and sleepy. She was wearing a rumpled purple Nike leisure suit and pink mules. Danee pulled at her while carrying a black trashbag full of clothes. A petulant look worried her face as he dragged her out of the building.

Colin had turned off the car's ignition; the Porsche overheated when idling. He was sitting in the driver's seat with the door open, and a few silent men and women were staring at him hard. One of the men said, "Yo, Danee, where you takin' yo Mamma?"

Another man said, "That white man kidnappin' yo Mamma?"

That made the little crowd laugh.

Danee threw the trash bag into the car's back seat and motioned for his mother to get into the passenger seat. She didn't want to.

"Get in the car, Mamma!"

Danee's mother stood her ground. "Why?"

"Because it's not safe here, and—oh shit!"

Fifty yards away, three large young men were hurrying towards them.

"Get in Mamma! Get in!" Danee pushed his mother halfway into the car, wormed his way into the back seat and shouted, "Drive! Drive!"

The passenger door was still open and only the front part of Danee's Mamma was fully in. Colin stepped on the gas, popped the clutch. The Porsche stalled.

"Oh my God!! Move, move, move, move!" Then, to his mother. "Get your butt in the car, Mamma! In the car!"

Colin twisted the key, the car hiccupped and started. The three young men had broken into a trot, and the small crowd of onlookers was gone. Colin got the car moving and heard one of the men yell, "Yo! Yo! Stop, mo'fucker! Stop!"

He didn't. The Porsche picked up speed and Danee shrieked, "Faster! Faster!" They turned a corner, then another, then a third, and found themselves on a main artery.

"Jeez," said Danee. "You all right, Mamma?"

"I lost a shoe." Danee's Mamma was wedged in the front seat. One stockinged foot rested on the passenger arm rest. "What am I gonna do with just one shoe?"

Colin glanced in the mirror and saw a black SUV weaving through the traffic. "Crap!"

Danee glanced out the back window. "Turn right on Vista! Turn right, now!"

Colin swung the car into the turn, heard a horn blast, crossed the yellow double line in the middle of the road and swung back. An aged Toyota beeped at him angrily. Its driver shouted something unintelligible.

"The garage!" Danee yelled. "Gotta get to Mr. Dioh's garage! Next left! Left on Chestnut! Left, left, left!"

Behind, Colin heard a car screech to a stop, more horns, and the metallic crunch of two vehicles impacting. He swerved around a van, passed a truck on the right and pumped his horn at a pedestrian crossing the road. The man high-stepped out of the crosswalk like a Steeler at the goal line and gave Colin the finger.

"Make it go faster! Faster, faster!" Danee yelled.

"It won't!" Colin shouted.

"Gotta get on Rhode Island Avenue," Danee shouted, "then we can get to the garage! Turn here! Right! Right on Clinton!"

Colin did. "Now straight! Straight! Then left on Rhode Island! Go faster!"

Colin took out his phone, handed it to Danee. "Call Mamadou! Tell him we're coming!"

Danee looked at the phone, hit the contact icon. "D or M?"

"What?"

"Dioh or Mamadou? D or M? It's a easy question!"

"D!"

Danee's Mamma was covering her eyes with her hands and whimpering. "We gonna die! We *all* gonna die!"

"No we ain't, Mamma! You keep quiet now!"

Mamadou picked up on the first ring. "Colin?"

"No! Me! Danee! With my Mamma! We got people chasing us! We're in Mr. Marsh's crappy old car! On Rhode Island! We're on our way! Gonna come through the back! The back!"

They careened through traffic. Twice Colin screeched to a stop inches from the bumper of another car, wrestled the Porsche into reverse, backed up, spun the steering wheel, and threw the car back into first gear. Danee was banging a fist against Colin's headrest. "Faster, faster, faster!" Colin yelled, "Shut up!" which stopped Danee for about a second. "Jeez! C'mon! Faster! Go faster!"

It took less than a minute to reach Dioh's neighborhood, but it seemed a lot longer. "Over there," Danee pointed. "Turn on Monroe, then go into the alley! Okay! Go, go, go!"

Mamadou was waiting in the alley and holding the Remington shotgun. Eight seconds later and two hundred yards away, the black SUV skidded into the alley. Mamadou waved the Porsche into a driveway that bordered the garage. He opened a side door, "Get in! Get in!"

When they were inside, he ran back into the alley. The SUV, a late model Ford Explorer, was barreling towards him. He swung the Remington to his right shoulder, aimed and fired one shot, pumped, fired another, then two more. The Explorer's front tires exploded and the thing slewed to a stop. Mamadou reloaded the shotgun and waited.

For a long while nothing happened, then the SUV began inching back, its two front wheels ratcheting against the pavement, the flattened tires making a blotchedy sound. Still in reverse, the SUV turned out of the alley, onto the street, and limped off.

In the garage, Colin was holding the Mossberg. Danee's Mamma was lying face down on the floor.

Mamadou asked, "You're all okay?"

Colin was pale. "Yes. I guess so. Jesus!"

Danee nodded. His hands were shaking. He glared at Colin, eyes hugely round and wide. "You *gotta* get a better car! They almost caught us!" He looked at Mamadou, "It kept *stallin'*! Stupid car! It wouldn't go any faster? What kinda Porsche only goes forty miles an hour!"

Colin opened his mouth to respond, then thought better of it. He said, "It got us here."

"Barely!" Danee was shaking his head violently. "Hardly at all! People was walkin' faster than we was drivin'!"

Mamadou touched the boy's shoulder. "Hush up now, Danee. That's enough."

Danee muttered, "I ain't *never* ridin' in that Porsche again. You get *killed* ridin' in that ugly car."

Danee's Mamma was still lying on the floor, hands covering her head.

"It's all right now. You can get up." Mamadou extended a hand and Danee's Mamma grabbed it. She carefully got to her knees, looked around, and struggled upright. Mamadou said, "You're Danee's mother. We spoke on the phone."

Danee's Mamma frowned, then smiled hesitantly. Mamadou asked, "Do you have a name?"

She nodded. "Eustacia. But I've never liked it."

"What do people in your neighborhood call you?"

She thought about it for a moment. "Some of the men call me Pussy."

Danee shut his eyes.

Mamadou said, "Why don't we just call you Danee's Mamma?"

That pleased her. She nodded, "Well, I *am* his mom…" She frowned, dusted herself off, adjusted her leisure suit pants and said, to no one in particular, "I lost a shoe," and then looked at Danee and added, "Where are we?"

"Have you ever shot a—" Mamadou didn't have time to finish. There was an enormous booming sound, glass shattering as a garage window exploded. Mamadou threw himself on Danee's mother and swept the boy off his feet with a swipe of his arm. Colin dropped to the ground, hugging the shotgun.

They heard a screech of tires. Mamadou wondered how an SUV with only two good wheels could make a fast getaway, and then realized that Rousseau's people had brought *two* trucks.

The four stayed on the floor another two minutes. Danee's Mamma made small keening sounds for about ten seconds.

Danee's eyes were saucer-wide. "They *shot* at us!" He looked down at his mother, knelt next to her and said, "Mamma? Mamma? It's all right!"

Danee's Mamma opened her eyes, then her mouth. Danee said, "Don't scream. It's okay."

Colin said, "I think they're gone." He shook his head. "Jesus Christ!"

Danee's Mamma looked at him disapprovingly, opened her mouth, shut it again.

Colin turned to Mamadou. "You were going to ask if I'd ever shot one of these things? Yes. Not this model," he laid the Mossberg on the workbench. "My dad used to take me hunting. But I was never very good. I always managed to miss whatever I was shooting at."

Danee's Mamma walked around the garage gingerly, avoiding the broken glass. She found a broom and automatically began sweeping, her one bare foot stepping around the shards. Her eyes had a faraway look and every three strokes of the broom, she stopped, looked around, and shook her head as if trying to get rid of an annoying sound.

Mamadou said, "I'm pretty sure the police won't come. It was just a drive-by and no one got hurt. I want to see what happened to the first truck. It can't have gone far on two wheels."

Danee said, "I'm going with you."

Mamadou shook his head. "Stay here with your mother."

Danee ignored him, turned to his mom. "You stay here and talk with Mr. Marsh. Mr. Dioh and I will be back in a couple of minutes."

They found the empty SUV with the two blown-out front tires less than a block away just as a flat-bed tow truck with Terry's Towing painted on the doors pulled up.

The driver positioned his flat-bed in front of the SUV. "Did you call this in?"

"No," Mamadou said. "Where are you taking it?"

The driver looked at the wheels. "Man, they just shredded those tires!"

Mamadou agreed. "The state of the roads around here is shameful."

"I guess." The driver squatted next to the Ford. "It almost looks like someone took a shot at these. There's little pellets all over the place..." He looked up at Mamadou who looked back without emotion.

"Well..." The driver stood and shrugged. "Ain't my business. Caller wants me to take it to the closest Ford dealership. That's in Alexandria, I guess."

He kicked at a demolished tire. "Those wheels are shot, too. Too bad. Custom jobs; a couple or three thousand just to replace them."

Danee and Mamadou watched as the driver placed two large hooks into rings bolted to the Ford's frame. The man threw switches and levers, and the tow truck's bed lifted up, tilted, and slid to the ground.

Mamadou said to Danee, "Let's go." To the driver he waved, "Have a great day."

The driver glanced first at the boy, then at Mamadou. "Yeah. Sure thing. You too."

Back in the AfriCars garage, Mamadou and Danee found Colin engaged in a monosyllabic conversation with Danee's Mamma.

"She says she wants to stay at home."

Danee looked at her. "Nope. Nope. Mamma, these dangerous people. They just *shot* at us! With guns!"

Danee's Mamma shook her head. "I been shot at before and I'm still here." She glanced at her feet. "And I had two shoes back then…"

Danee stared at her incredulously. "Well, I ain't *never* been shot at before, and I don't wanna *ever* be shot at again, and you're gonna do what you're told!"

They exchanged glares and Danee's Mamma said, "Oh, well." Then she opened her purse and rummaged through it. "Gonna need my medicine, though."

Mamadou frowned. "Medicine?"

"Her dope. I told you about that, Mr. Dioh. She needs her dope."

Danee's explanation was met with heavy silence.

Danee's Mamma said, "What? You ain't never heard of medicine?"

Danee sighed. "It ain't medicine, mom, it's heroin. That's what those people were shooting at us about."

Danee's Mamma wore a stubborn look. "They wasn't shooting at *me*. I didn't do nothin' to be shot at for. "

Mamadou corrected her, "They *were* shooting at you. They were shooting at all of us."

Colin looked at Danee, then at Danee's Mamma. "That's going to create problems. I'm sorry, but I can't have someone using drugs in my house."

Danee's Mamma made a face. "I was doin' real well until my own son and this white man kidnapped me, right in front of the neighbors, too. God knows what people are—"

"Mamma!"

"Well, you did! And people will talk, no accountin' what they'll say. And I lost a shoe, even…"

Danee ignored his mother and said, "How about Airbnb? I read on that in the library! Cheap, too!"

Colin shook his head, no.

"Why?"

"Well," Colin said, "For one thing, you need a credit card."

"She's got credit cards, don't you Mamma?"

Danee's Mamma nodded. "I *got* a credit card. I got *two* credit cards. But I know about this Airbnb thing, and I certainly ain't gonna stay in no house where I don't know the people! Get lost at night findin' the bathroom. Nope, unh-unh."

Mamadou cut in. "Perhaps we can put you in a motel on West Broad for a few days. You and Danee can stay with Colin until you have to…"

"Take my medicine," said Danee's Mamma.

"Right. Then I'll drive you back."

Danee's Mamma stood with her hands on her hips. "How come there ain't nobody askin' *me* what's best for me?"

Mamadou let the silence grow past the point of comfort. He raised his eyebrows briefly, and glanced at Danee, who shrugged.

Mamadou lowered his voice to just above a whisper. "No one is asking, because if you knew what was good for you, because if you did know, you wouldn't be prostituting yourself in front of your son and using drugs. Does that make sense?"

He was still holding the shotgun. He put it down next to the Mossberg.

"I'm sorry if I'm harsh, but a bunch of hoodlums just chased you around town, and then shot up my garage. They want to get to Danee. They'll get to you in order to get to him. Do you understand?"

Danee's Mamma nodded. She murmured, "Still gonna need my medicine. An' shoes."

For Ralph Charrette, life had never been so exciting. He was involved with a *dangerous* man; he was going to save the county millions of dollars, and though sane enough to recognize his actions would never be rewarded, he didn't care. *Something* had happened, he wasn't sure when or how or why, but he was a new man. Well, not a *new* man but a *different* man, and it was all thanks to the incomparable Charles Snow.

The word *incomparable* had struck Ralph Charrette the very first day at the gun range when Charlie Snow had approached, taken the lane next to his and with complete nonchalance fired off a full clip. Charlie wasn't a particularly good shot but it was the *way* he had handled the gun—without a moment's hesitation, smiling and so confident, as if he'd willed the bullets in the right direction. And he hadn't even bothered looking at the target after shooting! Charrette had never encountered a person so sure of himself.

Now he and Charlie were together, so to speak, in what Charrette felt for the first time was a guiltless relationship. It was thrilling and illicit and dangerous—everything Charrette had avoided until now.

At night, though, there were small moments when Charrette realized he might be in perilous waters; he'd think of everything being risked, and there would be some tremulousness, and then he'd think *Fuck it!* And feel good thinking it, like a warrior throwing caution to the wind. Yes. Ralph Charrette, *warrior!*

It was a serious departure, this fuck-it attitude. The very expression had a sense of the deeply forbidden. As a child, using such a word would have warranted serious punishment from his Baptist parents, and his new-found brashness would have driven his mother to tears and his father to rage. *Fuck them too*, thought Ralph Charrette, enjoying both the feeling and expletive more and more.

He cleaned and oiled the Hämmerli SP20. Maybe, when all the addicts were gone, he'd buy a Hämmerli for Charlie, so they'd have identical guns. And maybe buy matching Musto shooting jackets. The thought made him smile.

The gunmen didn't come back. Mamadou ordered pizzas, and in mid-afternoon Colin phoned Emily. She agreed to take a Lyft to the garage, pick up Danee and his mother, and take them back to Colin's apartment.

Danee made some comments on Emily driving the Porsche but was clearly glad to be taken someplace where people wouldn't be shooting at him. Save for a few heartfelt grunts, Danee's Mamma stayed quiet, though she frowned as she squeezed herself once again into the car.

When the three were gone, Mamadou said, "I have a feeling those men will be back tonight."

"We should call the police."

Mamadou smiled grimly. "I don't think so. Remember Rousseau?"

"But no one knows you had anything to do with that..."

"I don't believe in tempting fate, Colin."

"So you suggest..."

Mamadou picked up the Mossberg. "We wait."

Colin didn't like the idea. "They might not come."

"They will."

"How can you be sure?"

Mamadou unloaded the Mossberg and looked down the barrel. He sighted and pulled the trigger. The gun made a dry clicking sound. "I've known men like these all my life, Colin. They're cowards. They attack by night when they think they have an advantage. They'll come."

But they didn't. In the morning, both men were worn and gritty-eyed. Mamadou had sipped away the better part of a bottle of bad brandy and, much to Colin's amusement, complained of a thunderous headache.

Colin pulled out his iPhone, punched a few keys and said, "You're in luck. According to Google, there's an AA meeting just a few blocks from here. Starts in an hour."

Mamadou forced a wan smile, though he wasn't amused. "If they didn't come last night, it means they're planning something else."

Colin called Emily and was told she, Danee's Mamma, and Danee had spent a quiet night. Danee's Mamma was a fan of old movies, and the three had watched some until the wee hours. To the best of her knowledge, Danee's Mamma hadn't used drugs. "But I'm not exactly familiar with that stuff, Colin. She says she didn't, and Danee says he knows when she's been using and he doesn't think she has." There was a brief side discussion and Emily said, "She wants to talk with you."

Danee's Mamma's voice was scratchy. "Just wanted to tell you I didn't do anything last night. I'm pretty uncomfortable right now. Gonna have to do *something*, but it ain't gonna be in your house. And I wanna thank you for helping us, Danee mostly. He says you're a good man. I gotta go now."

Emily came back on. "I have to go to work, Colin. I'll see you tonight?"

He told her to give the apartment key to Danee. He'd be home within an hour.

Birch Carroll thought Bong Bong's drugs were excellent but had to be taken with care. Too little had no noticeable effect, too much gave him a blinding headache and a queasy feeling in his innards. But when he got it just right! Oh my! Just right was better than anything he'd ever felt with his pants on. Just right was floating an inch off the ground with the intellect of a giant and the confidence of a tiger. Bong Bong's powder made him smart, witty, possibly better-looking, and his back was pain-free.

He had gone so far as to call O'Reilley's show. He'd identified himself and been put through, and he and Bill had had a lively discussion and at the end, O'Reilly had said, live, to millions of listeners, "That was Birch Carroll, the Voice of Reason, and if you don't know who he is yet, you soon will!"

Yeah!

Still, on the way home, he found himself almost falling asleep at the wheel, and when he got home and peed, there seemed to be a pinkish hue to his urine. He tried to think back on food eaten recently and decided the blood orange at breakfast was the culprit.

He warmed a plate of mozzarella cheese sticks and marinara sauce, ate it, drank a beer, took out a legal pad, and planned the next days' shows. There were almost too many good issues to work with: the gun thing was coming back after a twenty-two-year-old unemployed truck driver had shot and killed eight people at a motel-truck stop. The Ay-rabs were still blowing each other up; that was always good for ten minutes. The Mexicans pouring over the border were worth fifteen, and the French, simply for being French, could be relied upon for five or six.

He cracked open another beer, dug out a tiny amount of drugs and snorted it. There was an instant rush followed by a slow and pleasurable descent.

A fat drop of blood fell on the legal pad. His nose? That hadn't happened since he was a kid! He wiped at it with a paper towel and after a few minutes the bleeding stopped. What was that about? He sneezed. A spray of blood stained the pad and the table. Jesus! He leaned his head back, held the paper towel to his nose. The sneeze itch went away.

He cleaned the table with a damp sponge and was surprised by the quantity of blood; the sponge was red through and through. Had to be the powder. Fucking little Chinaman! Maybe he'd do a few minutes on Asians, too.

He went to the bathroom, peed again. Definitely some red in his urine. The blood was heavier and made a streak in the center of the toilet bowl. Or maybe it wasn't blood, maybe it was the marinara sauce.

Probably it was the marinara sauce.

He was in bed by eleven, leafed through the latest issue of *The Weekly Standard,* watched an episode of *Heroes* on Netflix, and turned out the light. He dreamed of sex with the cute-in-a-chubby-way engineer.

In the morning his back was aching, but he wasn't bleeding from anywhere. He got dressed, snorted a minute amount, and copied the notes he'd written last night onto a clean sheet of paper. He stopped at Panera's for coffee and a whole wheat bagel.

He got to the station, read his emails and surfed through the conservative web sites, finding little of any interest. At eleven, he launched into his show. The first caller was a waste of time. The Voice of Reason wasn't interested in talking about the vast conspiracy involving doctors, insurance companies, and Big Pharma. Yes, it was there, but no, it didn't fit the show's soundbite format. The second caller wanted to address the POW-MIA issue. Really? Vietnam? A little dated, no? Carroll got rid of him quickly.

The third caller was just launching into an anti-immigrant speech when Carroll felt something in his gut give, as if a giant rubber band had snapped.

The cute-in-a-chubby-way millennial engineer in the control booth, her back turned, was pouring coffee from a thermos. She was eating a Danish when Carroll yelled, "FUCK!" and bent over double, clutching his stomach. She hit the dump button used to edit out a caller's inappropriate language. This emitted a beep on the output side, and the talk-show host normally would pick up the cue and explain the interruption. The engineer had never been forced to beep out the host himself.

Birch Carroll moaned, "JEEZUS FUCKING CHRIST," loud enough for his listeners to hear him very clearly. He fell out of the broadcast chair with a thump and rolled into a ball on the floor. The engineer went to commercial and within seconds the stations' phones lit up.

Birch Carroll, the Voice of Reason, was vomiting red stuff on the blue carpet. The engineer cued another ad and looped it, called 911, burst through the double doors, and lifted him so he was sitting up against a wall of the booth. Carroll threw up a mouthful of blood that stained her hands, sweatshirt and jeans. Then he lost consciousness.

The station intern's mouth was a tall O, but she went to music, then cued a series of ads. The station manager, who seldom paid much attention to Carroll's broadcasts, said, "What the fuck!" Then he saw the blood, took a step back and fainted, hitting his head on the edge of the mixing board and opening a gash that would require fifteen stitches.

By the time the ambulance arrived, Carroll was barely breathing. The engineer had punched in a repeat of a two-day-old broadcast, and both the receptionist and the intern, wedged in with too many others in the small space, were struggling to stay out of the way of the emergency people.

"What's wrong with him?" The engineer's jeans and sweatshirt were soaked where she'd tried to wash off the blood.

The EMT looked up. "Does he do drugs? Cocaine? Heroin? Does he take meth?"

She shook her head. "No. At least, I don't think so."

The emergency tech took a pulse, looked at the other EMT. "We gotta get this guy outta here, quick."

They did, leaving the station staff standing on the sidewalk. The engineer, her mouth tight, said "I'm going home. I have to change. I'm going to have to throw these jeans away. They're my favorites. Somebody's gonna reimburse me. I'll come back later. Maybe."

And so Snow and Charrette had launched *The Plan* on a very limited basis. Charrette had used his sources to locate enough scopolamine to stock a dozen or so dealers. The county routinely dealt with pharmaceutical houses for medical supplies delivered to homeless and animal shelters, rehabs, nursing stations throughout the county government properties, firehouses, and police stations. A modest shipment was delivered to the mailroom in Charrette's office building. Charrette picked it up on his way out to lunch, and passed it on to Snow.

Snow had selected a group of dealers, small fries for the main part, and had given them excellent prices on modest quantities of drugs he had doctored himself. *The Plan* had immediately demonstrated excellent results based on the limited tryouts.

He mentioned it to Charrette as they were eating steaks after time spent at the gun range.

"So maybe we need to get this thing moving big time," said Charrette. "Really moving."

"I thought we'd do another month or so of experiments. Before we fully involve my guy."

"Lobo," Charrette said with a hint of derision. He thought it was sort of a silly name for a grown-up and said so.

Snow paused for a moment, and then said, "You know what? We should get straight on this, just so there's no misunderstanding. I have a past... acquaintance with this man, with Lobo. He once threatened to have me hung from a tree by my balls." He made a face, shivered slightly, and continued. "He might have been kidding; I'm not sure he was, but the point is he could, and he'd hire someone to do it without a second thought. And then he'd come and watch, like it was an HBO Special. Are you catching my drift, Ralph? 'Cause it's very important that you do."

Charrette nodded, "I wasn't really making fun—"

"The thing is," Snow continued, "I'm lucky to be alive. Our former..." he paused again, looking for the right word, "Our former *relationship* could have ended very badly for me. Remember when I told you I had to go to the dentist? That was because of him. One of his people, big son of a bitch, slapped me around a little, just to make a point. I went there to sound Lobo out on our plan, and he listened to me, but first he had to make it obvious that he could have crushed me right then and there." Snow rubbed his jaw, as if the area was still painful. "He knows who we are. He knows who *you* are, Ralph." He let the sentence hang. Lately Charrette had been a little too cocky; it was time to let him know the stakes were getting increasingly serious.

"I get it." Charrette did, or thought he did. He'd faced some stiff opposition right here in the county, ruthless guys whom he'd carefully outwitted, like the group of Russians who had the county parks trash pick-up contract.

"Seriously," Snow insisted, "These are not people like anyone you've ever met. You got to respect them, and you can't have them believe you're even *smiling* behind their back."

"Yeah, uhhuh," said Charrette.

Charrette wasn't getting it; Snow could tell from the complacent expression on the bureaucrat's face. *Well, fuck it,* he thought. *Be an asshole.* Charrette wasn't going to survive *The Plan* anyway.

Gloria Rose Nachtalyan hoped her call to Colin about Bong Bong's demise might elicit some sort of protective instincts from the man who had been Clarence's AA sponsor. It didn't. The man thanked her for the information and suggested she call her own sponsor. She hadn't. In fact, she rarely called her sponsor at all because the woman had become sort of pushy and demanding and what did Gloria not need right now in her life? Pushy and demanding, was what.

She'd stopped attending the outpatient program at the rehab after a couple of weeks because by then she felt fine. She had no desire to drink or use drugs (well, maybe a *little* desire, but she was in control) and there weren't any people you might call interesting there. A lot of kids, from late teens to mid-twenties, and some older folks who called themselves retreads. There was one good-looking guy, but he stopped coming after the third session. And there were a few men and women, she was sure, who were simply lonely and got to talk about themselves.

This was also what she found at many AA meetings—lonely, bored people telling the same story over and over again. They drank. They ruined their lives. They got fired. Their spouses left. They hit bottom. They found AA. Things got better. They relapsed. Things got worse. They sobered up again. Halle-fucking-lujah.

She rarely spoke at meetings. What would she say? *My ex-boyfriend died in my apartment and I stuffed him in the trash chute?*

There were a couple of nice women with whom she'd gone for coffee a few times and mostly discussed the men at the meetings. Some of the women talked openly about themselves, too, where they'd been and how they'd ended up in the church basements, but Gloria was reticent. She freely admitted to drinking and doing drugs but hitting bottom? Not really, though the Clarence episode was a bottom of sorts. She was still working and making a nice chunk of money. She still had the apartment and the cats and the 1993 Lincoln, which attracted a lot of attention in the church parking lots. Truth was, Gloria simply did not feel she belonged with most of these AA folks because, when you got right down to it, a lot of them were... losers.

She'd hinted at having such thoughts to two of the women she sort of liked, and both had cackled.

"Nothing wrong with the word 'asshole'," said Jennifer, a portly woman in her late thirties. "A lot of them are, but it doesn't really matter. Take what you need and leave the rest, that's what I was told."

Added Jess, a rail-thin and veiny blond older than her age, "There are some nice ones, men, I mean, but part of the problem is that a lot of them are posturing. You know, saying what they think the group wants to hear. They just want so badly to be *part of*, to be respected. Probably because they were such fuckups in life."

"Right," said Jennifer. "Now they're *sober* fuckups!"

"Makes all the difference in the world," Jess added, and they all laughed.

Asked Jennifer, "You know how to tell when an alcoholic is lying?"

Gloria shook her head, no.

Jennifer and Jess said, in unison, "His lips are moving." AA joke.

Gloria did feel better without drugs and alcohol. True, there was a certain *sensation* she missed, or maybe it was an *emotion*. People in the meetings always talked about 'dropping the rock,' which, she thought, meant how relieved they were not to have to use anymore, but that feeling had so far eluded her. She was glad to be drug-free, but she was a little sad too. No, she was *a lot* sad.

She mentioned this to the two women who both nodded. They told her it was normal; they'd felt it too, the first year or so without. Gloria had kicked one of her best friends—cocaine—to the curb. Of course she'd miss it; cocaine and she had had a good thing going until they didn't anymore.

She was eating a salad by herself at Jason's Deli when she looked up and saw Mr. Snow and her boss, Ralph Charrette, enter the pub next door.

What the hell?

Gloria had begun eating at Jason's once a week because it was healthy and cheap, and she wanted to lose a few pounds. She tried, and mostly failed, not to eat too much potato salad and avoid the chocolate pudding, but her weakness was justifiable since she walked to the restaurant, almost a mile from her office. It was part of her exercise program for which she needed strength and calories.

Why was her idiot boss with Mr. Snow?

She returned to her office persuaded both men had been talking about her, positive she would be fired before the day's end, and terrified that somehow, her disposal of Clarence was going to come to light.

None of those things happened.

When Ralph Charrette returned, he greeted her as usual. Mr. Snow did not try to contact her. The police was not at her door when she got home.

So what was going on?

The paranoia stuck with her through the night and the better part of the morning, and she seriously thought of Bloody Marys as she was fixing her morning oatmeal. She spent the entire day in front of her computer screen looking busy but actually monitoring her boss's email. She sent Charlie Snow a bunch of meaningless figures, rehashes of numbers sent a month earlier and got a "Thank you, keep up the good work" response from him. In mid-afternoon, Charrette poked his mean little bureaucrat head into her door and said, "Gloria, I don't know what I'd do without you!" He did this once a month and was right on schedule.

The next day she kept digging, now confident whatever Mr. Snow and Charrette had met about did not involve her, but her gut told her Something Was Happening.

At three-thirty in the afternoon, as she was draining the last drop from her sixth caffeine-free Diet Coke, she noticed an invoice sent to Charrette on his private email account, which she was not supposed to access but of course had delved into for years. The man was as boring online as he was in real life. He got regular notices from Groupon, Myrtle Beach, Stauer, and Petco, even though he didn't have a pet, and was in regular correspondence with a gun nut from Waco, Texas. He also seemed to receive an above-average number of emails from women named Myrna or Suzanna or Kaylee who desperately wanted to send him their photos and were all buxom babes. And last were several ads to enhance his manhood. Two or three times a year, Gloria picked the most outlandish ad (Do You Want 10", 12" 14"!!!), filled out the online questionnaire, and gave Charrette's home number.

Charrette bought online stuff from Amazon and a few other sites, but she'd seen no earlier reference to VPD Inc., which stood for Virginia Pharmaceutical Distribution.

Hmm.

She double-clicked on the invoice.

Birch Carroll woke up in the hospital thinking he'd been in a car accident. There were tubes in his nose and he vaguely sensed something unpleasant in his penis. A catheter? Oh God! Had he injured himself *there?*

He wiggled his toes. Good. Relief surged through him. Whatever had happened hadn't left him crippled. His hands and arms seemed to work too. Even better. He could wiggle his head from left to right and up and down. He shrugged his shoulders. Everything hurt but everything moved. His dick still worried him. And his back was cramping.

There was another unpleasant sensation coursing through his body that he recognized immediately. He needed his drugs, badly. He looked around the room but couldn't find his clothes. He muttered, "Jesus Christ" and found the nurse call button next to his right hand. He pressed it, waited, and pressed it again and again.

A stout black woman in her fifties wearing a white uniform and a brown cardigan came through the door. "Back with us, I see." She said it flatly, almost, thought Carroll, with a hint of disappointment.

"What happened to me?"

She plumped his pillow without sympathy. "You overdosed. The doctor will be with you in a few minutes. She'll tell you more. She deals with a lot of junkies."

Junkie? thought Carroll. Who's a junkie?

She walked around the bed, inspected the catheter bag. There was an inch of bright yellow liquid pooled in the bottom.

"You're gonna have to drink a lot more water; it'll help clean your system out." She peered at him and smiled coldly. "I don't know what it is you took, but if I were you I'd check myself into a rehab when you get out of here. Get clean. Start going to NA meetings, maybe, or something. Another episode like that and you'll die, pure and simple."

Carroll tried to sit up, couldn't. "I'm no addict! I have to take meds for my back!"

Her smile got frostier. "Right, you're Birch Carroll, the Voice of Reason, right? You're the guy who hates everybody?" She lowered her voice. "Just so you know, I'm a black liberal, and I voted for Hillary." An afterthought, she added, "And I'm gay as hell!"

They stared at each other for five seconds, and Carroll said, "I need something for my back. My back really hurts."

She said, "That's too bad." Then she left the room.

The doctor was black too, a cheery woman in her mid-thirties with a pronounced Southern accent. She shook his hand, looked at his chart for a moment.

"Well, Mr. Carroll, you got lucky. If this had happened at home and you were alone, you'd be dead by now." She smiled as though this was good news. "I've been working here four years, and I have to tell you, I've never seen a reaction like that to drugs. But then again, considering what you ingested, I suppose that's not so surprising."

"My back," Carroll said. "I need something for my back. I was telling the nurse..."

She read from the chart. "Cocaine, some fentanyl, heroin, and scopolamine. That's a pretty interesting mix."

"A back injury from when I was in the service!"

She ignored him. "Oh, and a trace of flour, too."

"Flour?"

"Yes. Like bread and muffins? Do you bake, Mr. Carroll?" Now she was taunting him.

He pushed down on the bed with his elbows, scooted his butt back so his shoulders pressed against the pillows.

"I don't understand."

The doctor arched her eyebrows. "You ingested a very lethal dose of street drugs. A lot of people come in the ER, they've overdosed on heroin, or meth, or maybe pills. Fentanyl, too. You, it was like you raided a pharmacy." She replaced the chart in the holder at the foot of the bed.

Carroll pretended not to understand. "That nurse was really rude to me!"

The doctor was amazed. "Celia? Rude? I'm sure you're mistaken! She's one of the most caring nurses on the floor."

Carroll insisted. "She called me an addict!"

"Ah." The doctor pursed her lips. "Celia lost a brother to drugs a few months ago. She's not a big fan of junkies."

Junkies? That word again! "I'm not a junkie!"

"I'm sure you're not, Mr. Carroll." She walked to the door, turned back with a large white-toothed smile. "But I'd stay away from drugs if I were you. And flour, too."

18 A FEW DAYS AFTER THE GARAGE INCIDENT, Mamadou and Colin sat in a booth at the rear of the Korean-owned all-you-can-eat seafood buffet on Leesburg Pike. Colin had heaped his plate high with sushi and sashimi; Mamadou looked at it with distaste. "I don't know how you can eat that. Raw fish would make me ill."

"Not if it's fresh." Colin popped a strip of tuna into his mouth and chewed thoughtfully.

"And how do you know it's fresh?"

"It smells fresh."

"You trust the people in a restaurant?"

Colin nodded yes. "Why shouldn't I?"

Mamadou mock-shuddered. "In Dakar, I knew a health inspector, the brother of a fellow policeman. He would tell me about how the food was prepared, even in the best restaurants. After speaking with him, I began bringing my own meals to work."

Colin frowned. He wanted to say that there was a world between Dakar and suburban Virginia, but didn't.

Mamadou smiled, dabbed at his lips. He had loaded his plate mostly with cut fruit and vegetables, and then discovered the chocolate fountain with delight and dipped sliced strawberries, bananas, oranges, pineapple, and melon. "I know what you're thinking, Colin. That, of course, restaurants in Africa wouldn't be as clean, and 'yadda, yadda', as you say." Mamadou bit into a chocolate-covered strawberry and sighed with pleasure. "I'd bet most of our eating places are cleaner than yours. We don't use grease, we don't deep fry, and our food is mostly fresh."

Colin slid a sliver of ginger into his mouth and chewed thoughtfully. "Could be," he said.

"Positively," said Mamadou, finishing the strawberry. "And eating with wooden sticks," he pointed to Colin's chopsticks, "is really sort of primitive." Having made his point, he returned to the chocolate fountain. When he sat down again, his plate was almost full.

"So," Colin said, "I wanted to talk about what's going on. I'm a little worried."

He put his chopsticks down, wiped his mouth with a paper napkin. "What are you planning, Mamadou. I can't deal with more killing. Three years ago, it was the Zulu and his men, and Joe. Now that Haitian dealer. I have a bad feeling about this. I'm afraid you're just getting started."

Mamadou chased a wedge of peach around his plate, caught it and cut it in half. "If they leave us alone—me and Danee and Danee's mother—then that's the end of that. The Haitian killed Antwone. Now the Haitian is gone. We are even, an eye for an eye, as your scriptures say. But," he pushed the piece of peach around to gather bits of chocolate, "there is something happening with *your* people. Something is killing them. That old black singer, the man they found in the trash chute, that politician…. Aren't you curious?"

"I just don't want to be involved in any more murders." Colin lowered his voice on the last word.

"Ah, you see, this is where you and I differ, Colin. That Haitian killed Antwone, for whom I was responsible. It was my responsibility to see that this hateful person got what he deserved. And he did. In my country—"

Colin interrupted. "But you're not in your country! You're *here!* And *here*, you can't do that!"

Mamadou's smile was cruel. "But I did."

Colin closed his eyes and scratched his head. "Okay. I don't want to argue with you. I'm simply saying, please, no more violence."

"That would be wonderful," Mamadou agreed. He speared a chunk of banana. "But, as you say, just for the record, I did not instigate the violence. And I fear it's not over. The Haitian's men? I've seen them four times cruising my neighborhood. That is not a coincidence. Possibly they just want to intimidate me, but I believe they're planning something, and I do fear it will involve… violent activities."

"And how do you plan to deal with that?"

"The only way possible," Mamadou said, licking the last of the chocolate from his fork. "I will strike first. I will take the violence to them."

That night in bed with Emily, Colin said, "I don't know what to do. Mamadou's sure the bad guys are going to come after him and Danee."

She stroked his back, asked, "He's your friend?"

He stretched, nodded.

She kept stroking. "Then you have to do what you have to do."

That didn't help.

"I like the man, but I swear he scares me. The last time he and I took on a drug dealer…" And he told her the story of how Josie, his friend Catherine's daughter, had been kidnapped because the Zulu, a drug kingpin, had thought she knew something of his missing heroin shipment. She didn't; the Zulu had kept her in a cellar, feeding her crack cocaine in the hope of wresting from her knowledge she didn't have.

"It didn't end well. We got Josie out, but a friend, a man I sponsored, was shot. He died." Colin paused, remembering the night, the breaking-stick sound of gunfire, Mamadou's decision to rush from the scene and abandon Joe the Cop who, it turned out, was still barely alive and might have been saved. Or not. Colin still had nightmares.

"That's when I relapsed. It seemed the best thing to do was go to a bar and have a drink, then two, then ten. I passed out. My sponsor had to come and get me."

"Orin?" Emily had never met the man but had been told stories.

"Yeah, Orin. He'll still mention it from time to time, when he wants to prove a point."

"And the girl, Josie?"

"She's fine now."

Emily sat up, swung her legs off the bed, strode to the kitchen stark naked and returned with two Diet Cokes. Colin watched her leave and return.

"That's a terrible story," she said. "Now I'm a little scared of Mamadou, too." A few days earlier, Mamadou, DiAngela, Colin, and Emily had eaten in a Lebanese restaurant and all come out stinking of garlic. "But he is a charming man..."

"I'm afraid he's going to go out after this gang and that this time he'll be outgunned."

Emily sipped at her drink. "These are the people who've been putting out the poisoned drugs? The stuff that killed my grandfather?"

"Yeah. Pretty sure."

"Humph," said Emily. And then added, "Those are bad people. They deserve bad things to happen to them."

"So you think I should get involved?"

"No," she shook her head, reconsidered. "Well, maybe. I think you should help. There's a big difference between helping and getting involved. But I don't want you doing anything dangerous. I don't want anything to happen to you."

They were both silent for a moment. Colin got up, stepped into his jeans and stood by the window. "I never gave it much thought," he said, "taking the law into your own hands. Vigilantism. That's what it is, isn't it? But you know, your grandfather, he was a really good man, and the idea that someone would take his life, poison him like that, and nothing will happen, well, that's just wrong."

She smiled. "You're talking yourself into something. Come back to bed."

He did.

Two mornings a week, Lobo went to the Panera on Broad Street in Falls Church. One bodyguard stayed in the car, the other stood in line to order Lobo's asiago cheese bagel. There was another Panera closer to his neighborhood but it was near two county-run homeless shelters, and Lobo didn't like sharing his space with indigents. He resented their vacant glares and found their shopping carts full of plastic bags disturbing.

He only had two bagels a week because of the carbs. He'd put on a few pounds in the last few years, and overheard someone call him El Lobo *Gordo*, the *fat* wolf. The offending funnyman had not fared well, and now everyone commented on how *slim* Lobo looked.

He sat in the booth near the door, *La Opinión* spread on the table before him. Lobo didn't read much—his formal education had ended in the fourth grade—but he liked to appear well-informed, so *La Opinión* was shipped to him daily from Los Angeles.

The bodyguard returned with two bagels—one for himself—and four shots of espresso in a large take-out cup, no sugar or sweetener. He took a banana out of his jacket pocket and placed coffee, stirrer, bagel, and fruit carefully in front of his boss. Then he took a seat opposite Lobo, moving the table back slightly to accommodate his girth. Lobo shot him an annoyed look. The bodyguard shrugged, "*Perdóne, jefe,*" and moved to an adjacent booth.

An Ecuadorian busboy cleared dishes and wiped nearby tables. He owed a not insignificant sum of money to Charlie Snow, and watched Lobo and the bodyguard. He went to the men's room and scribbled some words on a napkin. He had already noted that the man he was watching always sat at the same booth, came in only twice a week, and was never without the second man who looked fat but moved economically. Later, the busboy would call Mr. Snow and relay the information, and Mr. Snow would lessen the burden of debt by a hundred dollars.

The busboy was staring. The larger man turned, hissed, *"¿Qué miras, pendejo?"*

The busboy retreated with a sickly grin. *"Nada, señor! Nada!"*

The man bared his teeth. They were big and even like rows of Chiclets gum. *"No te metas conmigo, hijo de puta!"*

Lobo frowned. He didn't like swearing, in any language. The busboy fled to the kitchen and spent the rest of his shift looking over his shoulder, long after the two men had left. The big guy looked like he might belong to Los Choneros, the Ecuadorian gang that back home in Guayaquil specialized in assassinations and drugs.

Things were developing elegantly and agreeably, thought Charlie Snow. It had taken some thought and effort, but the dominoes were nicely set. Lobo, Charrette, that woman, what was her name? Charrette's secretary? Gloria. That was it. A few more tiles at the head and tail of the line, and with an imperceptible nudge, the entire assembly would fall into place. He would fulfill a long-ago contract, make some money—maybe even a lot of money—and retire. There would be the satisfaction of a job well done and loose ends securely tied, all with a minimal investment on his part. He smiled. Is this a great country or what?

In the morning Colin dug the juicer out of the pantry. He was going to throw it into the building's dumpster when Emily came out of the bathroom wrapped in a large, white towel.

"What's that?"

He was almost out the door. "Juicer."

"Oh. What're you doing with it?"

"Throwing it out."

"Why? Does it work?"

He admitted that it did.

"That seems like a waste."

"It was a gift. I never use it."

"Lemme see." She came closer. He could smell the moisturizing soap she'd rinsed off her skin.

"Throwing away a gift is bad karma. Everybody knows that."

He sighed. "So whaddya want me to do?"

She smiled. "You could give it to me, but I don't have room in my place. It'll have to stay here."

He offered it to her, sighed. "Fine."

"Thank you, Colin! That's sweet so of you, giving me your juicer!" The way she said 'juicer' was almost pornographic. She pointed toward the kitchen. "Why don't you just put it on the counter?" Then she smiled lewdly and asked, "You got anything we could juice?"

SHOOTING VICTIM IDENTIFIED

A 36-year-old man was identified after he was shot and killed in a Manassas parking lot.

  Manassas police said Rodrigo Tomás, also known as Bong Bong, was found in the 2900 block of Wellington Road. Mr. Tomás was shot once and a police spokesperson said the murder may have been "part of a drug deal gone bad." He was pronounced dead at the scene.

Michael Wilkie

Later that morning, the phone rang as Colin was staring at the juicer. He'd rarely disliked inanimate objects, but the squat, round machine's refusal to disappear offended him. He picked up the phone, heard, "Um, hi. This is Gloria…"

Colin dropped into the sofa. The cushions sighed under his weight. "Hello, Gloria."

"Gloria Nachtalyan? The friend of Clarence, in the trash chute?"

"Yes, Gloria. I know it's you. Your name is flashing on the phone."

"It is? Um. Okay. Am I disturbing you?"

"I'm staring at a juicer."

"Excuse me?"

"There's a juicer in my kitchen and... never mind. What can I do for you?"

There was a longish pause. "I wonder, could we meet? There's some strange stuff happening. Here at my office. And other places. I was thinking, maybe we could have coffee? I get off at five, and there are a couple of places around here..."

Colin closed his eyes. "How about if I meet you on the trail, the W&OD. We can walk. I'm drinking too much coffee as is, and I need the exercise."

She thought about it for a moment, then agreed.

Colin said, "You know where the trail crosses Cedar Lane? Okay. In two hours. Bye."

He exhaled noisily, rubbed his eyes until stars appeared. The juicer stared at him.

19 "SO NOW I REMEMBER," GLORIA SAID, "Bong Bong was Clarence's dealer." She glanced sideways at Colin, seeing if he'd caught her lie. If he did, he didn't seem to care, but then he asked, "Wasn't he your dealer, too?"

Ah shit. "Well, no." She lied again and stared straight ahead at the path. "Well, maybe sometimes. But anyway, this morning, there was this tiny little piece in the *Post's* Metro section, and it said that a man called Bong Bong had been murdered, and it was probably drug related, and I thought, there can't be two people called Bong Bong dealing drugs."

"That's his real name? Bong Bong?" Colin was too curious to laugh. He repeated it. "Bong Bong?"

"I guess maybe after a while, you get used to it." She kicked at a stone and sent it skittering down the trail. "When I was in high school, there was a kid everyone called Boog. It was short for Booger."

"Jeez."

"So anyway," Gloria lied on, "I figure it was Bong Bong who sold the bad stuff to Clarence."

"That would make sense…"

"So I went on the Net and I did some research. I'm good at that; I do it a lot. Hey! Bunny!" She pointed to a small rabbit munching on grass. Then she made a face. "Did you know French people eat them? Bunnies?"

Colin did not answer that rabbit was something he'd eaten often. Instead, he said, "Really?" And tsk'd a time or two.

"So what happened is I found out my boss had ordered scopolamine through the mail and—"

Colin stopped walking. "Wait. Repeat that."

She took three more steps, stopped, walked back. "Scopolamine. And he was meeting with this sort of maybe shady man I know—"

"Gloria, start over. Go back to before you said 'scopolamine.' How'd you find this out? Your boss?"

"Well," Gloria took a deep breath and exhaled. "You're not going to tell anyone about this, right? Because, you know, I could get fired."

"Ah jeez, Gloria…"

"Ralph. Ralph Charrette. My boss. It wasn't illegal or anything. I just sort of monitored his email account."

"Your boss. His personal account."

"Yeah. Well, sort of."

Colin's phone dinged. He plucked it out of his pocket, said, "What? What? Jesus Christ!! Where are you? You're okay? Danee's okay too? I'll be right there!"

To Gloria, "Gotta go! Friend's been hurt." He started jogging back toward his car. She kept up with him. He wasn't panting but the words came in spurts. "Go home and… write it all down. Everything… Everything you… Remember. Email it to me."

She nodded and he broke into a sprint. He got to the car which for once started without hesitation. He squealed the tires in second gear and lurched toward Inova Fairfax hospital, two miles away on Gallows Road.

The nurse at the reception desk told him to go to the third floor, west wing. He got lost twice then looked down a hall and recognized the three small shapes of Dion, Dewan, and Darnell and the taller figure of DiAngela Jones.

Darnell reached him first, Dion trailing three feet behind. Dion said, "Mr. Mamadou done got shot in the leg, Mr. Colin!"

Darnell didn't bother to correct his brother.

"But he gonna be okay!"

"Yes," Darnell chimed in. "He's going to be all right. Nothing major was hit. The bullet missed the artery." Darnell had memorized what the emergency room doctor had told DiAngela.

She came to Colin and hugged him. "He's fine. They're tending to him now."

Now all three boys surrounded him. DiAngela Jones barked at them. "You all go sit over there." She pointed to a nearby waiting room. "I need to talk to Mr. Colin."

"Where's Danee?"

DiAngela pointed to her right. Colin saw the boy sitting on a plastic chair, his back ramrod straight.

He said, "Excuse me a second," went to the boy and squatted next to him. "You all right, Danee?"

The boy shook his head, no.

"You weren't hurt?"

Danee shook his head again. Then he whispered, "They was shooting at *me*. We just went to the store to buy some jeans, and we were leaving the store, and Mr. Dioh saw them coming in their stupid SUV, and he pushed me down, and I fell, and they fired out the window of the truck, and I skinned my knee, and they shot Mr. Dioh. But they was wanting to shoot me." Then he shuddered.

Colin saw a nurse hovering. She said, "The doctor gave Danee something. He was hyperventilating. I've been watching him. I wanted to put him in a bed, but he insisted on waiting for you. He'll be asleep in a minute." And as she said it, Danee closed his eyes and slumped in the chair. Colin gathered him, amazed at how little the boy weighed. The nurse said, "He'll be out for a couple of hours. There's another bed in the room where his dad will be." She gave him the room number, fifteen yards down the hall and across from the nursing station. "It's a two-patient room. Just put him in the bed closest to the window."

Colin did, took off the boy's shoes and tucked him in. Danee was frowning in his sleep but breathing evenly.

Back in the hallway, Colin noticed for the first time the two uniformed cops looking at him. They were talking to a third man, a cop, too, but in plainclothes.

"Jesus, Colin, is that you?"

"Haven't seen you since Joe's funeral. How've you been?"

Colin shook the proffered hand. "You got promoted? Not in uniform anymore?"

The cop's name was Ed Kuminsky, and Joe the Cop had sponsored him in AA. Since Colin had sponsored Joe, Colin was Kuminsky's grand-sponsor, but they hadn't been in touch since Joe's memorial service. Kuminsky was wearing a relatively sharp suit with too-thick brogans. "What're you doing here?"

"Friend got shot a couple of hours ago. Trying to find out what's going on."

"Us, too," Kuminsky motioned to the uniformed cops. "Drug thing, I'd bet."

"Not from my friend's side. He's an ex-cop. From Africa. Hates drugs."

Kuminsky looked only somewhat interested. "Africa, huh?"

Colin changed subjects. "Haven't seen you in the rooms. You still attending meetings?"

Kuminsky pursed his lips. "Not so much. You know, after Joe died... Not drinking though. Well, not much. Beer now and then, glass of wine with the old lady. I stay away from the hard stuff."

Colin thought it didn't look like it. Kuminsky's skin was the color of cooked bacon fat.

"You had, what? Three, four years?"

"Three-and-a-half," Kuminsky was looking at his brogans. "Hated every day of it. That's what I used to tell Joe, and he'd say for me to hang on, but I'll tell you what, it never got better, the cravings. So I talked to my doctor, to my old lady, they're pretty sure I'm not really alcoholic. It just got away from me from time to time."

Colin vaguely remembered that Kuminsky had once beaten up Mrs.

Kuminsky pretty badly. Joe had told him about it, how the woman had gone to the hospital but refused to talk about what had happened. Kuminsky went to three anger-management sessions led by the department's consulting shrink, and his record was expunged. He even got a diploma that he put in a Walmart frame and hung in his office.

"Your family okay?"

Kuminsky didn't answer, instead asked, "So this guy, your friend," he looked at a scribbled note, "Mamadou Dioh. He got into a shoot-out with some punks a bunch of years ago."

"Didn't know him then."

"Killed three of them. Self-defense. No charges were filed." Kuminsky peered at his notebook as if it might hold answers. "That's rare. Normally, there's always some sort of investigation when shots are fired, but with your friend, *nada*."

Colin shrugged. "I really don't know much about that. It's not the kind of stuff we talk about."

Kuminsky ignored him. "You think it might be the same people? A vengeance thing?"

Colin shrugged again, tried to edge away. "Really, Ed, you're asking the wrong guy."

"Because that's sort of weird, you know? If your friend doesn't have anything to do with drugs, how come people are shooting at him? Doesn't that seem strange to you?"

"I gotta go talk to some people over there, Ed. Good to see you; I'm glad you're well."

Kuminsky's mouth was open, and he snapped it shut. "Sure thing, Colin. I still got your number. I may call you."

Colin was already ten feet away. "Do that, Ed! We'll talk soon. Maybe hit a meeting together and have coffee after?"

If Kuminsky heard him, he didn't let on. He was still staring at the scrap of paper. He left a minute later, trailed by the two uniforms. "I'm going to get coffee. Be back in a few…"

Two of the triplets were asleep on a padded bench. The third— Colin didn't know who was who—was sitting and leafing through a tired golfing magazine. DiAngela Jones appeared to have dozed off but opened her eyes as Colin sat next to her.

She asked, "You think he's going to get into trouble?"

Colin rubbed his forehead. "Probably not. But the police will be curious. Did he ever tell you about his sister and what happened to her?"

"Some." She yawned. "Sorry. Been up a while. These three guys run me ragged."

"So you know he was involved in a shooting a few years ago, after his sister died."

"I don't know the whole story. I got the gist."

Colin touched her arm. "Go home. I'll get Mamadou to call you as soon as he comes out. Go home and get some rest."

She yawned again. "You sure?"

"Absolutely."

"Okay." She woke the two sleeping boys, got the third one to abandon the golf magazine, and kissed Colin lightly on the cheek. "You'll let me know? Soon as he's out?"

She left, trailing the three boys.

A half-hour later, an orderly followed by a doctor and a nurse, wheeled Mamadou down the hall and into his room.

"Danee?" Mamadou's eyes were frantic.

"Right there," Colin pointed to the adjacent bed where a small form lay under a blanket.

"*Merci Bon Dieu...*"

"He's fine. They gave him something to calm him, but he's okay. How do you feel?"

Before Mamadou could answer, the doctor said, "He's going to hurt for a while, but he was very lucky. I mean *very* lucky. Half-an-inch either way would have been... serious. The bullet missed both the femoral artery and his testicles." Then the doctor smiled broadly, slapped Mamadou on the arm and said, "Imagine that!" He shivered, "Brrr. Anyway, I'll check on you in a couple of hours. You'll be staying overnight, at least, maybe two nights. I want to make sure there are no infections."

Ed Kaminsky, back from his coffee break, followed them into the room, watched as the orderly and the nurse helped Mamadou into the bed. When they left, he said, "I need to speak with you alone, Mr. Dioh."

Colin made to leave but Mamadou stopped him. "Stay, please Colin." And to Kaminsky, he added, "It's perfectly okay. Colin is my brother."

Kaminsky looked at Colin, at Mamadou. "Interesting." He took out and opened his notebook and a pen, wrote the date and time at the top, and said, "I'm sorry this happened to you, Mr. Dioh, and I'm glad the wound isn't too serious. I'm told getting shot is never pleasant." He grinned like a wolf, "But then again, you've been shot at before, haven't you? You were involved in an... altercation with some gang members a few years ago."

Mamadou nodded. "That is correct. It was a home invasion that I managed to repulse."

"Quite successfully. Three gang members dead..."

"Yes, that is correct as well."

Kamisnky turned to Colin. "Were you involved in that?"

Mamadou answered. "He was not. We met for the first time at a later date."

"Can you tell me anything that might help us find the people who shot you?"

Mamadou gave it some thought, glanced at Danee's sleeping form in the next bed.

"The boy and I had gone shopping for him. I saw a large SUV, perhaps a Ford Explorer. A black man was driving with the window down. I saw the passenger lean over, then a hand appeared with a gun. I pushed the boy to the ground. There were shots, maybe three. My leg hurt. They drove away. Not fast."

"You didn't happen to see a license plate."

"I did not."

Kaminsky snapped his pad shut. "Not much there to go on."

"I'm sorry."

He nodded towards Danee. "I don't want to wake the boy now, but I'll want to talk to him. Kids see things, sometimes, that grown-ups don't notice." Kaminsky dropped the pad in a side pocket of his jacket, and then asked, "What's his relationship to you?"

Mamadou smiled. "Honorary nephew I suppose."

"You mean, like a Big Brother thing?"

"Yes, something like that."

Kaminsky nodded. "That's good. I'm active in the Boys' Club myself."

There was a silence that lengthened until Kaminsky said, "I'll be back in touch. Good to see you, Colin."

He left, and the two uniforms followed.

Mamadou said, dryly, "I'm glad the police approve of my actions."

On the next bed, Danee stirred, murmured, "Mamma?" in his sleep, and turned over.

"Did DiAngela come by?" Mamadou asked Colin, who nodded. "I called her right before calling you?"

"Before?"

Mamadou laughed. "She's prettier than you, Colin! Plus, I was concerned. I thought she and her boys would be safer here than elsewhere. Probably nothing to fear, but I didn't want to take a chance."

Colin pulled a plastic chair up next to the bed and sat. "So that's pretty much what happened? You saw them, they took a couple of shots and drove away?"

"Basically," said Mamadou, and then filled in the details.

He and Danee had gone to buy the boy some clothes. Mamadou spotted the Explorer just as he and Danee were leaving the store. "Same people who came by the garage. The SUV sped up, the passenger leaned out to take a shot, and that was that."

"You were lucky."

Mamadou touched the bandaged wound and winced. "The painkillers should start working soon, that's what the doctor told me. Anyway, for a few minutes I couldn't feel anything." He lowered his voice. "I thought they'd shot me in the balls! That would have been tragic."

"I'm sure…"

Mamadou laughed. "I've just become active again! DiAngela would be so disappointed!"

Colin smiled and put up an interrupting hand. "Please. Too much information!"

Danee stirred again. He mumbled something that ended with, "Stop that!"

Mamadou glanced at him. "I was really frightened for the boy."

"I'm afraid to ask, 'what now?'"

"Now?"

"Yes. What're you going to do?"

"Do?"

Colin shook his head. "Come on, Mamadou. Don't be dense."

"All right. Now, I'm going to let my leg heal. Then, I'm going to kill them." He said it with a toothy smile.

"Ah crap," Colin said, looking down at his feet.

Mamadou was still talking when the meds hit him. He dropped off in mid-sentence and began snoring softly. In the other bed, Danee woke up and shouted, "They're shooting at us!" Then he looked wildly around the room, spotted Mamadou and moaned, "Oh no!"

Colin stood, walked across the room and put a hand on the boy's shoulder, "It's okay, Danee. He's fine. He's resting."

Danee nodded, sighed, closed his eyes and asked, "Why's everybody shooting at us, Mamma?"

20 Danee's Mamma had returned to her own apartment, where she was plying her trade with moderate success. She had enrolled in a methadone clinic and went there every morning to get her dose and took pleasure in telling her dealer she didn't need him anymore. The methadone was nowhere near as satisfying as the real thing, but it did take care of the cravings and only cost five bucks a day as opposed to fifty for H.

She'd had a minor revelation while huddling on the floor of Mr. Dioh's garage. She was still young, barely in her thirties; she had done a piss poor job of raising a son and yet Danee was such a good boy; how had he turned out so well? Now, a handsome and well-off African man was willing to act as a father to Danee, and this was nothing but a miracle from her Baptist god.

True, the African had not spoken to her kindly while she was on the floor, but she'd never minded forceful men. Danee's father had been a forceful man until he vanished with all her coffee can money and was later arrested and jailed for a variety of meaningless crimes. Danee's Mamma was certain the African man would never do that.

And he had a Mercedes. The frantic drive in Colin Marsh's broken down sports car had terrified her, but she'd found the Mercedes a very pleasant ride. She could get used to that.

She wondered if the African man might prefer a thinner woman; that was doable. Tavana, who lived two floors up, had a DVD player and a stack of exercise DVDs. Maybe they could work out together. Meanwhile, Danee was the best link possible. He was now living with the African man. She missed him, he was her son, but it was for the best. He was safe, and if the African kept him, there might even be a future there. Maybe it was time for Danee's Mamma to visit her son, because a good boy like Danee should have an attentive mother. Everybody knew that.

Danee woke up fuzzy-headed and still confused. It took him a full fifteen seconds to understand where he was and why, and when he saw Mamadou sleeping in the other bed and Colin dozing in a plastic chair, his heart stopped.

He got up, shook Mamadou's shoulder. "Hey! Hey! You ain't dead, are you? C'mon, wake up! This is important! People are—"

Mamadou opened unfocused eyes. "*Quoi? Quoi?*"

Danee shook him again. "Kwa nothin'! Wake up! WAKE UP!!"

Mamadou tried to sit up. The pain coursed down his leg like molten glass. "Danee? Okay, okay. You're all right?"

Colin's eyes opened. He stood. "I need some coffee." He left the room.

Danee barely glanced at the white man, fully focused on Mamadou. He said, "Yeah. I gotta call my Mamma. What're we doing here? What's wrong with you? Oh. Jeez. You got shot, didn't you? Where? Can you walk? We have to go home. I have to call my Mamma!"

Mamadou grabbed the boy's arm, not a simple thing with the IV lines dangling down. "Shhh. It's okay, we're both fine. Well, almost fine. I got shot in the leg, right here," he pointed through the sheet.

Danee's eyes went even wider. "Ohmygod, you got shot in the *balls*? Did it hurt? Ohmygod stupid question, course it hurts and—"

Mamadou squeezed Danee's arm harder. "Shhh. Listen, not, not in the balls," he looked around to see if anyone else might have heard him. "Near the balls. It's okay, we'll go home tomorrow. Get my cell phone," he pointed to a plastic hospital bag where the nurse had put his phone, wallet, and some spare change. "Get it and call your mom. Don't scare her, just tell her we're fine and we'll talk to her tomorrow and explain everything."

Danee nodded, took the cell phone and punched in the numbers. When his mom answered he shouted, "Mamma! We been shot! I mean, Mr. Mamadou been shot! He's okay, but he got shot almost in the balls! I'm okay too, I didn't get shot anywhere so I'm fine. Yeah. The hospital. I don't know which hospital, wait," he looked at Mamadou's plastic bag. "Inova Fairfax. Yeah. Well, I don't know. Mamma? No, don't do that. We'll call you later, okay. We're both fine. Okay. Okay. No, Mamma, really, we're fine, I promise. Mamma?"

He looked at the phone reproachfully, as if it were an errant pet. To Mamadou, he said, "She says she's coming…"

Mamadou closed his eyes.

Danee's Mamma arrived at the hospital at exactly the same time as DiAngela and her triplets. They all rode the elevator to the third floor, unaware they were visiting the same patient until they stood in the doorway of Mamadou's room. Danee's Mamma asked, "Who're you?"

DiAngela Jones smiled, "A friend." Then, sweetly, "Are you Danee's mother?"

Danee's Mamma didn't have time to answer. Danee rushed out of the room and hugged her. "Mamma!" And then, "Hi, Miz Jones!"

Danee's Mamma looked at her son, "You know this lady?"

"Well sure, that Mr. Dioh's girlfriend!"

Danee's Mamma took the news with aplomb though she squinched her eyes a bit.

With everyone in Mamadou's room—Colin, Danee and his mother, DiAngela Jones and the triplets—things got both crowded and noisy. Mamadou asked Danee to take the boys to the cafeteria for ice cream. Then he said, "I'm sorry for this… confusion. Danee's fine. I'll be fine in a few days."

"But you got shot!" It had taken Danee's Mamma almost two hours to get to the hospital and she wanted answers. "Danee said you almost got shot in the balls!" She pronounced it *bahwls*.

DiAngela Jones eyes went very wide. She said, "WHAT??" She looked at Mamadou whose gaze focused on a ceiling tile.

"Is that true? Is that where you got shot?"

"Almost," Danee's Mamma said it again, as if the word felt good in her mouth.

"No." Both women were staring at him. "In the leg. I got shot in the leg."

"But near the balls," Danee's Mamma added, as if she'd been in the emergency room.

DiAngela's voice rose. "Will you *please* stop saying that?"

"Yes," Mamadou agreed. "Please."

"Just statin' facts. Man almost lost his gentles."

There was an extended silence. Both women were trying and failing not to look at the junction of Mamadou's legs under the cover.

"I'm grateful for your concern. I'm fine..."

Danee's Mamma nodded. "Well, sure." She stood, straightened the skirt that was just a bit too tight. "You still want Danee to stay with you?"

"Absolutely. This doesn't change anything. He's a wonderful boy."

She said, "Good. That's good. He likes bein' with you. He told me." She stuck out her hand, and DiAngela Jones shook it. "A pleasure to meet you," said Danee's Mamma.

"Yes. Likewise."

After the woman left, DiAngela said, "I do believe she might have had some designs on you."

"Humph."

"Well, she certainly was interested in your..."

He cut her off. "Humph."

21   Birch Carroll got his cell phone from the nurse by telling her he needed to call his aging mother who, he did not add, had died twelve years before. As soon as the nurse left his room, he punched in Leonard Baskey's number. Baskey answered on the second ring.

"Leonard? Birch Carroll here. I need your help."

Leonard respected Birch Carroll as a motivated voice for the right at a time when the leftist media's rants were altering the mindset of the country. Baskey thought if there were more Americans like Carroll, the country would be a better place. The problem was, Baskey the Pharmacist had suddenly become Baskey the Potential Terrorist, and the Department of Homeland Security now had him on its radar, all because he had disseminated a couple of stupid email messages suggesting a left wing politician might be better off dead.

The attention touched his pride. Homeland Security was the big leagues, even though he hadn't even initiated the kill-the-politician joke—a bad joke only a paranoid Federal bureaucrat would see as threatening—but merely received it and passed it on. That was what they got him for, passing it on, like he'd *passed on* plastic explosives or TNT or an AK to a nut-job.

As a precaution, Baskey had rid himself of every controlled substance in his home, garage, back and front yards, automobile, girlfriend's house, and parents' home. He had nothing save a small amount of powder given to him a day before by one of his contacts, an ex-cop with access to the Fairfax police evidence room. It had been an unexpected freebie from a fellow patriot, proof once again that good people stuck together.

Baskey went to the hospital with the powder in a baggie nestled in his BVDs beneath his scrotal sack. He'd learned from the Internet that most cops wouldn't touch him there; it was a guy thing.

He found Birch Carroll's room on the second floor of Manassas Hospital Center looking none the worse for wear. Carroll was truly happy to see Baskey, which made Baskey happy too, since he was a people-pleaser and he liked being liked by important men such as the Voice of Reason.

"You got something?" Carroll couldn't keep the excitement from his voice. "Because I got to tell you, my back is killing me and these people here," he waved his chin in the general direction of the nursing station, "these people don't give a rat's ass about a patient's discomfort. Plus, the nurses and doctors are a bunch of liberal bigots."

Baskey nodded, "Yes, I've noticed that in the past, how people in the medical professions are lefties. Anyway," he turned around so Carroll couldn't see him retrieve the baggy, "This should help you out."

Carroll glanced at the door, then held the baggy up to the light. "This sorta of looks like the stuff that put me here."

Baskey said, "Oh no, this is safe. I got it from a very trusted source that I've been dealing with for years."

They talked for a bit and Baskey said he'd be happy to pick up Carroll when Carroll was released. Carroll thanked him effusively for everything and, as soon as Baskey left, snorted a tiny amount of the powder. He was about to give it a second go when half of the radio station staff arrived with Mylar balloons and a bouquet of flowers from Trader Joe's.

There was more talking, and the cute-but-chubby engineer kissed him on the lips and whispered, "Get well soon," as if she might have something in mind. After about fifteen minutes, Carroll faked a yawn and closed his eyes and someone said, "You're exhausted, we'd better go," and he nodded like someone who really was tired, and they left too.

Carroll checked that the room's door was closed and took the baggy from beneath his pillow. He dipped his index finger into the bag, brought a small mound of powder to his nose, and snorted once in each nostril. The effect was immediate. He felt as if his heart had been slammed by a sledge hammer wielded by a giant. He gasped and tried to catch his breath but couldn't. He peed on himself as his right hand flailed to find the nurse call button. He hit it repeatedly and within seconds a nurse arrived. The heart monitor squealed, showing rapidly diminishing peaks and valleys. The nurse saw that Carroll's eyes were almost popping out of their sockets even as his body jerked and twitched and convulsed. He foamed at the mouth and his nose was running with blood. His chest heaved once, twice, three times, as if a large hand inside was trying to push out. His throat made strange hacking sounds, and then it all stopped. By the time the guys with the paddles came, it was too late.

They spent fifteen minutes trying to revive him, and though his sympathetic nervous system responded to the electric shock by arching his body on the bed, Carroll was gone.

The autopsy would show that his heart had virtually exploded in his chest due to a fatal dose of heroin, cocaine, flour, and scopolamine. Since this was the same concoction that had brought him to the hospital in the first place, a brief investigation would follow focusing on the radio station staff that had visited. Had one of them slipped Carroll the drugs? They all denied it, noting Carroll looked good, if tired, when they came by.

No one had seen Leonard Baskey, though one nurse vaguely remembered someone going into Carroll's room and staying there a few minutes. No charges were ever filed. Carroll, the final report said, had either been given drugs by a visitor or brought drugs in with him—addicts were known to sew secret pockets in their garments where they could hide contraband. This was not far from the truth.

Michael Wilkie, the reporter at the *Post*, called early. "Hey, you still interested in strange drug deaths?"

Emily stirred next to him. Colin looked at the clock. Six a.m. "I might be if it weren't so early. Hang on, lemme go to the kitchen and start come coffee."

A minute later, in the living room, he asked, "So who died?"

"Guy called Birch Carroll. Familiar name?"

"Nope. Should it be?"

"That's because you're not a right wing asshole. Carroll is, or was, one of those Rush Limbaugh types, called himself the Voice of Reason. He had a show that was moderately successful in the Delmarva area."

"Never heard of him."

The microwave dinged. Colin took out the mug of water, dumped in a teaspoon of Bustelo instant coffee, added sugar and stirred.

"Died yesterday at Manassas Medical Center. No cause publicly given, but a friend who's a night nurse said it was definitely drugs. In fact, Carroll had been admitted earlier on some sort of an overdose. It involved—get this—flour."

"Flour? As in bread and rolls flour?"

"Yeah. They pumped his stomach, got him stabilized, but as soon as he was alone he took a big hit of the same stuff—probably brought it in with him—and croaked."

"Flour, huh?" Sometimes dealers cut their stuff with flour, but it wasn't the best of adulterants since it tended to clot. Sucrose, starch, or powdered milk were better.

"Sort of interesting. Hang on." Colin heard the snick of Wilkie's lighter and an inhale. "His obit will be in tomorrow's paper. But listen, what I really called you about, have you ever heard of Erowid?"

"No. What's that, some new designer drug?"

"It's a website run by a couple of unusual people who call themselves Earth and Fire…"

"Oh boy."

"Listen," Wilkie said. "They've been building this site since the nineties. They want to classify *all* the street drugs people take and their database is huge. Even the feds use it, so I thought, if there's some weird stuff out there, maybe they know about it."

Colin swallowed a large mouthful of coffee and winced. Too hot. "So you're going to look into it?"

"Oh hell no," said Wilkie. "I'm just doing you a favor. Maybe you should see what's there. Oh, and there was a story about them in *New Yorker* about a year ago."

"*New Yorker?*"

"They have an archive and you could look into it. It's free."

"Yeah. I know."

"Right," Wilkie exhaled loudly. "You're a researcher! I almost forgot." He hung up without sounding apologetic.

Emily was still sleeping. Colin fired up the computer, punched in Erowid.com, changed it to .org.

The website was basic. He navigated through several pages, found one for heroin, went to that. Saw *Heroin cut with scopolamine* and read a Center for Disease Control report on a rash of scopolamine- and heroin-related emergency room visits in New York. He checked the date of the report. June 1996. Humph. Then in 2002, another report headlined, *Unknown Heroin Contaminant Causes Leukoencephalopathy.*

He looked the word up found that leukoencephalopathy had something to do with degeneration of the brain's white matter, and the myelin sheath that insulates nerve cells.

When he went to the search box and typed in 'Heroin additives,' the site told him there were twenty-three pages of results with 672 entries.

Emily woke up, kissed him on the cheek, took two bites from a day-old Danish, showered, dressed, and left.

He spent the better part of two hours clicking through the information, amazed at the wealth of material there. Much of it focused on the safety or danger of using certain drugs, and he wondered how well known the site really was. He liked to think he was better informed than the average citizen about drugs, yet he'd never heard of Erowid.

In the afternoon, he drove to Mamadou's apartment. The African greeted him at the door, hobbling on two crutches.

In the not-too-distant past, there'd been a sliver view of the Potomac, but developers had put in another high-rise luxury condo, and now the river's only presence was a persistent waterway smell, not always unpleasant. "I don't mind," Mamadou had told him. "It reminds me of Dakar."

Mamadou sat with difficulty, splayed crutches resting on the couch. "The doctors say there'll be no permanent damage. I should be able to get rid of these things in a week." He nodded towards the crutches.

Colin smiled. "Well, there's a couple of women who'll be happy to hear that."

"God. I couldn't believe it when Danee's mother arrived! When did women start talking that way?"

"You mean talking about your balls?"

"Not you, too. Please." Mamadou looked genuinely disconcerted. He shifted slightly trying for more comfort. "You know it wasn't me those people were after, it was Danee."

"I figured. His friendship with Antwone."

For a moment, Mamadou's face fell. He struggled for composure.

"Mostly, Danee told me, he and Antwone talked sports and cars, not drugs." He paused and his eyes teared. "Antwone complained that I wouldn't let him drive." He looked at Colin, his voice a sad question mark. "But I couldn't let him. He didn't have a license, no insurance…" He trailed off, then pointed to a large television set in a corner of the living room. "Danee found Antwone's things in a closet. I was going to give them away, but…" He shrugged. "He set up the Xbox and plays the games. He likes the same ones, where he gets to race expensive cars and crash them. Antwone liked doing that too. It's strange."

"Must be painful."

"Like getting shot," Mamadou said and grimaced. Colin smiled and nodded. "Yeah."

The door flew open and Danee blew in like a small uniformed tornado.

"I gotta go to the libary. Hi Mr. Marsh! Can you drive me? Mamadou can't cause he got shot," he paused, "in the leg. But I think

I know, I'm pretty sure, anyway, and if we go to the library I can find out for sure."

Mamadou put one cop hand up as if stopping traffic. "Danee! Stop. Start over, slowly."

Danee took a breath, nodded once. "Okay. I've been thinking about this since you was shot, and there was this book we both liked, me and Antwone, with cars, really expensive ones, like Ferraris and Lancias and Bizzarrinis and—"

"Porsches," Colin threw in.

Danee frowned, "Yeah. But not like yours."

Mamadou bit back a laugh. Colin didn't laugh, but he did smile.

"So the last time I saw Antwone," Danee continued unfettered, "he told me, 'D, whatever you want to know, it's in the book.' And it's been bothering me, what he said, and today at school there's this kid whose dad has a Ferrari, one of the cheap ones, a Dino but not a good Dino, more like a Fiat that look like toys, and he dropped the kid off, and then all of a sudden it came to me!"

Danee looked triumphantly from Mamadou to Colin and back.

Mamadou nodded and asked, "What came to you?"

Danee's eyes were bright, "See, it's just like in shows, where they leave clues where you can't find them, and that's what Antwone did, I bet. He left me a clue."

"A clue to what?"

Danee opened his mouth as if to say, "Are you the dumbest man on Earth?" But didn't. Instead, he said slowly and with great patience, "A clue why people are chasing us around and shooting at me, cause I know they wasn't shooting at Mr. Dioh, they was shootin' at me cause they think I know something, but I don't. They think maybe Antwone told me something', but he di'n't, cause Antwone, he was sort of embarrassed about working with that Rousseau man, and he knew I didn't, you know, *approve*." He took a breath. "If we go to the libary—"

"LiBRAry," Colin and Mamadou said in unison.

"LiBRAry! Jeez. Okay, liBRAry then I can look in the book and see if there's a clue."

Colin looked doubtful. "This isn't a game, Danee, or a television show."

"Well no shit—I'm sorry, I meant, yes sir, I know it ain't no game. People don't shoot no real bullets in no game or chase you around in cars a lot better than the one you're in."

Colin looked at the floor, then at Mamadou. "Sounds a little unlikely. Colonel Mustard leaves a sign."

Both Mamadou and Danee looked at him blankly.

"Never mind."

Mamadou peered at the boy. "You're sure of this, Danee?"

Danee folded his arms across his chest. "Yessir. I'm sure."

Mamadou looked at Colin, who shrugged in turn. "I can take him, I guess."

Danee said, "Can we go in Mr. Dioh's car? Just in case?"

So they did, Colin secretly admiring the Mercedes' ease of handling while verbally abusing it.

"Mushy response," he said to Danee while wiggling the steering wheel.

"But a nice soft ride," Danee responded.

"I guess. If you like that sort of thing. It's kind of an old-lady car. But don't tell Mamadou I said that."

Danee made a face, "Your car, my butt's three inches off the ground, and I can feel every little bump in the road. No offense, Mr. Marsh. This is a whole lot better. Smells good, too, not musty like… Turn left here," he pointed. "There's some parking spaces behind the building."

The library was clean, well lit, and sparsely populated. Danee waved at a portly lady behind a desk and she smiled back, gave Colin a cursory look, and returned to the stack of books she was checking in.

"That's Missus Greene. She's worked here forever. She's real nice. She cried when she found out about Antwone and gave me a lecture on drugs." He turned a corner into a row of shelves. "Like I needed it."

He stopped, inspected a shelf. "Ah crap. Sorry. I mean darn. It should be right here," he pointed. "But I don't see it."

"What?"

"The book I'm looking for. On cars, that Antwone and I always looked at. Really cool expensive ones. I wonder if someone checked it out?"

They both scanned the shelves, checked the other aisles as well. Danee said, "I'll go ask Missus Greene if someone took it." He was back a minute later shaking his head. "Nope."

They spent another five minutes looking. Danee said, "Maybe somebody stole it."

Colin asked, "Antwone was taller than you, right?"

Danee nodded. "Some. Not a lot."

Colin roamed the stacks until he found a rolling footstool used by librarians to reshelf books. He climbed on it, ran a hand on top of the shelf that had the car books and earned an arm full of dust. He moved the footstool down the aisle, did it again. The fourth time, his arm hit something. He reached and retrieved a thin volume. "This it? *Million-Dollar Classics*?"

Danee took it from him. "Yo! That's it!" He stared at the cover, then fanned through the pages and stopped in the middle. "Motherf--! I was right! I knew it! I *knew* it!"

He pulled a sheet of paper torn from a spiral notebook and folded in half, then opened it. "Yeah. It's from Antwone."

He glanced at it, shoved the page into a back pocket of his jean. "Let's get out of here, go back to the apartment."

In the car, he pulled the sheet out and held it up. He whispered, "Shit," and shot a quick glance in Colin's direction. Colin pretended not to notice there were tears in the boy's eyes. Danee began reading aloud.

"D, man, I hope you're not reading this cause if you are it means I'm in trouble. I can't talk to The African cause then he'd know I've been working for the Rousseau man, and he'd be real disappointed. So if you're reading this, and I'm not around, here's a couple of things

*you should know and you can talk to The African and explain I wasn't doing nothing wrong but I needed money for stuff. Anyway, it's this guy Rousseau who's been putting stuff in drugs and it's making people sick and killing them sometimes. He's doing it with the help of a couple of white men and some big drug dude. And I found out about it, Rousseau told me, he likes to boast about how important he is. There's someone call Lobo, or something like that, and they plan to kill like a whole bunch of people, and I think they've already started cause I know some people is dead already. Anyway, if you're reading this, and I hope you aren't, you got to go and talk to The African and tell him what's going on, cause I can't. Tell him Rousseau's a mean mother**cker and he got an associate called Meat and he should be careful of him too, cause he's a mean mother**cker too and pretty smart, I noticed that. Your friend, Antwone.*

Back at the apartment, Colin thought Mamadou's skin had turned grey. "That's Antwone's writing." He held the piece of paper between the thumb and forefinger of his left hand, away from his body.

"It was in the book, just like I thought!" Danee tried and failed to keep the excitement out of his voice. "Just like I said," he nodded.

Colin asked, "When do you think Antwone wrote this?"

Danee shrugged. "Don't know for sure. Last time I saw him was a while back. Maybe two or three weeks before he, well, you know…"

"Before he died?" Mamadou reread the note.

Danee nodded. "I guess."

Mamadou let the sheet of paper float to the floor, held his head in his hands. "If he'd talked to me, we could have gotten him out of trouble. He'd be alive."

The three, two men and a boy, were silent for a long while, then Mamadou looked at Colin. "At least Rousseau… got what he deserved."

Colin nodded. "He did."

Danee opened his mouth to say something, then didn't.

"Did Antwone mention this other man, Meat?"

Danee sank to the floor and sat cross-legged. "No. I would've remembered. What kind of a man has a name like Meat? Gotta be either real big or real mean; probably both."

Mamadou looked at Colin. "I wonder if this Meat person has taken over Rousseau's people."

Colin frowned. "Emily was right, the addicts are the target. I thought maybe it was all coincidence. New drugs, more potent street stuff. New dealers. I don't think I allowed myself to think it really might be deliberate."

Danee opened his eyes wide. "Man. I wouldn't want to run into a man called Meat."

Mamadou said, "I'm going to try to."

Danee pondered the name. "I guess they couldn't call him Burger, or Pepperoni. That's not really scary. But Meat..." He shuddered.

Mamadou stood with difficulty, maneuvered his crutches, and straightened the creases on his trousers as best he could. "Danee, you did well. Thank you. Now go do your homework. You can play Xbox afterwards. Colin and I have to talk."

Danee frowned. "I can talk with you! I know stuff!"

Mamadou repeated, "Homework." Then added, "You and I will talk later. Don't leave the apartment. DiAngela and her kids will be here in an hour. Let them in if I'm not back."

Danee stood, picked up the backpack he'd dropped by the front door and placed it on the kitchen counter. He opened it, pulled out several books, muttered, "Homework. Yeah. Like that's gonna solve everything."

Meat was smarter than his name implied. He was a large, balding man whose entire life had been lived outside the law, and he liked to joke that his mother's husband was *not* his natural Daddy. Few people got the joke, so he tried to explain it. "See, my momma was screwin' some other guy; she was committing 'dultery, which is a crime. So from the very start, I was a *illegal* Nigrah."

Most listeners still didn't get it, and for those who did, it wasn't particularly funny, but they laughed anyway. Meat had that effect on people.

Smart as he was, Meat had figured out almost immediately who'd killed Rousseau. It wasn't the Filipino guy, Ping Pong or Dong Dong, or Hong Kong, who ended up being collateral damage. And it wasn't a woman, as had been rumored.

No.

It was that kid Rousseau had taken a shine to, Antwone. Well, not exactly Antwone, but most likely that African dude Antwone spoke about all the time, the man who'd taken Antwone in.

Antwone ran errands, washed cars, had a lip and big ears. Rousseau was much into impressing people, and he'd really liked the kid, talked to him like it was his little brother and boasted about how he was going to clean up the neighborhood, har har. Antwone repeated what he'd been told to a friend because that's what kids did.

Rousseau had said way too much, and Meat told him so. Meat suspected Rousseau's inability to maintain a discreet silence regarding certain actions had something to do with the Haitian's hurried departure from Florida.

At any rate, Rousseau, realizing his error and not being the sentimental type, had decided the Antwone kid had to go. Had to be, as Meat had once read in a spy novel, *terminated with utter prejudice.*

That should have been it. Kids OD'd all the time, but there was this African man, and who the fuck knew what an African guy would do. They were into weird stuff, old-timey retribution like in the Bible. Meat was certain the African dude had sought vengeance and terminated Rousseau with utter prejudice, too. That had left a vacuum in the organization. Organizations detest a vacuum, so Meat filled it.

He took over by beating the crap out of one guy, buying the allegiances of two more, and making a third disappear, not at all as complex as it might seem. The Washington area had hundreds upon hundreds of acres of parks, woods and, recently, coyotes feeding on squirrels and rats.

Meat now ruled, and he did so with an iron fist-velvet glove philosophy. What he wanted above all was for Rousseau's group—it had no name though he had toyed with The Meat Grinder—to sink into obscurity as far as the law was concerned.

One of his first moves was to impose some rules on the rented house in Mt. Pleasant that his people used as a base. There was to be no dealing of *anything* within four square blocks of the house. Nor would there be public drunkenness, using of controlled substances, loud music, or any other obstreperous behavior that might bring on unwanted attention. No women. People would not carry weapons in the house; they would check them at the door in a large wooden box brought in for that very purpose. They would be polite with the neighbors and maintain the small front yard. No littering, no women, no drugs. "No fuckin nothin," said one relatively new member.

"That's right."

"Seeyit," said the new man, though not very loudly. He had tried, and failed, to stare Meat down, and there the confrontation had ended.

There was much to do and large amounts of money to be made unobtrusively, and unobtrusive money beat noisy money every time. People with noisy money attracted attention. They bought Caddies and Range Rovers and five-hundred-dollar shoes and *wanted* to be noticed. Meat favored footwear from Payless and two- or three-year old Ford Explorers. His only automotive conceit was expensive mag wheels, which he got from a Glen Burnie chop shop in the Maryland suburbs. And he liked watches. Meat wore a well-made Rolex Yacht-Master replica he had paid $200 for from the Perfect Watches online store.

Meat had never agreed with Rousseau. He thought killing off addicts was ridiculous, like destroying your customer base, but Rousseau countered by saying that in the long run, there would be even more users and they'd be willing to pay more. Meat wanted to say, *Bullshit!* but didn't.

He glanced at the almost-as-good-as-a-real-one Rolex. It was time to attend to details.

Lobo sat at his favorite booth in the Panera near Columbia Pike and buttered his asiago bagel. This was bagel number two, the last one of the week, and he arranged it on his plate and stared at it for a moment. His four shots of espresso steamed in a ceramic cup. Lobo liked to build the small anticipation. At the next over booth, his bodyguard chewed contentedly on his own bagel. Lobo noticed that the bodyguard's jacket was fully buttoned up, making access to his sidearm difficult, and at that exact moment, Charlie Snow pulled out his silenced Glock 26, a honey of a small compact handgun designed for concealed carry. Charlie Snow shot the bodyguard twice in the forehead, the gun making a tiny popping sound. When Lobo turned, Charlie smiled at him, said, "Hi, Lobo! Great morning, isn't it?" Then he pulled the trigger again twice, and Lobo expired without a sound but with a mouthful of bagel.

Charlie slid out the restaurant's side door, bumping shoulders with a young black man. He apologized but kept moving, climbed into the waiting Toyota stolen from a parking lot earlier that morning. He nodded at Ralph Charrette, who was behind the car's steering wheel and wearing a ridiculous black watch cap low over his forehead. Charlie got in and said, "Drive."

Ralph pulled out carefully, no squealing tires. He made a full stop at the sign, looked both ways and accelerated steadily until they were doing three miles above the speed limit. Five minutes later, Charlie told Ralph to stop the car and pull to the curb. He took the Glock from his pocket and shot Ralph twice in the right temple. There was hardly any blood, just a couple of very small holes that showed red. Ralph didn't even slump. He was sitting straight up, one hand in his own lap and the second on the steering wheel. He looked surprised but not displeased.

Charlie made sure the car was parked legally. He wiped the inside and outside door handles with Armor All. He stuck the Glock in his waistband. Lastly, he used the Armor All wipe to take five small baggies of drugs from his own pocket, and dropped them into a side pocket of Charrette's jacket. He gave the car a last look and walked fifty yards, then turned off onto a trail that meandered through a patch of woods. A day earlier in this same place he had spotted a tall maple that had recently fallen. He dropped the Glock beneath the tree's upended roots and kicked dead leaves into the hole. He returned to the street and glanced inside the Toyota. Ralph was still there, staring straight ahead.

Charlie walked to a nearby Burger King, nodded at the kid behind the counter, and went into the men's room. He washed his hands thoroughly, took off his jacket and stripped off his white tee-shirt to reveal a second tee-shirt beneath it. He balled shirt number one and dropped it into the waste bin, burying it beneath the damp paper towels earlier customers had used to dry their hands.

He checked his face and hair closely in the men's room mirror. Sometimes blood sprayed out, but not this time. He decided he did not look like a man who had just earned a great deal of money to eliminating another man. He ordered French fries and a small drink and sat by the window. He stayed there fifteen minutes. He didn't see a single police car.

The young black man's name was Tee, and he hardly noticed the white guy who bumped into him. He entered the Panera, got his bearings and spotted the two men he'd been assigned to kill. He had a cheap made-in-China CZ replica in the front pocket of his hoodie and he fingered it nervously. This was much more demanding than taking down the Asian dealer; there were witnesses, a lot of people eating and drinking and talking. He spotted his quarry, stopped, squinted. Something was wrong. Both were... dead?

The first scream cut through the noise and was followed half-a-second later by the crash of a dropped tray full of coffee cups. Then there was a second scream and a third, and the young man turned and ran out the door. He kept running—he was in wonderful shape—until he saw a Starbucks. He stopped and took a deep breath to compose himself. He sat at an outdoor table away from other customers. He made the sign of the cross, something he hadn't done in years, then he speed-dialed a number. After a moment he said, "Meat? Zat you? Aw, man, you ain't gonna believe what happened."

Meat didn't care what had occurred. He was pleased at his young man's actions. The kid has scoped the situation out quickly and reacted correctly. As to Lobo's death and that of the man's bodyguard, shit happened. The drug world was in a constant state of violent flux, though the mayhem rarely happened at the Lobo level in a franchise restaurant. Mostly it was soldiers and low-level dealers who felt the brunt of the savagery. And the users, of course, all those people who passed away, most times quietly, with needles in their arms.

This, Meat knew, had been a well-planned assassination by someone who had studied and knew Lobo's movements and been willing to take chances. The fact that Meat's young man had been tasked to do the same thing at the same time was almost humorous, but then again, shit happens.

In the morning Meat gathered the *Washington Post* from his house's front stoop and turned to the Metro section. He spotted the story of the two murders on B1, and read it quickly. There was little new information. A smaller piece reported the killing of a Fairfax County bureaucrat discovered sitting upright in a rental car. Meat though, *hmm*, then turned to the comics.

Meat was the only member of his group to read the paper, save for Dollar Bill, an obsessive follower of the stock market and subscriber to the *Wall Street Journal*. Dollar Bill actually made a little money playing the market but lived off his earnings as a level-two distributor, one rung below Meat and two rungs above the average street dealer. Dollar Bill was also an excellent trigger man, smart, cool, never known to panic even in the worst of situations. He was methodical and unemotional. It was he who had watched Antwone die. Dollar Bill could be counted upon to take care of business, and business now called for the quick and efficient removal of the bothersome African, the other kid who was Antwone's friend, and whoever else unfortunately happened to be in the way.

In Colin's bed, Emily rolled over and punched on the news. She was interested in the weather, that would dictate what she'd be wearing, but she caught the tail end of the local news, something about the murder of a local drug lord and his bodyguard. She elbowed Colin awake and froze the television image with the remote, then backed it up. The newscaster, a blonde with flawless hair and perfect teeth was saying, "…Geovany Sandino, known locally as Lobo. According to police there were more than twenty-five customers in the restaurant when the incident occurred, no one took notice of the shooting though one person claimed to have heard 'a sound like a beer can popped open.' Police told us this may have been the sound of a silenced handgun being fired. Back to you, Brian!"

Colin sighed and made a grab for Emily but she evaded him.

"Sandino," she said. "That's one of the names you ran across, Colin."

Colin rubbed his eyes. "It is?"

She made an annoyed sound in her throat. "Yes. Call your friend at the paper. Ask him if there's anything more."

Colin glanced at the bedside clock. "He won't be there."

"Call him at home."

"Emily, please." He tried to reach for her again but she fended him off. "Nope. Call him. Find out what he knows." She smiled and got up. "I have to go home before work."

He raised an eyebrow.

"I'm not going to show up at the office in yesterday's outfit, Colin." She slipped into her clothes. "Dinner tonight?"

He got out of bed, hugged her and felt himself stiffen.

She laughed and pulled away. "None of that. Call your friend."

He did an hour later and woke Michael Wilkie up.

"Jesus Christ, Colin. We aren't that good friends that you can call this early."

"It's 9:30."

"It's 9:30 at night or 9:30 in the morning?"

"Morning. 9:30 in the morning."

Colin heard the snick of Wilkie's lighter and a sharp inhale.

Wilkie exhaled, "What can I do for you, Colin?"

"Those murders at the Falls Church restaurant yesterday. What do you know that wasn't printed?"

Wilkie was silent for a moment, then said, "Well, there was one person who saw something. A woman was waiting for a fresh urn of coffee, and she told police that she saw one man hurry out, a white guy, and bump into a black kid. Then the black kid looked into the restaurant, she said; she thinks maybe he saw the people who'd been shot, and he turned and ran out."

Colin sipped at his coffee. "Okay. Not much there."

"There's more. A mom with a couple of kids in tow saw a bald man get into the passenger seat of a Toyota, then the car drove away. She knew it was a Toyota because she and her husband have the same one, different color."

"There are what, 10,000 Toyotas in the area?"

"I've saved the best for last. Hang on a sec."

Wilkie was gone for a minute. "Coffee. So guess what was found about three miles away with a dead guy behind the wheel?"

"A Toyota?"

"You're so smart, Colin! Yeah. Actually, the same Toyota that the mom saw."

"And the dead guy?"

"One Ralph Charrette. Middle level county employee."

"Can you spell it?"

Wilkie did. Colin thanked him and tapped the tip of his pen on the note pad. Charrette. He knew the name.

In the hallway everyone was gathered around the Coke machine, some whispering, one or two talking aloud. Gloria had avoided her coworkers though a couple of them had actually grabbed at the sleeve of her jacket. She'd shrugged them off angrily, cursed under her breath, and made her way to her office. Once there she'd locked the door from the inside, then collapsed in her chair.

Her boss? *Her asshole* Ralph Charrette, found shot dead with two bullets to the head in the driver's seat of a stolen Toyota? *Her* she-was-almost-sure-he-was-gay *supervisor*?

Holy crap.

It had started in the parking lot. A woman she barely knew had accosted her and asked, "Is it true? Is it? Mr. Charrette?"

Gloria didn't know what the woman was talking about. "What about Mr. Charrette?"

The woman regarded her with oversized round eyes. "Ohmygod you haven't *heard!* Dead! Mr. Charrette! Shot! The police are here. They're questioning people!"

Gloria had shaken her head and walked on. At the elevator, a man she routinely saw in the cafeteria said, "Good Lord, Gloria! What is this world coming to?"

She'd led him to a corner table away from the food line. "What's happened to Mr. Charrette?"

The man had looked around as if he were a suspect and whispered, "He was murdered! In a stolen car! My God!" Then, looking at her curiously, had added, "Really? You hadn't heard?"

The man had a brother-in-law on the Fairfax Police force and so had details. Gloria listened, mouth slightly ajar in shock and bafflement. *Her* Ralph Charrette?

She took the elevator back to her office. It had to do with that order of, what was it? Scopolamine? She sat, stared at the monitor screen. The Fairfax County seal—four lions, a horse, and what looked like a covered picnic basket.

The phone rang. She stared at it for a moment, then hesitantly picked it up and, out of sheer habit, said, "Ralph Charrette's office?"

The voice at the other end said, "Gloria? This is Colin Marsh. Clarence's sponsor? We have to talk."

She said, "We do?" And immediately felt stupid. Of course they had to talk. She added, "I'm sort of busy right now…"

He understood. "I'm sure you are."

They made arrangements to meet in the evening and just as she was hanging up, someone knocked on her door, opened it, and stuck his head into her office. She looked up, annoyed, to see the same detective who'd come to her apartment after Clarence's death. Her insides froze; she forced a tremulous smile, and grabbed the edge of her desk with both hands to stop them from trembling.

The cop was as surprised as she was. "Ms. Nachtalyan! I thought I remembered the name!" He smiled tentatively, shook his head. "I'm sorry for your loss." He sat and asked, "May I sit down?"

They peered at each other for a moment. She said, "A tragedy. I just can't understand it. Ralph was so… *law-abiding!*"

The cop nodded. "Yes. I looked in his office. Commendations and plaques. A well-respected man."

Gloria nodded, then shook her head. "Absolutely. I can't imagine what happened."

"Ralph Charrette. French?"

"French Canadian, I think. Originally." She wiped at an eye. "A fine American."

The cop looked around Gloria's small office. "Nice people, the French Canadians."

She shrugged. "I wouldn't know. Ralph was the only one I've ever met."

The cop found that mildly interesting. "Really?"

Gloria shrugged. "I've never been to Canada."

"Beautiful country," said the cop. "Just beautiful."

There was a ten-second silence, than Gloria said, "I don't know what I'm supposed to do from now on. I mean, my boss is…"

"Dead," said the cop. "Just like the guy in the garbage chute."

She gave him a sharp look. He shrugged. "I didn't mean anything by that. It's just unusual, you know, that I meet the same person in two different cases.

"So anyway, is there anything you can tell me? Did he have enemies, your boss? Anyone you can think of?"

Gloria pretended to think. "No. He was pretty mild-mannered. But I know nothing of his private life. He liked to do target shooting. I know that."

The cop's eyebrows went up. "Really? Target shooting? Hmm."

Then Gloria said, "This probably doesn't have anything to do with anything, but a few months back, he got some people mad at him. Russian people, who lost a contract with the county."

The cop sat up. "Russians?"

Gloria nodded. "Yeah. I forget the name of the company. They were trying to get the trash pick-up contract for county parks. Their bid was too high. They got turned down and called Ralph a few times. I think they shouted at him. He was definitely surprised. Bothered. That's not how we do things in Fairfax."

The cop repeated, "Russians."

Gloria nodded.

"You have a number?"

She shook her head, no. "I'm afraid not."

The cop shrugged. "Nothing else you can think of?"

She said, "Afraid not. This is a pretty quiet place. Boring, even."

He stood, reached into his pocket for a card and handed it to her. "Anything you can think of, call me." Then added, "Or even if you can't think of anything. Maybe we can get coffee or something."

She smiled. "I will." But she knew she wouldn't.

Halfway out the door, the cop turned around. "The man in your trash chute? His name was Clarence. Clarence Bensonhurst. Does that ring a bell?"

Gloria kept her smile and knit her brow as she pondered the question for a meaningful moment. "Clarence. Bensonshirt?"

"Benson*hurst*."

She thought about it. "Nope. Never heard of him. Sorry."

22   MEAT HAD HUGE HANDS, HANDS LIKE A LEFT-FIELDER'S glove, his Mom had said that even when he was a little kid. Now he held the ballpoint gingerly, drew a line down the center of the blank page and, on the left side, he wrote in an elegant cursive script:

African Guy X
African Guy's Kid X
African Guy Kid's Mother X
White Guy in Sportscar X

Four people. Getting rid of them would clean everything up, and put to a final rest Rousseau's ridiculous plan to kill off addicts—addicts! their customer base—to rest once and for all.

That, thought Meat, was the trouble with foreigners like Rousseau and Lobo. They came from somewhere else with troublesome foreign ideas and tried to alter the way things were done. Meat had little respect for people who wanted to change things. He thought the stream of life should run placidly, and people throwing rocks into the stream disturbed the flow of normalcy. He did not miss Rousseau, and indeed for a short while had considered killing him himself. It was funny how things worked. Meat hadn't lifted a finger and Rousseau was dead. Maybe there was a God.

The thought made him smile but only briefly.

Dollar Bill and the young hood assigned to do Lobo but thwarted were both good soldiers, and the youngster could learn from the older man. Dollar Bill would talk the boy's ear off about how to wisely invest in this and that. They would shoot and kill the necessary people, for which Meat would give them each a not insubstantial bonus over their regular earnings. Dollar Bill would invest in asphalt shingle stocks because he had read a hurricane was slated to hit Florida. The boy would spend his money at a club with a couple of girls and chug Remy Martin.

In fact the boy asked for an advance, a few hundred dollars, and Meat gave it to him. The boy did indeed go to a club, ordered a bottle of Remy from which he drank steadily. He told two young girls who had joined themselves to him that big things were in the offing. He would be an important man in a matter of days. He lifted the hem of his hoodie and showed the girls the butt of a gun, and one of the girls laughed at him and said, "Who you gonna use that on, big man?"

The boy considered the comment and answered, "Some African dude been bothering my associates, is who."

The other girl smiled and said, "I *like* Africans. 'Specially the ones who speak French. They do know what they're doing."

The boy decided the girl needed to be put in her place. "You let me know if you like them Africans when they're full of holes." Then he drank deeply from the Remy, emptied the bottle and ordered a second one.

Neither of the girls went home with the boy.

The next morning, the younger of the two girls called a cousin, who called a brother, who called Aunt Mim's house and talked with her for ten minutes, mostly catching up on what had happened to whom and when. After hanging up, Aunt Mim pondered the conversation for a moment. The caller was an in-law who'd gotten into trouble a year earlier and been bailed out of jail by George. The in-law then got a job thanks to Mim's contacts and now walked the straight and narrow.

In the bed she never left, Mim said, "George?"

George looked up from the tome he was reading.

Mim said, "I think you should ask Mamadou to come and visit. There's stuff happenin'."

"And so, Mamadou," Aunt Mim concluded, "I think there's somethin' goin' on, and you may be in danger, and George agrees."

George nodded without looking up, then took off his glasses and wiped them with a silk handkerchief. "Definitely. We can't presume to say for sure that it's you they're after, but it'd make sense. You've—let's say *affected*—the trade Mr. Rousseau was plying, and now that man is no longer around." He placed the glasses back on his nose and avoided Mamadou's eyes. "It is to be assumed Mr. Rousseau's disappearance has left a vacuum and..."

"Nature abhors a vacuum," Mamadou finished the sentence. George smiled. "Aristotle. Very good,"

Aunt Mim beamed. "Such an educated man!"

George turned serious. "I would be on guard." He took a square of paper from his breast pocket, handed it across Mim's bed to Mamadou. "Mr. Rousseau rented this house on Kenyon Street in Mount Pleasant as a gathering place for his people. I believe the man called Meat lives there now. The members of the..." George paused, looking for the right word, "... organization are often there as well, according to someone familiar with them." Mamadou stared at George, then at Mim. Mim was smoothing the bedspread covering her wide body. George had a glint in his eyes. He added, "I would be pleased to go with you should you invite me. I'm old, and somewhat weakened after Mr. Rousseau's intemperate behavior, but you may still find me useful."

Mim sat up in her bed and glared at her partner. "Are you crazy, old man? You ain't going nowhere near them people! They almost killed you once!"

George stood and straightened his tie. "Hush Mim." Aunt Mim recoiled. Mamadou's eyes widened. He'd never heard George talk back to her. "They almost killed me. That's precisely why I'll go with Mamadou. I'll be fine." More softly, he added, "Don't you worry even a little bit. I'd never leave you alone."

Mamadou saw Aunt Mim's mouth open, then shut. Her eyes grew misty and she wiped at them with the hem of a sleeve. Then she nodded. "So you take care of this crazy old man, Mamadou. He crazy as a loon, or maybe a fox. Don't let nothing happen to him."

George smiled at them both. He sat back down, careful of the crease in his pants, and went back to reading. Then he looked up and said, "Do you know American football, Mamadou?"

Mamadou shook his head. "No. I've watched a time or two, but it's slow and confusing."

George agreed. "It is, for the most part. Boring and violent, too, which I don't at all like. But there is one thing worth learning from the sport. The best defense is a good offense."

Mamadou was puzzled. "I'm not sure—"

"You ponder that, young man. Give it some thought."

Back at the garage Mamadou sat in AfriCars1 and considered the options. There weren't many. He tuned the radio to WETA and listened to something with violins and horns. A very white voice told him he had just heard Concerto 17 in something-or-other by a French-sounding name. He barely listened. Antwone's face swam before him, and a jumble of rage, sorrow, guilt, and fear enveloped him. Fear? Where did that come from? He traced the emotion and soon Danee's face supplanted Antwone's. Mamadou seldom feared for his own well-being. What frightened him was what could happen to others, what had happened to his own sister, Amelie, whom he had not properly protected from the evils of their new land, and to Antwone, whom he had failed as well. And now it was Danee who was in danger, who, too, might fall victim to a drug dealer.

Sitting in the darkened car, Mamadou sensed the vaguest of a plan emerge. He closed his eyes, focused on an image of DiAngela Jones and her triplets and smiled. He allowed himself a momentary joy, then chased the thought away, promising to return to it later. The best defense is a good offense. George's words, which made sense after a moment's deliberation. He bounced the notion around. Yes, he thought. Yes, that might work.

The sound of the garage door opening startled him. Danee walked in, too-baggy pants cinched tight around a skinny waist, new basketball shoes unlaced.

Danee looked around and at first didn't spot the African. When he did, he peered into the limousine's driver side window and asked, "That you, Mamadou? What you doing in there?"

Mamadou sat up straight, frowned deeply and said, "Inspecting your work! These cars are supposed to be clean!"

Danee tilted his head to the right, a move Mamadou knew meant an argument was coming. Danee said, "They ARE clean! I did them yesterday with Armor All. Vacuumed 'em, cleaned the windows! Those cars are cleaner than when they left General Motors!"

Mamadou pointed to a non-existent blemish on the car's dashboard. "That's not clean!"

Danee peered in. "I don't see nothing!"

Mamadou looked closer. "Hmm. Maybe you're right. Must be the light."

Danee rocked on his heels. "That car is *clean!*"

Mamadou stepped out of the car, towered over the boy. "So why are you here?"

Danee nodded to the other car. "I need to do the interior of 2. Didn't have time yesterday to do it as good as I wanted."

Mamadou stepped out of the limo. "Good. You do that. I have to go to AutoZone and buy some things. I'll be an hour. Don't let anyone in. When you're through with the car, you can start on your homework."

Danee shrugged and muttered. Mamadou stared at him. "What?"

Danee returned the look. "I said, 'Yassuh'!" Then he added, "Seems everybody tell me what to do. You. Mr. Colin. My Mamma. Even Mr. Colin's girlfriend. She says I talk too much and should catch my breath sometimes."

"She's right."

As soon as the African left, Danee went to the small office, opened the lower desk drawer, used a screwdriver to remove the false bottom the African had built, and took out the Beretta and the box of ammo. He replaced them with a set of cheap Craftsman sockets and a wrench that weighed about the same. Then he went outside, looked to make sure the African wasn't there, and slid the gun and ammo beneath an old piece of tarpaulin that had spent several winters by the side of the garage.

Danee had known about the gun since his second day working for Mamadou. He had figured, rightly, that no business would exist in this neighborhood without a weapon of some sort. He knew it wouldn't be hidden in an inaccessible space, so he went for the obvious and it had taken him less than a half-hour to find the gun. Danee was a smart kid and knew it, and he didn't want to be a smart dead kid, like Antwone. *Something* was going to happen, and it would involve the bad guys, and the African, and maybe Mr. Marsh. It might even involve his own Mamma, and she'd need him to protect her. All the men would be armed. Now he was too.

That night Mamadou, Danee, Colin, Emily, DiAngela, and her boys all came for dinner at Colin's apartment, and Emily made pasta with pesto from Trader Joe's. George was there as well but refused to eat, claiming Mim could not stand the smell of garlic on his breath. Emily volunteered to make something else but he smiled shyly and shook his head. "I only have one meal a day."

Much to Danee's displeasure, the children sat around the coffee table away from the grown-ups. When they'd finished eating, Danee and the triplets were sent to watch television in the next room while the adults acted as if everything was normal when it was obvious things were not normal at all.

Danee gave the triplets a dollar each to be quiet, then as innocently as he could, went to the kitchen for a glass of water. The adults fell silent until he'd gone. Back in the bedroom, he drank the glass of water in one long gulp, then pressed its rim against the door. He put his ear to the other end and heard one of the women say, "… conspiracy ever." Then the African said something too, about "… your grandfather, and Antwone, and hundreds of others…"

Danee strained to hear but got mostly muffled sounds. No laughter though; the adults were being serious. After a while his attention strayed to the television show, something about giant ants in Africa. The triplets had questions he answered with invented facts that impressed two of the boys but failed to sway Darnell who said, "He's making things up."

Danee protested. "Am not!"

Then Dewan said, "I gotta pee!" and his brothers chimed in; they had to go too, so Danee took them into the bathroom and by the time they all returned, the adults had stopped talking and were clearing the table.

When everyone had left, Colin said to Emily, "I'm not sure about all this."

She said, "I understand. I have my doubts too. But they did kill my grandfather."

23 GEORGE TOLD AUNT MIM EVERYTHING WAS GOING to be all right, but he could tell she didn't believe him. He'd never managed to lie to the woman, not once successfully ever since they were small children living in a black-only slum building next to a river that stank of dead fish and spilled diesel oil. He said it again, "It's going to be okay."

She looked at him with the saddest eyes he'd ever seen on her and said, "Don't you lie to me, old man."

The triplets were sleeping pell-mell on a comforter spread on the floor. Danee was also asleep, or, thought Mamadou, pretending to be. He led DiAngela to the balcony and closed the sliding door. It was a cool night, and the smell of the Potomac just reached them, slightly acrid, slightly salty; it made Mamadou think of the Senegal River he'd visited as a child with his parents.

DiAngela linked an arm into his and said, "You're sure about this? I'll support you regardless, but it's frightening, what you're planning to do. I want you to be safe."

He leaned against her, felt a quiet strength there. "I'm a lot more worried about George than anyone else. He's an *old* man, and if anything happens to him…" He let the sentence hang.

DiAngela said, "Mim and I are very distantly related, did I tell you that? She and my grandmother had people in common. I remember maybe twenty years ago, she and George came to my house, and my mom spent the entire day cooking and cleaning. It was like having the Reverend King come to dinner. And you know, George was already an old man. Looked exactly as he does today. My mother said he was, well, almost legendary."

"Legendary?"

"I don't remember the details. But he got into a shootout with some very nasty people, hit a couple of them, and then he ran out of bullets, I guess, and he went after them with a penknife. *A penknife!* And they ran away." She laughed, a bright sound. "Can you imagine that? That little old man?"

Mamadou could.

Over the next week, Colin and Emily spent hours on the internet and used every tool at their disposal to identify the members of the late Rousseau's group. Emily employed data mining tools Colin had never heard of. They gathered prison and jail records, court transcripts, newspaper articles, video clips, mug shots, information on known acolytes, apartment leases, birth certificates, drivers' license numbers and traffic citations, parking tickets, known aliases, employment records, unemployment benefits, and former addresses. Emily shook her head. "I do this all the time and I'm still amazed at the amount of stuff publicly available."

"You're really good. I thought I was, but you put me to shame."

She smiled, liking the compliment. "I've been doing this a while."

"So have I," Colin replied.

"And I may have more resources at my disposal." She paused, grinned. "The things I could tell you about you!"

"You didn't!"

Her eyes didn't leave the screen. "Of course I did."

George took the Metro and the 42 bus from his and Mim's house to Mount Pleasant. He carried his cane and a thin briefcase and held a clipboard under his arm. He passed the house on Kenyon Street twice that day and noticed all the blinds were drawn save one. The first time he walked past the house, he noted a man looking out at the street from behind the one uncurtained window. The second time he walked past, the watcher left his post momentarily and returned with a second man. They both looked out the window at George who smiled, waved, and went on his way.

That evening, George, Colin, and Mamadou had a three-way phone conversation during which George said, "Mim agrees. Ladies should not be involved."

Mamadou said, "Good. We are, how do you say, on similar chapters?"

Colin corrected him. "On the same page. But you both know how Emily and DiAngela will react."

"Like women," Mamadou sighed.

"You might not want to say that out loud," Colin said before hanging up.

Two hours later, Emily was glaring at Colin. "You know," she said in a very low voice, "this is the first time you've really pissed me off. I hope it doesn't happen too often."

She left his apartment and slammed the door hard. It sounded like a gunshot.

"So this is what I've decided," Mamadou told DiAngela Jones.

"Is that a fact," she smiled.

"I think it's for the best."

She nodded. "Do tell." Her smile was steady and brittle. Her teeth shone.

He had been lying on the couch in her townhouse with his head in her lap; she dislodged him with a quick bounce of her legs and got to her feet.

"Colin agrees with this?"

He looked at his shoes, noting they needed a shine. "Yes. We talked."

She kept smiling. "Did you now? How nice."

There was an edge in her voice he chose to disregard.

She hugged him briefly. "Time for you to go home."

That caught him by surprise. "Oh. I thought I might—"

She smiled. "No. I don't think so. Not tonight."

He found himself on the stoop of her house, holding his shoes in his left hand and not sure how he'd gotten there. She patted his butt as she would one of the triplets' and closed the door behind him. He heard the decisive click of a latch, then the throw of a deadbolt.

Women.

There were nine men, all black and ranging in age from early forties to late teens. By now the group knew their names. The big one was Meat; the skinny dangerous-looking one was Dollar Bill; the youngest was nicknamed Tee; and another one, slightly older, was Cue. One man was hospitalized following an emergency appendectomy, and two were in jail awaiting trial. The last two were traveling, one to Florida and the other to Los Angeles. The four in the house had a total of 106 arrests for crimes ranging from manslaughter to possession with intent to distribute. Meat had been in correctional facilities in Delaware, Pennsylvania and West Virginia. Both Tee and Cue had served minor sentences in Maryland, and Dollar Bill had spent a total of ten years in three states for a variety of offenses. When Mamadou questioned the need for such in-depth research, George quoted Lao Tzu. "If you know the enemy and know yourself, you need not fear the result of a hundred battles." The quote did not impress Mamadou.

On the appointed day, Colin, George, and Mamadou took the Mercedes into town and parked it a block from the Mount Pleasant house. George got out first with his clipboard. He made his way up Kenyon Street, climbed the stairs to the house's front porch and rapped on the door with his cane.

Still in the car, Colin said, "Emily is furious."

Mamadou nodded. "So is DiAngela. She told me I had to leave her house."

"Do you think it was…?"

"Yes." Mamadou's voice was tight with anxiety. "We made the right choice. If Emily and DiAngela had come, we would have worried about them. It would have been distracting and not helped us."

They got out of the car, their weapons hidden beneath the jackets folded over their arms.

"Just so we're clear," Colin said, "we're gonna take them and call the police. That's what we agreed on, right? No shootung."

"Unless the bad guys shoot first," Mamadou said.

The bad guys did.

Weeks before, Emily and DiAngela had exchanged not only phone numbers but truthful opinions on each other's man.

Emily: "Your guy scares the bejesus out of me."

DiAngela: "That's one of the reasons I like him. I'm with him, no one's gonna mess with me or my boys."

Emily: "Colin, he's sort of different. He *ponders* stuff a lot. I don't think he's a violent guy, but sometimes I wonder what might set him off."

Now, they sat in Emily's Volvo and could see Mamadou's Mercedes.

"Tell you what, though," DiAngela said. "I don't know where they get off telling us to stay at home while they go out there and hunt down the bad guys."

They were parked a hundred yards away and watched Colin, Mamadou, and George exit the Mercedes. George went off by himself to the house. Mamadou and Colin waited a short while and followed him at a discreet distance.

Less than thirty seconds later, the women saw the German car's trunk lid open slightly, then more, and watched as Danee peered from the trunk and climbed out.

"What the hell is he doing there? He's supposed to be in school!" DiAngela whispered, "Oh my God! Is that a gun in his hand?"

Danee climbed out of the Mercedes trunk. He looked around guiltily and retrieved the Beretta he'd taken from Mamadou's garage. He stuck it into the waist of his jeans where it nestled like some evil foreign thing against his stomach. He could almost feel its malevolent vibrations. He sucked in his non-existent gut.

He shook with fright and remembered a television program about how children in Africa scared off hyenas by making themselves taller, wearing ridiculous hats made of straw or balancing buckets of water on their heads. The thought wasn't helpful.

He took a deep breath, squared his shoulders and walked a block toward the house. He hid behind a tree and saw Colin and Mamadou. Then he darted into the alley he thought must run behind the house.

George knocked on the door. He had reasoned that an old man would be perceived as less of a threat than a tall Senegalese or a medium-sized white man. No one answered. He knocked again with the same result, then nodded his head. Colin and Mamadou began climbing the front porch steps. George stepped to the side, allowing Mamadou access to the door.

Inside the house, Cue, the kid who'd killed Bong Bong, saw the three men through the window. No one ever came to visit, ever, and he grabbed and fired the shotgun without even realizing it. He fired through the window, shattering it, and was surprised when a shot was returned, hitting him squarely in the center of the chest. It felt as if someone with a huge fist had punched him in the solar plexus. He sat down heavily on the couch, touched his shirt, and was startled to feel something wet and sticky on his fingers. He looked at the blood—his blood—without much comprehension, then closed his eyes and slumped forward.

Colin's ears rang. He saw George sitting on the porch floor, splay-legged and rubbing his forehead. Mamadou was holding a large pistol and aiming inside the house. Colin said, "Ah shit."

Dollar Bill was reading the *Wall Street Journal* in the kitchen and agonizing on whether he should rid himself of some AI stocks that had shown promise three weeks earlier but now were tanking. He'd seen this happen before, only to watch shares rebound and double in value. Playing the market was a tricky thing, he told everyone.

When the first shot boomed through the house, Dollar Bill sat straight up as if someone had jammed a poker up his butt. It took him a few seconds to focus on his shotgun, which was leaning against a corner of the room.

Meat was in the bathroom leafing through a three-month old *Maxim* when he heard the shots. Those were BIG sounds, shotguns-in-enclosed-space sounds and he didn't bother with thoughts of investigating. He dropped the *Maxim* to the floor, pulled his pants up to his ample belly, and blew out of the bathroom without flushing. He crashed through the kitchen, past Dollar Bill who was trying to focus on something in the corner, and barreled through the house's back door, holding his unbelted pants with one hand and trying to take a small revolver out of their right side pocket with the other.

Danee had just crept into the backyard and didn' see Meat coming. The big man hit him like a runaway garbage truck. The boy flew in the air, dropped his stolen gun and landed on his back in the dirt. The air whooshed out of his lungs. His glasses sailed off his face and landed six feet away. He sat up with his vision blurred and head ringing. He waited for his heart to burst out of his chest.

Dollar Bill grabbed the shotgun. Half his mind still considered dumping the AI stock, the other wrestled with what he'd just seen. Without thinking, he fired and took out the kitchen window. There was no reason to do this, but he did it anyway.

The window glass exploded out, showering Danee with shards and splinters.

Meat, a few feet away, stopped, concentrated on the kid and on the firearm next to the kid and finally got his pistol out of his pocket. He aimed in the kid's general direction and fired once. The shot threw up a small cloud of dust from the backyard's red dirt, five inches from Danee's leg. Danee yelped, rolled into a ball, and covered his head.

Inside the house, there was another loud BOOM. Meat yelled, "Motherfucker!" and glanced briefly in Danee's direction. He got off a second round that went wide and bolted out the backyard's gate. For a large man, he was surprisingly fast.

Danee got to his feet feeling nauseous but brave. He grabbed Mamadou's gun and stood in the backyard, undecided and swaying, his vision murky. He darted a look at the house, another at the opened gate. Out of breath, shaking and terrified, shards of glass in his hair, his legs buckled and he sank to the ground, his back resting against the chain link fence bordering the yard.

Blood seeped from his scalp and forehead onto his face and he could only think of what his Mamma would say, how scared she might be and how her voice would rise almost a full octave if she saw him.

He stood and retrieved his glasses. One lens was gone, the other was cracked. He put the glasses back on his nose and, still half-blind, felt a sense of the familiar. He stripped off his tee-shirt, wiped the blood from his face, and tied the shirt around his head. After a moment, he got to his feet, unsteady and listing to the left. He could hear voices inside the house but the shooting had stopped. His legs were still jelly.

Meat, twenty yards away, stopped in mid-stride. The kid might be worth something. He retraced his steps, stared at the boy who stood frozen, large gun useless in his small hand. Meat spat a curse, swatted the weapon away, and grabbed the boy by the back of the pants. He tucked him under one arm like an Easter ham and began running again. Danee's small weight didn't seem to hamper him. Meat reached a nondescript six-year-old Chevy Malibu parked by the mouth of the alley. He ripped open the rear door and threw Danee in.

Emily and DiAngela both heard the booming sound of shotguns. Angela opened the Volvo's passenger door, but Emily pulled at her arm. "Wait! Wait!"

They saw a large black man run to a car parked in an adjoining alley, then throw a shapeless mass through the rear passenger door.

"Was that...?" DiAngela's voice was hushed.

"Yes!"

"Danee?"

"Yes!" Emily twisted the Volvo's ignition key and floored the accelerator just as the Chevy erupted from the alley.

DiAngela yelled, "Lemme out! Lemme out!" She wrested a small gun from her purse. "Gotta make sure they're all okay!"

Emily glared at her. "You crazy? You wanta get shot?"

Charlie Snow was amazed, sometimes, at how things worked out. Careful planning, even more careful execution, attending to details, discipline, paying close attention to all these fundamentals almost always resulted in a successful endeavor. Certainly, there were exceptions to the rules, but exceptions were just that—out of the norm, unexpected.

He had just been paid a very nice sum of money for the "termination with extreme prejudice" of Lobo, the tooth-loosening Aztec motherfucker he'd been contracted to eliminate some time ago. It wasn't the full amount promised since the delivery date had been missed by more than a year, but still. A *very* nice sum.

Charrette, his erstwhile partner, was gone as well, with enough white powder on his person to assure his murder would be seen as drug-related. Which it was, but not in the way the police might see it. There were a couple of loose ends to deal with—Charrette's secretary, what's-her-name, and Meat and his people, whom he was on his way to see.

He was contemplating using a small amount of his recent windfall to purchase a Hämmerli SP20 22 caliber target pistol like the one Charrette had owned. This was a *nice* gun, and he could almost visualize himself at the range squeezing phenomenally accurate shots into the splatter targets.

He was not paying a lot of attention to traffic when a Chevy Malibu pounded through a stop sign at his left at better than forty miles per hour. Charlie Snow swerved to the right but it was too late. He clipped the rear deck of the Malibu, which half-spun into a parked compact with a metal-rending sound.

Meat staggered out of the Malibu, unsteady on his feet. He was holding his right hand over his right eye and Charlie Snow recognized him immediately.

"Sonofabitch," Snow muttered. He pasted a solicitous look on his face and got out of his car. "You ok?"

Meat turned slowly and faced Snow, and when he did, Snow gave a quick glance around, saw no one, drew his gun and shot Meat twice in the head. Meat dropped like a side of beef. Snow approached the car, looked inside.

"What the fuck?"

In the kitchen Dollar Bill put down the shotgun and yelled, "Whoever's out there, I give up! Don't shoot!!"

He wasn't entirely aware of the rationale; too many things had happened in the blink of an eye. A loud explosion, followed by what he knew was a gunshot. And Meat, a genuinely fearsome man, fleeing rather than fighting, his departure displaying a rare lack of decorum. Meat was struggling to pull his pants up as he ran. Lastly, there was the AI stock. Dollar Bill had been toying with the idea of going straight for a while. He had made money on the market—quite a bit of money, actually—and come to the conclusion stocks were safer than dealing drugs. He was getting older, well into his 40s, a bad age to get shot at.

He yelled again, "Yo! Mu'fuckers! Don't shoot! I ain't armed! I give up!"

Danee was in the back on the floor. The crash had banged the boy's head against the passenger door and bright spots swam in his blurry vision. He heard two shots and thought they were aimed at him—everyone was shooting at him these days—but he felt no pain, so after a moment, he looked up. The pinkish face of a white man looked down on him and said, "What the fuck?"

"Stop the car! Stop the car!"

DiAngela Jones had seen the crash, seen the white man shoot the big black guy, seen the big black guy drop to the ground, seen the white man approach the wrecked Malibu and point his gun inside the car.

She fired from the Volvo's open window at the white guy without aiming, the gun making a fearsome sound and kicking in her hand. The white guy was twenty feet away.

"Ah shit," Charlie Snow said. "I'm sorry kid." He took a deep breath, aimed his gun at Danee's head and tightened his finger on the trigger. Something sharp bit into his neck. He jerked backwards and the shot went wild.

On the second floor of the house, in the room above the kitchen, the second kid, Tee, was watching Oprah. The shotgun sound knocked him off his chair.

He reached for the pistol he kept in the drawer where all the remotes were and suddenly realized the pistol would not be there. It was under the driver's seat of the car he'd driven a day before to the old neighborhood intending to do some harm.

Tee had heard an old rival was back in town and there was some unfinished business he needed to attend to, i.e. shoot the mo'fucker, not necessarily to kill, but to remind him that he was neither forgiven nor forgotten.

The expedition to Michigan Avenue, Northeast, had not been successful. No one had seen the other kid, and a few neighborhood acquaintances had accused Tee of abandoning the nabe and going uptown.

Tee had stashed the pistol under the seat when a couple of cop cars with wailing sirens had passed him, and then he'd forgotten about the gun altogether.

He heard Dollar Bill yell something, and then repeat it. There was no more gun fire.

Tee opened the door and peeked out. A small, elderly man was standing at the foot of the stairs.

Tee said, "Yo!"

The old man looked up and smiled. "Come on down son, we need to talk."

Tee hesitated. The old guy said, "Ain't nobody gonna hurt you, boy. You got my word."

"Where's Meat?"

The old man scratched his head. "Last I heard, he went out the back door. That's what your friend Dollar Bill said."

Dollar Bill chimed in, "Just like a fuckin cannonball! Left the rest of us to fend for ourselves." Then he added, "Fucking fat mo'fucker."

Tee said, "Lemme see Bill!"

George stepped aside and Dollar Bill leaned in so Tee could see him.

"Where's Cue?"

There was an overlong silence, and Dollar Bill said, "He's kinda shot."

Tee had never liked Cue, who was loud and always had to have the last word in an argument. He wouldn't mind if Cue was shot. He asked, "Cue alive?"

Dollar Bill didn't answer.

Tee said, "So he dead."

Dollar Bill shrugged. "Kinda."

DiAngela Jones kept squeezing the trigger and watched as a bright red spot appeared on the white man's neck and a stream of blood spurted. Then her gun clicked empty.

The white man's eyes were open. He appeared unpleasantly confused, mouthed, "Well fuck me." He was leaning against the Malibu, then began a slow slide to the ground.

DiAngela bounded to the damaged car, stepped over the white guy and noted a froth of red on the man's lips. She wrested the passenger back door open. Danee slid to the pavement. She grabbed him by a shoulder and with strength she didn't know she had, pulled him to his feet. Her mouth worked silently; she squeezed him tight against her, then pushed him back, slapped him hard once and would have struck him again if Emily hadn't caught her arm. DiAngela Jones looked around wildly, and yelled, "Why aren't you in school!"

24   THE NEXT DAY COLIN WOKE UP TERRIFIED. The police would come. He'd be arrested, and Emily would be an accessory. Mamadou might be deported, and Danee returned to the mean streets of the housing project. George's heart would stop, and Aunt Mim's heart would soon follow.

Actually, Mamadou would skate. The man had an unerring way of talking himself out of any situation. But he, Colin, would get nailed. The night before there had been a brief story on Fox 5 News and a disinterested DC detective had shrugged his shoulders. "We'll do our best to find the criminals," he'd said, but his tone of voice implied the opposite. There was little interest in pursuing anyone in a matter that involved only other criminals. When the reporter asked about the white man found dead alongside the black dealer, the detective's voice had taken on an accusatory nature. "What? You think only black people are involved with drugs." The Fox reporter, a toothy blonde with an overbite, had backed off.

Over a bowl of Shredded Wheat, Colin explored aloud all the possibilities of being apprehended until Emily snapped, "You're driving me crazy! Go to a meeting."

So he went. His inability to share about his predicament made him more anxious.

When he returned to the apartment, Emily was gone and had left a note. "Call Wilkie back. See you for dinner."

Colin delayed calling the reporter back, fearing an inquisition. When he finally did, Wilkie asked, "You didn't have anything to do with those three people getting killed downtown, did you?" Then he answered his own question. "Course you didn't."

"What three people?" Colin feigned ignorance badly.

"Two black guys and a white one. One, the black guy was nicknamed Meat, according to the police. A badass dealer. But the interesting thing was the white guy."

Wilkie paused for effect. "His name was Snow, and he is, was, a cop. His name's come up in a half-dozen Internal Affairs investigations. Drugs and payoffs, mostly, but nothing ever stuck, and he left the DC force about a year ago."

Colin heard the snick of a lighter and a sharp of intake of breath, then a long, slow exhale. Wilkie sighed with satisfaction.

"Anyway, a couple of sources told me Snow was a person of interest—nice euphemism, isn't it—in the killing of that white county guy, Sherbet? No. Charrette. Found shot in the head in a parked car. They were, pardon the expression, asshole buddies." Wilkie snickered, inhaled.

"Hardly politically correct," Colin said.

"Fuck political correctness," Wilkie exhaled again. "That crap is how we got into the sad mess we're in." He took in a lungful of smoke. "I digress. Anyhow, the cops got a bad egg out of the way, one of their own, no less, and pretty much are gonna write off Sherbert's—Charrette's—murder, and the two black guys were nasties, so everyone's happy."

"That's sort of callous."

"Oh for God's sake, Colin. To quote our eminent president, don't be a baby."

"You're quoting *Trump?!*"

Wilkie was silent for a moment. "I apologize. Really, I do." He sounded like he meant it. Then, with a note of wonder, "I don't know what got into me. Anyway, I thought I'd ask if you had any special insight on these... events?"

"Me? Why me?"

Colin could almost hear Wilkie shrug. "Rumors in the rooms. You know how people talk sometimes. Anyway. Forget I asked. You be well, stay out of trouble, maybe take your new girlfriend to Florida for a week. You know, get some air." And he hung up.

Colin stared at the phone a long time and decided he'd go to a noon meeting too.

Twenty-four hours later, on a moonlit night, Mamadou went to see Aunt Mim and George. The large woman was in her bed, propped up on pillows, with a cup of herbal tea. Chamomile, Mamadou guessed. A plateful of bagels was on her nightstand. He bent down and pecked her on the cheek.

"George here," she nodded in the direction of her companion who was sitting in his armchair with Volume 1 of the Encyclopedia Britannica on his lap, "has decided he's gonna read all 32 volumes."

George nodded. "Got a bargain. Fifteenth edition, the last one printed, and I only paid $250 on eBay."

Aunt Mim made an annoyed face. "So now I'm gonna have to listen to him talking all day about this and that, and he's gonna bore me to death."

George didn't look up. "The way you smoke and drink, I'm gonna outlive you."

Aunt Mim said, "George!" But she was smiling.

She turned her attention to Mamadou. "George said everything went well?" It was both a statement and a question.

Mamadou lowered himself into a chair near the bed. "It did."

"Don't want to know any details," said Aunt Mim, "but the general thought in City Hall, I was told by a lawyer friend there, is that someone did Dee Cee a favor. That Meat fellow, he was a nasty man." She paused, added, "Is that boy okay? Danee?" Aunt Mim's eyebrows arched.

"He is. A few cuts but he'll be fine."

"You gonna take care of him?"

"Yes. He's a good kid, and he'll turn into a good young man."

"And his Mamma?"

Mamadou sighed. "That's another story."

Aunt Mim lit a Tareyton, expelled a long stream of smoke. "I swear, that dope is gonna kill all the young ones." She paused, sucked on the Tareyton again. "There's a place in Maryland that can take her. Near Baltimore. It's a three-month stay. The director owes me a favor."

Mamadou dipped his head. "Thank you."

She fell silent and George turned a page in the encyclopedia and muttered, "Imagine that!" under his breath. Then Aunt Mim looked at Mamadou speculatively, "You gonna stay with that nice woman, DiAngela? I *do* like her."

He smiled. "I like her too."

"You gonna see her soon?"

"I might."

"Bring her by. And those cute little kids, too. Can you imagine that? Triplets? She gotta be a strong woman!"

In the morning, Mamadou called DiAngela and arranged to pick her and the triplets up in an hour. In his apartment, he collected all the guns, packed them in a duffel bag and dropped the bag into the trunk of the Mercedes, thinking how Danee was a pretty foolish yet courageous kid.

He went to DiAngela's house and gathered the tribe, then returned to Mim's neighborhood.

DiAngela had obviously lectured her sons on the dire consequences of ill behavior at Aunt Mim's. Once in the house and facing Aunt Mim's bed, Dewan, Dionne, and Darnell stood at attention, and held their breath, though after a minute, Dionne began to shuffle his feet. His mother recognized the danger, scooped him up and rushed him to the guest bathroom where he vomited. Darnell and Dewan struggled to keep a straight face.

DiAngela returned, smiled at Aunt Mim. "I'm so sorry, Aunt Mim. He gets nervous."

"He gotta a weak stomach," added Dewan.

"He *has* a weak stomach," corrected Darnell.

George looked at Darnell and nodded. "Good grammar is important," he said, and returned to the encyclopedia. Darnell beamed.

"You young people go out and enjoy lunch or something, leave those boys here. There's toys in the basement, they'll have a good time."

The triplets looked questioningly at their mother, who nodded. Aunt Mim pulled out the drawer in the night-table next to her bed, reached in and took out a hundred dollar bill. She held out to Mamadou who, after a moment's hesitation, took it. "Thank you."

DiAngela admonished the three to be good. George stood, evened the crease in his pants with two fingers, and asked, "You guys play video games?"

Back on the sidewalk with DiAngela, Mamadou said, "It's too early for lunch. And there's something I need to do."

They got into the Mercedes and he drove through the city, cut across Georgetown to Canal Road, took a left at one of the lock houses, bounced down a cobblestone street and through a short, dank tunnel. He parked, got the duffle bag from the trunk and slung it across a shoulder.

DiAngela stood with her hands on her hips. "Why are we at Fletcher's Boat House?"

Mamadou said, "I told you. I need to do something."

"What's in the bag, fishing gear? I'm not dressed for fishing." She frowned. "Hell, I don't even like fishing! Worms and hooks and slime. And you always end up smelling bad."

They got a rowboat. The rental guy in the little shack that also sold bait, cold drinks, and candy bars, looked at the duffel bag. DiAngela said, "Fishing gear." The man shrugged.

Mamadou rowed to the middle of the river, where he let the current carry them. He reached into the bag, took out a shotgun and let it slip into the river. Then two handguns, boxes of shells, a rifle, another shotgun with a sawed off barrel, a shiny revolver, more shells, a scope, a silencer.   All slipped into the water. When he was done, he smiled broadly, "Now I want lunch."

He rowed back to the pier. The rental guy looked at them again and DiAngela said, "They're not biting today."

Danee had twelve stitches in his scalp from the flying glass, and his mother was on the verge of apoplexy. He stopped her raving, his voice carrying a new authority.

"Mamma! MAMMA!"

Danee's Mamma fell silent. She opened her mouth to resume her rant, but Danee pushed her Quarter Pounder closer to her hands, and she picked it up.

"Mamma, listen to me, okay. I'm fine, they just little cuts. They don't even hurt." He took a bite of his fish fillet sandwich, looked around the McDonald's where they were sitting, and lowered his voice.

"You're gonna go into a rehab, okay? This nice woman, a friend of Mr. Mamadou, she gonna take care of it. You gonna get clean, and stop using, and stop being a ho."

She flinched but stayed quiet.

"I'm sorry, Mamma, I know that's a bad word, and it probably hurt your feelings. But I want you to stop the drugs and the men, okay?"

He turned his head to hide the tears in his eyes. "You're my Mamma, and I want you to be around a long time, and if you keep doin' what you're doing, that ain't gonna happen."

She looked at him, slowly nodded.

"We gotta chance now, me and you. You know how you always say, bless this and bless that? Well, we been blessed."

He took a huge bite of the sandwich, drank a mouthful of Coke, swallowed, and cleared his throat. "And I'm gonna come and visit you every week. Every week, and when you're clean we're gonna get us a nice apartment somewhere, maybe in Virginia, near Mr. Mamadou. And you can go to school. Mrs. Mim said…"

"Mrs. Mim?"

"Everybody calls her Aunt Mim."

Danee's Mamma's eyes were spectacularly round. "Aunt Mim? How do you know Aunt Mim?"

"I don't, but Mr. Mamadou and she is good friends, and he told her about you, and she wants to help."

"Oh my God," said Danee's Mamma. "Oh my God." She stopped chewing and a small trickle of McDonald's sauce escaped the right corner of her mouth.

Now Danee sounded surprised. "You know Mrs. Mim?"

Danee's Mamma wiped her mouth carefully. "Boy, there ain't a black person in Dee Cee that don't know her, or about her. She *famous*." She said it again, "Famous!" Then she asked, "Why she want to help me? I ain't nobody."

"Cause Mr. Mamadou likes you, and he told her about you."

"He likes me?" Now she was *really* interested and her eyes widened a bit.

Danee made a face, scrunched up his lips. "Not that way likes you, Mamma. He got a girlfriend. She really nice and has three little kids. You saw her at the hospital, remember? Anyway, you gonna go to rehab. It's all arranged."

"When?"

Danee looked out the window and saw Mamadou's Mercedes pull up. The big man got out of the car and walked into the McDonald's.

"Now, Mamma," Danee said. "We going there right now."

From Best Selling Author, **Thierry Sagnier**

The Colin Marsh Mystery Trilogy
For lovers of crime thrillers

THIRST
Amazon Bestseller
Available in paperback and on Kindle

A mystery thriller set in Washington, D.C. where a fortune in drugs is missing. Finding the drugs starts with finding the girl. An ex-reporter with contacts and a nose for asking questions, Colin Marsh finds himself in the middle of drugs, dealers, kidnapping, and shoot-outs in this first of the Colin Marsh thriller series as he tries to save the life of his girlfriend's daughter.

> A fast-paced crime novel with fallible characters, good-guys and bad, that prevent any of the action from becoming predictable.
>
> **—Goodreads**

DOPE

Available in paperback and ebook

In *Dope*, Colin, Marmadou, and a handful of AA friends battle a conspiracy to poison thousands of addicts. Revenge, redemption, mayhem, and dark humor play out with insights into addiction and the shadowy world of dependency and exploitation. Enjoy the twists and turns.

> Sagnier builds characters as solid, griatty, and as broken as a D.C. street, with prose that lights up like monuments on a starry night.
>
> **—Michael J. Sullivan,**
> Best-selling author of *The Riyria Revelations*

VICE
2021 Release

In *Vice*, the third book in the Colin Marsh trilogy, Colin Marsh and Mamadou Dioh are faced with a new highly addictive drug promoted by Captain Bang, a shadowy dealer whose way of dispersing the drug is not illegal. A renegade AA group preys on young men and women, and a disappearance has the recovering community terrified. Both men face challenges never imagined and must choose between the law and their need to protect the people they love.

Thierry Sagnier is a writer whose works have been published both in the United States and abroad. He is the author of *The IFO Report,* (Avon Books), *Bike! Motorcycles and the People who Ride Them* (Harper & Row) and *Washington by Night* (Washingtonian Books). He is also the author of *Thirst,* a thriller based in Washington, D.C.'s mean streets and the first book of this trilogy. *Writing about People, Places and Things* is

a collection of essays chronicling Sagnier's thoughts on writing, family and friendships, and cancer.

In 2016 he wrote *The Fortunate Few,* recounting the memories of the men and women who served with the International Voluntary Services, the precursor of the Peace Corps. *L'Amérique,* the tale of a French family coming to America in the 50s, was published in 2018 by Apprentice House Press, which also published his novel, *Montparnasse.* He is currently working on sequels to *L'Amérique* and *Montparnasse.*

Thierry Sagnier was born in France and came to the United States in his early teens. He has worked and written for *The Washington Post* and several other newspapers and magazines, produced videos and short films for the Canadian Broadcasting Corporation, and was a columnist for Canada's *Le Devoir.* He was Senior Writer for the World Bank and traveled the world to write about that institution's projects in developing countries.

His plays have been produced in the D.C. area, performed by Tada Theater in New York, and featured by the East End Fringe Festival in New York.

His novel, *Montparnasse,* was nominated for a Pulitzer Prize by Apprentice House Press.

He currently lives in Virginia, USA. www.sagnier.com

www.ingramcontent.com/pod-product-compliance
Lightning Source LLC
Chambersburg PA
CBHW031941110726
47902CB00001B/258